The Hour Past Midnight

The Hour Past Midnight

SALMA

Translated from the Tamil original
by
LAKSHMI HOLMSTRÖM

zubaan

ZUBAAN
an imprint of Kali for Women
128 B ShahpurJat, 1st floor
NEW DELHI 110 049
Email: contact@zubaanbooks.com
Website: www.zubaanbooks.com

First published in English by Zubaan 2009
Originally published in Tamil by Kalachuvadu Pathippagam as
Irandaam Jamangalin Kathai

10 9 8 7 6 5 4 3 2

ISBN 978-81-89884-66-6

Zubaan is an independent feminist publishing house based in New Delhi
with a strong academic and general list. It was set up as an imprint of
India's first feminist publishing house, Kali for Women, and carries forward
Kali's tradition of publishing world quality books to high editorial and
production standards. *Zubaan* means tongue, voice, language, speech in
Hindustani. Zubaan is a non-profit publisher, working in the areas of the
humanities, social sciences, as well as in fiction, general non-fiction, and
books for children and young adults under its Young Zubaan imprint.

Typeset by Tulika Print Communication Services
Printed at Raj Press, R-3 Inderpuri, New Delhi 110 012

The Hour Past Midnight

(Irand'ám jámattin kadai)

These nights
following the children's birth
you seek, dissatisfied,
within the nakedness you know so well,
my once unblemished beauty.

You are much repelled,
you say,
by a thickened body
and a belly criss-crossed with birthmarks;
my body, though, is unchanging
you say
today, hereafter and forevermore.

My voice, deep-buried
in the valley of silence,
mutters to itself:

True indeed,
your body is not like mine:
it proclaims itself,
it stands manifest.

Before this too,
your children, perhaps, were born
in many places, to many others;
you may be proud
you bear no traces of their birth.

And what must I do?
These birthmarks cannot be
repaired, any more than my own decline —
this body isn't paper
to cut and paste together, or restore.

Nature has been
more perfidious to me
than even you;
but from you began
the first stage of my downfall.

More bizarre
than the early hours of night
is the hour past midnight
when dreams teem.

It is now, at this midnight hour
the tiger which sat quietly
within the picture on the wall
takes its place at my head
and stares
and stares

Author's Note: Speaking Silence

(from the preface to the Tamil edition, translated by Aniruddan Vasudevan)

Four years ago, during one of those moments over which my loneliness lay unfurled, I started writing this novel with some degree of planning. As my desire to speak the silences that my society incubated and my keenness to fill the empty pages in contemporary Tamil literature grew, so did the pages of this novel.

The women who inhabit this novel are those who journey with me in my world. They bear realities that are not contained by the images that society has created for them. They desire, just like any other human being, to live and love their lives. Traversing the spaces within the boundaries that are permitted them, they seek and find their joys, dreams, secrets, and sorrows. My writing here has not been determined in any way by concerns about pleasing or inconveniencing anyone. Throughout the novel, all that I have tried to show is how things are, and how they are so persistently.

Though a reader might feel discouraged at times by its length, the novel has a timeframe of less than a year. In this and other choices my primary vision has been to emphasize the frozen time within which the women in my novel live. I am also firm in my conviction that I shouldn't be anxious to answer any questions that arise about the novel.

It is beyond doubt that women can face nothing but injustice in a world that refuses to see the common humanity beyond the barriers of caste, religion, gender, and sexuality. It is no exaggeration when I say that the long gap between the completion of the novel and its publication was determined by the notions of purity and sanctity within which women are silenced and by the norms of this society and literary world that dictate what we can say and not say.

I would not have completed the novel if not for Kannan's friendly nudging and encouragement. Whenever I was bogged down by the pressures of domestic life and found no desire to write, Kannan's support helped me move forward.

I am very grateful to Kalachuvadu Publications for bringing out my writing, which would otherwise have stayed hidden and cowering inside me. They have published many of my writings and have shaped me.

My father Samsudeen, my mother Sarbunisa, and my sister Najeema are always with me and feel a sense of pride in my actions, the meanings and implications of which are not always clear to them. I am filled with love when I think of my dear children, Saleem Jafar and Amjad Najeem, who give up the time that they would like to spend with me so that I can write.

Translator's Acknowledgments

My thanks to Salma for patiently answering all my questions; to Rukhsana Ahmad and Arshia Sattar for many valuable insights; to Rizwi Faizer for sharing with me her experiences as a Tamil Muslim in Sri Lanka, and to Nalini Devdas and Afzal Friese for reading the manuscript. Thanks too, to the Roja Muthiah Library, Chennai, for tracking down two important texts, *Adabu maalai* and *Pen butthi maalai*.

❧ 1 ❧

Through the classroom window, Rabia watched the falling rain. At a little distance from the classroom, adjacent to the playground, stood the Asaari well endowed by the carpenter community; it was amusing to watch the raindrops falling steadily on the high parapet surrounding it and dripping away. The water that dripped into the well would be good for drinking, but the water that drained away ran into the gutter. Every now and then, the breeze blowing through the window flung a handful of raindrops at her face, making her feel overwhelmed by joy. Supposing she had heeded Amma and not come to school today...? It was well-known that on rainy days no teacher, man or woman, would arrive at the school or conduct any lessons. Rabia and her friends would ridicule them, giggling amongst themselves, 'They are scared they'll get drenched when they change class-rooms at the end of each lesson-period.' The teachers' fears transformed the day into one of rejoicing for the children. They spent their time delightedly, exchanging stories and running competitions.

'Ei, Rabia!'

She turned round with a start, hearing her name called. The classroom monitor, Uma, said, 'Someone is here, looking for you. Better go and see what it's about.' She stood up, wondering who it could be, walked past the other children and came to the door. Their driver, Mutthu, was standing there, sheltering under an umbrella.

'Amma told me to come and fetch you.'

'Why?' asked Rabia.

'How would I know? Come, let's go,' he said, the tone of his voice urging her to hurry. But she had absolutely no desire to leave the rain-enhanced classroom.

'I can't just come away like that, Muthanné. I'll have to ask permission from the teacher first. You go home; just leave the umbrella for me.'

'Nothing of the sort. Ask permission straightaway and come home with me. Amma will be very angry with me otherwise. Come on. Come at once. Let's tell them and go.'

But she insisted stubbornly, 'No, I have to do some writing first. Otherwise Teacher won't let me off. But you please go.'

Reluctantly Mutthu gave her the umbrella and left.

Rabia felt a rush of relief. A little later she would go home, walking all the way. She'd go home with the others, getting wet in the rain, splashing and paddling through the newly formed pools. The very thought of it made her happy.

'Why would they want to send the car for you? Don't you think it might be something important?' Uma asked. There was a trace of disappointment in her expression.

'I'm sure it won't be anything like that. They must have sent the car for me because they are worried I'd be drenched in the rain, that's all' she answered in an offhand way, went back to her desk and sat down.

Rabia noticed the look of envy on all her classmates because of the car that had come for her, and which she had sent back; she felt a rush of pride. From the corner of her eyes she checked to see whether Ramesh was watching her. She was disappointed that he was not.

Madina, sitting next to her, remarked, 'What a good thing you said you wouldn't go. We'll walk home together and have a lot of fun.'

'Of course. That's exactly why I wouldn't go in the car,' said Rabia, turning away once again to watch the rain falling outside the window. The sight of the flowers dropping from the pannir tree, weighed down by the rain, was very beautiful. On her way home, she must remember to gather up all the flowers and put them into her bag. She loved that pannir tree the most, out of everything in the school. She loved to sit under it and read. Every time she looked at it, she felt an inward surge of surprise at its huge size. Often she had asked her Amma why there wasn't such a tree anywhere else in the town. Amma would put a stop to her in a few words: 'How should I know, di? There just isn't, and that's that.' She determined to ask Periamma the answer to her question, that very day. Periamma came from the town; she wasn't a rustic like Amma.

Even though she had the umbrella, by the time she reached home, after school was over, she was drenched through. The minute she saw her daughter, Zohra was overcome with fury. She didn't scream or scold, but the irate expression on her face revealed her feelings quite clearly.

'So you can't be bothered to come home when we send for you! What rubbish were you learning, anyway? Because of your stubbornness we are still stuck here'. But when Zohra came close to Rabia, she was shocked into a standstill.

Rabia's white blouse, wet through, revealed her entire upper body. Zohra was startled by the sight of her daughter's breasts, surely too well-developed for her age. She grabbed Rabia by the shoulder and shook her hard. 'Is this the state in which you come back from school? Oh Allah! Everyone must have seen their fill of you. Shouldn't a female child have some sense of shame? Do I have to teach you even this much?' Complaining loudly, she began to dry Rabia's hair with a towel.

Rabia didn't quite take in the meaning of Zohra's complaints. Wondering at her mother's words, she gazed down at herself. Wet through, her upper chest was clearly outlined. When she saw this, she herself began to feel embarrassed.

Zohra finished drying her daughter's hair. 'Go now, go and change your clothes and get ready. We have to go to your Kuppi's house. We thought we shouldn't go away by ourselves and leave you alone in this house – and this is what you do in return!' Muttering to herself, Zohra went off towards the kitchen.

Once again Rabia felt a spurt of joy. Exultant that they were going out, and that she didn't have to study that evening nor go to the madrasa, she ran at top speed to her room, shut the door and began to change out of her school uniform.

Rahima Periamma peeped in to ask, 'Have you just come home, Rabia?' She ran up and hugged her aunt. Looking straight up at her, she asked, 'Why are we off to Kuppi's house?'

'Do you know that Zunaida Kuppi has just died? That's why,' replied Rahima. 'Well, you hurry up and get ready now. Your Amma is cross with you already.'

Rabia wasn't all that keen on Kuppi, so the news of her death didn't make her feel particularly sad. Hastily she pulled out a long skirt and blouse out of her clothes-shelf and put them on. Her long hair wasn't quite dry yet and felt damp still. Thinking to herself her mother would scold her if she knew, she braided her hair haphazardly and in haste, then ran to stand by the front door, all ready to go.

Once again she heard her mother call out, 'Rabia', and hurried towards the kitchen. 'Here, drink this milk. When you're done, take this carrier in your hand. We'll just put on our dupattas and join you,' said Zohra, drawing the bolt of the kitchen door.

Rabia drank her milk and went back to the front door. There was still a thin drizzle outdoors. From the house opposite, Faridakka peeped out of her window. 'Rabia, where are you off to? I suppose you are all going to the funeral?'

'Yes, we're going to Kuppi's house,' Rabia answered.

As soon as he heard Farida's voice, Mutthu got out of the car which was parked close to the front door. But just as soon as he turned round to look up at the window, Farida drew her head in hurriedly.

Mutthu began to laugh. 'Why is this, Rabia? Am I some sort of ghost or evil spirit? Is she so scared she has to hide away at once?'

'Faridakka's come of age, hasn't she? Then how can a man see her? She mustn't come before men, you know that?' Rabia spoke self-importantly.

Amma and Periamma came outside. Mutthu sat down in the driver's seat. Rabia was about to climb in, ahead of the others, but first Zohra handed her a davani, saying, 'Here, put this on'. She took it and blinked in a puzzled way, as if to say, 'What's this for?'

'Ss! Your chest is showing, you know that? There'll be any number of people in a house of bereavement. Are you going to stand in front of all of them, looking so disgraceful? Your uncle will scold, besides. A girl must be modest, you know? Do as you're told, now,' Zohra hissed into her ear.

Rahima Periamma, for some reason, was angry. 'Why are you hassling the child like this? Has she suddenly become a grown woman or what? You're always finding fault with her,' she reprimanded Zohra. To Rabia, she said, 'Wrap this round yourself for the time being, just to please your mother.'

Zohra herself draped the davani on Rabia. The car drove off, as soon as they climbed in. Both her Amma and Periamma had covered their bodies entirely with their white dupattas. Rabia squeezed between them, shrunk into herself.

* * *

The deceased Kuppi's house was only two streets away. They were there within five minutes. A big pandal had been erected in front of the house. Many men sat there silently, on the chairs provided. Although it was only five in the afternoon, it had darkened early, because of the rain. Amma and Periamma climbed down from the car, covered their faces so that only their eyes showed, hurried past the men gathered there, and entered the house. Rabia walked more slowly, embarrassed by the new davani, pulling at it on all sides and adjusting it as she went. The sound of the wailing from inside the house filled her stomach with dread.

Rabia entered the house hesitantly, trembling a little. The smell of incense rose up into her nose, increasing her fear. In the middle of the hall, where the sound of weeping came from all sides, Kuppi's corpse had been laid out on a big bench, her legs stretched out towards the west. The sight of the body, covered in a white cloth, made her shudder. Afraid that she would lose her hold on the carrier, she gripped it tightly, trying to bury her fears there.

Slowly she crept towards her mother, keeping close to the wall until she reached her. She sat down between Amma and Periamma. Under the bench they had placed a maldova tin filled with salt, into which an entire packet of incense sticks had been stuck. As she stared at the smoke rising from the incense sticks in a great cloud, her entrails seemed to churn.

Amma had gathered Nafiza Macchi into her lap, and was patting her back to comfort her. 'Don't cry, Nafiza. This was all that was ordained for us. Don't cry.'

But Nafiza would not stop weeping. She cried out in a loud voice, 'Oh my mother, you gave me birth, and now you've left me orphaned! You've left my father alone in the world! Who is there left for us now? Oh Allah, how could you refuse to look upon me!'

As she wept aloud, unable to bear it any more, a few other women joined her, raising their voices too, in lament. Nafiza Macchi's fair, round face was swollen with weeping. Her loosened hair fell over her forehead, hiding her face. Great sobs came from her, as she lay on Amma's lap. Meanwhile, Rabia was staring at Periamma, longing to be relieved of the carrier. Telling herself she must hand over the carrier and run outside as fast as she could, she said softly, 'Periamma, I'm feeling scared. May I go outside, please?'

Rahima understood the child's fears, took the carrier away from her, and whispered, 'Yes, go on then.' Then she tried to support Nafiza into a sitting position. At the same time, she called out, 'Yemma, is there anyone who will pour this coffee into a tumbler, please, so that I can give this girl a drink?'

Rabia was hugely relieved. She got up, walked past the crowd swiftly, and came outside. She cast her eyes about, all around, looking for a convenient place where she could sit down. Having considered which of the two unoccupied steel chairs was the best, she picked up the black one, carried it noiselessly, and placed it against the wall. Because of the rain, the entire floor was covered in mud and mire. She sat down carefully, holding her skirt well above her calves.

Kuppi's husband, Kamal Maamu, was sitting a little distance away. She looked at him carefully, to see if he was crying. He sat with his head bowed in sorrow, but he wasn't weeping. She asked herself why the tears had not come to his eyes. She had asked Amma once, 'Yemma, don't men cry, ever?'

'Why are you asking me this?'

'No, it's just that I've never seen men cry. Didn't Allah make them with tears in their eyes?'

Amma said, 'Idiot! Men mustn't cry. They never cry. They are not like women.'

Rabia began to get bored. She looked around, her eyes searching for Ahmad. At least if he were there, they could spend their time chatting together.

* * *

Zohra and Rahima were trying to compel Nafiza to drink some of the coffee in the tumbler. 'You've been crying continuously like this since the morning, what is going to happen to you? At least drink a mouthful, amma. Your mother died well, as a vaavarasi, while her husband is still alive. Who can be so fortunate, tell me?' they said, to comfort her. But after a couple of swallows, Nafiza shook her head violently, as if she wanted to ward off a terrible sense of guilt. Once again she lay down on Zohra's lap, wailing, 'My own mother who gave birth to me, Oh when will I see you again?'

Rahima raised her voice a little and scolded her. 'What are you doing, weeping uselessly like this? If you continue to weep,

won't your Amma feel bad where she is now? Isn't that a sin?'
At this reprimand, Nafiza's wailing lessened a little.

Rahima's stomach churned lightly. There was a pervading
odour of incense smoke mingled with human breath and smell.
The room was jammed with people, preventing any fresh air
from coming in. She pulled her dupatta up to cover her face so
that no one could see, and screwed up her nose.

Kader came in and said loudly, 'Mm, do the last preparations
now, ladies, all of you. The burial has to take place at Maghrib
time. Bathe the body now.'

Rahima was relieved at her husband's words. Now she began
to hurry the others to prepare for the funeral. She rose to her
feet and called out, 'Get up please, ladies, everyone. We have
to carry the bench to the bathing place.'

At once, four or five women carried out another bench that
was resting against the wall, and returned to carry the body, as
well. As soon as they left, Nafiza began to weep even more
loudly.

Asiamma and the others who would bathe the body, tied a
sari across the courtyard, forming a screen. A bowl of Lux
soap stood there, already mixed. They bathed the body, and
began to wrap it in the white shroud that had already been
ritually cleansed and prepared. Rahima was aware of the men's
anxiety that the burial should take place before it started to
rain again. If it were delayed till after Maghrib, it would be too
dark; too difficult to get to the cemetery. If the electricity were
to fail, there would be even more problems.

The whole house filled with silence. A silent sorrow seemed
to pass over every face there. The ritual of bathing the body
had created a moment for each woman present to reflect upon
her own death. Every face there revealed a helplessness; and a
fear that one day, inevitably, the moment of that final departure
from home must arrive for everyone.

Zohra thought of her own mother. Why could not
Aminamma too have died before her husband, a vaavarasi?
When she considered the harshness of her mother's

widowhood, the tears flowed from her eyes, involuntarily. Suddenly she lifted her hands, and raised her voice, pleading, 'Allah grant a good fate to all women, and call us away before our husbands. Grant us a good death like this one.' Several voices, full of sadness, joined in, with a heartfelt 'Ameen'.

The body, ready for its burial, was laid out now, in the middle of the hall, on a palm leaf mat placed on the bench. The way the corpse lay, tightly wrapped and tied from head to foot, leaving only the small and shrunken face open, disturbed Rahima in a strange way. To protect herself from that tormenting feeling, she tried to compel her eyes to look in another direction – but failed.

Asiamma's voice rang out, 'Whoever wants to look at her face for the last time, do so now, amma.' Immediately, voices were raised from all directions, filling the house once more. Everyone was moved to see Nafiza running up to fall on her mother and kiss her face, crying out aloud. Two women took hold of her and moved her away forcibly while some of the men came with a bier, laid the body on it, covered it with a green cloth and carried it outside. Asiamma raised her voice and began to chant the prayers of final farewell, her hands uplifted.

After that prayer, the house was still once more, as if it were built up of a silence that could not be shattered. Women began to collect their dupattas and shawls, put them on and say salaam to the others, preparatory to going home. Nafiza sank against the wall, exhausted from all her weeping.

Rahima and Zohra exchanged glances, wondering whether they would have to stay until the men returned from the burial when the final prayers for the dead would be said. Quietly and without being seen, Rahima took Zohra's hand and pressed it, at the same time signalling with her eyes. She and Zohra said salaam to the other women and came outside. Rahima remembered to bring away the carrier which was by her side.

Both women were extremely tired. As soon as they stepped outside the house, Rabia stuck her head out of the car and waved to them. Zohra climbed into the car and asked at once, 'Where were you all this time? I never saw you inside?'

'I felt scared, Amma,' Rabia replied.

'So were you outside all this while, among the men?' Zohra asked in agitation. But Rahima was irritated, and intervened. 'Pach,' she said, 'Can't you keep quiet? It was quite wrong to bring her at all, in the first place. On top of that must she stay inside the whole time?'

Nobody said anything after that. Seeking comfort, Rabia leaned against her Periamma's shoulder.

᠀ 2 ᠀

Rabia woke up very early in the morning. She usually set off at dawn, more eager to pick up the fruit which lay scattered beneath the badam tree, than to recite the Koran at the madrasa. All the other children were the same. They competed with each other to get there first; to gather the greatest number of fruit.

Zohra's voice stopped her as she picked up her head-scarf and Koran as usual, and began to set off at a run. 'What is it, Amma?' she asked, coming to a stop at the front door.

'Did you wash yourself properly before touching the Koran?'

'I did, Amma,' replied Rabia, climbing down into the street and starting to run. There would be no one at the mosque after the dawn prayers, only the Modinaar Bawa, who gave the call to prayers, busy about his work. Rabia was very fond of him. When she arrived there in the morning, he was usually seen stirring water into the earth he had sifted on to a large iron plate. Rabia always went and squatted next to him.

'What's this for, Modinaar Bawa?'

'Wait, child, I'll tell you,' he'd say. He'd give her a tumbler, saying, 'Here, go and dip this into the water trough and bring it to me.' She would dash off to fetch the water.

'Now tell me, what's it for?' she'd repeat.

He'd scratch his beard lightly and say, 'You see, it's a game, like when you play at cooking, with your pots and pans. Now watch!' He would sweep the ground in front of him very thoroughly, and lay out the wet earth with his spoon, spacing out the mounds in neat rows, like a line of iddlis. She knew he was not telling her the truth. She would catch hold of his hand and plead with him, 'Don't try to fool me, Bawa. Why do you make these mud-iddlis every day? Tell me why?' Even though the eager expression on her face made him remorseful, he would say nothing, but laugh quietly. When he laughed he looked very odd to her, with his short beard and moustache, and his teeth showing through his dark lips.

It was a mystery to Rabia and her friends that he made these mud pies every day, and that the men folk who came to pray at the mosque would each pick up a mud pie before disappearing into the toilet. One day, Ahmad asked them in a mocking tone, 'Ei, di, do you girls know what they call those things?' His boisterousness and loud behaviour seemed to proclaim that he knew an important secret, and that if they wished to share it, they should plead with him appropriately.

Madina and Rabia conferred between themselves and agreed they didn't want to learn anything from him. They knew he would be truly humiliated if they just ignored him.

'Well, di, don't you want to know? Come on, ask me,' he said, rolling his eyes and trying to intimidate them.

'We don't want to know anything, da. Go away, or we'll tell the Hazrat, do you understand?' Madina threatened.

Ahmad went away and sat in a corner, but his tongue twitched, as if it were determined of its own accord, to tell them what he knew. He tried his best to control himself, but failed. Turning round to face the wall, he addressed himself to it.

'It's called "delakatti"! There are some idiot girls who don't even know that much, the ignorant wretches,' he complained. But Rabia and Madina had ears that day only for the new word.

Rabia had often come across the word, when her father, Karim, was talking to her mother about people he knew; it was used by him as a term of abuse. 'He is no more to me than a delakatti; I can fling him off whenever I choose.'

She had been watching Mohideen Bawa all this time as his hands dipped into the mud mixture and poured it out very neatly. Suddenly she was anxious because that morning she saw no fruit lying beneath the badam tree.

'Bawa, why is there no fruit today?'

'How can there not be? Look there! The senior Hazrat has picked them all up himself. Go and get yourself some.' He pointed to the senior Hazrat, who had removed his turban and placed it on his lap, and was sitting with his daspih prayer beads in his hand. Rabia ran up to him happily. As she approached him, he looked at her with eyes full of kindness, and invited her, 'Come here, amma.'

'Asalaam aleikum, Hazrat-nga,' she said, politely, sitting down beside him.

'Aleikum salaam. And what are you here for, madam? Wasn't it to get some fruit?' Mischief bubbled over his face.

'No, no, I just wanted to come and see you,' Rabia said, dropping her head shyly.

He looked very small and shrunken, with a thin body and wrinkled skin. His back was hunched. His eyes seemed to look out of deep hollows. A very long nose and flowing beard. He had thrust his fingers into his beard and was combing it out. He was very fond of children. Often he gathered up the fruit by himself, shared it out among all of them, and enjoyed watching their delight. All the time, he would tell his beads, muttering, 's'Allah' as he chewed on his betel leaves. For their part, the children loved him too. If any family had a child who became sick, they would give it water which had been blessed by the Bawa at Maghrib prayers, and the child would never fail to recover. Even if Uma or Ramesh fell ill, their families would bring them the holy water. Uma always said, in surprise, 'Why, Rabia, is he a great saint, an avulia or something? My fever left me at once. It didn't even respond to Dr Saravana's needle.'

Nobody liked the junior Hazrat, Rabia and Madina, least of all. When they chanted from the Koran, if they mispronounced a single word, he pinched their thighs. It was not just to punish them, Rabia felt, that he touched their thighs. He only hit the boys with the cane in his hand. As for the girls, he pinched their thighs. Even to look at him filled her with shame and repulsion. To make things worse, he often invited her to sit next to him, saying, 'Rabia, come and sit by me. Your mother has sent word that I should teach you really well.' Often he would stroke her cheek and pinch it. At such times, Rabia wanted to cry. She would say to Madina, 'I can't bear to learn the chanting from this fellow.'

'It isn't just you. I can't stand him either,' Madina would agree.

Because he hit them soundly, the boys didn't care for him, either. Ahmad said, 'This fellow never married. Nor did he have children. Then how can he show any affection? He beats us as if he is a wild man from the jungle.'

But Rabia was cross with Ahmad, then. 'Don't abuse the Hazrats like that, you'll go to hell. Don't you know that hell-fire can never touch those parts of your body where the Hazrat's cane has fallen on you?'

He replied, 'That's fine if I go to hell. What if I get into heaven? What will be the use of all the beatings I get here?'

'Go away, da, you idiot. Why should I talk to you?' Rabia lost interest.

The hauz, the water trough, was what Rabia loved most in the courtyard of the mosque. Set at floor-level, it was where all the congregation washed before prayers. Lots of fish were allowed to breed there. The fish swam in and out of the water-weeds, lurking and playing; and Rabia's chief concern was to bring them to the surface so that she could watch them. She never forgot, every day, to spend some of her pocket money on puttu, which she bought from the boy who sold it outside the mosque. Sitting by the side of the hauz, she would break it into pieces, and scatter it on the surface of the water. At once all the fish would rise up, scurrying and fighting. It was a daily ritual with her to watch and relish this scene. When Ahmad went and told her mother about it, she got a proper scolding.

'I send you to the mosque-school in order to learn to recite the Koran, not to play about. I was intending to give the Hazrats new clothes and a gift of money if you finish reading the Koran before you come of age. But you, all you do is idle about,' her mother scolded. In exactly the same tone, every day before she left for mosque and as soon as returned, her mother admonished, 'Wash your face and powder it now. You are nearly old enough to come of age.'

That morning, while the madrasa was being held, Kuppi's family distributed a rupee to each child there, because of the Katab Fatiha rite of the third day after the funeral. The children were overjoyed. A big crowd gathered at the Kaja's shop opposite the madrasa, ready to buy a variety of snacks.

Madina whispered in Rabia's ear, 'Don't go and spend this money.' Rabia blinked, not understanding what her friend meant. Madina explained, 'It's money from the house of the dead. We mustn't keep it. Let's throw it away into the water flowing down the hauz.' Without letting anyone see them, they flung their rupees away. Rabia was not very happy to do this. At least she could have bought puttu for the fish the next morning. But she did as she was told, believing that if Madina said so, there would be a good reason for it. Between Madina and herself, nothing was hidden or kept secret. Except for only one thing: the fact that her young aunt, Firdaus, had been given a talaq by her husband, and had returned to her mother's home. Rabia's mother, Zohra, had warned her sharply not to breathe a word of this to anyone at all.

Rahima Periamma had been angry. 'How long can you keep such a thing hidden? If not today, it's surely going to come out tomorrow. What are you saying to this innocent child?'

Rabia was bemused, and stood there staring at them, not

knowing what the shouting was about. What did 'talaq' mean? Who should she ask, in order to find out? She didn't know. Perhaps she should ask Ahmad?

⟐ 3 ⟐

Firdaus, awakening to the sound of cock crow, knew by the undisturbed darkness surrounding her that it was very early morning; not yet time for the Bajar prayers. Her eyelids, swollen from crying during the hours she lay awake, felt heavy. Far away, she heard the faint sound of a child crying somewhere. Suddenly she was confused about where she was. Through the darkness she groped at the wall above her head. The almirah, which her finger touched, above the bedstead, informed her that she was in her mother's house. Her throat felt choked when she remembered that within a month the most important events of her life had happened, and were now over. Hereafter, there was nothing left for her to hold on to. It had taken her a whole month to become fully aware of this fact: everything was finished. Hereafter she could not appear in the outside world. The whole town would jeer at her, speak ill of her, treat her with contempt.

But it would have been a worse horror, had she been forced to live with Yusuf. She could never, never have accepted that. She had made her decision because she knew she could bear any hardship other than that. Her mother and Zohra Akka had pleaded with her to the best of their ability. They even wept in their distress. She would not give in. And finally they agreed they would ask for a talaq.

However hard she thought about it, Firdaus could only conclude that her beauty was the chief reason for her situation. She often said to herself, 'Why was I born with this beauty? Why should I be destroyed so completely?'

On the day of her wedding, the entire town had said the

same thing. All the women had whispered in her hearing. 'What a monstrous thing this is! Is this the best they can do for her, with her looks?'

One woman said, derisively, 'Well, he's from abroad, isn't he? He has lots of cash, probably. So they didn't waste time bothering about suitability and all that. Do you see what I'm saying?'

She was aware their words were meant to provoke her, but she listened all the same, as she sat there with her head bowed down. Her heart beat fast. Tears streamed down her eyes as she sat with her drooping head, hidden behind her veil and her head-dress of flowers. The bridegroom, his silk veshti rustling, came and sat by her. The haji-amma told him to touch her hair and chant the salawaat in praise of the Holy Prophet. When his hand touched her, she wanted to disappear; to withdraw within herself, entirely. A feeling of repugnance had filled her, even before she saw his face. She continued to sit there, her head drooped forward. Then the haji-amma picked up a hand mirror, lifted aside the flowers covering her face, and told the bridegroom to look at his bride's reflection. Firdaus, however, could not see him yet. The haji-amma tied the tali around her neck, and proceeded with all the rituals by herself. Firdaus began to feel an urgent need to see her bridegroom's face immediately.

She was asked to measure out some rice from a vessel. She looked at his hands as they knocked over the grain she had set out. Shocked by the sight of those fingers – very dark and long, shrunk to the bone – she could not bring herself to continue measuring the rice. The women surrounding them urged her, 'Come on girl, measure it out a couple of times more; it's getting late.' Hardly conscious of what she was doing, she carried on; and so she finished everything she was told to do.

The bridegroom's party had eaten the feast, and were ready to leave. The bridal gifts were loaded into a lorry and sent away. They were preparing to take away the bride and groom.

Firdaus was in her room, clasping her mother tightly. It took a very long time to persuade her to come away. Although there was a great deal for mother and daughter to say to each other, at that moment the two could only weep. When Firdaus hugged Amina and wept, it was obvious she did not want to go. It was clear that she was very frightened.

That night when they were alone in their room, the instant Firdaus saw Yusuf's face in the pale light, she said. 'I'm not going to live with you. Don't touch me.'

When she thought about it, she herself was shocked, even now. How could she have been be so daring? How could a village girl like her have had the courage?

Indeed, it seemed that the whole town was frozen with shock. Amina could scarcely leave her room; very rarely did she go outside her house. She wept all the time, berating herself for having such a wild and defiant child. Zohra tried to counsel her younger sister not to be so foolhardy as to ask for a divorce.

'How is your beauty going to help you? Your life will come to an end this way, you know that?'

She replied, weeping, 'Akka, just to look at his face repulses me. I can't bear his wolf-like features and sickly body. I can never, ever live with him, Akka. I'd rather kill myself.'

Amina said, 'Yes, it might be better to do just that. This is a disgusting business.'

But Firdaus was aware that it was not only Yusuf's looks that made her refuse to live with him. She was also goaded by what amounted to a frenzy to defeat her brother-in-law Karim who had chosen this man for her. Karim, who had taken over all the responsibility for the family after her father's death, brought everyone under his control. He insisted his word was law. Nothing was allowed to happen without his permission. Everything that happened was by his favour. Whatever he did was right. No one should question it.

One day, soon after the marriage had been arranged, Zohra and Karim were together in the room upstairs. Firdaus heard

Zohra ask her husband in a soft voice that betrayed her concern, 'Were you certain you liked this man before you actually fixed up the match?'

'What does that mean?' Karim asked, in his turn. 'Look here, it is true the bridegroom isn't much to look at. But he's got plenty of cash; that's the main thing. Tell me, in these days, and in this world, who looks for suitability and all that? Besides, considering the position your family is in, it's a great thing that these people even agreed to be your in-laws. There's no father here; there aren't even any brothers to give the appropriate bridal gifts. Somehow they agreed, because of me; in the hope that I would have the odd piece of jewellery made for her. Tell me what I can do, if I let this chance slip?'

Her brother-in-law's voice sounded very certain of itself.

'And so, must we marry her off without a worry, as if we are paying off a debt? We hoped you would take the place of a father, and seek out a good family for her.' Zohra's voice seemed to cower within her, full of suppressed sobs.

'Don't cry, amma. That child might overhear.' Karim, upset in his turn, tried to comfort her.

Firdaus's dreams dissolved that instant as she stood there at the bottom of the stairs, listening.

* * *

She heard the sound of footsteps as a group of women passed by, on their way to bathe in the river. Firdaus longed to join them as she usually did. They would all go to that stretch of the river that lay beyond Ibrahim Rowther's garden. If they set off as early as this, they could be certain to return home before sunrise. Because they were all girls who had come of age, they had to be back home before the men had begun to stir. Of course it was difficult to avoid stepping on the faeces that lay in piles all along the way. Only a month ago, she too had walked with the other girls. They would all agree, the previous evening, when exactly they should set off in the morning. During her holidays, Rabia too would come along. Even if she was afraid, she would hold on tightly to her Chitthis hand, and stand in the water until dawn broke, playing about and singing, 'Just a pot full of water and a flower blossomed...'

Hereafter Zohra would not visit them. Nor would she bring Rabia with her. That is, not until her anger died down. But even if Rabia were to return some time in the future, she would not be able to enjoy the pleasure of bathing in the river. The child would really mind that. Besides, that tender heart would not understand why Firdaus could no longer take her to the river, and would be confused by the sadness pervading this house. In some ways, it seemed to Firdaus that she had emerged from her nightmare. At the same time she wondered whether she was deceiving herself, whether what she believed to be true was a lie, after all. After her long silence, she broke into sobs while the stars faded away from the sky and daylight began to spread.

ᴄ 4 ᴄ

Rabia came home from school, kicked off her sandals in the courtyard and dropped her satchel on to a chair with a thud, saying, 'Allah!'

'Rabia, come here,' her mother called.

'Mm... I'm coming,' she answered without enthusiasm, going to stand in front of her mother.

Zohra looked her up and down, frowning. 'Go and wash your face properly, with soap. Then, after you have had your coffee, you can do what I tell you.' She went back into the kitchen.

The very thought of washing her face made Rabia feel uncomfortable. And that wasn't the end, was it? She had to powder her face after washing it. It was only after that the look

of disapproval on her mother's face was likely to shift a bit,
Rabia thought, as she went into the bathroom. She took the
soap in her hands, squeezed it hard and rubbed the suds into
her face to her heart's content.

She stood in front of the mirror, powdered her face, staring
at her reflection until she was satisfied at last; then went and
presented herself to Zohra. 'What did you want, Amma?'

Zohra, waiting, the cup of coffee ready in her hand,
expressed herself satisfied with her daughter's appearance.
'Drink this coffee first. After that you have to go and borrow
as many mortars, pestles and sieves as you can from all our
neighbours. Tomorrow morning we'll be pounding rice.' She
added, teasing Rabia, 'Now you won't get a wink of sleep the
whole night long, will you?'

Instantly Rabia asked, her faced suffused with delight, 'Is it
going to be the Ramzan fast soon? Are we going to prepare the
rice flour?' She gulped down her coffee in a trice and sped off
towards Madina's house to start her rounds.

A couple of weeks before the month of Ramzan began, all
the houses in town would start to pound rice and make sweets.
Rabia would get more and more excited as the month of fasting
drew near. She decided to ask her mother exactly how many
more days they had to wait. When she reached Madina's house,
she found the front door locked and hesitated a moment. Then
she peeped through a side window and called out, 'Madina!'
No answer. She returned to the front door and gave a couple
of loud raps. From within, she heard Madina's mother, Sainu,
calling, 'Who is that?' Then Sainu appeared herself, pushing
open the door a little and sticking her head out. 'Oh, it's you,
is it?' she said, opening the door wide. She stood aside, allowing
Rabia to go through.

'That is... my mother wants to borrow your mortar, pestle
and sieve so that we can pound our rice.' Her hesitant tone of
voice betrayed her uncertainty. Would they lend these things
or not? Immediately after she had spoken, her gaze strayed

away from Sainu and towards the interior of the house. Sainu
was aware that Rabia was looking for Madina, and laughed
mockingly. 'Why, amma, you parted from each other just now,
after school. You are yearning to see her again, already, aren't
you?'

Picturing herself blushing with shame, Rabia stuttered, 'No,
it's nothing. Please give me the things soon; I have to go.'

'Come inside. They are stacked in the courtyard; you can
have them.' Sainu turned and led the way inside. 'We pounded
our rice just today. All the mortars, pestles and sieves that we
borrowed from our neighbours are gathered together right
here. So you don't have to go wandering about to any of the
other houses.' She added, 'But there are so many bits and pieces
here. How can you carry it all? You go home and send one of
your servants.'

Rabia was surprised by the concern that was apparent in
her tone. All the same, she had a stubbornly held wish to do
this chore all by herself, so she answered in a rush, 'No, no, I
can do it myself. I'll carry them all home, one by one.'

She hurried into the courtyard and touched the tall pestles
which were leaning against the wall just beside the well. Farida
called out from within, 'Careful, girl, careful. They're going to
fall over!' She ran up to Rabia and caught her hand.

When Rabia turned towards her in a bewildered way, Farida
went on, 'Wait, let me hand them to you one by one. You
don't try and pick them up.' She laid the first pestle across
Rabia's arms. 'Here, take it home carefully without dropping
it on your foot or anything.' Then, as if she had made up her
mind suddenly, she grabbed it back and replaced it carefully.
'No,' she said, 'better not. Better ask one of the older folk to
come and carry these. Fatima will have to see to it. You had
better carry only the sieves. Why should we ask for trouble?
Those pestles are really too heavy.'

Rabia was deeply disappointed. But Faridakka had declared
she wasn't up to it. What to do now? She muttered, 'Such

concern, as if I'm a little baby.' But hiding her disappointment, she stacked the sieves one on top of the other, balanced them on her arms and carried them home.

* * *

That night, Rahima Periamma looked up in surprise to see Rabia creeping into her room. 'Let me sleep with you tonight, Periamma,' Rabia pleaded. Rahima smiled and teased, 'Well madam? What's up madam?'

For a second, Rabia hung her head shyly at her aunt's teasing. Then she looked up and said, 'Periamma, as soon as you are up in the morning, will you wake me up too? I want to watch the rice being pounded. If I ask Amma, she won't let me.' As she spoke, Rabia couldn't bear the pleading tone of her own voice.

'Is that all? I imagined it was something quite different.' Not quite comprehending what was behind her aunt's mischievous smile, Rabia quickly leapt into the bed and rolled away to one side, saying, 'I'll go off to sleep then.' She made haste, for fear her aunt might change her mind.

Rahima woke her up very early indeed: it was only three in the morning. 'Come on, let's go and wash the rice.'

Her mother and aunt began to wash the rice which had been measured out in big silver tumblers, and lay heaped in the paved courtyard. Now and then, Zohra threw a stern glance at her daughter, which said, 'Why do you have to do this?' Rabia understood, but pretended not to notice. Rahima scooped the washed rice into baskets to drain, poured out the remaining water into the cattle troughs, and then washed the rice again, repeatedly, until it was transformed into a gleaming white. Gasping for breath, she straightened up and rested for an instant. 'It's got to look white and shining, just like our Rabia.' Rabia was squatting on the paved courtyard, watching. She knew that Periamma hadn't really meant her. She thought to herself, 'Say it should look like Wahida Akka.'

Her legs were tormented by mosquitoes, and she scratched away at herself, muttering, 'ush…ah'. Zohra complained, 'It's our fate to do all this, but what on earth possessed you to wake up at this unearthly hour and sit here?' Almost immediately, there was a rap at the door and her mother hurried towards it, calling out, 'Who is it?' Satthappan stood there, flanked by the hired women. Zohra opened the doors wide, inviting them to enter. Satthappan sent the women inside first, locked the door behind him and came into the courtyard.

'How is it going? Have you washed all the rice? Is it soaked properly?' He went up to the anda containing the rice, scooped up a handful and gazed at it. Then he threw a couple of grains into his mouth, chewed on them and announced, 'Mm. We can make a start.' He took off his shirt, rolled it up with both hands and walked around the courtyard, looking for a safe place to put it away.

Rabia watched him intently, not once blinking her eyes. He walked in a peculiar sort of way. Even the way he spoke, dragging his words a little, seemed odd to her. It seemed as if she were watching a woman. But then, he wasn't exactly like a woman, either. Confused, she turned her eyes away from him and towards the coolie women. There were six of them. They picked up a pestle each, and began to pound the rice which they flung into the mortais.

By the time Satthan too began to pound, wearing only a cloth about his waist, dawn had just begun to break. 'Hm, come on women, hurry up now. No star-gazing! Let's see how quickly you can get on with it!' He began to throw the pestle into the mortar, lifting it higher and higher.

Rahima Periamma urged him on. 'Why, Satthappa, no songs as yet? Come on, you start them off!'

'Let them get on without any singing for a while. When they start to tire, then I can start off, can't I?' he replied, with some pride. 'Hm, throw it this way, throw it well,' he called out, urging the workers on. The women in the team suppresses their giggles and pounded in unison, to a steady rhythm and a loudly hissed 'ss... ss'. Zohra gathered together the pounded rice and spread it out to dry on a mat laid on a bed strung with coir-rope.

Rabia was transported as she listened to the rhythmic sound of the rice-pounding. Weeks before the beginning of Ramzan, the harmony and rhythm of pounding rice would sound from every house, resonating throughout the town. Unable to contain her excitement now, she kept running between the kitchen and the courtyard. Fatima was sifting the finely pounded rice flour on to a cloth which was spread out in a room next to the courtyard. She called out an order. 'Rabia come and sift the rice flour that's just been pounded.' Eagerly she accepted the job and sat down next to Fatima. Satthappan who had been resting for a moment, leaning against the wall, called out, 'Appa-di, how this heat is tormenting me. Give us a little water, please, thaayi.' He added, complaining, 'Clever woman you are, passing off your job to the Master's daughter!'

'You shut up, Satthappa, and let her get on with it. Otherwise she'll just be running about uselessly, here and there. And after all, who do you think is going to eat all the idiappam and paniyaaram that will be made from this flour we are labouring over? It's not going into the mouths of servants like us, but theirs, that's for sure.' Fatima spoke sharply and laughed.

Satthappan held his chin, miming surprise. 'What a woman!' He addressed the other coolie women. 'Did you see this, what she gets up to? Did you hear how she talks?' He went up to Zohra, swaying from his waist, and drank the water from the chombu she handed to him.

Rahima, who had been quietly sifting the flour all this time remarked playfully, 'Oh this Fatima! She'll say all this, and more than this! Do you know that, Satthappa? But come on then, give us a song so that we don't all get bored.'

Rabia could see Fatima's face beaming with pride at Rahima's words. But then, Zohra came out of the kitchen, calling out, 'Come on, everyone, drink your tea first.' She saw

Rabia chewing on the raw rice and reprimanded her. 'Adi, are you eating raw rice? Won't it upset your stomach?' She was cross with Rahima as well. 'And there you are, happily watching her. Just look at the state of her!' She sat down to do her share of the sifting.

Fatima rose to her feet and poured out the tea for everyone. 'Hurry up now. Finish all the pounding before it gets too hot. I'll light the fire and get everything ready to roast the flour.'

'Well, well, the sun is already high in the sky. Everything in due time; it's not as if this job is new to us.' Satthappan sat down cross-legged on the floor and drank his tea. Rabia kept on gazing at him, steadily. She watched him continuously as he stood and walked and spoke. Her mind buzzed with all the questions she would ask Rahima Periamma later.

Fatima rolled three big stones into the courtyard to make a hearth, lit a fire, and picked up the big earthenware pan in which the flour would be roasted. She was just about to place it on the stone hearth when Zohra called out, 'Wait, I'm coming.' Leaving off her work, she took the pan from Fatima's hands, and laid it on the fire herself, saying 'Bismillah'. She scooped up some of the flour onto a vessel, took it to the fire and tipped it into the pan. 'Bring the ladle, Satthappan,' she called out. Then she returned to her sifting. Rabia watching all this, noticed how Fatima's expression changed during her mother's intervention.

Satthappan sat on a wooden plank in front of the fire and began a song as he stirred with the ladle. The women threw their pestles faster and faster to the rousing rhythm of the song. Rahima and Zohra looked at each other gleefully. Coming to a stop suddenly, in the middle of his song, he called to the others, 'Quick! The flour is just done. Take it off and put it to cool. Once it's cooled down, you can finish the whole thing by sifting it a last time.'

Rabia continued to be fascinated by him. From whatever angle she looked at him, he seemed like a woman, with his long nose, wide forehead and well-defined eyebrows. Unable to

stand it anymore, she brought her lips close to her aunt's ear.
But Rahima had settled down to sift the flour which had been
roasted and cooled; her glance was stern. 'Not now,' it seemed
to order Rabia. Disappointed, the girl went back to her place,
and began to chew the raw rice-flour that she was sifting. Seeing
this, Zohra shouted, 'Don't stuff your mouth, you little devil,
you'll choke and die.'

The sizzling sound of the roasting flour mingled with
Satthappan's singing. Rabia could not follow a single one of
those songs. She couldn't remember hearing any of them in
the films she had seen; yet she enjoyed them so much. The smoke
and the dust made her eyes water and she rubbed at them with
her long skirt. The entire house felt sticky. All of them looked
like ghosts; the flour covering their hair and their bodies.
However hard they tried to dust off their hair, they looked
strange, as if they had all suddenly gone grey. She wondered
how it would be if she ran out into the street just as she was,
and showed herself to Madina. She gave up the idea at once,
remembering her mother's warning earlier that day. 'If people
see all this flour spread out to dry, they might cast an evil eye
on us. So you must not open the door, on any account.'

It was very nearly mid-day. The coolie women and
Satthappan had ranged themselves in the shady pathway,
unable to bear the heat anymore. Their faces, so eager and
enthusiastic when they first arrived, looked tired and wilted
now. Rabia felt very sorry for them. She went quietly up to her
mother's side and asked, 'What about some food for them?'

'Yes, we must certainly feed them,' Zohra agreed, and called
out towards the kitchen, 'Here, Fatima, serve them their meal,
now.' Then she said in a low voice, to Rahima, 'Ei, Akka, you
haven't noticed anyone who stands right in line with her
tradition, have you?' She waited a moment, and then indicated
Rabia with her eyes. 'Take a look!' Rabia couldn't understand
what was going on, but felt shy, all the same. 'Go on, Amma,'
she said, fondly.

'All right, all right, come on. Let's go and stir up the mixture for athirasam. Fatima has the jaggery syrup on the fire.' Rahima now hurried into the kitchen, followed by Zohra. Her enthusiasm flaring up again, Rabia leapt to her feet and joined them.

Rahima held the pot of syrup firmly between her feet and began to stir it with a ladle, while Zohra sprinkled the rice flour in, gently, very gently. The smell of the syrup pervaded the entire house, and filled Rabia with rapture. The fasting month was approaching; all this was to celebrate the revelation of the Koran, the very first chanting of the Fatiha. She was wildly excited. Standing behind Zohra she watched intently as Rahima Periamma's hand guided the ladle as it whirled round and round the pot. She felt a huge desire to take a handful of the swirling batter, velvety smooth like butter; gold-coloured. Amma wouldn't let her eat it though. 'You'll be ill if you eat too much sweet stuff,' she'd say.

But Periamma understood the yearning in her eyes. She dropped a small piece from her ladle on to a plate, saying, 'Here, Rabia, try a bit of this and see if it tastes right.'

'Why are you giving her this, now? We'll soon be stirring the athirsam dough made with sugar-syrup. Let her have some of that.' Zohra spoke as if she had some special reason in mind.

Rabia was irritated by her mother's words. 'No, this is fine for me,' she said hurriedly, reaching out to take the plate.

Zohra and Rahima were both perspiring all over from the heat of the hearth; they were soaking wet. Now they lowered the sugar syrup from the fire, and began to work all over again. Suddenly, Rabia didn't want to stay there any longer. She returned to the courtyard, to watch Satthappan and the coolie women. Weren't they anxious to finish their work and go, she wondered. She felt uncomfortable, just watching them.

Satthappan smiled at her affectionately. 'Why are you standing there looking so sad, Master's daughter? And why have we not seen the Master? He hasn't come home for his mid-day meal yet!'

Her father and uncle wouldn't come anywhere near their

house, not even by accident, on rice-pounding days. She knew
that they had said that the house would be in chaos, and that
they would prefer to have their meal sent to the shop. She said
to Satthappan, ' The thing is… their meal has been sent to the
shop.'

Seeing her hesitate as if she wanted to ask them something,
but didn't dare, Ramayi and Ponni spoke up. 'What are you
thinking about? Why don't you tell us what it is?'

Her eyes wide with surprise, she came closer and said, 'It's
nothing, really. That is, I wanted to ask whether your arms
hurt or not?' She spoke in a whisper, as if she didn't want her
mother to overhear.

Satthappan fell about, laughing. 'Just look at this child,' he
said. Afraid her mother would come out, she didn't wait for
an answer, but ran away and hid in the kitchen.

Throughout that evening, her mother and aunt rubbed
ointment into each other's legs, turn by turn. Even so, Amma
tossed about all night, unable to sleep for the pain. It was
always the same. Rabia felt very sorry. 'Amma why do you
have to work so very hard to pound the rice?' she asked
anxiously.

'We have to cook idiappam for the men to eat, when they
break their fast, don't we?' said Amma, in answer.

Her legs ached, too. She had gone from house to house,
returning all the mortars, pestles and sieves. But it was for her
mother and her aunt that she felt really sorry.

∽ 5 ∽

The heat was fierce that day, even in the early evening.
It was a day that was more important than any other. Not
only for Rabia, but for all the other children, too. In a little
while, darkness would cover everything. It was then that the
Ramzan moon would appear in the sky. The month that
followed was one of celebration. Even to die in the month of

Ramzan was said to be a blessing. For if one were to die at that time, a direct passage to heaven was a certainty. Rabia had heard her mother say this. When the fast ended, every evening, there would be plenty to eat, in every house. The happiest thing of all was that during this month, Allah would imprison all the devils, and keep them tied up in the skies.

From late afternoon, Rabia, Madina and some other friends had found themselves a stone each in the waste ground next to Rabia's house and had seated themselves there. Rabia was scratching away at her ankles, where the mosquitoes were biting her. Madina asked, 'What do you think, Rabia? The crescent moon will definitely show up this evening, won't it?'

For some reason, she was uncertain; fearful that the moon might disappoint them. Seeing the expression on Madina's long face, Rabia wanted the crescent moon to appear, at least for her friend's sake. Anxious to dispel that dispirited look at least for the time being, she said consolingly, 'It will come. Of course it will come. Even if we can't see it, they'll announce it over Radio Ceylon, won't they?'

'Have they pounded the rice in your house?'

'Yes, of course. On the day after they did it at yours. Have you forgotten already?'

'See, I forgot about it entirely,' said Madina, tapping herself lightly on the forehead.

Rabia watched the sky silently for a while, but soon became bored. Her neck was hurting, besides, so she turned towards her friend. 'Madina, come on, let's play Sand or Stone.' Madina felt no great desire to play, but agreed because Rabia asked.

Guessing that Madina had agreed only reluctantly, Rabia forsook the idea of a game. 'No', she said, 'let's not. There's no one around here to play with, what can we do?' She looked about her. She wanted Madina to believe she had decided against the game because there really were not enough people there to play.

Madina accepted Rabia's words and squatted down on her

stone once more. 'Where are all the little fellows from the Frog's and PKL's families? They are usually to be seen playing just here, every evening, the little devils!' Madina muttered this in a tone that suggested she was disappointed Rabia could not have her wish.

A cow from ORAS's house stood opposite them, chewing cud. Foam and spittle dribbled from its mouth, down to the ground. It stared at them profoundly, with its brown eyes, as if it harboured some unknown purpose. It swished its reddish tail, attempting to drive away the flies which covered its swollen and pregnant stomach. Watching it with pity, Rabia wondered briefly whether there was any way of driving away such a swarm of flies. The flies were clinging to the poor cow's neck as well. Each fly was as big as a bean-seed. Not a single one of them was tiny.

It looked as if it would calve in a couple of days. Rabia remembered the old lady from the ORAS family telling her mother this. She was eager to see the calf being born, at least this time. When the cow was in the throes of labour last year, Zohra had dragged her away, saying, 'It will scare you.'

Madina shook her by the shoulder. 'What are you thinking about?'

'Nothing, really, 'she said, but added, 'Just look at that! How many flies are tormenting that cow, poor creature!'

'Phew! You've noticed something amazing, haven't you? Do you think there are only flies on cattle? There will be ticks as well, you know that? But in any case, let's sit a bit further off. When she swishes those flies off, she might scatter them on us.' Madina spoke with concern and sarcasm at the same time. There was a trace of mockery in her voice which said, How can you feel pity for a mere cow? Rabia pretended not to notice, and gazed up at the sky. Madina shooed the cow until it moved some distance away; then she returned to her former seat. They were surrounded by the smell of the dust which the cow's hoofs had raised when it walked away.

Madina looked at her friend, wearily. 'What's this; there's no sign of the moon yet.'

Rabia said in a reassuring tone, 'It will show up. You wait and see.'

The sky stretched away to the horizon, absolutely clear; there wasn't even a speck of cloud to be seen. It was the colour of a faded blue sari that her mother had set aside for spreading out vadaam to dry. When it finally did appear, there would certainly be no place for the new moon to hide.

Only towards the south, and in just one place, there was a small heap of clouds looking like the dirty suds which gathered beneath the washing stone when Fatima washed their clothes. She liked to poke at the suds, even though Fatima kept on telling her off. Now, a little further off, a shred of a cloud sat by itself, all alone, as if it had quarrelled with the rest. She felt sorry to see it, but laughed at herself the next instant. 'Ché, it isn't human, it's only a cloud. Why should I feel sorry for it?'

'Oi, hurry up, you fellows!' A gang of boys came thudding through the passageway adjacent to Rabia's house. Startled, Rabia turned round and saw Ahmad and Iliaz appearing through the dust cloud behind her, shouting and yelling. They stopped short in front of her, gasping for breath and saying, 'Ss ... Allah!'. The other boys from PKL's house, who had come running along with them, rushed off homeward, yelling themselves hoarse. 'Each to his own home, to eat avarakka rice, to the house of the newly-born, to eat biriyani rice!'

Madina covered her nose with the palm of her hand and said, grimacing irritably, 'Saniyans! Look at the dust they have raised in their wake'. Ahmad was oblivious to the fact that she had included him when she said 'saniyan'. He sat down on a stone at a little distance from them, and began to stare at the sky as if he had some special intent.

The girls were tired of staring at the sky for such a long time. It was only after the moon appeared that preparations could begin for the early morning sahar meal, eaten before the fast began. Before they started cooking, it would be Rabia's job to go to the shop for bananas and eggs. She rose to her feet and shook off the barely visible dust from the back of her skirt. 'I going home for my dinner, I'm hungry,' she told Madina, and started off. 'In that case, you'll tell me, won't you, when they broadcast on the radio that the moon has appeared?' Madina shouted after her.

It gave Rabia great pleasure that Madina counted on her and asked her this. She felt special, not just one of the rest. Besides, she was asking her in the presence of Ahmad. 'Oh, of course I'll tell you,' she replied loftily.

But Ahmad wouldn't mind his own business. 'Why do you have to tell her, specially? In a little while Modinaar Bawa will announce it from the mosque, over the mike. These girls just want to show off in front of me.'

This infuriated Rabia and Madina, but they stalked off homewards, making no retort.

* * *

The month of Ramzan had just begun, and the girls were fasting on the first day. They would not be allowed to fast on all thirty days. Their families would allow them to do so only on the most important days: the first, the fifteenth, the twenty seventh, and the last. Rabia's uncle would protest all the time, telling the rest that the girl was growing up, and should keep the fast throughout the month. Her mother would never consent to it, though.

There was no cooking to be done in the morning, and no madrasa either. The two girls arrived at their school very early. Uma would join them only after some time. Not even a single teacher had turned up as yet. In fact, the whole school looked empty. They stood under the mango tree. Rabia, leaping on to a low branch that nearly touched the ground, wondered what her mother would say if she were to see her, and smiled to herself.

Still smiling, she felt the back of her green uniform skirt, checking whether it felt sticky. Then, satisfied it was not, she balanced herself on both hands, and swung gently back and forth. Madina, climbing on to the branch after her, couldn't understand her gesture, and looked at her quizzically. There was a trace of anxiety on Rabia's round face. But Madina didn't comment on it.

'Well, Rabia, what did they cook in your house for today's sahar?'

Rabia thought for a while and said, 'It was the first sahar, wasn't it, so there was only dal and a side-dish. What about you?'

'Exactly the same. What time did your wake up for the sahar?'

'Do you know, I was up at three,' said Rabia, proudly. 'Didn't you see the Sahar Muzafar announcing sahar, then?'

'I woke up only at four o'clock, Rabia,' Madina was remorseful. 'But what about you? What did you do so early in the morning?'

'My mother sets her alarm clock, and is up as early as 2.30. The noise wakes me up, too.'

'But why so early? What does she do?'

'It's only then that she can finish everything in time. First she'll light the fire and cook the rice. While it's cooking, she'll do her olu ablutions, and say the night-time tahajjat prayers. By the time she's seen to all the other chores, it will be four, won't it?'

Rabia remembered how hard it was to force herself to eat the sahar meal. She had sat down between her father and uncle, extremely proud that she was going to keep the first day fast. Telling herself that she wouldn't be able to eat or drink until the following evening, and that she must fill her stomach now, she loosened the waist string of her skirt and retied it. She stopped her uncle from serving her, and piled up her plate with rice saying, 'I'll do it myself.' She was so pleased with herself.

She poured the sambar all over the rice until it was drenched, thinking to herself, 'If I eat up all this, I won't feel the tiniest bit hungry the whole day.'

'Don't spill, don't spill,' her uncle warned, worried.

'I won't spill,' she assured him, pouring on some more, and putting her hand in the middle of her plate to mix the sambar with the rice.

Her uncle watched her intently. 'Here, stop it, will you? Is that rice you are mixing, or is it cement? Hasn't the Holy Prophet told us to mix the rice properly, only in one corner of the plate first of all, and to eat it slowly, little by little? Should you plough your food about, like this?' His voice was gentle and stern at the same time.

Rabia was deeply ashamed. 'Very well, Periattha', she said shyly, bending over her plate and placing a handful in her mouth.

He watched her a little longer, and then called towards the kitchen, 'Rabia's mother, please come here.' Not knowing why he was summoning her mother, Rabia stopped eating and gazed in bewilderment at her father and uncle.

'Here I am, Macchaan.' Zohra came towards them, her sari pulled right over her head. She stood half-hidden next to a pillar. Rabia's father continued to eat, showing no concern. Now Rabia stared at her mother and uncle alternately.

Zohra addressed her brother-in-law. 'The sahar time will end soon, and you haven't even begun to eat.' She sounded worried.

'We'll eat; there's still time,' he said calmly. 'But what is this, Rabia's mother, you are failing to teach this girl any of our proper practices.' His voice and expression were dense with disappointment.

Zohra stared; she didn't understand what he meant. Unable to reply, she turned her gaze on Rabia, silently. Rabia, for her part, not knowing what she had done wrong, looked at her mother, piteously.

'Look at her, there's no cloth covering her head. What sort

of practice is it, tell me, to sit down to eat without covering your head? She mixes up all her rice in one go, makes a complete mess of it and then eats. She doesn't seem to know the benefit of mixing it a little at a time, just before each mouthful. See how many grains of rice are scattered right around her plate. I don't know whether she even said "Bismillah" before starting to eat. Bring up this girl child with some idea of right learning. Teach her to respect what is good conduct and proper behaviour. Let her learn which things we are commanded to do and which things we may aspire to do.' He spoke in one breath, his voice gentle and caring; his hand stroking Rabia's head lovingly.

Zohra stood stock-still, unable to say anything, her gaze entirely fixed on her daughter. That gaze said, 'You irresponsible slut, because of you I have earned a bad name.'

Rabia's eyes darted through to the inner rooms, searching for her Periamma. Grains of rice lay squashed between her fingers. She looked up at her uncle. He returned her look, smiling kindly, and taking a handkerchief from his lap, spread it over her head. 'Eat,' he said, helping himself to some rice. He looked satisfied; he had said exactly what he intended. Karim stopped eating for a moment and said, with an air of bringing everything back to normal, 'Hurry up and eat, it's getting late.'

'Zohra, come and take this appalam,' Periamma called from the kitchen. Rabia looked fearfully at her mother, who sped away.

* * *

A dog from Kattaiyan's house rushed around the school grounds, barking loudly. The noise brought Rabia to the present, and she followed the dog with her eyes as it raced towards the foothills of the mountain. She muttered, 'Crazy creature! Why is it running so fast?' Poor thing, it wasn't going to get its mid-day meal from her that day, she thought, and looked above her at the rustling leaves. A squirrel, rushing about amidst the branches, stopped for a moment and looked at her with jewel-eyes. Its eyes seemed to say, 'It was you who commanded me to stop.' Rabia lifted her left arm above her head and said, 'Shoo.' Frightened, the squirrel gave a single leap and disappeared. Her eyes searched for it everywhere among the branches, and at last came to rest on the flowers, strewn in a carpet, beneath the tree.

'Amma-di, look at all these flowers!' she exclaimed, seizing Madina by the thigh and giving her a shake. Madina, searching for something among the pages of her book, glanced down quickly, muttered in agreement, and returned to what she was doing.

'We're going to have lots of mangoes in our garden this year,' Rabia murmured, flooded with happiness,

Their head gardener, Pandi, would bring cart-loads of mangoes, spread them out on the sacking-covered floor of one of their store-rooms, and sort them out into separate piles according to their species. There would be ten cart-loads in all. He usually brought two cart-loads a day, covered the mangoes with straw and more sacking, made sure that all the holes in the room were stopped up with cloth so that no rats could enter, and fastened the door tightly shut. Once in two days, Amma or Periamma would go in, lock the door and check whether the fruit had ripened. They would never allow Rabia inside. When she protested, insisting on going in with them, Periamma rebuked her sternly. 'If a single rat gets in, everything will be ruined, Rabia; don't be stubborn.'

Rabia was embarrassed now, as she remembered how proudly she stood in the street, watching Pandi carrying in the mangoes from the bullock cart. When her uncle heaped the ripe mangos into baskets, and sent Mariyayi to deliver them to all their relatives, how she would sit there, watching and yearning. Meanwhile, her mother, walking to and fro, always grumbled, 'Don't go and gorge on too many mangos. They are heating! You could get your period suddenly.'

Rabia consoled herself now, 'So what's the good of so much

fruit? Who's going to eat it all? Not me, certainly. Why on earth do I have to grow up? Why can't I be a little girl, always?' She asked Madina, 'What are you looking for? You've been searching for a long time.'

'It's nothing. I have a five-rupee note somewhere. I remember I put it into this book, but I can't seem to find it. That's all.' Madina sounded regretful at having lost her money. Besides, Rabia thought, she must be truly sad she did not see the Sahar Muzafar.

For a while, both girls were silent. The breeze blew gently, comfortingly. Rabia watched the wilted mango blossom drifting down to the ground. Suddenly she remembered to ask, 'By the way, have you done your homework?'

'No,' said Madina, indifferently.

'Won't Sir beat you?' Rabia was alarmed.

Madina laughed. 'I'm keeping the fast, aren't I? Sir certainly won't hit me.'

All the teachers refrained from beating the children during the month of Ramzan: a small concession that was deeply appreciated.

Giving Madina a fond tap on her head, Rabia said, 'You are a fine one!' But her voice betrayed her regret that she alone had finished all her homework, to the point of giving herself an aching arm.

ᕕ 6 ᕗ

Amina woke up with a start, at midnight. Involuntarily her hand moved, groping at the mat next to her. As soon as her fingers touched Firdaus's warm body, she was overcome with relief, and muttered, 'Ya, Allah!' For how long must she carry the burden that Firdaus had become? The thought made her choke with sorrow. She could not sleep for fear that despair would drive the girl to destroy herself.

Memories came to her, suddenly, of her parents and her

younger sister; and the way in which her own marriage had been arranged. Her father, Kani Rowther, was so dark-complexioned, you could have touched him and used your finger to make a black pottu. Her mother, on the other hand, was fair-skinned and beautiful. Any room she sat in was lit up, as if by a bolt of lightning; her colour had the glow of a lantern set within its niche. Yet there never was an argument between her parents.

It was always a celebration in their house, when Kani Rowther returned from one of his business trips. He'd spend the money he had made extravagantly, causing a great stir in the whole town. He'd buy four sheep heads at the butcher's and parade down the street, holding them by their ears, two in either hand, in full view of everyone. The women walking past would say to each other, 'He's full of himself, isn't he?'

When he found time hanging heavy on his hands, he would sit under the pipal tree and play cards. Ismail would join him at his card games, on these occasions. Once, when they were joking with each other, Ismail got up suddenly, saying, 'I don't like to play for money, Maamu. After all, it's not as if I need the money, is it?'

'Then what should we play for, maapilé, tell me,' said Rowther, in a merry mood.

'Let's play for your daughter. If I win, I marry her,' Ismail said.

'Do you think it is a hardship for me to give you my daughter? But in any case, let's play and see.' And Rowther began the next game.

That evening, Amina came home from school, and was standing in the street, nibbling at a snack, when Rowther arrived, singing with happiness. 'Come here, my girl, come to your Attha,' he called. He peered into the kitchen, twisting his moustache and shouting enthusiastically, 'Ei, Kadija, come here, hurry up, I've been arranging a match for your daughter!'

Kadija came out hastily, wanting to verify what she had half-heard. A grindstone had fallen on her foot when she was a

child, so she could not walk straight; she had to drag her leg
along. She came up to him and sat down on the small mat
which was spread on the floor. 'What were you saying?' she
asked, eagerly.

'You know Ismail from the Big House? Well, he asked if I
would let him marry our girl, and I said, yes, da, of course;
marry her!' He laughed loudly, as if to say, 'What do you think
of my smartness?'

He was surprised that, contrary to his expectations, Kadija
did not express any great joy. Hiding his disappointment, he
watched her keenly while he spoke in a bantering tone, 'So,
aren't you going to say anything?'

'It's not that. But she's only just ten years old. I'm wondering
why we should hurry, that's all. And then, this Ismail, he was
married before and lost his wife; he must be over thirty-five,
now.' Hesitantly she expressed her disapproval, and waited
quietly for his reply.

'Is that all it is? I imagined it was something much more
important. Come on, di. Is this a proper reason? You are
carrying on as if it is something unknown to this world.
Anyway, I've given him my word. The nikah is to be held next
week, on Friday. Very well then, off you go now and make me
some tea.' He shook out his cloth, wrapped it around his
shoulders and walked off to the front thinnai at a brisk pace.

When the wedding took place in the next few days, Amina
understood nothing about what was going on. The procession
of the bridegroom on his prancing horse, and the lavish
wedding feast were such as to astonish the whole town. Kani
Rowther's smartness in making such a grand alliance was the
envy of all; he had grabbed hold of a fine tamarind branch,
laden with fruit, they said. But it was the same Rowther who
came to grief after he arranged a match for his second daughter
Maimoon; this time, through his business contacts.

Within two months of the marriage, Maimoon returned
home. She sat in an upstairs room, huddled close to the storage
bin, declaring she would never consent to live with her husband.

However much Amina and Kadija advised and then pleaded with her to return to him, Maimoon would not. 'I can't' was all she would say. Reflected by the light of the lantern, they could see the obstinacy and resolve in her tender face. That expression also sent out an order that they should not speak of it anymore.

Kani Rowther felt more keenly than Kadija that the family had been shamed. He forgot his laughter, his songs and his jokes, and stayed within the four walls of the house, paralysed. Kadija wept for his sake alone. 'We are women, after all; we are used to staying at home. But he is a man and he can't even get about; it's become impossible for him even to step into the street.'

Whenever Kani Rowther looked at Amina, tears gathered in his eyes. 'My child,' he muttered to himself. He began to think of her as the one who sacrificed her own will in order to accept the bridegroom her father chose for her. In those days, when he did not go out into the world or conduct any business, the family was sustained only by the favour of Ismail and Amina. He was overcome at the thought of his son-in-law's goodness.

Although he did not wish to carry on trading as before, he wanted to find a way of earning a living by working from home. So, every morning, after breakfast, he would carry his wooden seating plank into the courtyard. He would sit there and open up a bundle of incense sticks which he bought wholesale, and separate them into sets of four. Then, out of a small wooden box, he would take out little bottles of scent and arrange them on the floor beside him. He would open and sniff each one in turn, and shake out a few drops of attar into the palm of his hand. He would spread this mixture on to the incense sticks, four at a time. He would sniff them again to check that the perfume was as it should be. When he was satisfied, they would be arranged on to a winnowing tray, and placed in the gentle warmth of the courtyard, to dry.

All day he wrapped bundles of ten attar-scented incense

sticks in rose-coloured silver paper, and packed them away in a cardboard box. He didn't want anyone to help him in this task. He did it all by himself, humming songs to himself in a very low voice. There was a deep sorrow in that voice that wrung the hearts of those who listened, and stopped them from talking to him or interfering in his work. Later he would put away all the scent bottles into their wooden box.

Amina loved to observe those bottles. They were each of a different and beautiful shape; each had a different stopper. He would pick each one up with his trembling fingers, make sure it was securely closed, and put it away with care. Every few days a tradesman known to Rowther would arrive, pay for the bundles and take them away. The pride on her father's face as he received that money with his shaking hands made Amina's little eyes sparkle with tears.

And then, suddenly one morning, Maimoon vomited. Kadija came running to Amina's house to fetch her. On their way back, she said in a faltering voice, 'Please talk to her. The wretched child won't listen to anything I say.' As they hurried along the street, hurricane lanterns in their hands, they seemed to be surrounded by dust and darkness. Even as she took care to tread carefully, Amina wondered how she should reply if anyone were to ask her, 'Where are you off to, Amina, at this hour?' At her young age, when she was having enough trouble giving birth to her babies and running a family, here she was, bearing the brunt of Maimoon's problems as well. It was because of Maimoon that it even struck Amina that it was possible for a woman, once she was married, to consider an option other than living with her husband. And Maimoon had brought such shame on her family that they could not show their faces in town. After all that, what need was there for her to live any longer, Amina wondered.

They arrived home and quietly pushed the wooden door open. Anxiety gnawed at Amina: her father must not know anything of this; he would be entirely broken. This, on top of Maimoon's divorce, would surely deprive him of his life. The

sound of a dog barking in the street frightened her. If Zohra
were to wake up at this time and cry, Ismail too would wake up
and look for her. She went into Maimoon's room thinking to
herself, it was enough for the mother-in-law alone to be
informed; let us not have any further unpleasantness.

* * *

But in the end, she had asked their farm-hand, Marudu, to get
the bullock cart ready some days later. His wife, Murugi, had
told them about the midwife who lived in the next village.
'There's nothing she can't manage.' She had offered to go and
fetch this woman herself. Although it was only the next village,
it would be ten at night by the time they returned. And that
would be a suitable time for what they intended. So Marudu
and Murugi arranged to leave in good time.

Darkness began to spread everywhere. Amina fed Zohra
early and put her to sleep. She had planned it all for that day,
because Ismail was away on business, conveniently for them.
Even so, she was full of an uncontrollable fear. Her mind
couldn't quite take in the awfulness of what was going to happen
shortly. But, here in this village, she couldn't think of any other
way out but this. Her sister must be rid of the burden in her
womb; that was all. What if it became common knowledge
that she was pregnant? The very thought of it made her heart
beat fast. This was the only thing to do, given that the girl was
in no position to bear and bring up a baby. Ismail had said he
would arrange another marriage for her. They were only
waiting for the idda time following a divorce to lapse. If she
went and had a baby meanwhile, what would happen?

As soon as the town was quiet, she stepped into the street. It
was convenient too that there was very little moonlight.
Although the road was not a difficult one, she watched the
path carefully. She had not dared, this time, to carry a lamp to
light her way. She was afraid she might be seen. Although she
only had to go to the next street, she walked into the darkness

very fearfully. Her body, sagging with sorrow, crept along the street as if it were sinking into the horror to come.

She passed the houses of the Hazrat, the 'podum ponnu', the 'enough girl' (so named in the hope she would be the last girl in her family), the Kaattu Bawa, the tailor. Only the Chélladurai and Ponnayya houses left. She kept reminding herself of each of them, in turn. Her fear grew hugely, each time she saw someone asleep on their front thinnai, seeking some fresh air. Involuntarily she repeated to herself, 'Allah, Allah,' as she walked on as noiselessly as she could. She wished with all her heart that even the pale moonlight that filtered down from the skies had not been there. She walked on, oblivious of her solitude, not minding the wind that blew past her on the silent road. The wind's whistle, which usually frightened her, only increased her awareness of the need to hurry.

Amina reached the house, opened the door, and hastened towards the backyard. Murugi and an older woman were squatting down on the stone thinnai there. They rose to their feet the instant they saw her. She put a finger to her lips, signalling to them not to say a word. The back door of the house was not locked, only closed. It gave as soon as she pushed it. Amina entered first, and turned around. When they had followed her inside, she locked the door behind her, and looked for her mother. Kadija sat in the hall, leaning against a pillar, waiting for them. As soon as she saw them she stood up clumsily, clutching at the pillar. Amina whispered, 'Where is she?' Kadija gestured to indicate that Maimoon was upstairs, and began to lead the way there. She walked slowly, in utter weariness.

Kadija felt pained by Amina's vengefulness at this terrible hour, but at the same time, her eyes filled with tears as she thought, 'My beloved daughter, my golden girl, how resolute you have to be at so young an age.' At once she also thought of Maimoon's extreme youth, and began to lament aloud, 'Allah, how could you have put a child in so tender a body?'

All four women climbed up the wooden steps, one behind

the other. There lay Maimoon, curled up asleep, a dimly lit lantern beside her. 'Allah, when I look at her, I am gripped with fear,' Kadija said, pressing her sari against her mouth to hold back the sobs. 'Now, now, don't cry please,' Amina comforted her, trying hard not to betray her own terrors.

Hearing her mother's sobs, Maimoon woke up and looked about her, perplexed. In the dim light, they could see her young body trembling. It was only then that Amina looked directly at the midwife. She seemed about forty-five years old. Her sari was wrapped about her bare upper body; she did not wear a blouse. Studs in her ears, with sparkling red stones. Both hands had scorpions tattooed upon them. There was an expression of indifference in her features and her eyes, which implied, 'This is nothing new to me.' That expression actually put courage into Amina. It was almost as if the woman was smiling mockingly at Amina and Kadija and saying, 'How can you possibly be scared about such a trifle!'

'All right, it's getting late, so let me get on with it,' she said, placing down the bag she held tucked under her arm. She drew out a yerukku twig, a ball of thread and finally, a tin of ointment. The way she proceeded gave Maimoon an impression of efficiency. Maimoon watched silently, unblinkingly. She watched, speechless with fear and helplessness.

The midwife dipped one end of the twig, stripped of leaves, into the dark ointment in the tin. She tied a piece of thread tightly to its other end, and then wound the thread around her own hand so that her fingers gripped the twig firmly. She looked up at Amina and Kadija as if to ask, 'Shall I do it now?' Amina felt at that moment that something slipped from her heart and dropped away. A feeling not so much of loss as of total helplessness; a sense as if she had been forsaken by God; a loss of trust, a notion that anything might happen, overcame her suddenly, and she caught her sister in her arms, weeping. And Maimoon began to sob in silent spasms along with her, a terrible shudder spreading all over her childish frame. The midwife's harsh, strong hands held Amina by the shoulders, and pulled her away. Amina came to herself, wiped her sisters face with her sari end, and attempted to put courage into her sister. 'Don't be frightened, amma. It's nothing. I only wept because something suddenly came to my mind. Now, hereafter, there won't be anything more for you to worry about. All your troubles will be over, amma, won't they?'

The midwife hurried them again. 'Right, right, it's late now. When will I finish, and when will I go home?' But as the others were about to leave the room, Maimoon begged, 'Akka, won't you stay with me, please?'

'Of course I won't leave you. Of course I'll stay with you,' Amina said, taking Maimoon's hand in her own.

The agonizing pain that Maimoon suffered after the ointment was applied continued on and on, into the early hours, until dawn broke; the four women holding her down to stop her from screaming. Terrible memories of that hellish time would wrack Amina for a long, long time. Maimoon's life ended that day, along with the baby that dropped from her body as fragments and shreds and clots of blood. The next day, when the outer world rocked with the news of Gandhi's murder, their town was shattered by the news of Maimoon's death.

* * *

Amina felt her anguish choke her throat, causing her a fierce pain. She sat up, her pillow wet with tears. Her memories had taken her on a long journey, from which she had just returned. The cock's crow and the call to prayers indicated that dawn was breaking. She looked at Firdaus's face as she lay beside her. It seemed to her it combined Kadija's beauty and Maimoon's stubbornness. Like Maimoon, Firdaus too had left her husband and come home. Feeling fearful and frustrated, she rose up, leaning wearily against her arm. She remembered it was time for prayers.

❦ 7 ❦

'Rabia, is Ahmad here, di?' Nafiza called from the front doorsteps.

'No, he's not,' she called back.

'Where could he have vanished, at this time in the morning?' Nafiza came in and looked about her. 'Why hasn't anyone got up as yet?' She sat down next to Rabia, and began her complaint. 'It's the way of the world, isn't it? Here I am, I've just eaten the sahar meal, I want to stretch out a little, but does this fellow allow me to lay my head down? I filled the muzafar box with coins, and I asked the boy to go and distribute it among the beggars while I lay down for a bit, but of course he's gone and disappeared. All right, he's gone, but should he leave the front door wide open? What if beggars enter the house and steal everything? And of course he's taken the box of coins with him. I thought it was likely he might have turned up here. But he's not here either. Who knows where he has lost himself? If I don't sleep after the sahar meal, I tend to get heart-burn. And heaven knows where the muzafar mob turns up from. They pester the life out of us for these thirty days.' Nafiza poured all this out at one stretch. 'Well I'll be off. If he turns up, tell him I was looking for him.' Then she added eagerly, 'By the way, have they chosen your new clothes for the Feast Day?'

Rabia didn't know how to answer. Not quite knowing what would please her mother, she said evasively, 'Mm? Actually, I don't know...'

Nafiza left, saying, 'I suppose your mother will be cross if you give anything away.' She was disappointed her strategy to find out about the new clothes had failed. At the same time, she had to praise Rabia. Even though she was only little, she was smart.

Watching her go, Rabia was proud of herself on two counts. First, she had not given away anything about the new clothes. Her mother would be pleased with her. Amma had warned her not to tell anyone: people would be jealous and cast the evil eye. Second, she knew now about Ahmad stealing the muzafar box. This one fact was enough to break his nose for him. Suddenly she could not contain her jubilation. She wasn't sure whether he would cave in when confronted about it, but she was prepared to try.

Her head felt as if it would burst. She wanted to run to Madina and tell her about it immediately. Madina would be delighted. For an instant she considered what to do, then she ran out into the street. She bolted the front door from outside, and ran across to the house opposite. There was another important piece of news she had to tell Madina as well. That very day her Periamma's daughter, Wahida would be coming home for the Feast Day. She stayed in the big town, usually, at her Ummumma's house, and went to a convent school there. She had to share with Madina her delight at Wahida's homecoming.

* * *

Ahmad leaned his foot on the ground and brought his cycle to a stop. He brushed the mud off his shirt. He had fallen down and stained the front part of it with red earth. He wiped the sweat off his forehead with his collar. His knees were grazed and hurt him. He rubbed spittle all over them. He was very pleased with himself because that day he had managed to ride his bike very competently, even if he had fallen once. He really wanted Madina and Rabia to watch him riding past. But they were nowhere to be seen. Where could they have vanished? They would definitely beg him to teach them to cycle. He was determined to refuse them and to put on a superior air. 'Why, anyway, should these females learn to ride?' he asked himself. How they made fun of him the other day saying he had stolen the muzafar money! He was humiliated by the memory, even now! It was all because of his mother, he thought resentfully. How he had tried to retort! But they had not let up. He had even been driven to say, 'I only took the money from my own house; I didn't steal yours, did I?' After all, he had helped himself to a few coins only because he was so keen to learn to ride a bicycle. He was annoyed that they should tease him so much for that. Now, if they saw him ride past with aplomb, they would be stunned. And they wouldn't dare to mock him again.

It was almost time to return the cycle to the shop that hired it out. If he wanted it for an extra hour, he would need more money. He had spent all his, already. He didn't know the time, but surely it would soon be the hour for them to break their fast. He must ride the cycle to his father's shop, collect some money and buy bajjis and vadais for his mother from the shop next to the mosque. He began to cycle as fast as he could.

He cycled quickly along the street where the shops were, applied his brakes and came to a stop in front of the mosque. Because it was time to end their fast, men were gathering in groups there. The mosque stood at the centre of their town; all three main streets met there. The crowds were largely moving along the street where the shops were. Ahmad decided to go home along one of the other streets. He calculated which would take him the longest, and determined to go that way. Feeling very proud of himself for cycling for such a long time, he gazed at the street ahead of him. He saw Madina and Rabia leaving the Kaja's stall next to the mosque, and turning homewards. Both had packets of bajjis and vadais in their hands, the newspaper wrapping shiny with oil. They also held carriers in which they had collected that evening's 'nonbu kanji'.

Ahmad cycled up to them nonchalantly, stopped and asked, 'Where have you been?' Smartly, Madina answered, 'Don't you know? We've been collecting the kanji and vadais to break our fast.' They showed no signs whatever of noticing his cycle. He was seriously annoyed by this. Such haughty girls, he grumbled to himself. 'I'm going on the same errand,' he informed them. 'So late? The nagara will sound in just ten minutes; they won't give any more kanji after that. That's it; your mother will give you a proper scolding.'

'Hm, what do you mean, ten minutes? There's only five minutes left. But I'm not like you, am I? I can be there on my bike in a split second.' He knew very well that if he let this opportunity go, he might not get another chance to get his own back. Even then they chose to ignore him. He was profoundly disappointed.

'OK, I'm off,' he called, cycling away.

Madina and Rabia laughed together. So he was riding a cycle. A fine cycle, it was! They too would learn to ride one soon. But though they said this to each other, they could not suppress the questions, How would they do it? Who would teach them? Rabia was also anxious that she might have gone too far in mocking Ahmad. He certainly looked very grand to her, as he rode that cycle. And actually, there was nothing he didn't know. He could make kites and fashion carts out of the shells of palmyra fruit. He was brilliant at making paper covers for textbooks. He knew all sorts of things. Rabia was always surprised when she remembered all this. But Madina would never allow her to say a good word about Ahmad. It even seemed to her sometimes that Madina set out deliberately to denigrate Ahmad. Perhaps she felt that by admitting Ahmad's skills she also admitted her own failures?

The sound of the nagara, struck by the Modinaar Bawa in the mosque, came to them, magnified by the mike. It seemed to pierce through their ear-drums. It was time to end their fast, yet they hadn't even reached home. Anxious, they began to run as fast as they could.

As she ran, Rabia remembered how, on every Ramzan Feast Day, after Modinaar Bawa and the other men had set off to the prayer grounds outside town for the Ramzan sermon and prayers, she and the other children would strike the nagara gong and enjoy themselves. But they were never able to make it sound this loud. 'This year I'm going to strike it as loudly as this; just wait and see.' The resolve urged her to double her speed.

❧ 8 ❧

Wahida's homecoming, it seemed to Rabia, made their entire house float on happiness. Most of the time she didn't want to leave the house or go out. She even forgot to play. Even when her friends came to summon her, she didn't wish to join them. 'My Akka is here; she's come home from town. So I can't come and play,' she said, sending them away.

Wahida laughed. 'Ei, from now on I'm going to live here for ever. So you go and play,' she said. But Rabia refused, fondly begging, 'No, Akka, let me stay here with you.'

Rabia's affection made Wahida happy. After this, she would not return to her grandmother's house to continue her education. But although she claimed to Rabia that she would be at home forever from then on, she didn't believe it. It was apparent her father wanted to arrange a nikah for her after the sixth day of the following month. Her mother, however, opposed the idea. Why should a girl get married immediately after her SSLC examination she asked; is it written in her fate that we should give her away when she is so young, as if it were the olden days still?

Wahida was confused by it all. In this town, once a girl came of age, she was not even allowed to cross the threshold of her house and step out. If strange men entered the house, she must not appear in front of them. It was because of all this that Rahima had sent her daughter away to her parental home, to study at the madrasa there. Even though Rahima's mother was not alive, her father lived there. There were enough servants to run the household. Wahida could gain a good education and attend Koranic school at the same time. But now, returning to her home town, she had to spend her entire time within the house. The talk of marriage, coming on top of this, really distressed her.

Wahida spent a lot of time telling Rabia about her life in the big town, and Rabia had many questions to ask. Most of the things that Wahida told her were astonishing. Most surprising of all, were the number of cinema theatres that seemed to be there, all of which held matinee shows. Here there was only one theatre, and only one evening show. There were performances during the day only at Pongal, Deepavali and Id. Her family thought about it a thousand times before allowing her to go to a film show. How nice it would be if there were morning performances all the time!

She asked Wahida, 'So who goes to the films there, during the day?' But Wahida could not answer that. When she was not at school, she stayed at home most of the time, there in the big town, too. There was no way she could mention cinemas and films to her grandfather. Nor would Nanna ever allow her to go. A girl who was of age should behave with propriety; first you get married, then you may go to the cinema as you choose, he would say. You can go where you please, then. Is the cinema going to disappear or what? Wahida tried her best to answer Rabia's questions, using all the information she could. But Rabia was never satisfied. 'Didn't you go to the cinema at all, while you were there? But you went out, didn't you, you went to school?'

'You idiot, we are allowed out only to go to school. Otherwise, it is exactly the same there as here. We have to stay within the confines of the house. I've come of age, haven't I? If I were a little girl like you, I could go about as I pleased. Anyway, will you do a job for me, and stop all this chattering?' Wahida gave a fond tap to her head. But Rabia couldn't make it out. So did one have to stay inside the house, even in the big town? From watching films, she had assumed that the girls there could come and go as they pleased. She was deeply disappointed.

'Very well, Rabia, please do something for me. Go to the library and fetch some books for me to read. Will you do that?' Wahida broke into Rabia's thoughts.

'Right now?'

'Yes, please. I have to pass the time, haven't I? I'll give you the money for the subscription. Pay it in and bring me the books I have listed.'

Rabia asked eagerly, 'Akka, when I come back, may I bring some of my classmates to meet you?'

Wahida's eyes widened with surprise. 'Why? Why would they want to meet me?'

'They just say they want to see you, that's all.' Rabia felt shy to say this. Wahida wanted to laugh, but nodded her head all the same, implying yes, of course, let them come.

Rabia was overcome with pride and happiness. For how many days she had been boasting to her friends about her cousin's beauty and brilliance! Let them see for themselves, today. How lovely her Akka looked ! Amma always said they would be hard put to find a husband to match Wahida's glowing colour, her height and her straight nose. Rabia often placed her arm against her cousin's, to compare the two. She wasn't half as fair-skinned as Wahida, she was sure. Rabia would measure Wahida's long hair with her small hands and then check her own, despairingly. 'Ché, why can't I be as pretty as you, Akka! Look how big my nose is. And even Ahmad teases me sometimes for being so dark!'

At such times, Wahida gathered Rabia into her lap and embraced her. 'Idiot, idiot! When you come of age like me, and have to sit at home in the shade all the time, your skin too will lighten like mine. Now you run about in the sun all the time. Of course your skin is tanned.'

This was the chance for Zohra to intervene and have her say. 'Well said. She's always running about everywhere, just like a boy. And then, does she at least wash her face and powder it at the right times? Not a bit. She's always to be seen with her face streaked with oil.'

Rabia prepared to go to the library. She washed her face very well, with soap. When she saw her reflection in the mirror, it looked bright. Wahida had combed her hair, and plaited it beautifully in two; she had put mai into her eyes. When she powdered her face, it struck her that she too was pretty. She looked again and again at herself. Just as she was about to set off, Wahida brought two silken roses from the garden and tucked them behind her ears. Rabia felt shy. If Ahmad were to see her now, decked out to this extent, and so suddenly, he would tease her mercilessly. All the same, she was pleased with the way she looked. 'I'm off now, Akka,' she said, deciding to go across to Madina's house to invite her to go to the library with her.

She reached the opposite house in a couple of paces. But she hesitated to go inside. Would Madina's mother object? She stood quietly for a while, her hand against the closed door. Then she took hold of the big iron hoop which hung against the heavy door, tapped it against the wood, making a gentle sound, and waited again. Appadi, what a heavy door it was! No thief could ever break into this house. She was disappointed that nobody answered her knock. Thinking to herself that they might not have heard her, she pushed hard with both hands. The door opened inwards, with a creak. She put her right foot forward and stepped in, cautiously. Her eyes swept around the hall.

Madina, sitting on a sofa next to the courtyard, looked up at her in surprise. 'Where are you off to, all dressed up and decked out?' she asked.

Rabia felt shy. 'I'm going to the library. Will you come with me?'

Madina's elder sister, Farida, needed to exchange her book, too. 'Go on, di, Madina; go with her,' she urged.

'Very well, Akka, I'll go. But will you give me a rupee?' she asked, seizing the opportunity.

'Yes, I'll give it to you,' Farida promised, taking her book down from the shelf. She sent Madina away saying, 'Go and wash your face and powder it, just as Rabia has done.' Then she asked Rabia, 'What are they cooking at your house today? Something special, I'm sure, in honour of your cousin's homecoming.'

'I don't know, Akka. Everyone in the house is fasting. I'm the only one who isn't. I don't know what they are cooking.'

Farida nodded, listening to her. There was something very

pretty about her short, fair figure, her round face, her attractive eyes, and the way her lips moved as she spoke. Rabia was very fond of her. She treated her as she did her own cousin, Wahida.

'Rabia, do you like the skirt and davani I'm wearing? They've chosen exactly the same material for Madina, for the Festival Day.'

Madina, squatting by the well in the courtyard, washing her face, was eager to hear Rabia's response. She twisted round and looked at her friend.

'It's very good. Where did you buy it?

Madina was delighted. 'Do you really like it, Rabia?' she called out, wanting to be sure.

'This material came from Singapore, Rabia. Our elder brother sent it from there. I had a set tailored for myself last month. We set aside the rest of the material so that it could be made into a paavaadai and jacket for this girl. But she's been complaining since yesterday that it's not at all nice.'

'Why, what's the matter with it, it's really pretty, isn't it?' Rabia looked at Madina. Madina was good looking too. Anything she wore would suit her and look pretty on her.

'No, it's not that. I wanted something like the skirt material they bought you, with the gold patterns. But Amma says I can have that for Bakr-Id if I want.' Madina explained. Madina approved profoundly of every movement that Rabia made. She wanted to do everything in exactly the same way; to buy everything she bought. Farida knew this very well. The close friendship between the girls quite astonished her.

Rabia was exactly the same as Madina in this respect. If ever anything happened in their family, or if ever they cooked something special, she would come racing across to the house opposite, to share it with her friend. At times the older people would laugh amongst themselves and declare they would have to find a single bridegroom for the two girls; only that would work.

'Very well, Akka, we're going now,' they said.

Farida asked then, as if it had struck her suddenly, 'By the way, Rabia, what's happened to your family car? It doesn't seem to be in use?'

'It's been sent off to town for some repairs. It's been gone for a week now. Mutthannan took it there.'

Sainu was just about to enter the house as the two girls were leaving the front steps. She looked at them with a quizzical expression, wanting to know where they were going. 'To the tuition master's house,' said Madina, as they fled away, like birds.

They were out of breath from running so fast. They stopped at the corner of the street to recover themselves. Madina declared, 'It's a good thing we didn't say anything to Amma. Otherwise there would have been scoldings all round. Why do these donkeys want library books, she'll shout. It's enough if they chant from the Koran during the fast days, she'll say.'

'In my house, my Periattha is always telling me to take the Koran and chant from it during the fast days. I've finished eight chapters since the fast began. What about you?'

'Me?' Madina hesitated for a moment. 'I've finished twelve. Faridakka has finished all thirty and has started all over again.' It seemed to Rabia that Madina was embarrassed in some inexplicable way, to admit this. As if to reassure her friend, she said in a comforting tone, 'See, I'm going to read four more chapters today and catch up with you.'

But for how long could one keep chanting the Koran? When she was bored with it, Farida would pick up a novel, without the knowledge of her mother. Madina too would bring home comics, magic tales and children's stories from the library, and read them. And Rabia was always to be found with them. This made Sainu complain, 'Whatever can these little minxes be up to, shut up in that room like brooding hens?'

✑ 9 ✑

Rabia stood at the street corner, hesitating a little. Ahmad's house was right there, two houses away from Madina's. She wanted Ahmad to see her that day. Her eyes swept towards the front of the house. Madina pulled her away. 'Why have you stopped here? Come on, let's go, it's getting late. It's so hot as well. Look how I'm sweating.' She stroked her hand across her neck and wiped it against her skirt. The girls walked on. It was the month of Panguni, and blazing hot.

Madina asked, 'It seems they are going to get your cousin married? My mother was talking about it.'

'I don't know. Periattha says they should marry her to Sabia Kuppi's son. But Periamma insists there's no hurry. I really don't know what's going on.'

'But they live in the same village as your grandmother, don't they?' Madina asked, frowning. 'Ayyé, isn't it an uncouth sort of place?'

But Rabia couldn't accept that. Somewhat resentfully, she insisted, 'It's only a small place, but I'm very fond of it.'

'I didn't mean it like that. But Wahida studied in a big town, didn't she? How will she fit in there? She might not like it. It's different for you, you have your grandmother's house there. Your grandmother and Chitthi live there. Of course you'll like it there. But what about Wahida?' Madina sounded doubtful.

She spoke in such an adult manner that it struck Rabia she might be right. 'I don't know' she said, choosing to end the conversation. It seemed to her unlikely that Wahida's marriage would happen so soon, anyway. She knew her Rahima Periamma very well. Unlike Rabia's mother, she wasn't easily frightened; she wasn't silly. She knew how to think and act independently. Kader Periattha would never go against her word.

Uma's house was on the way to the library. Rabia wanted to invite her to go with them. She suggested it to Madina, who agreed. So they went up to the small tile-roofed house. The door stood slightly ajar. They sat down in the front thinnai, while Madina called out loudly, 'Uma! Uma!'

A voice asked from within, 'Who is it?' Uma's mother pushed open the tinned door and peered outside. Her eyes widened in surprise when she saw the girls on the thinnai. 'Come in Rabia, come in Madina. Why didn't you come right inside? Why are you sitting out here?' She held the door wide open for them.

The reason for her excitement was that her son Mutthu worked as a driver for Rabia's family. For their part, the girls felt a little embarrassed by the respect she appeared to show them.

'It's only... we wanted to see Uma, is she in?' asked Madina.

'Of course she is. I'll call her right now,' Uma's mother said, raising her voice and calling out her daughter's name.

'Here I am!' Uma came running out. Her mother explained, 'There were a few vessels that needed to be scrubbed today. She was just doing that. I was washing the clothes. Where are you both off to, with your arms full of books?'

'My cousin is home from town. She wanted some books from the library. That's why we're here.'

'Oh, has Wahida arrived? When did she come? Mutthu didn't even tell me, otherwise I would surely have come to see her,' said Amudamma. Her expression showed her care and affection. Uma was the same. Whatever their difficulties at home, she never let it be known publicly. And at school, she gained the most marks. She joined them now, having washed her face while they were talking to her mother. They said goodbye, and left the house together.

* * *

Ahmad stood outside the library. He must have seen them from afar, and decided to make trouble. From where he stood, Uma's dark skin seemed almost to shine in the sunlight. 'Ei, darky,' he called out. All three girls looked up, then Uma dropped her head immediately. Madina was furious. 'So are

you so fair-skinned, da? Dogs can be fair-skinned too,' she flung
at him.

'I'd certainly agree with that. Are you lot going off to act in
a cinema or what? It certainly looks like that, from the amount
of powder you've smeared on your faces.' He contorted his
face at them.

'Get away, Mudevi,' Madina said. They were at a loss as to
how to get back at him with equal effect. Rabia spoke to the
others sharply saying, 'Let's go, what's the point of talking to
him?'

It upset her very much that he had ridiculed them. Why did
he behave like that? There were so many things she wanted to
share with him; so many games she wished to play. But it was
impossible, because he always made trouble like this. She could
have caught dragonflies and bees and butterflies with him,
during the holidays. He knew so many games: he could ride a
bike, he could make kites. She still remembered the cart he
made for her out of palmyra fruit shells, when she was little.
But recently he had changed a lot. He was always mocking or
teasing or ridiculing them. Even if she wanted to make peace
with him, he wouldn't let her get anywhere near him. She
wondered sadly what she could do.

Ahmad had followed them into the library, and was heard
to say, 'Who's coming to the cinema? It's Sunday today. There's
to be a matinee show.' Rabia turned around. He was talking to
his friends, Iliaz and Razak, but making sure the girls overheard
him. Madina and Rabia knew perfectly well that none of the
three boys had any interest at all in the library. They were
aware that Ahmad had followed them only to tease them, and
so they turned away quickly to find some chairs.

It was only a year since the library had been opened in their
town. Rabia had been very happy on that opening day. She
remembered her delight at the chance to read as many comics
as she liked. The library consisted only of a single room. It had
five or six wooden almirahs in which the books were arranged.
If anyone asked the librarian why it was such a tiny place, he

would say, 'It's only just been opened. There'll be plenty of books arriving in a year.' Rabia always felt very sorry for him. He had lost his leg in an accident and had to have a wooden leg. If anyone needed a book, he himself would search it out for them. He never complained about the girls, however long they stayed.

'You read, my dears, you read. Do you know how happy it makes me to see you coming here to read? You are no trouble to me at all. Just because I am crippled, you mustn't feel bad to ask me to look for a book. I'll look it out for you in an instant, you know!' He always said this, every time he saw them. All three girls were moved by his enthusiasm, and his attempt to chase away any embarrassment they might feel about asking him to search for the books they needed.

During the hour or so that they were there, he would interrupt his own work every five minutes, to thump across to them on his wooden leg, and ask in his splendid voice, 'Is there any book you want, amma? Tell me and I'll get it for you.'

On many occasions, he would have set aside books for them which he was sure they would enjoy. 'See this! When I was arranging the books yesterday, I came across it by chance. I put it by for you. Read it and see.' He would hand it to them, proudly. It was he who introduced them to Madanakamarajan stories, Vikramadityan tales, *A Thousand and one Nights*, and Detective Sambu. Rabia knew very well that all the books he gave them to read would become favourites of hers.

There was a water tank above the library. The entire town's drinking water was supplied from it, through a series of pipes. An iron ladder was fixed to the building, so that it could be reached easily. Next to the building stood a pipal tree and a water tap, making it a perfect place for them to play. Sometimes they would climb up the ladder, peer down into the tank, and scoop up some water with their cupped hands, and drink. It was a huge tank, one part of which was always left open. They were always afraid of being caught when they dipped their hands into the water. The water looked dark because of the tree's shadows, and the water weeds. Pipal leaves, yellow and withered, floated on the top. They would climb up the ladder, hold on tightly to the pipe that was next to it, and slide down very slowly. This game would go on until they were exhausted.

On that day, however, they had no wish either to read or play. Cinema songs came floating on the air from the theatre nearby, and fell on their ears. There would be a few more songs now, and then the show would begin. The question why there should be a matinee show on that particular day nagged at all three of them.

A little while after Ahmad and his friends left the library, Madina asked, 'Shall we also go to the cinema?'

'We might, but...' Rabia hesitated.

'Is it the money? I've got some. The rupee that Farida gave me. At thirty-five paise a ticket, it will be just enough.'

'We'll be five paise short,' Uma calculated. 'Shall I go and ask Amma?' She was delighted, eager to see a film with them.

'Yes, but just five paise will do, mind. Run!' Rabia chased her off. She didn't have the heart to ask her for more. Uma hurried.

'Rabia, if they find out about this at home, we'll be in bad trouble,' said Madina. Rabia was scared, too. Amma had warned her she must not go to the cinema during the fasting month. 'Right though this month, they say, we must only store up good deeds. They'll really scold us if they come to know. And then, there's Ahmad, isn't there, to tell on us? What shall we do?'

'But he's also going to be at the cinema, isn't he? We'll threaten to tell his mother; that should keep him quiet.'

This suggestion gave Rabia courage. 'In that case, there's no way they'll know. So let's go then,' she said enthusiastically.

They took out the books that Farida and Wahida had requested, and came out of the library. Uma came running up to them, breathless. She held a fifty paise coin in her hand. 'How come you got so much money, di?'

'My mother gave it herself. Let's buy some peanut sweets

and murukku. But I'm thirsty; let's drink some water before
we go.'

After Uma finished drinking, Rabia went up to the tap. They
were all thirsty. She lifted up her skirt and tucked it up between
her knees so that it wouldn't get wet. But when she bent down
to drink from her cupped hands, the water dripped all over
the front of her blouse. She was annoyed when she realized
this. 'So what? It will dry off soon. Come on, hurry,' urged
Madina, walking on ahead. Rabia thought of her mother. How
cross she would be if she could see her! Shouldn't a girl have
some shame, look how it's all showing through, she'd say. Rabia
hurried on, hugging her books against her chest.

Next to the library, there was Ganapathy Pillai's eucalyptus
grove. The Palani Theatre was just past that. A little further on
there was the school. They could hear the last song from the
theatre. All three quickened their pace. As for Rabia and
Madina, a pleasurable sense of anticipation competed in their
minds with guilt and fear.

Ahmad was standing at the theatre entrance. He had been
certain that the girls would turn up. As soon as he saw them,
he smiled triumphantly. They pretended to ignore him and
hurried to the women's ticket booth. When they saw through
the window that there was no one there, they looked at each
other in surprise, not knowing what to do. Slowly it dawned
on them why Ahmad had been smiling in that fashion. There
was no other way. They would have to go the men's ticket
booth. They returned to the front gate. Ahmad came up to
them and asked, 'Why, haven't you bought your tickets yet?'
Only Rabia answered 'No,' in a low voice. They were aware
that he wanted them to ask for his help.

Rabia didn't pause to consult the others. They absolutely
needed his help now. She hoped that by avoiding a quarrel
with him on that day at least, she might stop him from telling
on her. At the back of her mind she knew that if not that day,
he was bound to come out with it at some time. But she also
thought that if the punishment that must surely follow were

deferred for just a few days, it would be a little less fierce. So it was best to pacify him for the time being.

Very humbly she pleaded with him, 'Ahmad, please will you buy our tickets for us?' He could scarcely contain his sense of victory. He told himself, 'At last these haughty girls are brought to book.' To Rabia he said, casually, 'Oh, certainly, why not? What tickets do you want?'

'Just the bench seats. Thirty-five paise tickets.' She handed him the money. He took it and went away.

When he had gone, Madina muttered, 'Ché! How could you have talked to him and asked him to get the tickets for us?' But though they all regretted having to do that, none of them wished to go away without seeing the picture, after all.

Rabia realized, suddenly, that they had not even checked what picture was showing. She spelt out the name on the poster stuck to the front of the theatre. An unknown actor and actress were standing in a tight embrace. She didn't recognize the man. Was it Jeyashankar or Shivaji? But Uma put an end to her dilemma. 'What does it matter who it is? It's a picture to see; that's enough.'

Ahmad returned with the tickets. 'Right, come on, let's go in,' Madina said. As they stood at the gate, waiting to hand in their tickets, Rabia begged Ahmad not to tell anyone that they had come to the pictures that day. When he said, 'Ché, would I do that?' he seemed to be really kind.

The ticket collector looked at the three girls with a curious smile. 'Well girls, come to see the picture, have you? Go in then, go in.' He opened the tin gates for them. The instant they entered, they could perceive nothing in the half-light. There were certainly plenty of men occupying the men's seats. But the women's seats were totally empty. Madina began to get frightened. 'I'm scared. There's no one here. How can just the three of us sit here?' She held on tightly to Rabia's shoulder. The picture had started to run on the screen. Rabia hurried towards a bench. 'Come and sit down,' she said. The three of them sat huddled together.

To their surprise, a series of ugly and deeply embarrassing scenes appeared on the screen. Two women seemed to be bathing all the time. The girls were deeply shocked by it all. Sometimes they actually had to bury their faces in their laps to avoid looking at the screen. They were well aware that the men turned around frequently to look at them. Every time they looked up, they could neither avoid the shameful scenes shown on the screen nor the sharp glances of the male audience. The sheer humiliation of the situation they found themselves in made them wish to die that very instant. On top of all this, Rabia's stomach churned at the thought of her family and her mother.

Madina asked, 'Shall we just leave quickly and go home?'

'We can't', said Rabia. 'They've locked the gates. They'll open them only when the picture is over.'

For her part, Uma was not in quite such a desperate state as the other two. She felt a little bit braver because she, at least, had taken her mother's permission. Besides, she wasn't doing something deeply sinful by going to the cinema in the month of Ramzan. She jumped to her feet with relief, ready to go home as soon as the picture finished. Rabia pulled at her and made her sit down again. 'Wait, di. Let's wait for all the men to go out before us. They'll only stare at us if we join them now.'

Ten minutes after the theatre emptied, the girls crept out quietly. Their faces looked changed, shocked and terrified. Ahmad had gone. Outside, it was baking; the sun dazzled their eyes. Madina's hand gripped Rabia's, as they walked along the street. Uma alone appeared to go her way, without being tormented by guilt. Rabia trembled inwardly, more out of shame than fear. Both she and Madina felt too disgraced even to look at each other, but walked on, their eyes downcast, heads bent low. What would they all think of her, Rabia wondered – Amma, Periamma, Akka, Periattha? She felt disgusted with herself. Must she go home at all? The question tormented her. It would be better to do something to herself and to die in the eucalyptus grove with its regimented trees standing row upon row. It flashed across her mind that if you died during the month of Ramzan, you would certainly go to heaven. She would be reprieved; the sin she had just committed would go unpunished. But the very next moment she saw in her mind's eye the spangled paavaadai she was going to wear for the Festival. She reproached herself for her foolish thoughts. She bent down to pick up a handful of eucalyptus leaves, crushed them between her fingers and brought them up to her face and smelt them.

'Why are you dreaming? Do hurry up' Madina's voice was lifeless.

'No, I was thinking that we needn't go home straight away. Why don't we stay in the library until three? They know that this is the time the morning show gives over. If we go home later, we can say that Ahmad is lying and that we were actually in the library the whole time.' Rabia was desperate to postpone the punishment that was surely in store for them. And so they did as she suggested; leaving the library only at three.

* * *

As Rabia dragged herself up the front steps of her house, she was greeted by a voice saying, 'Come in, madam.' Startled and confused, not quite recognizing the voice, Rabia looked up and confronted her mother. The last shred of hope that Ahmad might have kept quiet vanished. Trembling all over her body like a tiny chick, Rabia stood paralysed, unable to take a step forwards. Making it unnecessary for her to move, Zohra strode towards her, her face flushed with fury. Rabia wondered whether she had ever seen her mother so angry. She stood stock still and faced her mother silently, knowing it was of no use whatsoever to lie that she had been in the library all along.

'Ei, so you have been to the pictures have you, bitch?'

The first blow fell on her cheek. Rabia was silent as the rest of the blows rained on her body; her eyes alone circled the house, looking for her Akka and Periamma. Her anxiety that they too might know what she had done even stopped her from feeling the pain. She thought too, that in all the days she could remember, this was the first time her mother had hit her. Then she understood the full extent of her wrong-doing, and began to weep loudly.

Rahima heard her weep and came running out of her room. She threw her arms around Rabia, exclaiming, 'Che, leave her alone. The child didn't know what she was doing.' She went on, 'Enough now; leave it alone. If the men come to know, we will all be disgraced.' She took Rabia away into her room. But for a long time after that, they could hear the sound of weeping from Zohra's room.

～ 10 ～

Kader, sitting at the cash-box in their shop, felt much troubled in his mind. He was anxious not to fail in his promise to give Wahida in marriage to his sister's son. He was afraid too of provoking Sabia Akka's anger. If this marriage did not come off, she would make a list of all his failings from beginning to end, and scold him for all of them. Sabia and Rahima had never got on together. Sabia complained everyday that he had followed his wife's advice and spoilt Wahida with all that education. If ever Sabia planned to visit them, Zohra and Rahima would immediately start to worry about all the things she was likely to find fault with, deliberately upsetting and disturbing them. Sabia was concerned to maintain her status in her parental home, and she did this by finding fault all the time with her younger brothers and their wives. She seemed to believe it was the only way to establish her position.

Yet she could be loving, too. She would say to Rahima, with real concern, 'Here's this girl who's come of age; instead of keeping her at home and looking after her health, how can you leave her in your parents' house? What need is there for a girl to study so much? It isn't even as if your mother is alive, is it, to look after her properly? How is she going to eat and relish what the servants cook? How can your father take charge of all that? What can he, a man, do? You shouldn't be so obstinate, you know!'

But it was Zohra who feared Sabia's words even more. As for Rahima, she never took them to heart. She would go about her business, her fair-skinned, round face flushed and shiny with annoyance, silent and tense. Kader would try and advise her as best he could, explaining that Sabia spoke out of her love for Wahida, and so Rahima should not be offended. Rahima might have accepted this, but she still did not like the idea of Wahida's marriage to Sabia's son; not one little bit. So Kader was hard put to work out how to handle the situation. He had decided to consult his younger brother, Karim. Karim had gone home for awhile, and would be returning to the shop shortly.

Kader gazed at the street. It was blazing hot; he was tired and sweating. Inside the shop, Mariyayi was peeling onions. Servants were filling the cleaned onions into big sacks. The work went on at a casual pace. Because the heat was at its height, there were not many customers. Throughout this month they sold a good amount of onions, which people needed to cook the nonbu kanji. They bought great piles of them. But people bought them only if they were sold cleaned, their dry skins removed. Mariyayi was better at doing this than anyone else they knew. Kader looked at her sharply. She was about forty years old, with the strong body of a labourer, and an attractive face.

Karim had had a relationship with her for many years. Both in their house, and outside it. And this was common knowledge. Zohra had objected for a long time, but finally let it go. Kader too had kept quiet about it. The woman's house was on their estate. It was she who looked after their gardens and their cows with great care. It seemed they were a pride and joy to her. She considered her relationship with Karim as a special privilege to the extent that she even accepted his arrangement to have herself sterilized. In comparison with Zohra, it had to be said, she did not have some kind of spell-binding beauty. 'But who knows what it is all about,' Kader muttered to himself. He was sweating. He tapped his pen, then wiped his face and neck with his handkerchief. Then he saw Karim climbing down from the TVS number 50 bus. Karim entered the shop, thrust his head into the inner room asking, 'Well, are you all getting on all right with your work?' Then he came and sat on a stool opposite his brother.

Kader gazed at his younger brother for a moment. He saw a slim, fair-skinned body. Wide jaws, flat nose and tiny eyes: exactly the same features as their father. Karim was not a quiet man like Kader. He was easily aroused to anger. He was impulsive too, making his decisions instantly. Consulting him might help him, Kader, to be more firm in his resolve. Having waited for the instant Karim turned to face him, Kader gently approached his subject.

'I am thinking of arranging Wahida's nikah after the sixth day of next month,' he said, looking directly at his brother. Karim returned that look with an expression which said, 'So, what about it?' He was astonished that Kader wanted to consult him first.

'Rahima doesn't like the idea. What's the hurry now, she keeps saying. As for Sabia Akka, she says her son is due back from Singapore right now. She's urging me for a quick reply. I just don't know what to do.'

Karim couldn't understand why his sister-in-law objected to the match. 'Doesn't she like him?'

'Sikander is fifteen years older than Wahida, you know. That's why.'

'Pooh! Is that a good enough reason? I thought it was something serious. There's nothing unusual in that, is there? It happens in many families. Our sister's son must marry a girl from our house; that's the way it is. Otherwise, we lose our kinship ties. Don't we have to consider all this?' Karim had the notion that his elder brother listened to his wife rather more than he should. He was very certain that men should not give an inch to women. He was very proud of that belief.

'And it isn't just that. I too am not entirely certain about this match,' Kader admitted.

'You can't always be thinking about age difference. Segu's daughter is seventeen years younger than her bridegroom. It's the same with Farukh's girl. Once the girl is married, and has a couple of children, it will all work out fine. Akka has a lot of our property. She has a house. The boy works abroad. More than anything else, there are our kinship obligations. Just go ahead and arrange it for any day after the six day fast following Ramzan, and be done with it. Above all else, you've promised to give them the girl. You can't break your word now.' Karim said all this with his head lowered, without looking directly at Kader.

Kader agreed that what his brother said was right. There wasn't anymore time to worry about it all. He told himself that all that was left was to console Rahima that it wasn't anything new or extraordinary. He felt at peace. It was not only unnecessary to ask her for her consent, to do so might place far too much importance upon her and her judgement. If he began to make the arrangements right away, she would come to realize her opinion did not count that much. He could see no other way out.

* * *

After the Tarawih prayers, Kader sat down on the mat which was spread out for him in the hall and ate his meal silently, not saying a word. He was in a dilemma as to how exactly to begin. He finished his meal, gazing alternately at the entrance door and at Rahima who sat in front of him. For a moment he turned to look towards the kitchen, which was adjacent to the courtyard. Zohra was busy about something there. 'Rabia's mother, can you come here a moment,' he called.

Not knowing why her brother-in-law was summoning her,

Zohra dropped everything instantly, crossed the courtyard in a few steps, and came into the hall, pulling her sari well over her head. Leaning against a pillar, she asked, 'What is it, Machaan?' Her mouth was dry before she could finish speaking the words. She pressed her slender frame close against the pillar.

Rahima could not yet understand what was going on. She looked at her husband and Zohra in turn.

'Are the children asleep?' he began. 'And why was that child, Rabia, still playing outside at the time of the evening prayers? She is always to be seen standing about near the shop by the mosque, idling away and playing with the other children. I've seen her myself, several times. You women could make sure Wahida reads out the Holy Book at Maghrib time, couldn't you? Hereafter, please do it everyday. You must make this a habit. Tell Rabia to do so as well.' His voice was firm, implying he would listen to no excuses.

Kader looked at the courtyard, and past it, to the front door, wondering why Karim had not yet come home. At that moment his brother entered, pushing the door open and locking it behind him; then vigorously kicking off his sandals. For a moment Karim wondered if he should go straight to the bathroom, and even took a step in that direction. Then he saw his brother and sister-in-law seated in the hall, and Zohra standing next to them, leaning against a pillar. He realized they were waiting for him, and went towards them instead.

'Do you want to eat?' Kader asked

'No, I'm not hungry,' he replied, removing his cap, folding it away into his shirt pocket, and sitting down with his back against the wall.

'Must you sit down on the floor in your clean prayer clothes?' asked Kader.

'It's all right; they are dirty already.'

Rahima looked at Zohra, as if to ask, 'Do you know what this is all about?'

At last, Kader cleared his throat and began. 'Insha Allah! I

have decided to hold the nikah for Wahida and Sikander soon
after the six day fast following the crescent moon. Pray for
them.'

Instantly, Rahima's fair face darkened and tightened. She
could not reveal her annoyance in front of Karim and Zohra,
so she merely raised her voice a little, and asked firmly, 'What
is it you are saying?'

'Why are you getting so excited about it? If you have a
daughter, you must give her away in marriage sometime or
other.' Kader sounded soothing and authoritative at the same
time. He did not like it one bit that he had to announce this
event in this way, in front of Karim and Zohra. But he was
forced to do so, because he did not have the courage to deal
with it when Rahima and he were on their own.

'How can you make such a decision without consulting me
first?' Rahima's plump body was shaking with anger and
humiliation. Her throat was choked. Tears stood in her eyes.
Zohra and Karim were deeply embarrassed. Karim bent his
head and made as if he were intent on pulling off the dry skin
on his heels with his nails.

Her tears and frustration clearly upset Kader. All the same,
he wanted to be finished with this business that very day. He
gave Zohra and Karim a look, as if he were ordering them to
smooth things over, and rose to his feet swiftly. 'Nobody need
cry. Put your trust in His design, that's all. Nothing will happen
unless He wills it,' he said, and disappeared into his room.

Karim felt truly uncomfortable about staying on in the
room. He got up without a word and walked off towards the
bathroom. He was aware that Kader had waited all this time
for his brother's arrival, then finished it all off in a trice without
bothering to seek anyone's advice, and taken to his heels.
'Heaven knows why he's so concerned about his wife's opinion.
A single tear and the fellow trembles with fear,' he grumbled
to himself. He folded his lungi knee-high, tied it up, and began
to wash his feet.

Zohra too was disappointed. Clearly Kader had begun to

speak only after quite a lot of forethought. But instead of discussing it with them calmly and arriving at a considered conclusion, he had run away.

As for Rahima, she continued to sit there silently, not uttering a word. When she agreed to a sterilization many years ago, on her doctor's advice, she had not asked Kader about it first. After it was done, he had refused to speak to her for some time saying she had gone against the Shariat. Rahima had tried hard not to make an issue of it. She knew perfectly well that Kader would never, at any time, have allowed a sterilization. He was incapable of taking a single step that was contrary to the Shariat. As for her, when her doctor declared it would not be safe for her to have another baby, she had quietly agreed to the operation with the support and aid of her father. She could not think what else to do. In the course of time, Kader had got over his resentment. But then, after that, their second child and only son, Sahul, died. After Sahul died Kader was plunged into grief. Rahima had put all her effort into assuaging his pain.

She thought now that Kader was a much better man than Karim. He truly wished for this marriage to happen. She could only oppose it up to a point. Besides, both of them doted on Wahida. Kader would never do anything that would cause her harm. Only God knew what was destined for the child. Let His will happen. Rahima consoled herself in this way. She did not wish to upset her innocent daughter by the expression on her face, and so she turned her attention to her other chores.

ℰ 11 ℨ

It was about eight o'clock in the morning. As it was a Friday, Amina prepared to set off to the river, for her bath. She tied up the clothes that needed washing, into a bundle. She placed her packet of soap and shiyakkai on top. Nobody would accompany her to the river, that day. Her neighbour, Sabia, had planned to go with her. But it turned out her son was arriving unexpectedly, that day, from Singapore. Lucky woman, she had succeeded in arranging for her son to marry Wahida, her brother's daughter, exactly as she had hoped. This Allah fulfils the dreams of only a chosen few. It's as if they have him in their hands. And it wasn't Sabia who had told her all this. Zohra had told her mother about it, on her last visit home.

It was always pleasant to have a companion when she went to the river. The conversation made the walk to the river and the washing of clothes less tedious. Now there was no one to keep Firdaus company at home, either. And Amina was not happy to leave her on her own. She had accepted a Hindu family as tenants of the house she owned on the other side of the road. She was told the man was employed as a teacher in the local school. He had a wife and child. If she had been able to talk to the wife and make her acquaintance, she could have asked her to keep an eye on Firdaus. Now there was no alternative. She must leave Firdaus in the house and lock the door from outside. Having made up her mind, Amina picked up the lock and key.

Firdaus felt angry and ashamed as she realized what her mother was doing.

'Why must you lock it outside? Can't I bolt it from within?' Her voice betrayed her annoyance.

'You don't know anything. We mustn't ever give any cause for people in this town to gossip. Don't you know that they are waiting for any chance to make up stories about you, knowing how vulnerable you are? You just stay inside and get on with your work; that's enough.' Amina spoke sharply, went outside and tried to pull the door shut. She couldn't do it. She hurt her foot and the toe began to bleed slightly. Firdaus herself had to help by pushing the door from inside.

Such a heavy door! How carefully Ismail had considered each detail when he was building this house for her. She remembered the teak wood he had bought, and how proudly he had given the instructions for it to be made. That very evening, Maimoon had climbed down from the bullock cart with her mother-in-law. At first, Amina and Ismail had been surprised to see them, but pleased, too. Amina welcomed them, 'Come in, Maami. What brings you here at this time?' But Maimoon's mother-in-law wore a look of distress. She walked into the house silently, and sat down on the mat that was spread there. Maimoon disappeared immediately into one of the rooms at the back of the house. Realizing that something had changed drastically, Ismail spoke in haste to Anthoni Achaari who was measuring the wood. 'Very well, let's talk about the door tomorrow. Come and see me in the morning.' The carpenter left at once.

Once he had gone, Maimoon's mother-in-law began to speak. 'I only came in order to bring your sister back. I'm going now.' With these few words, she began to walk off, taking no notice of the other two. Amina, rushing to stop her, stumbled over the wood lying in the corridor, and Ismail had to help her up. He could understand her anxiety, but scolded her all the same.

'Why are you so anxious? What has happened now? Let that amma go away if she wants. We'll find out about everything in good time.'

Amina had torn the nail of her big toe, it was pouring blood. He tore a strip off a piece of cloth which had been tucked into the crossbeam, bandaged her foot and stopped it from bleeding. Drops of blood had dripped from her foot and spread across the wood. Amina felt no pain. Her mind was in a whirl. She could not comprehend what was going on. Maimoon, meanwhile, would not emerge from the room at the back. Ismail, however, kept very calm. 'When it is a bit darker, you must go and leave her at your mother's house. We'll talk about it tomorrow and decide what to do,' he said, and went out.

* * *

The whole town was astounded by the house that Ismail was building. Look how proud of himself he is, for having married a young girl, they said, eaten up with jealousy; he'll do anything to please her. His mother, too, muttered such things all the time. She sat comfortably by her grindstone chewing betel leaves and muttering. Although the spittoon stood ready by her side, she never would use it. This was a particular trick of hers: she believed that listeners would not be able to make out her imprecations if she pronounced them with her mouth full. She would stand at her courtyard and survey the new building that was coming up opposite the house which they then occupied.

'Hm! What's wrong with this house that he must build himself a two-storey mansion? Isn't this enough for the likes of her and the miserable state of her? But that's the promise she got out of him. What can I do? The Holy Prophet alone should take him to task!'

One day, Ismail pulled up a stool and came to sit in front of her. He brought out a packet of sweets which he had tucked into his lungi, and presented it to her. She accepted it with her trembling hands and laid it on her lap. He felt very sorry to see her old and wrinkled form and sunken eyes. With affectionate concern he asked, 'Amma, is there anything you find wanting, here?'

Biviamma didn't know what to say. Her only son was asking her this, with such love. In all her life, her son was the only fortune and happiness she had known. When she was given to Farukh Mohammad as his third wife, he was fifty-five years old. She was twelve or thirteen. He was tubercular besides. The whole town had been disgusted that such a match should take place. But her mother, a widow beset by poverty and helplessness, had said, 'If I lose this chance, I don't know how I am to see her safely ashore. Rather than die of starvation in her mother's house, let her at least fill her belly. Besides, if she has a couple of children, then well and good; what else can there be in a woman's life? All she can do is bring up her children and stay at home. What's the use of wealth and property?'

Farukh Mohammad had married her only for her company.
His first wife had died, and he had divorced his second wife,
complaining that she was barren. Now, needing someone to
look after him in the last years of his life, he had married Bivi.

Just fifteen days after the wedding, Bivi menstruated for the
first time. In that first year of marriage, two things happened:
Ismail's birth, and, hastened by the disease, Farukh's death. It
was astonishing news, and the talk of the town that within one
year, Bivi went through four important occasions, each
requiring an observation of 'forty days'. At the end of the first
forty days of her marriage, her lap was filled with new clothes.
The new clothes still carried their gloss when the next forty
days were observed, following her coming of age. After that,
when she was still carrying Ismail, came the forty days following
the death of Farukh. And finally there were the forty days
following the child's naming ceremony. All four occasions came
and went within a year.

After she was widowed, any number of men tried to
approach her, under the impression her youth would allow
her to be led astray easily. But she never gave in to anyone. She
renounced all her feelings, and channelled all her attention
into bringing up her son until he was grown up. It was almost
as if she had taken a vow. The whole town praised her for her
resolute dedication.

This was the son she had borne, cherished and brought up.
She was overcome with pride. 'Why do you ask me such a
question, son? What can I lack? Nothing, nothing at all. Allah
has given me a kind and considerate son. I have a granddaughter
like a golden doll. What more do I want?'

Ismail knew his mother and Amina didn't get on. Most
certainly this was not Amina's fault but his mother's. She could
not endure it that Amina enjoyed the happiness she herself
never experienced. Her position as a mother-in-law combined
with the loneliness of old age had provoked in her a bitter
hatred of Amina. Ismail began again. 'No, Amma, it seems to

me you don't like the idea of the new house I'm building. Do you want me to stop it? If you don't want me to do it, I won't.'

She understood what her son was saying. 'It's true, ayya. Why do we need such a vast house? Isn't this one good enough? Then why go for anything else?' She said her say and spat into the spittoon. Her tired and wrinkled face showed her anxiety that the spittle in her mouth would stop her from speaking clearly enough.

Ismail knew perfectly well how to handle her thereafter. He appeared to agree. 'Very well, Amma. Of course this house is big enough for us. It was I who lost my head.'

'If that's the case, then who made you lose your head?' the old lady asked, in a knowing manner. She was delighted that she had got his wife into trouble now.

'Amma, now we have a baby, Zohra. Look at her, isn't she just like you? Shamsu Chacha was saying the other day that you were exactly like her when you were that age. He said she is the very image of you. I even named her Zohra Bivi because I said she is so much like my mother. Don't you dote on her too? Now you tell me, is this house big enough for her to run about and play? I wanted to build her a new house with shining, polished marble floors, and watch her walk on them as if my own mother were running and playing. Mustn't I see that? She is your granddaughter, your only son's child. If I had known you didn't approve, I would never have embarked on this building. I'm not building it for Kani Rowther's daughter. Would I do such a thing for that beggar man's child?' He put in a word against his wife, for good measure.

His voice sounded highly emotional, as if he was much moved. Of course he would never forget the difficulties his mother had undergone. Biviamma took her son's hands and pressed them to her chest. It was enough comfort to her that her son remembered all her sorrows and kept them in mind. 'My raasa, you are like a father to me. Stay well always, appa! You understand what is in my heart,' she said, weeping. From that time, to the day she died, she never said anything against the new house.

Amina remembered that for a long time she and Ismail used to say that the grand completion of the new house, and their getting the first connection when the town was electrified, all coincided with Firdaus's birth. The whole town knew Ismail as 'Two-storey-house Ismail'. Even the small children called him that.

Tears gathered in Amina's eyes. She didn't even feel the pain in her feet. She couldn't bear to think that his beloved daughter's life was now in ruins. She wondered whether he could have borne it, had he been alive. Troubled by the thought, she walked along the footpath toward the river, accompanied by her shadow.

***

It was the interval between the Asar and Maghrib prayers. Firdaus sat on the small platform next to the kitchen hearth, sunk in her thoughts, while a comforting evening breeze blew. As it was a Friday, she had washed her hair and put on a sari which could be described as reasonably new. They said it was good to say your Friday prayers, wearing new clothes. She knew her mother would insist she should wear only old clothes the next day, and consoled herself that she would be allowed to look pretty at least one day in the week. She ran her fingers through her hair as it was blown about, and revelled in its length. She loved the beauty of her heavy tresses falling below her waist when she walked about. She was aware that whoever met her never failed to complement her on her hair, and this made her more than a little vain.

The smell of jasmine came floating towards her, and she walked towards the well, past the washing stone and into the garden. She went up to the jasmine bower and checked carefully to see where the flowers were. The flowers peeped out singly, here and there, out of clusters of leaf-sprigs covering the creeper. 'How can we hope for a real show of flowers, when the leaves are so dense,' she asked herself. Every year, before the flowering season, she would thin out the dense leaves. That way, they were assured of plenty of flowers. How could she remember to do it this year? And in any case, she thought, what use would it be, even if the jasmine were to flower plentifully? Her mother wouldn't allow her to wear even these few. She felt deeply depressed.

Silently she groped among the leaves and picked the flowers one by one. Every now and then she carried her lapful of flowers to her face, breathing their scent deeply, immersing herself in the fragrance for a moment. She kept thinking of her mother. When would she return? It would be better to pick the flowers before that happened, she told herself, hurrying. She ran inside, dropped her load on the thinnai by the hearth, reached for the needle and thread tucked into the crossbeam, and threaded the flowers hastily. She kept wondering why her mother had not yet returned from Sabia's house, to end her fast. Just as well; let her take her time. She plaited her hair in a hurry, tucked the flowers inside, and then bundled the plait into a knot so that the flowers were hidden. She thought of Siva, suddenly, and glanced towards the front door. It was locked. A guilty shudder went through her as she wondered whether she should open the front door and gaze at the house opposite.

These days, she always left one of the front doors open in the morning and at four thirty in the afternoon, while she went about her chores. She was happy that the layout of the house aided her purposes so well. The kitchen was built as a separate block, to one side of the paved courtyard, with the main house standing on the opposite side. The courtyard linked the two, and the entire structure was surrounded by a big wall, with a tin gate. From the kitchen, you had to enter the main house through some steps and the heavy teak door. During the rainy season, Firdaus found this arrangement very annoying. 'Who would build a separate kitchen like this? You have to cross the open courtyard every time you go in and out. My clothes get drenched,' she would grumble. Now, definitely, she did not wish to complain about the architecture of the house.

Ever since she saw Siva, her mind was in a flutter. Now she crossed the courtyard frequently, just to catch a glimpse of him in the opposite house, through the open tin gate. Amina scolded her, 'Why can't you think of all the things you need for the cooking, woman, and take the rice, dal and everything from the big house in one go? Instead of that, you keep running to and fro the whole time.' But Firdaus was careful not to let her mother find out the real reason for her behaviour.

Most of all, it was convenient for Firdaus that Amina did not wake up from her afternoon nap at four thirty. It was just about that time that Siva returned from school. She would leave the front door slightly ajar, and stand by it, her body half-hidden, but her face in full view, gazing into the distance, as if totally unaware of his arrival. Only when he was very near, she would look as if she had woken up with a start, suddenly aware of his presence. Then she would draw her head in with a delicate shyness, and disappear rapidly. This happened everyday.

The realization that he noticed and admired her excited her to the point of intoxication. She partly understood why this was so, and partly did not. She imagined how it would be if he were with her that evening. She wondered immediately whether it would ever happen. She felt the pain of being denied the companionship she craved, young as she was, with only the torment of a continuing loneliness ahead of her. Firdaus wanted to weep.

Hearing the sound of Amina's footsteps, and the front door opening, she went into the house quickly, climbed the stairs, and walked up to the terrace above. Amma knew this was where she would be, if she was not downstairs. She would not search for her. This knowledge consoled Firdaus. As it darkened, she felt a little more comforted. A few stars and the crescent moon shone in the sky. She leaned down and peered into the street.

Siva sat in the front thinnai of his house reading, the baby held in his lap. A yearning that he should lift his head and look up at her filled her heart and made it heavy. The fragrance of the flowers she had left unpicked wafted over the breeze to her; her hair loosened from its knot and fell across her face, abrading it, troubling her in a strange way. She wondered how that evening could so awaken all the womanly impulses that lay frozen within her; she touched her skin, aware of her hair standing all on end; she turned her gaze on him once more. Seen in the bright electric light, the fineness of his body, clad only in a banian and lungi, filled her with such desire that it frightened her. 'How can I think such thoughts during the fasting month,' she muttered to herself, sinking to the floor, burying her face in her hands, and beginning to sob silently.

↶ 12 ↷

Sherifa was sweeping the front veranda of her house. Her arm ached. It was Rahimakka family's turn to provide the nonbu kanji which was distributed to all, to end the day's fast. Rabia had come earlier, to summon Sherifa and her mother Saura to help prepare the meal. She must finish her chores quickly and go there. Saura was still asleep; fasting made her weak and drowsy. I need not wake Amma, Sherifa thought. Noiselessly she opened the front door, bolted it from outside, pulled her sari over her head, stepped into the street, and walked two houses along to Rabia's family home. She hesitated for an instant in the long veranda, carefully examining the large, paved courtyard and the wide corridor immediately beyond. Her eyes scrutinized each of the rooms leading off from the corridor, resting briefly on each, and moving on. She was greatly relieved when it became clear that there were no men in the house.

The utter silence made her begin to wonder why Rabia had come for her. But just as her feet crossed the threshold, she could make out Zohra's head. Zohra, scooping onions into her palm-leaf tray from the pile heaped up in a shady corner of the courtyard, heard footsteps, turned round and said, 'Come, come, Sherifa.'

'Here I am, Akka,' said Sherifa, sitting down next to Zohra.

'Wait, wait,' protested Zohra, 'Are you going to sit on the ground in your clean prayer-sari? I'll send for a wooden plank.' She called out in the direction of the inner rooms, 'Rabia, oh, Rabia!'

It was Wahida who came out. A Koran lay open, spread out on her hands. She came up to them, asking, 'What is it you want, Chitthi?'

'What are you doing here?' asked Zohra. 'Don't interrupt your chanting. You carry on with it. And where did that one disappear, just when I need her to help me?' She went off in the direction of the kitchen.

Sherifa, who had sat down on the ground, meanwhile, smiled at Wahida and asked, 'Are you well?'

'I'm fine, Akka,' returned Wahida.

'Why do you hold the book open in your hands, don't you have a Koran-stand?'

'I have one, but I didn't bother.' Wahida smiled. 'I'll go back to my chanting,' she added, in a tone of voice that said goodbye.

Sherifa said to herself, 'She's a well-behaved girl, with good manners, just like her mother.'

Zohra brought the wooden plank herself, grumbling aloud, 'Where has that Rabia disappeared to?' Hearing her, Wahida called out from her room, 'She's gone to call Nafiza-Akka, Chitthi.'

'Oh, she's gone there, has she? Fine, in that case she won't turn up again until the sun is well into the sky. Heaven knows what keeps her there. There's a battle royal going on between her and Ahmad. So why she hangs about there, I don't know.' Zohra came and sat down opposite Sherifa.

To one side of the hall, garlic, onions, tomatoes, coconuts,

green chillies, and all the vegetables needed for the meal were
stacked, some still in sacks, some spread out on mats. Zohra
complained, 'The coolie women haven't turned up as yet.
We've got to start straightaway if everything is to be ready on
time.'

Sherifa agreed, and asked at the same time, 'And why is
Rahimakka not to be seen about?'

'She has a slight headache,' said Zohra, 'I've asked her to lie
down for a bit. Let her rest now; she can help us later.' The two
women began to top and tail the onions, using a chopper.

'It seems your Wahida is going to be married? I heard
something to that effect,' Sherifa remarked in a while.

Thinking to herself that the gossip was about to start now,
and would accompany the entire day's work, Zohra replied,
'Yes, after the six day fast following the festival.' She was a little
embarrassed to speak about wedding matters with Sherifa.
Sherifa's beauty and grace were enough to break anyone's
heart. How could Allah have thought it fit to make her a widow
at such a young age, she thought, resentfully.

At that moment Mariyayi arrived, bringing two women
workers with her. Instantly, Zohra felt as if a load had been
lifted from her mind. After this, Mariyayi would take over the
responsibility for everything, and do it all. Zohra need only
supervise. And indeed, Mariyayi settled down to work, at once.
She told the workers exactly what needed doing, and began
scraping the soaked ginger. Zohra scolded her affectionately,
'Why so late, Mariyayi? We should have finished half the work
by now.'

'And do you think I've been idling away in the fields or what?
I can only come when I've finished with the cows and calves
and everything else. You're a fine one,' she answered sharply
in her turn. Sherifa looked at Zohra and smiled slightly. There
was an insinuation in that smile that Zohra did not fail to
understand. She too smiled, in return. And her smile intended
to say, 'Well, would you find such a good worker, however
hard you looked all over the world?' There was no indication,

in that smile, of any disapproval whatsoever, regarding Mariyayi and her own husband.

Nafiza came into the house, 'How is it all going?' Rabia and Madina's sister-in-law, Mumtaz, were with her. Zohra welcomed them all. 'Come in, please, all of you. Mumtaz, when did you get back from your mother's house, amma? We've seen no signs of your return.'

'I only came back yesterday, Anni,' Mumtaz said, as she and Nafiza placed themselves in front of the scattered garlic and onions and began peeling them. A while later, she remarked, 'Your family is giving the meal today; so when will it be our turn?'

Nafiza looked at Mumtaz, tilting her head sideways and giving a sarcastic smile. 'Amma, did I hear you enquire when it will be your family's turn? Well, well, well...' she dragged out her words. 'If you had asked your mother-in-law this question, you would have got it good and proper. You speak as if you are a newly married bride who has just set up house. You donkey, you have a fixed date every year, don't you remember?'

Mumtaz said, 'People forget, don't they? You're a fine one...' She laughed, and the entire house seemed to become animated.

Zohra asked Nafiza, 'Have you finished your cooking, or do you still have to do it?'

'It's a fast day, after all. Ahmad's father and I are fasting. I've only cooked a little rice for Ahmad and Rafiq. There's a little left over from the curds I set for the early morning sahar meal. And there's some sambar in the fridge. What else do they want?' replied Nafiza. She carried on, 'By the way, have you chosen your clothes for the festival, yet? You are going to have a double expense this year, aren't you? Clothes for the festival as well as clothes for the wedding.' She stopped short, watching Zohra and wanting to know how much she would give away.

'Yes, that's right,' Mumtaz chimed in. She had only just returned from her mother's house, and the news of the wedding

had reached her already. Thinking to herself, 'What a town
this is; and how gossip gets about here,' Zohra answered aloud,
'We've only chosen the festival clothes for the children. We
still have to go to Madurai to select ours. It's only the tenth
day of the fast; we can take our time.'

'Well, come on then; show us what you've selected for the
girls,' Nafiza asked eagerly.

'Wait, I'll bring them,' said Zohra, going inside. Rabia's
expression betrayed nothing. Nafiza observed her with a
mischievous smile. So what did you tell me when I asked you
the other day, that smile seemed to say.

Rabia, for her part, was furious with her mother. 'Look what
she is doing now,' she thought, 'after warning me strictly the
other day, not to tell anyone.' For Zohra now returned with a
bag which she placed before Nafiza. All three women – Nafiza,
Sherifa and Mumtaz – took the clothes out and handled them.
There were two sets each, for Wahida and Rabia. A long skirt
and blouse for Rabia. The same for Wahida, with the addition
of a davani. One set would be worn at the Laylathul Qadr
prayers on the twenty-seventh day of Ramzan, the other set
would be worn for the Id festival ending the Ramzan fast. All
three women loved the slippery feel of the satin, and the glinting
gold-thread work of the skirts. All the same, they were
disappointed at not seeing the saris chosen for the adults. Nafiza
thought to herself, they must surely have chosen the saris too;
they just don't want to show them to us yet. She asked, 'Akka,
where did you shop for all this?'

'Where else but at Hasim Moosa's?'

'Didn't you go to the cinema, then?'

'Oh, so you are urging me to go to the cinema during the
fasting month, are you? Would I commit such a sin?' Zohra
spoke sharply, but her voice betrayed a trace of regret that she
could not go to the cinema.

If ever anyone in their town fell ill, or if they needed clothes
for a special occasion, they would set off for Madurai. On those

occasions, the women would certainly take the opportunity to go to the cinema. It was only during the fasting month that it was impossible.

Nafiza spoke again. 'Akka, you know this daughter-in-law of mine, Rabia. I don't know anyone as clever as she is. I asked her whether your new clothes were ready, and she told me she didn't even know! Never mind. She's my future daughter-in-law, isn't she? The smarter she is, the better for me. Isn't that so, Rabia?' She winked and smiled at Rabia. Everyone laughed at this, and Rabia, overcome with shyness, ran away and hid behind a pillar, flinging her arms around it.

'Who stitched this jacket for Rabia? The puffed sleeve isn't set properly at all. Look how it's all drooping and wrinkled ... looking like something else,' teased Mumtaz.

'Oh, so you've started your silly talk, have you? Nobody can find comparisons like you do,' Zohra laughed.

'Macchaan has gone abroad, hasn't he? This girl is all frustrated here. That's why she says these things.' Nafiza gave a playful knock to Mumtaz's head.

Nafiza retorted, 'You are a complete innocent, aren't you? If anyone puts their hand in your mouth, you won't even bite!' And she repeated, 'You take a look at this jacket yourself. It looks exactly like I said.' She laughed once more.

Rabia lowered her head, thinking to herself, how can they use bad language like this!

Mariyayi was scraping ginger against the wash-stone in the corner of the veranda. The heat was intense now, making her sweat profusely. She took her sari end and wiped firmly around her neck. She helped herself to a tumbler of water from the trough and splashed it on her face, careful not to let her hands touch her face. If she were to do so with ginger all over her hands, her skin would burn. The thought of some tea was comforting. Staying where she was, she craned her neck in the direction of the women seated indoors and called out, 'You could stop your jabbering for a moment and give us some

coffee, or whatever is going. I've got a headache, here.' There
was a touch of authority in her voice.

Nafiza winked at Mumtaz and teased Zohra by assuming an
expression which said, 'Look how this landlady-person talks
to us!' Needling Zohra, she said, 'Go on, go on, amma. Go and
give the mistress of this house something to drink.'

But Zohra took it casually. 'Pach,' she said, 'Shut up, you,
you're another! Do you think you can annoy me with your
teasing? I've decided that the one good thing your brother did
was to bring this lady here.' She rose to her feet and went
towards the kitchen, saying, 'If anyone else wants tea, please
speak up! Don't feel shy if you weren't able to go to prayers,
and had to break your fast.'

It was four days since Sherifa had started her period. She
could not have her ritual bath until the seventh day; it was
only then that she could attend prayers and resume her fast.
But she was too shy to say any of this aloud, and stayed silent.
Zohra asked Sherifa pointedly, 'Are you fasting?'

'Yes, Akka, I am.'

'You can't be, though. You didn't come to yesterday's
Tarawih prayers at our house. Why are you trying to cover up
the truth? We are all women here, you crazy girl!' Zohra chided
Sherifa playfully and went into the kitchen.

Rabia, peeling onions, felt a stab of doubt. She wondered if
she could ask Nafiza what it meant that Sherifa wasn't
attending prayers. No, definitely Nafiza would laugh at her.
She thought of Wahida, and ran to her room.

Wahida had put away the Koran, having just finished her
chanting, and was adjusting her davani. Rabia went up to her,
held her by the waist, and looked up at her. Wahida embraced
her in return with an expression that said, 'What's the matter?'

'There's something I don't understand. Will you explain it
to me?'

'And what is it that Rabiakutty can't understand?'

'What does it mean to say you can't go to prayers? It's

happened to Sherifa.' She pulled away from Wahida, expecting an answer.

'Ayyaiyé – you're only a little girl, you shouldn't know all that,' Wahida said, laughing. She took Rabia by the hand and brought her in front of all the other women. 'Nafizakka, your daughter-in-law has a question for you. Please give her an answer,' she said, sitting down with the others.

'What's worrying you? Shouldn't you ask me instead of going and bothering your sister?' asked Nafiza.

'Oh, it's nothing.' Rabia ran away into the street, embarrassed.

Zohra brought the tea and handed it round to the workers and to Sherifa. 'Let it be, Akka,' protested Sherifa. 'I'll drink it later. How can I drink in front of all of you who are keeping the fast? Wouldn't it be wrong?'

'In that case, go inside and drink your tea there. Then you could wake up Rahimakka and bring her here. She's lying down in that room there,' said Zohra. When Sherifa had left them, she added, 'Poor thing, she's such a good girl. And Allah has gone and done this to her.' The others nodded in agreement.

Mumtaz began again, after a little while. 'Well, Akka, how are the arrangements for Wahida's wedding going on? It seems that it's only taking place because of Macchaan's insistence, and that Rahimakka doesn't like the idea one little bit? People are saying all this in town.'

Zohra thought to herself, 'Of course these two must have something to gossip about, otherwise their heads will burst. But must they come out with all this in front of Wahida?' But aloud, she only said, 'No, no, nothing like that. Wahida is still very young; we wanted to wait a little longer.'

Nafiza was not satisfied with this, however. 'Just because she's young, it doesn't mean she doesn't know how to lie down. You're a fine one! Listen, Wahida, if you have any doubts about anything, don't hesitate to ask us, we'll teach you everything. Mumtaz even has a cassette; if you ask her nicely, she'll show you. The bridegroom will see to what's left,' she declared. Wahida's fair complexion blushed blood-red as she rose to her feet in haste and fled from there.

Zohra was annoyed with Nafiza and scolded her. 'How can you talk so crudely in front of her of all people?'

But Mumtaz only laughed. 'As if girls of her age are so innocent! She's going to be married within a month; don't you think she will sleep with her husband then?'

'Let her learn about all that at the right time. What's the hurry now,' Zohra admonished her.

Mariyayi finished her tea, washed her stainless steel tumbler, put it away in the kitchen, and joined them. 'All the ginger is scraped and washed. Shall I pound it in the ural, now?'

'What's this? You're asking me as if you don't know anything! You've done all this for years together, and you're asking me now as if you were married yesterday and are learning about the family for the first time!'

'It's not that I don't know; I only asked for the sake of exchanging a few words,' said Mariyayi in a complaining tone as she went away to drag the large stone mortar into the centre of the veranda.

Meanwhile there was a suspicion that was churning around inside Nafiza's head. 'Do you actually give her tea in one of the tumblers that you yourselves use?' she whispered, with an expression of disgust.

'Ché ché! We've bought her a special steel plate and tumbler for herself, because we were sure she'd get angry if we serve her in an aluminium lota,' Zohra assured her.

Nafiza gave a sigh of relief. 'I was just wondering,' she said. But Mumtaz gave a cackle of laughter. That mocking laughter was suggestive in a new and different way.

'And why are you laughing like that, di?' Zohra asked her.

'Oh, it's just that I was thinking, you've kept aside a separate plate and so on for her, haven't you? None of you will touch it. But Karim Macchaan goes to her, doesn't he? Do you refuse to touch him?' She laughed some more. Zohra was stunned into silence, not quite knowing how to respond to Mumtaz's remarks. Nobody said anything for awhile. Nafiza broke the silence. 'She talks as if she's found out something amazingly new. As if it is such an extraordinary thing for a man to keep a mistress? As if we can call all men virtuous!' She shook her head, taking Zohra's side against Mumtaz.

Mumtaz, for her part, could not endure to see Nafiza setting herself up as an advocate for Zohra. She also understood what was behind Nafiza's words, which were spoken as a kind of self-defence. Her head would surely explode, she thought, if she didn't expose Nafiza. She began again, lamenting, 'Whatever it is… All right, perhaps we have to accept that men will have their way with their mistresses. What I can't understand is how women can bring themselves to sleep with many men. I can't think what sort of creatures they must be.'

Nafiza too knew, perfectly well, what Mumtaz was insinuating. She tried to ignore the barbed words which were directed at her.

Just as the conversation had reached such a dangerous point, Rahima appeared. She came and sat down with the others, saying, 'Welcome, all of you.' She went on, 'It looks as if half the work is finished. I was the only living creature unable to help you. The rest of you have been so good, you put goodness itself to shame!' After a while, she said, hand held to her cheek, 'Did you hear the news about last night? While the Tarawih prayers were being said, it seems a group of Kafir boys went past the mosque beating their drums and making mayhem. See how extreme they are becoming!' Her round face wore a tense expression, as if she could not bear the shock of it.

'Yes,' said Nafiza, 'I too heard about it. This is something we have never seen in these parts! They have never gone past the entrance to the mosque beating their drums. Ahmad's father says this is all the work of their leader, Arumugam. Now who can we go and complain to?'

'Hm, the times are really bad. What else is there to say? It seems there was some kind of boundary dispute between our

Headman Moosa, and Arumugam. It seems those fellows are dragging a personal dispute into community relations,' Zohra commented.

The conversation drifted off in a different direction. The women got on with their work, swiftly. A hundred coconuts were scraped and sent to be machine-ground; the pounded ginger was handed over to be ground together with garlic; onions, chillies, fenugreek, coriander and mint were all prepared and made ready and dispatched to the mosque, along with the firewood. Everybody was kept busy until all the work was complete.

Ω 13 Ω

Nafiza felt as if her whole body was overcome by fatigue. Her tongue was dry. She thought she might have a bath and say her prayers, but could not. She went and lay down quietly, instead. Somehow, her heart seemed empty. She kept gazing at the wings of the fan, whirling above her. She wanted to weep, yet found it impossible to do so.

Mumtaz had chosen to reveal just a fraction of her true opinion about Nafiza; spoken just a few words, and gone her way. Now, however hard Nafiza might try, those words could not be ignored. She had to accept that she no longer came within the boundaries of what was defined by others as right conduct; she had been pushed outside those boundaries. At the same time, she did not see how she could give in to other peoples prescriptions with regard to everything in this life. Of course, the world would not be able to comprehend the deep connection between herself and Aziz. But she could not imagine leaving him, ever.

Did her husband, Bashir, know about it, and yet pretend not to know, or did he truly remain ignorant of it? She could not make it out. She had a deep affection for Bashir, too. She had no reason whatever to dislike him. The distance between them was only because of their difference in age. Theirs was a marriage that had been arranged to keep the property within the family. He continued to be loving towards her, and she, in return, was always affectionate in her behaviour towards him. But between her and Aziz, a relationship had developed, far beyond that. She could not bring herself to believe it was wrong. For some unknown reason, it had grown and developed and it was her great comfort. She did not have the wisdom to think about it or comprehend it any more than that, she told herself.

It was very nearly Asar time. Busy with her thoughts, she had not realized how quickly time had flown. Unless she began on her chores straight away, she would not finish in time. Ahmad was not to be seen. She must send him to the mosque as soon as he turned up, to fetch the nonbu kanji and buy vadais. Bashir would certainly come home, to break his fast. He always enjoyed sitting down to eat with his sons and Nafiza. On the other hand, it made him extremely angry and upset if either Rafiq or Ahmad stayed away, playing with their friends. He was so fond of his boys.

She heard someone at the door, and peeped out of the kitchen. Rabia had come, a carrier in her hand. 'Well, Rabia, it seems you have brought your maami something or the other?'

'Amma sent me with the nonbu kanji,' Rabia said with pride.

'What a fortunate thing! I was just about to send someone to the mosque, to fetch the nonbu kanji, but here, you've actually brought some. Leave it here. I'll send Ahmad with the carrier, later.' She went on, 'Rabia, I'm going to ask you something. Will you answer me truthfully, and not hide anything?'

Rabia was in a quandary. What could she want to ask her? She looked at Nafiza with an expression that said, What is it?

'Don't be scared, di, amma, it's nothing serious. I wanted to ask why you don't go to your Ummumma's house regularly, nowadays. You used to go at least once a week, didn't you?'

'I don't know, Macchi, Amma never sends me these days.'

' But that's what I'm asking you. Why not?'

'Amma seems to be very angry with Firdaus Chitthi. It's because of that.'

'Why is she angry? Because she refused to live with her husband and came away home. Isn't that why?'

Rabia felt extremely awkward. She didn't know how to answer. Avoiding any further questions, she said, 'I don't know about all that. I must go now'. She flew away like a bird, and told herself, as soon as she was in the street, 'Appada, I've escaped.' She breathed a great sight of relief.

Nafiza was disappointed. She didn't get the chance to learn all the details about Firdaus's situation. She didn't know, now, who else to ask. She felt troubled when she thought about the girl. It wasn't only in the olden days that they arranged marriages without considering the compatibility of the couple concerned, and ruined the lives of young girls; it was happening now, too. They only seemed to consider money and kinship. Who thought of the matching up of age or looks? Such is women's fate, Nafiza muttered to herself; who ever asked a girl for her opinion? She went to have her bath.

* * *

Rabia, escaping from Nafiza, ran at breakneck speed. She was breathless from having taken the front steps of the house, two at a time. She stopped at Madina's house to draw breath. She was sweating all over. She lifted the end of her skirt, bent down, and blotted her forehead. The main reason she had gone to Nafiza's house was to see Ahmad. Where on earth did he go? She wanted to play with him all the time, and to stay with him. But he wouldn't ever allow her to join him. She thought she must make up with him from now on. She hoped that he might teach her to cycle. Madina was still reluctant to agree with her, though. She must bring her round somehow.

The women were beginning to gather as usual at Rabia's house, for the Tarawih prayers. It was only after the men had all left for the mosque, that the prayers would begin here. It was always either Zohra or Rahima who led them. Since almost everyone attending would have completed their olu ablutions in their own homes, Rahima now began to get ready for the prayers.

Clean prayer mats had been laid in a row in the hall. You should never step across or on them, even by accident. If Rabia ever did that, her mother would be very annoyed. She went and sat on the sofa in the corner of the hall, and watched all the women who were assembling. Madina's mother and sister-in-law, Mumtaz, had arrived earlier. Now Nafiza, Saurakka, and all the rest arrived, one after the other. 'Where's Fatima? Is she not here?' Nafiza asked Rahima.

'For the past two days she's had a lot of work. She's not very well, and is staying at home. That's what it is,' Rahima said.

'Oh, I see,' Nafiza caught sight of Rabia. 'Why are you sitting there, all by yourself? Go and sleep, why not?'

'As if her eyes are likely to close,' Rahima remarked, fondly. 'She's got to watch everything. Yes, why don't you go and sleep?' Rabia felt shy. She hid her face against her knees.

'Ahmad and Rafiq are at home. Why don't you go and chat with them until the prayers are over?' Nafiza offered.

Rabia shook her head, meaning, No. She glanced at Zohra, doubtfully.

'Are you afraid because of your mother? She won't say anything; go on,' Nafiza encouraged her.

Zohra had just come in, having done her olu cleansing. Since she hadn't as yet prayed the olu nabil, she could not speak, but simply made the sign of takbir, raising her hands up to her ears and then crossing her arms.

At least if Madina were here, they could have chatted together, Rabia thought. But Madina was always asleep by eight. How did she manage to do that? The prayers had begun. The entire house fell silent. The only sounds were of their bangles and anklets as the women knelt and rose intermittently. Rabia felt bored. It would be so much better to be chatting with Ahmad. She thought it might be a good opportunity, in Madina's absence, to make up with Ahmad. But at the same time, she was afraid that her mother might be cross with her. Emboldened by the presence of Nafiza Macchi, she got to her feet and opened the door gently. The street lights were on, so she wasn't afraid. Remembering that a dog might enter the house and go into the kitchen, she pulled the front door and shut it tightly. Satisfied, she stepped into the street.

In a trice she had reached Ahmad's house and pushed open the door. Ahmad peered out to see who it was. 'It's me,' said Rabia, running across the courtyard and into the hall. He was sitting on a bed strung with rope, reading. He looked up at her as if to ask why she had come. She sat down at a little distance next to him, holding her skirt closely about her. 'I just came. Aren't you asleep, then?' she asked, somewhat hesitantly.

'No, I'm reading.'

'What is it?'

'Nothing that you need know.' He shrugged his shoulders.

She felt humiliated. For a while she didn't say anything. Sri Lanka's Rupavahini was showing on the television. Rafiq was watching ardently, lying on his stomach; his legs skywards. He hadn't even noticed her arrival. She began again. She pleaded with him with a piteous expression, 'I want to make up with you from today. Will you let me join in when you are playing?' She was sure he wouldn't deny her.

He looked at her for a moment with his little eyes. He flicked his hair to one side, with his fingers, and with an air of conceding gracefully, said, 'OK, OK, I'm ready to make up too.' He knew perfectly well that if he missed this chance he wouldn't get another such victory. But what about Madina?

'But what about her? She's not going to make up with me, is she?' he asked, in an indifferent tone.

As for Rabia, in her delight that he was prepare to make friends, she put on an innocent expression and said, 'Oh she? I don't know about her.'

He warned her strictly, assuming an authoritative tone, 'In

that case, let me tell you one thing. Listen well. I will talk only to you. I'll allow only you to join in our games. I'll teach you to ride a cycle, provided you don't go and teach her. Remember all this.'

Well, that's enough, she thought; I don't have to worry any more. Just as well he hadn't said, 'Unless you are her enemy, you can't be my friend.'

She didn't want to say anything more for a little while, but turned to look at the TV. A play in Sinhala was being shown. She began to watch it avidly. In their house, her uncle had stowed the TV in a cardboard-box and put it away in the store-room. He said you should not watch TV during the month of fasting, it was a sin. He was always like that. Every year he would pack away the TV on the day before Ramzan began and say, 'For this month at least go and add to your stock of good deeds.' Remembering this, she felt remorseful.

Rafiq still lay on his belly, his legs lifted skywards. Wanting to show herself in the best light to Ahmad, she remarked, 'Its Nandana-Vindana, isn't it?' Then she rebuked the younger boy, 'Rafiq, put your legs down.' Rafiq, startled, turned his head, transferring his gaze from the TV screen to her. Ahmad looked surprised as well, wondering what she meant.

'You shouldn't point to heaven with your feet should you? Because that's where Allah is. That's why.' Her voice was full of concern for Rafiq. And sure enough, the very next instant, Rafiq, frightened by what she said, lowered his legs.

Rabia wanted to know how Ahmad reacted to this. Surely he must think the better of her. But why was he refusing to talk to her properly? She began again. 'Why didn't you go to the prayers with the others?'

'I need to revise for my exams, don't I? And then, Amma went off to the prayers, telling me to look after this fellow. But why aren't you revising?'

'I've finished revising everything. I even recited it all to Wahidakka, so she could check me.'

He was surprised. 'But she studied at an English-medium

Convent, didn't she? Does she know Tamil as well?'

'Oh, of course she does, she knows English as well as Tamil. We only know Tamil.' She liked to boast about her cousin.

Ahmad did not say anything. He bent over his book, riffling through its pages. There were so many things he wanted to know, to find out. He had decided that there shouldn't be a single fact in this world of which he was ignorant. Many women must come and learn from him, ask him questions, just like this Rabia here. Everyone should say he was their leader, the best of them all.

Rabia watched him carefully. He was only wearing a banian on top of his trousers. A lean body and long legs. It must be because of that he learnt to ride a cycle so quickly, she thought. For whatever reason, she really liked him. It would be good if she could spend a lot of time with him. But she could not stop herself from feeling hurt that he took no notice of her.

'I must go,' she said, standing up.

He lifted his head and looked at her for a moment. 'Why so soon? The prayers haven't finished yet,' he said. She was overjoyed by his words. She was about to sit down on the bed again, but remembered her mother. Knowing she must expect a scolding from her, she said, 'No, I must go. I'll come again tomorrow. Amma will be looking for me now.' She set off home at a run.

Ahmad was very surprised. Why on earth was she so shy? He knew very well that however much he teased her, she still remained very eager to play with him. He too, took a great pleasure in provoking her. His mother always said, 'You are never happy unless you get her into trouble.' But it was Madina who really made him angry. He grumbled to himself that he would bring her in line, one way or another. In another week, their exams would be over and the long vacation would begin. Then, if she had no companions at all to play with, she must come and join his group of her own accord. Having determined this, he returned to his revision.

ᔆ 14 ᔆ

Mariyayi was pulling out hay from the rick, with a
long-handled crook. When she had as much as she
needed, she leaned the crook against the fence, gathered up all
the hay into an embrace and took the bundle to the cowshed.
Slowly, casually, the cows rose to their feet and approached
the hay, while she went to sit under the shade of the neem tree.

Since the previous day, she was overcome by a feeling of
bitterness and frustration. She thought about the life that was
left to her. When she was helping to prepare the nonbu kanji at
Karim's house yesterday, she had half-heard the gossip and
banter of the women gathered there, but had pretended not to
notice, and let it go. What, in any case, could she have done
about it? Tears gathered in her eyes at the thought. She felt
unbearably sad that Karim had not even thought fit to tell her
about the marriage arrangements for Wahida. In the end, she
was only the mistress to whom he came when he desired her;
she was not the reigning queen, she told herself. All the same,
Karim saw her everyday; why could he not have told her about
it, even in passing, as a piece of news? Then she wondered
whether she was assuming a right that went far beyond what
was owed to her.

For wasn't this the life she had assented to and sought for
herself, after all? How could she either complain, or assume
any right? It was a great folly to cultivate huge hopes and
expectations on the strength of Karim's desire for her. When
she first began living with him, her mother had pointed out all
the reasons why she should not, and had wanted to take her
away elsewhere. But she was so infatuated with him, she had
refused, stubbornly, to listen. Did she think about all this then?
When he arranged for her to have the operation which would
prevent her from having his children, she had consented
willingly. So what was new now, she tried to ask herself, in
consolation. When his fire burnt out, he might even leave her.

'Well, so what? The only aid and support for the poor are their own arms and legs. There will be place enough for me to labour for myself and eat my own kanji,' she muttered to herself.

Karim was inside the little tiled-roofed house, lying on the bed. Realizing it was a while since she disappeared, he called out from within, 'What are you doing out there? Come and press my legs.' She shook out the end of her sari, as she rose to her feet and came inside, murmuring, 'No shortage in these demands, anyway.'

'You seem to be muttering something. Speak up if you want to say something. At least let me hear you,' he said, turning to look at her.

'It's nothing. What am I going to say? I'm the inferior one, aren't I?' she said, sitting down at his feet, and pressing his legs. He could see clearly the sadness of her expression.

'Why, what's happened to you today?' he asked

'They say Wahida is to get married. You kept it all from me, didn't you? You never said a word.'

Before she finished he cut in, laughing. 'Oho, so that's it, is it? Yes, so what about it? You've heard about it now, haven't you? Do I have to bring you the news formally, with betel leaves and nuts? Why are you making a big issue of it?'

His indifferent tone, slightly mocking, made her feel even more humiliated. 'Why, do you think it wouldn't be correct to tell me formally, in the auspicious way? But what right have I? I'm only your kept woman,' she said, beginning to weep.

He stared at her, not understanding why she was so worked up. He tried to pacify her. 'I didn't keep it from you deliberately; it's just that I forgot to tell about it.' He went on in a slightly more hectoring voice, 'So what should I do now? You will be the one to oversee all the jobs that need doing. You'll wear the sari that is presented to you. What more do you want?'

Mariyayi felt a sudden pang. What he said was true enough. He knew her place well; better than she did. Why could she not understand that? She pressed her sari firmly against her face and wiped her tears. She calmed down, knowing he would not like it if she wept anymore; he might very well walk off in anger. They were both silent for a while. Only her hands continued to work, pressing his legs. She wiped her nose from time to time.

Karim felt sorry to see her in such a state. From time to time, he considered, she would forget who she was, and her place. When she was reminded of it, she would subside. She was easily beguiled, too. She always brought all the earnings from the garden, without loss or waste, and handed it all over to the family. She sold whatever she cultivated, tomatoes, cotton or vegetables of any kind; as well as milk and eggs from the chicken she reared. As soon as she had collected a certain sum of money, she handed it over to him. He never liked to take it from her. 'Keep it,' he would say, 'it's your own hard-earned money.'

'Why do I want to save it? Who do I have?' she'd say and insist on handing it over. She took pride in this.

The house was quiet. Except for a crow calling constantly from a tree outside, and the sound of the water in the well lapping in the breeze, it was silent. It was he who broke in. 'Well, now that your daughter is getting married, what are you going to do for her?'

Instantly her face flooded with joy. 'Me? I've saved a little money. Shall I buy a ring that will be just right for her?' she asked enthusiastically. Enough; now she would be overflowing with happiness. Just because he said 'your daughter,' meaning Wahida. This was sufficient to keep her going for many days. Crazy woman, Karim said to himself.

'By the way, shall I tell Zohra to choose a sari for you, or shall I get one myself, when I'm in town next?' he asked, hoping to mollify her even more.

'Let Akka do it herself.' Her black expression had left her, and she looked very attractive, her face suffused with delight. What an honour it would be, to receive a sari which Zohra herself had chosen for her! The thought of it was truly thrilling.

Every year, it was Zohra who went to town and selected new clothes for her, in celebration of the Id feast. Since she began

living with Karim, she had given up new clothes for Deepavali.
She didn't wear a pottu on her forehead any longer. She wore
the black beads she had bought for herself in the market,
around her neck. In her imagination, she lived like a decent
Muslim woman. As far as she was concerned, Karim was her
husband. She held single-mindedly to the belief that his joys
and sorrows were her own. To this day, no other man had so
much as touched her. They knew she was Karim's woman, and
kept away. She took pride in the knowledge that no one believed
her to be a prostitute, and that therefore no one had ever
approached her improperly. She felt satisfied with this single
privilege.

She felt deeply uncomfortable when she considered how the
women of her community were treated by the men of this
village. These men were never content to eat and stay quietly
at home. They had any amount of money, besides. So one man
wants this woman today; the other tomorrow. And can she
refuse him? And how many women became pregnant and had
to go to Rosie Nurse to get rid of the child! She sighed
profoundly at the thought.

She recalled something that Karim told her once. The village
headman, Moosa, had the habit of asking any woman whom
he fancied to stand in a corner and urinate in that position. He
would choose only those women whose urine fell at a distance.
If it fell close by, he would taunt the woman of having had too
many children and grown old, and would drive her away.
Karim fell about laughing as he recounted this. Apparently his
friend Ismail had told him this story. It angered and repulsed
her, though. She quarrelled with him over it. 'How can you
say such obscene things! It's disgusting, disgusting!' she said,
knocking herself on the head.

'Why do you have to be so disgusted, di? I told the same
story to Zohra, and she just laughed with me. Why don't you
see the joke, instead of making such a fuss?' he said. It was as if
he was putting her on the spot and saying, 'As if you are such a
respectable woman!' Zohra herself was prepared to laugh at

the joke, to share it with her neighbours and to report that they had all found it hilarious. Why should she alone pronounce it obscene?

Karim broke into her thoughts. 'Well, you seem to be in a deep meditation?'

'Oh, it's nothing,' she replied, continuing to press his legs for him. Karim shut his eyes. He was tired. The fasting made him drowsy, but he could not sleep. He had come here in the hope of a peaceful nap. Wahida's prospective bridegroom, Sikandar, had arrived home from abroad. He would have liked to visit them in their home, but unfortunately, his mother-in-law and Firdaus lived next door. He was in no state of mind to see them.

The very thought of Firdaus spurning the husband whom he, as the elder son-in-law of the family had made it his business to arrange for her, filled him with fury. He might excuse her, for she was just an ignorant girl, but what could he say about his mother-in-law? What happened to her common sense? Should she not have insisted that the marriage was the result of her son-in-law's honourable and decent effort, and forced the girl to go back to her husband? 'Fine woman,' he muttered to himself.

They claimed the bridegroom was not suitable! What did it mean, suitable! And who was struggling now, with a daughter who had to be kept hidden away? He tossed on his bed, muttering, and remembered the bridegroom, Yusuf, and his family. They were the wealthiest family in their village. They had only come after Firdaus because of their contact with him. He had taken the initiative and made the match in the knowledge that his father-in-law was dead, and his wife's family was struggling. He had been anxious that if this match fell through, they would be hard put to find another as good. Because the girl was so beautiful, Yusuf had been generous enough to leave it to the bride's family to provide the dowry and jewels that they could manage. Had it been anyone else, he would have made out a list of needs: so many sovereigns' worth;

so many thousands; so much for the husband's sisters; so much dowry. In this case, Karim had calculated that they would be spared the expenses and the bother and, at the same time, she would go to a good place. But this was how it all ended! It pained Karim greatly that now they could not even face Yusuf and his family. From now on he was determined never to step across the threshold of the family who had treated him and his decisions with such disrespect. Of course it was unfortunate that if he went to visit Sabia Akka now, he would have to come away without going next door. And Sabia would not fail to spread this news to everyone in town. That would hurt his mother-in-law, Amina, very much. Worse still, Zohra would weep her heart out here, saying, 'You seem to have gone there just to humiliate my family.'

Karim thought about it. He would cause more problems by visiting Sikandar than by staying at home. Of course, Sabia Akka would shout at him and say, 'So it's so difficult, is it, to come and see my son?' That wasn't going to be a big deal, he thought; he could handle it.

He thought once more of Firdaus. How daring of this chit of a girl! For how many days did he and Zohra stay with her and try to advise her? Would she give in one little bit? On top of everything, he felt humiliated by the way she blamed it all on him: 'You only chose him because you didn't want to lose your money, you made sure you wouldn't be left with all the bills.'

Did I do any of this out of bad intentions? Did I do anything outlandish, unknown to our community? Have we arranged this marriage between Wahida and Sikandar because of their compatibility at all levels? Is there the least compatibility between Nafiza and Bashir? 'You have to look around you and learn the way of the world, otherwise you have to stay like a frog in the well,' Karim muttered to himself. He felt anxious and regretful, but at the same time, he said aloud, 'Everything must happen as He ordains. Who can do anything to prevent it?' He was aware that it was nearly time to end the day's fast, and sat up.

She got up from the bed and stood aside, making room for him, while he strode off without even saying goodbye. Sunk in his own thoughts, he went straight to the motor-cycle which stood outside, started it and rode off. After he had left, she stood there in the same place for a long while. Her heart was full of anxieties. Until he returned, she would be alone there, with only the trees and the chicken for company. In earlier times, she never felt her solitude as a burden. But now, more and more, she hated being alone. It was only now that she realized the folly of having listened to him, and agreed to the sterilization. But in any case he would never have allowed her to bear his children. At the start of their relationship, when she became pregnant, she had been very hesitant to tell him. He had been shocked, and sat there silently, for a long time. Then he said, 'Go and get an abortion.' Because she had expected it, she just looked at him quietly. He was absolutely stern. 'There is no option. Everyone in town knows that you are sleeping with me. If you have a child, there will be no doubt in anyone's mind that it is mine. How will that look? Just think about it yourself. If you were sleeping with many men, no one would be certain that the child that is growing in you is mine. And it wouldn't affect me that much. Now, on the contrary, everyone will be certain the child is mine, and that isn't right. Do you remember when Mohiuddin the butcher's mistress had a baby that was the spitting image of him? You know how he wanders about, in that witless way? People know he is Mohiuddin's son and they make fun of him. Don't let that happen. I'll give you the money. Go to the hospital in the next town, and have it aborted.'

His voice was firm, and contained the warning that she must not, on any account, cross him. She had only two options: either to abort the baby and be sterilized at the same time, or to leave him and go away for ever. She could not begin to

imagine how she could leave him. Her love for him was endless.
With all his good looks and wealth, it was she whom he desired:
the thought gave her a certain arrogance.

There was also some justice in what he said; she could not
ignore that. She agreed to the abortion because she could see no
other way. But nowadays, she was often tormented by the
thought that she had no one of her own.

～ 15 ～

Rahima woke up at daybreak, that day. Usually, on fast
days, she would have a nap immediately after the Bajar
prayers, and wake up at her leisure in the morning. But on
that day she had a great deal to do. She had woken up Zohra as
well, and sent Rabia to fetch Fatima. Fatima appeared, still
half-asleep. 'What is the matter, Akka, you're up very early?'
she remarked as she walked in, her hair still uncombed. Her
short stature and her middling-brown skin gave her the look
of a young girl. 'But she is only a young woman,' Rahima said
to herself. She said, casually, 'Yes, di, there's plenty to do today.
Sabia Akka and our nephew are visiting us today, from the
village. Wahida and her father went to invite them for the Iftar
feast, remember? That's what it is.'

Fatima was excited. 'Is that the news?' She loosened her hair,
gave it a couple of shakes and twisted it up into a knot. She
tucked her sari up knee-high, and set off to the kitchen to start
on all the chores.

From then on, she would be as busy as a spinning-top. No
one would be able to intervene. She would insist on taking on
everything herself. But this keenness of hers was only manifest
during special events in the household. On routine everyday
matters, she tended to be casual, answering back a thousand
times before she completed a single piece of work. Rahima and
Zohra tended to tease her, claiming that on special days, it was
as if some sort of jinn had entered her. She usually joined in the

laughter, saying, 'Yes, there has to be some excitement which drives you to work.'

Rahima and Zohra had agreed on the menu the previous day. There would only be Sabia and the bridegroom as guests. There was no need to cook a great feast. They must fry vadais and bhajjis to break their fast; boil some beans for a sundal, make a payasam. There would also be the nonbu kanji, as well as dates, apples and oranges. That would be enough! After that, for the evening meal they would make idiappam, and serve it with chicken kurma and fried chicken. There would also be iddlis, dosai and a meat soup. They thought they should toss the idiappams lightly in oil. If they began on their cooking immediately, they would just about be ready in time. Besides this, they would have to include them in the preparations for the next morning's sahar meal.

Just the thought of all this made Rahima feel exhausted. She gave a great sigh, saying, 'I wonder when we'll finish all this.'

Fatima teased her, 'Yes, but there's all the chores to do with the wedding, still to come. You have to make all the sweets and snacks for the in-laws and get the dowry and wedding gifts ready. How can you afford to get tired already? You forget that there's a mountain of work ahead of you.'

'But we'll hire some help for all that, won't we? On top of that, there's you, and there's Mariyayi. You'll do it all in a trice, won't you?'

Fatima was gritting her teeth and scrubbing hard at the cooking vessels. 'Look at all this stuff that's burnt on! It's never going to shift. Only my hands will wear away, it seems. What's the good of your having all this money! You don't have the wit to cook on a gas cooker. If you get yourselves one, you won't have to scrub off all this muck, will you?' Fatima twisted her features into a grimace.

'Yes, we have gas cookers in all the houses in town. But is it easy to buy gas cylinders in this village?' Rahima was anxious to pacify Fatima. 'Besides, Zohra is scared of those things. She thinks they may explode on her!' Rahima laughed.

'It's true, I've heard that those things can be dangerous. Of course, this fine lady is so proud of herself because she worked for awhile in the tahsildar's house in town. How she goes on about this and that gadget they have in their house instead of getting on with her business!' Zohra gave a playful swipe at Fatima who sat on the floor, scrubbing the vessels.

'Ah,' called out Fatima, pretending to cry. 'By the way, what went on when you were peeling onions for the nonbu kanji the other day? I heard something about it … '

'If you haven't filled yourself up with all the town's gossip, you won't sleep, will you?' remarked Zohra.

'Who can hide anything from me?' Fatima asked proudly. 'Someone said something to me. Let's say that crow which is sitting on the edge of the tile told me. So why don't you come out with it?' Fatima spoke with a mock sternness.

'Keep quiet!' Rahima signalled Zohra with her eyes. Zohra spoke up, with a hint of warning. 'It was nothing, amma. Your friend Sherifa must have told you about everything that went on here that day. That was all. Nothing important. And don't you go and report it to anyone else.'

Fatima stopped working on the vessels for a moment. 'As if I have no other work except to wander about spreading gossip. What do you think? I heard something, so I thought I would ask you about it. If you don't want to tell me, then don't, that's all.' Fatima was cross.

It was best to leave things alone, Zohra thought, busying herself with something else. She was also afraid that if she were to anger Fatima with further talk, then everything would be ruined.

They were all busy throughout the day, without time even to sit down once. Kader had suddenly asked them to send some of the feast as well as the smaller items for ending the fast to the Hazrats at the mosque. Rahima had grumbled a little. 'We are always sending food to the Hazrats. Do we have to add to our work today by including them?' Kader had quelled her with a stern glance. Now everything had to be cooked in greater quantity. They felt as if their backs were breaking. Sabia and Sikandar arrived by the evening. The whole household began to hum, the moment Sabia entered. It was some years since they had seen Sikandar. Rahima and Zohra came to the front of the courtyard, their saris pulled over their heads, stood half-hidden by a pillar, welcomed him with a single word, and returned quickly to the kitchen. It was not the custom for a mother-in-law to come in front of the prospective groom. Wahida had vanished upstairs since the afternoon. She refused to come down. Sikandar seated himself on the sofa, feeling shy. Had there been some men to keep him company, he would have felt less embarrassed. Rabia came running home from elsewhere. She could smell an expensive scent perfuming the air and knew instantly that the guests had arrived. She desperately wanted to go and take a close look at her Macchaan. She crossed the courtyard without glancing at the hall and peeked into the kitchen.

Sabia was saying something loudly and laughing away, while her mother and aunt stood by. As soon as Sabia saw her, she stopped what she was saying and welcomed her proudly, 'Come here, my little niece! Haven't you seen your Macchaan? He's sitting there on the sofa, all by himself. Go and join him.'

Zohra laughed. 'Don't go and stand in front of him just as you are. Tidy up your hair. Wash your face and wipe it well, and then go,' she said in her firm voice. But Rabia rushed into the hall without answering. She wanted to see Wahidakka's future husband immediately. Otherwise her head would splinter into pieces and scatter away. The lights were on in the hall, though it was not yet dark. She hid behind a pillar and gazed at him.

He was wearing a white veshti and shirt, and sat with his head bowed. Although he wasn't as fair as her Akka by any means, he looked handsome enough, with a sharp nose, curly hair and a medium-sized moustache. He was tapping his foot on the ground as if deep in thought. She looked at his feet. His soles were clean and looked very white. He is very clean and tidy, just like Akka, she told herself. But she was very slender; he was big-made, a little plump even. So what, she thought. She felt very shy to go in front of him. But then, she was not of age as yet, so why should she feel shy? She had just about plucked up enough courage to go up to him slowly when she heard her mother calling out to her. 'Rabia, come here!' She returned to the kitchen quickly.

Zohra asked Rabia and Fatima to spread a subra on the floor and to arrange on it all the snacks for the ending of the days fast. Fatima began to bustle around. They spread mats on all four sides of the dining room and placed the subra in the middle with all the food and the fruits arranged beautifully upon it. Rabia wanted to sit down and start eating at once. The aroma of the food filled her nose and her mouth began to water. But her father and uncle had not returned home as yet. It was almost time to end their fast, though.

Sabia came into the dining room. Fatima stood in a corner, checking that everything was in order; nothing forgotten. Sabia frowned when she saw her and drove her away, saying, 'If your work is done, why don't you go and stand in the kitchen. What business do you have here, just when the men are about to come in?' Fatima was deeply ashamed. She took herself off into the kitchen, without saying anything.

Rahima heard what Sabia said, and was embarrassed. The older woman went on to complain, 'These women will never learn to place everything correctly.'

Rahima comforted Fatima quietly, saying, 'Don't take anything that woman says to heart.' Then she murmured to herself, 'Who knows how my daughter is going to suffer at this woman's hands.' Fatima's face looked drawn and downcast. Rahima felt very sorry to see her like that, squatting on the kitchen floor, next to the bench there.

When Rahima first came to this house as a bride, Fatima was only a little girl. In those days it was Nuramma, who came to the house to scrub their vessels. Nuramma slaved away night and day, denying herself everything, in order to make a good marriage for her daughter. She would never allow Fatima to do any work. She said, frequently, that her worries would be over once she had given her fatherless daughter to a good man. Rahima's mother-in-law, Jamila would assure her, 'You only have one daughter. Won't I get her married? My husband makes sure all the young girls of this town are looked after. Why should you get so upset?' But Nuramma would never be comforted. With great difficulty she saved tiny, tiny sums which she gave Jamila for safe-keeping, and was at last able to get Fatima married to a distant relation of hers.

He lived with Fatima for six months together, at the most. Then one day, he vanished. To this day, no one knew where he had gone. There had been no news from him. It was now not less than ten years since he disappeared. Fatima herself reported that someone had said he was living somewhere near Bombay. But she never made a great deal of fuss about her position. If anyone spoke of him, she would only say, Let him go his way, Mudevi! She had her small child, and her mother, Nuramma; and so her days went by.

How could that woman bring herself to be so spiteful towards Fatima? Was there no kindness at all in her heart? Women should understand women, Rahima said to herself.

Zohra emerged from the bathroom, having done her olu ablutions, and hurried her. 'Akka, go and do your olu. Fatima, you too. Macchaan and the others have arrived, to break their fast.' Rahima shook herself free of her memories, pulled Fatima to her feet, and dragged her along with her, into the bathroom. Zohra, oblivious of what had gone on, and not quite understanding why Rahima was pulling Fatima, called out loudly to Rabia. Rabia came running up, calling out, 'Here I am, Amma.'

Zohra filled two vessels with different foods and gave them to Rabia. 'Run along and take one of these to Nafiza's house, and the other to Madina's house. When you come back, you must take some of all this to Wahida, who is still upstairs. Don't forget to take her some water as well. It is time to end our fast.'

Kader and Karim welcomed their nephew by embracing him shoulder to shoulder, and saying Salaam. They brought him into the dining room, and invited him to sit down on one of the mats. Sabia was already seated there. At once they sat down next to her, welcoming her and asking after her welfare. Sikandar was a little hesitant at first, but Karim pulled him down to sit by him saying, 'Why do you feel shy, come and sit down.' He added, 'Do you need to do your olu?'

'No,' Sikandar assured him, 'I have done it already.' He took a cloth cap from his pocket, and put it on.

Sabia called towards the kitchen, 'Why not come and join us here, amma, you two?' She knew very well they would not join them, but called them all the same, for courtesy's sake. Zohra answered from the kitchen, 'It's all right, we'll stay here. Please help yourselves; don't stand on ceremony. Please ask nephew to help himself, as well.'

Rahima put her head out, and added for good measure, addressing her husband, 'Look after them, won't you?'

In the kitchen, Fatima, Rahima and Zohra seated themselves around a plank. Rabia took the food that was set aside for Wahida, upstairs. As soon as the nagara was heard, sounding from the mosque, everyone raised both hands, chanted the Fatiha, and ended the days fast by eating dates. They began their meal after that.

Sabia laughed as she ate. Karim and Kader looked at her, as if to ask why. 'It's just that Allah told us to keep this fast in order to understand the importance of going without food. But during the fast we are not meditating about hunger, are we? We spend our time planning the meals to come; we cook different dishes, and later we eat them. It's as if we've been thinking about food the whole day.' She laughed again.

'What you say is true in a way. All the same, having kept our fast dutifully, how can it be wrong to end it honourably, with different kinds of food? Aren't all these the gifts that Rahman has ordained for us, his children?' Kader spoke, swelling with pride. He was always praising Allah's grace.

Karim and Sikandar ate silently, Karim observing his nephew all the time. No one felt inclined to say anything more, but concentrated on the food. Rahima and Zohra glanced at Sabia through the kitchen window now and then, and laughed between themselves. How can one put so much food into an empty and starved stomach? 'There's all that food waiting to be eaten after the evening prayers, as well. Is that a stomach or is it a cauldron? Ah, Allah!' Fatima was pleased to hear them laughing at Sabia. Her face lost its tightness, and looked wide and bright.

In the upstairs room, Rabia was eating vadais with Wahida. She had remembered to place a towel on her head before she began to eat. She was wondering whether she should say anything about the bridegroom to her cousin. It seemed to her that Wahida didn't like the idea of getting married. Once, when the elders were talking about the forthcoming marriage, Rabia noticed that Wahida looked very unhappy. Then she went upstairs, lay down and wept. It took a long time for Rahima to plead with her and comfort her. Rabia wanted to laugh at her. 'Why does she refuse to get married, silly thing! How grandly they are going to dress her up in a silk sari, put jewels on her and garland her! As for me, when they arrange my wedding, I shall laugh with joy!' she thought to herself. Suddenly she thought of Ahmad and felt shy.

Wahida began to speak. 'Who all have come from the village, Rabia?'

Rabia was so excited, it seemed that lightning sprang from her eyes. 'That is, it's just Sabia Maami and the bridegroom who have come. You can smell perfume in the air, can't you? It's the bridegroom who's wearing it. And then, you know, he's very handsome to look at! The soles of his feet are very white and clean. If you saw him, you'd really like him, you know that? Come on, try and have a peep at him,' she rattled on at great speed.

Wahida was uneasy and confused. For the whole of the past week she had been frightened at the thought of getting married. Today she was strangely disturbed. She was overwhelmed by an eagerness to see the man who was about to marry her. At the same time she felt terribly shy. She had only seen him when she was a little child. She could not call to mind his features, his face. Try as she would, she could not imagine what he looked like. There was not the faintest memory left for her imagination to work on.

Rabia broke into her thoughts. 'Akka, it seems he has travelled by plane and everything. There will be lots of bottles of scent in his house, won't there? It seems he might even take you to all those countries, by plane. Madina said so. It seems her brother works in the same place too.'

Wahida didn't know how to reply. She was wondering solely about how she might get a look at him. Since she first menstruated, Zohra had threatened her saying, 'Never ever come before men who are other than our family. If you see their faces, or they see yours, your face will lose its light and go dark.' Because of that, she had never come within sight of men outside the family, nor had she looked at them. When visitors came to the house, they always pressed the bell. On the instant she heard it, she would take to her heels and hide inside her room. It was not in this house alone that this happened. In every house in the village, girls who had come of age ran and hid in exactly the same way. It was just the same in her Ummumma's house, too. She had attended the Muslim girls' madrasa and always went about wearing purdah.

But on that day, her mind was tossing about without reason. All her thoughts circled around him. What did he look like? How was his hair? Was he short or tall, dark or fair? If she asked Rabia, she was afraid the little girl would blurt it all out downstairs to her mother or aunt, and make it all ugly.

Zohra called from downstairs, 'Rabia, come down with your Akka. The men have gone to the mosque for prayers.'

When they came down, Zohra told Wahida to go and see Sabia Maami immediately. Sabia was in the prayer room. The instant she saw her, Wahida began to tremble. She waited quietly in a corner until she could make her salaam. The way Sabia prayed looked very peculiar. Her legs were apart, positioned oddly. She breathed hard as she lowered and raised her body. When she prostrated herself, it was as if a tortoise peered out from its shell and then drew its head inside again. Wahida wanted to laugh, but controlled herself.

Meanwhile, Rahima summoned Fatima who was sweeping the hall and preparing it for the Tarawih prayers, in order to give her two big containers full of food for her son, Iliaz, and her mother, Nuramma. She wanted to send her away before Sabia finished her prayers. If Sabia saw her giving away this much to Fatima, she would never hear the end of it. Rahima was afraid of causing needless trouble.

Sabia finished her prayers and her chanting, greeted Wahida immediately and embraced her warmly. Holding her close, she pulled her along to the sofa and made her sit beside her. 'How are you? We haven't seen you all this time; where were you hiding? Why have you grown so thin?' she asked. Then she called out, 'Zohra, is the bag I brought with me somewhere there? Just bring it here, will you?'

Sabia sat close beside Wahida, who gazed at her large body; her round, fair and lively face. She noticed her resemblance to her father. Sabia put her hand inside the plastic bag that Zohra brought to her and drew out a string of flowers in a package and tins of biscuits and chocolates. She placed these on the floor beside her, and then took out the saris that were beneath. There were three saris, made of shiny satin-type material, covered with a design of stars and crescents. Besides all this, there were two bottles of scent for the men and material for shirts.

'Here, take all these and put them away; they are presents that your nephew brought from abroad,' she said, laying them all out on the sofa. 'These saris are for Rahima and you. There's one for Wahida as well. Choose one each.' She turned to Wahida. 'You like your sari, don't you?'

Wahida didn't know what to say. She nodded her head silently. She didn't even understand the question. Zohra and Rahima took one look at the saris and smiled at each other. The pattern on them was crude; the colours too flashy. But how could they say that? Without making any comment, Rahima gathered them up in her arms saying, 'Why did you go to all this trouble?' If she didn't accept them immediately there would be trouble: Sabia would complain loudly that they had humiliated her and ignored her gifts.

'Well, do you like the saris? These ones he has chosen for the two of you are of high quality, he says, and very expensive. He's put aside another box of saris and materials. But all that's for his wife, he says. All that's more high-class than this. And it's all for my daughter-in-law.' She fondled Wahida's chin, speaking playfully to her.

Wahida's head only sank lower. Zohra wondered what splendours the high-class materials might possess. Rahima's face reflected exactly the same thoughts. Sabia had nick-names for Zohra and Rahima. Sometimes she addressed them by these names in order to tease them. When Sabia was a child, there were two coolie women called Nalli and Padavi, who worked for the families in their village. They were both married to the same man, but they never quarrelled. The entire village was astonished by their solidarity, and wondered that co-wives could be so fond of each other. The solidarity between Rahima and Zohra reminded Sabia of Nalli and Padavi. Sometimes she would call them by those names.

Now Rahima felt it necessary to say something about the slippery material she was holding. Perhaps it would be disrespectful to say nothing at all. So she spoke briefly, for the sake of form, 'The material is very good. The colours, too. They show up well, unlike those pale English shades.' She had a social grace which kept her real feelings well hidden.

Rabia watched them all this while, standing there with her arms around a pillar. Her eyes were focused on the tin of sweets, yearning after it. Surely Sabia Kuppi would summon her and hand it over? Wahida, glancing at her mischievously, wanted to smile.

'I had put aside some headache ointment and some sea-weed as well, but just as we were leaving, that Mudevi turned up and made me forget it, look,' Sabia complained, meanwhile. 'I'll bring it with me when I come next time.' She added proudly, 'Sikandar's father went to the shop himself, in order to buy it for his brothers-in-law.'

Rahima suppressed a smile. Even if he had sent it, would Sabia have the heart to hand it over? Wouldn't she have sent it to the Burma Bazaar in town by now, and sold it for what she could get? She, in her turn spoke as if she realized that Sabia was deeply upset and needed to be comforted. 'Never mind! We'll see about it later. Do you have to give it to them right away?'

Neither Rahima nor Zohra had picked up Sabia's reference to that 'Mudevi', nor asked whom she meant. Thwarted, Sabia felt as if her head was bursting. But, so what if they didn't ask; she would speak out, anyway. 'It's her, I mean, that Mudevi. My sister-in-law, my husband's sister, who's gone to the bad. Once you've given a girl away in marriage, does it mean it ends there? Her husband left her and the children in dire straits. Then her husband's family plucked away the children because they didn't even have kanji to drink. So she's come back here, to bring shame on all our heads.' She was breathing hard by the time she came to this loudly told and confused tale. 'Adiyé, Rabia, go and fetch your Maami some hot water to drink,' she urged the little girl. Then she stretched herself out on the sofa, saying, 'Very well, I'm going to put my head down for a little while; I'm feeling very tired.'

There was a sudden sense of relief. It was as if a raging wind and rain had suddenly come to an end. The two women rose up and began to put the final touches to the evening meal. But both were aware of a kind of tightness around their hearts. Wahida was desperately considering how she might catch a glimpse of her future husband during the evening. Rabia alone was without a care in the world: she picked up the tin of sweets and began to eat.

⮞ 16 ⮜

Nuramma's mouth watered when she saw all the different items of food that Fatima had brought. It was many days since she had seen such an array of foods displayed at one time. In her old age, it seemed, her palate was adrift all the time, yearning for something to eat. But what could be done? It was difficult enough to get sufficient kanji to fill one's belly. What else could they do, when one woman slaved away in order to keep three souls alive, she muttered to herself. Iliaz was away somewhere, playing with his friends. Fatima had gone to look for him. Nuramma was desperately hungry. How could she keep on waiting; it was long past the prescribed time for ending the fast. She pulled out the small wooden seating plank and sat down. Her knees ached. 'Ya, Allah,' she said, pressing her legs to relieve the pain.

She served herself some idiappam and kurma on to an aluminium plate and began to eat. It was delicious. When Zohra was first married, her cooking wasn't up to much. In those days, Karim used to fling away the plate of food that she put in front of him, very frequently. Zohra, devastated, would weep and weep. Now, it seemed Jamila Amma's culinary skill had been well learnt by her daughter-in-law, Nuramma thought. In those days, when Jamila cooked a meal, its aroma would fill the whole street! Nowadays, it seemed to Nuramma, all kinds of delicious smells came from every house, whatever they were cooking. Heaven knew what they were all up to. It's all fate, she thought, and finished eating. As soon as the food entered her empty stomach, she began to feel faint. She dimmed the light in the lantern and decided to sleep a little, sitting in her chair. Fatima, gone in search of her son, had not yet returned. 'Where has he vanished, the good-for-nothing layabout? The poor woman has slaved away all day, and can't even lay her head down,' she said, closing her eyes and trying to sleep.

* * *

The street was pervaded with darkness. A couple of street dogs could be heard, howling in the distance. No moon nor stars in the dark sky. Suddenly she heard the sound of a cauldron being rolled along the narrow, two-foot wide lane separating her house and Saura's. A sound as if a heavy bronze cauldron, full of gold coins, was being pulled along. The noise of it being dragged so effortlessly woke Nuramma, who was half asleep. It was a very long lane; it would take at least ten minutes to move it from one end to the other. And nothing seemed to stand in its way.

What a racket! Nuramma was curious. Should she open the back door and peep out? But, ammadi, she had heard that the jinn would kill anyone it saw standing in front of it, with a single blow. Remembering this, she changed her mind. She listened carefully, wondering at whose house the noise would stop. But no, the cauldron seemed to roll up and down the street without stopping, until at last the noise ceased abruptly.

Nuramma was disappointed. Why could not the jinn leave the buried treasure in her house, tonight at least? She had been hearing this same noise for many years. She was exasperated by the jinn which wandered about, unable to make up its mind where and with whom it should leave the treasure it safeguarded. How could it have the heart to walk past this house with its fatherless child? She had asked herself many times whether its heart had blackened, perhaps. She was certain of one thing, though. The treasure would certainly arrive at their house one day or other.

Once, long ago, when Fatima was a little girl, she had been

sitting in the front room, playing seven stones with her friends. It was about mid afternoon. The sunlight falling on the front courtyard dazzled the eyes. Board games, pallaanguzhi and daayam, lay nearby. Tamarind seeds, used in the games as counters, were scattered everywhere. Saurakka, who had been playing daayam for a long while, had just left. Nuramma thought she should go to Jamila Akka's house to bring away some food, before Fatima began to clamour with hunger. She had finished all her chores there, earlier, in the morning. Jamila had told her then, to return later on, to collect the food. If Fatima grew hungry, she would be in agony. Poor child, she was fatherless, she thought, pitying her. She needed a father to see her safely set up in life, didn't she? What could Nuramma, a woman, do? She was always anguished by a sense of fear and responsibility. How was she to bring up this child, unhurt, unblemished? She was never free of this worry, night or day.

It was then that she heard that sound. The noise of thunder. In the front courtyard, a flash of lightning tore through the sunlight, and suddenly, is if it fell from heaven, a bronze cauldron fell into the courtyard, glowing brilliantly. Within a second, as she sat there petrified not knowing what had happened, the cement floor of the courtyard split, the cauldron fell through and the floor closed over it; the house returned to a frozen silence. Fatima, not understanding what was going on, screamed, 'Amma', and ran up to her and fell into her lap, terrified; Nuramma embraced her tightly. The other children who had been playing with Fatima were equally shocked by the terrible noise of the thunder, and stood cowering against the wall.

It was after she came to herself that she began to comprehend what had happened, and then she began to lament. Her lament came in a downpour of tears: for some reason, the jinn who had brought the treasure to her had suddenly changed its mind and taken it away, having given her just a brief glance of it. To this day she would weep, remembering what happened. She believed the jinn would return it to her one day. She would

console herself then, saying, if not today, it will certainly give
it one day; let my child live without hardship.

From that day to this, she lived in that hope. But time went
by, and nothing ever happened. Her own body was losing its
strength. How much longer would she last? Of course she would
rejoice if the treasure came to them in her lifetime, and she
could see a life of freedom opening up for her child. Her
daughter, Fatima, grew up fatherless. Then Fatima's husband
abandoned her when she was yet a young girl, leaving her
without support. Now, Fatima's son Iliaz, too, was without a
father. How could He have the heart to ascribe such a fate to
them? What had He ever done for them, that they should be
grateful to Him? Why should I ever pray, she asked herself,
resentfully. Mosquitoes were biting her legs to shreds. She sat
up, driving them away.

Fatima lay curled up on a mat in the front room. Iliaz lay
within her arm. Nuramma walked up slowly, in the dim light,
and stood by them. She wondered whether she should lean
down and wake Fatima and ask her if she had heard anything.
But she would be angry. Fatima tended to get annoyed very
quickly. Then she would snap at her. Don't you have anything
else to do with your life, she'd ask. For how long will you keep
on asking me this, she'd say. Or she'd say contemptuously,
what nonsense, as if jinns ever wander about during the fasting
month. She gave up the thought of waking Fatima, and went
to the backyard instead, to relieve herself, and wash afterwards.
The whole town seemed immersed in silence. In a short while,
that quiet would be dispersed entirely. All the houses would
wake up to prepare for the sahar meal, and the street would
come alive.

At a distance, she could hear faintly the Sahar Muzafar Bawa
reciting baytus and sounding his small drum to announce that
it was time for the sahar meal. Now he would go round all the
streets in the town. A young boy accompanied him, holding a
hurricane lamp. He collected a good lot of donations along
the streets, in the morning. He made a good income right

through this month, for no one gave him less than ten rupees.
Twice in the week, on Fridays and Mondays, he made his round
in the mornings. There was no lack of special foods, either. But
it was all over by the end of Ramzan. After that he always
returned to his own village. And then he was only seen the next
year, during the next month of fasting. He had been coming to
their town every year, since Fatima was a small child. A man
with a good heart. He knew about the affairs of each family
here. He never failed to ask whether Fatima's husband had
come back. When they said no, he always consoled them saying,
'I'll pray to Allah to give him good sense.' But Fatima always
cursed, cracking her knuckles, 'Heaven knows where that evil
wretch has gone. Is he likely to come back now?'

Nuramma was racked by a fear that Fatima was at an age to
go astray. She thought that there was something different about
her behaviour in recent days. She combed her hair carefully,
and dressed it with flowers. For some reason, she laughed and
smiled a lot. Her face looked bright, not drawn and faded as it
usually was. Once or twice, Nuramma had seen her daughter
chatting and laughing with Murugan who worked in Bashir's
shop. She had asked Fatima, 'What were you saying to that
low fellow?' Fatima had snapped back, 'Nothing.' Since then,
Nuramma had begun to watch over her daughter. What would
she do, if Fatima, driven by the desires of youth, did something
foolish, and something bad happened?

Beset by all these thoughts, Nuramma knew that there was
no hope of any more sleep. She took up her betel box, came
out into the courtyard and began to chew, sitting on the
grindstone.

⌐ 17 ⌐

Rabia and Madina were walking along the main street
on the way to their school. Rabia, wondering for a moment
whether they should follow the route which would take them

there directly, asked aloud, 'Which way shall we go?'

'Oh, let's take the direct route,' said Madina. 'I have some money, we could buy something at the stall to munch as we go.'

'But then, shouldn't we go to Uma's house and pick her up, first?' Rabia was doubtful.

'We could, but if we go that way we won't be able to buy snacks.' Madina hesitated. But she came round quickly. 'Very well then, never mind. We can still get some of the snacks they sell just outside the school, under the tree.' She started along the short cut that split off from the main street with Rabia following.

Even though it was still early in the day, the sun was scorching already. Rabia quickened her pace. 'Madina, hurry up, I can't stand the heat.' Madina, agreeing, matched her pace to Rabia's.

The portia tree which stood beside Accountant Sethu's house shed a cool shade, and Rabia wanted to linger there for awhile. She asked, as if seeking permission, 'Shall we stand here for a bit? It's pleasant, here.' But Madina walked on, ignoring her, 'Pach! Never mind all that, it's getting late. The bell will go soon.' Rabia was resentful. Saying to herself, 'So what will happen if we just stand there for a moment', she walked past the tree unwillingly. She walked on, kicking up the dead leaves which had fallen on the ground, and remembered that her mother would scold her. She would say, 'Is that a way for a young girl to walk?' Involuntarily she began to walk differently for awhile before chiding herself, 'Yes, but Amma isn't here, is she, so why should I worry.' She began kicking up the leaves again.

When they reached Uma's house, they called out to her from the thinnai, outside. As if she had been waiting for them, Uma came running out immediately, saying, 'Here I am.' Rabia had lost her Konar revision notes and was worried about preparing for the exams. She had hoped to borrow Uma's. Uma, of course, had learnt everything well beforehand, and could recite her notes back to front. Rabia knew she would not need them

now. Madina too had a set of notes, but Rabia could not ask
her; she would need them herself.

'Uma, I need your Konar notes. Will you lend them to me?'
asked Rabia.

'Mine? But I gave them to Prabha just yesterday. She's lost
hers, she said. Why didn't you ask me before?' Uma was very
sorry. It meant a lot to her that Rabia had asked her for help,
and was deeply frustrating that she could not give it.

'But I've got mine, haven't I? We could study together, you
and I,' said Madina.

'No, but I need a set of my own, because I need to recite
them to Wahida Akka when she is free,' Rabia insisted. She
suddenly remembered Ramesh. She asked, 'Uma, shall we ask
Ramesh? His house is right behind yours, isn't it? He's a clever
boy too, isn't he? He's sure to have learnt all the notes by heart,
already. Do ask him for me.'

But Uma replied smartly, 'Go to Ramesh's house? I won't
go there, ever.' She looked deeply shocked at the very thought.
Rabia was surprised. 'Why ever not? Why can't you go there?'

'That is... My mother has told me I must never go there.'

'But why? That's what we are asking. Has your mother
quarrelled with his mother or what?' Madina demanded.

'Ché, it's nothing like that. No, no. They were chatting to
each other just yesterday, even. But she's told me never to go
there.' Uma was adamant in her refusal to go.

Rabia could see no way out. She got up to go, saying, 'I'll go
and fetch the notes myself. Just wait for me.'

The next street ran behind Uma's house; the first house on
the opposite side was Ramesh's. Ramesh was in the same class
with them. He was very bright and did well in all his lessons.
His father worked in the Electricity Board, and so their house
was known to everyone as the Current-kaaran's House.
Ramesh always appeared a bit shy to Rabia. Whenever he met
her eyes, he would lower his head. On the other hand, when her
eyes were turned away, he would gaze at her. Because their desks
were next to each other, she was aware of his gaze. At such times,

she felt shy, too. Now if she hesitated to go to his house, she would not be able to get hold of his notes. She decided to go, because she couldn't think of any other way out.

It was a small tiled house. The courtyard in front had been cemented over, and had a kolam drawn over it. There was an old man, of about fifty, lying down on the front thinnai. Except for his foot, which seemed to be shaking by itself, he lay still, his face covered with a towel, his arms folded under his head. Up on the roof, a sparrow had built its nest under the tiles. Rabia could catch a glimpse of it, up there. For awhile she stood there, watching. A couple of stalks of straw had come away from the nest, and hung loose. She was sure there were chicks inside.

'Who are you, amma, little girl? What do you want?' She was startled by the voice, and turned round. The old man was sitting up. His hair was entirely white. His pale face was adorned with a slight moustache; his teeth were stained. He looked at her kindly and asked again, 'What is it, amma? Who are you looking for?' He had a good, strong voice.

'I'm looking for Ramesh, Thattha,' she said softly.

His eyes widened with surprise when she called him Thattha. 'My hair has all gone grey, hasn't it? That's why you are calling me Thattha, aren't you? Never mind, never mind.' He stroked his hair with his hand. Then he stood up, tightened his veshti and straightened it out. He turned towards the inner rooms and called out, 'Ramesh!'

Ramesh came out, calling out, 'What is it, Appa?' Seeing her there, he stopped short, wondering what had brought her to his house. By this time, a beautiful middle-aged woman followed him outside. She must be Ramesh's mother, Rabia thought, unable to take her eyes away from her. A face in which everything was perfectly proportioned; which had a very attractive sereneness about it. A fair and smooth figure, as if it were kneaded out of flour. She came to herself when the woman asked, 'Come, amma? What is it you wanted?'

'That is.. I wanted to ask Ramesh...' She pointed to him. Now he came up to her and asked, 'What did you want?'

'I need your Konar notes. Please can you lend them to me?'

Without a moment's hesitation, he answered, 'Of course; I'll get them for you,' and ran inside.

Ramesh's mother asked, 'What's your name, amma?'

'Rabia,' she answered, softly.

'Are you in the same class as him? Come inside. Will you have something to eat?'

But by this time, Ramesh's father had recognized her. 'Aren't you Kader's daughter?'

She shook her head vehemently. 'No, no. I'm his younger brother Karim's daughter.'

'Oho, I see. I recognize the features now,' he said, and introduced her to the woman. 'Shanta, do you know who this girl is? She is Grocery-store Karim's daughter.'

Now the woman too recognized her. 'Is that so,' she said. 'You wait here and take the notes from him. Why don't you sit on the thinnai, if you would rather?' She took Rabia by the hand and led her to the thinnai. Rabia sat down and pulled down her skirt to cover her feet. She felt a little embarrassed and wished Ramesh would hurry up. She was aware that Ramesh's parents were gazing at her and lowered her head yet further, staring at Shanta's feet. They were beautiful, with long, fair, shapely toes on which she wore toe-rings. She thought to herself that Wahida Akka's feet too were like this.

'Will you come and eat?' Shanta asked her husband.

'Later will do. I'm not hungry now.'

Rabia could hear someone slipping off his sandals outside the front door and turned round to see who it was. A fine looking man wearing trousers and shirt was climbing up the steps leading to the thinnai. He saw Rabia, and seated himself on the thinnai running opposite hers. 'Appada, how hot it is so early in the morning,' he said in a low voice. He called out, 'Shanta, will you serve me my meal?'

'Right away,' she answered. Then, 'You haven't asked who this girl is.'

'Yes, who is this? Do I know her?' He looked intently at

Rabia, trying to recognize her features. But it was Ramesh's father who introduced her as Grocery-store Karim's daughter.

'Oho, is that so? Then she comes from a well-known family. What brings you here? And why are you sitting out here?' He sounded very surprised. 'So are you in the same class as Ramesh?'

'Yes,' answered Rabia. What on earth was Ramesh doing, for so long? Her eyes wandered towards the rooms inside. She was determined to run away the minute her hand closed around the notes

'Your father and I know each other very well, do you know that? I used to come to your house very often, sometime ago. Not so much nowadays. But we still meet along the streets and talk to each other. We used to send sweets to your family every Deepavali, Adi eighteenth and so on. And he used to give me the special snacks for Ramzan and Bakhr Id with his own hands. Do you know that?' The newcomer was vociferous.

She blinked, not knowing how to answer him. Ramesh's father understood her confusion and came to her aid, relieving her of the need to say anything. 'Why are you bothering her with all this. She's only a little girl, how would she know?'

True, many people sent them sweets at Deepavali time. The whole house was full of them. It was celebration time for her; she ate to her hearts content. Her mother, as usual scolded, 'Don't eat so many; you will menstruate too soon if you fill yourself up with sweets.' Who was going to listen to that? And anyway, Amma never said anything to Wahida who was home for the holidays, however much she ate.

Ramesh's voice broke into her thoughts. 'Here they are, take them.' he held out the notes towards her.

'I'll return them as soon as I've studied them.' She took the notes, jumped off the thinnai, climbed down the steps and set off, saying to them all, 'Then, I'll be off; goodbye.'

When she returned to Uma's house with the notes, Uma looked at her with admiration. 'Not bad at all! You went and fetched them all by yourself!'

'Well, you refused to go, didn't you?' Rabia complained.

Uma was embarrassed. 'Don't be cross with me, Rabia. It's just that Amma has forbidden me to go there. That's why I couldn't go. Besides, Amma is here now, at home. If I went, she would know, definitely. She'll give me a terrible scolding.'

Rabia, surprised, asked again, 'But why? Has she quarrelled with Ramesh's family?'

'Ché, it isn't that. I told you, she often chats with Ramesh's mother. She even goes to their house. I'm the only one who is not allowed. Because Ramesh's mother has two husbands, it seems.'

Neither Rabia and Madina could quite understand what she was saying. 'How is it possible for her to have two husbands?'

'That's what I'm saying. You too must have seen them. There are two men. I know them quite well,' Uma said.

'But Ramesh's mother looks as if she is a very, very good person. And she is so beautiful, besides.'

'Yes, of course. And she is very affectionate towards me as well. She comes to our house sometimes. She gets on very well with us. But I don't understand any of it.'

They were all silent for awhile, walking towards the school. Madina felt as if her head would burst. Many men had two wives; she knew about this and had seen it. But she had never known a woman who had two husbands. How could it be? Who could explain it to her? It struck her that she might ask Rabia to find out from her Periamma. If they dared to ask her own mother or Rabia's mother, for that matter, they would only be flayed alive. But Rabia's Periamma was prepared to answer any questions that were put to her.

The very same thought was running through Rabia's mind simultaneously. She determined to ask Rahima Periamma all about this business the same night, and try to understand it. Then she thought of other things she needed to talk about. She had to tell Uma and Madina that she had made friends with Ahmad. But how was she to begin?

They were silent for a little while longer. Then Rabia began, 'Madina, I have to tell you something. You won't be cross with me, will you?'

Madina looked at her sharply. What could it be, that made her hesitate so much? How could Rabia be embarrassed to speak about anything to her? She had been aware recently that Rabia had often been on the point of saying something to her, but had stopped herself at the last moment. All the same, she didn't ask now, what it was, and neither did Uma. They walked on, waiting for her to come out with it of her own accord.

'That is, Ahmad and I have made up. If you two make up with him as well, then he'll let all three of us join in all his games, won't he? Please make friends with him,' Rabia pleaded.

Both Madina and Uma were shocked at her words, that much was clear by their expression. Madina spoke first, 'How could you have made friends with him? And that too, without telling us! Haven't you the slightest shame?' Even though she was furious, she could not bring herself to reveal her feelings entirely. She was annoyed by Rabia's folly. She was also saddened that she could have done such a thing, without even saying a word to her. At the same time, she also understood that part of the reason for Rabia's behaviour was her eagerness to learn to cycle.

Now Uma broke in, looking distressed, 'If you want to go and talk to him, then do it. I won't ever make friends with him. How badly he spoke of me!'

'Its only when we're quarrelling that he says all that. Once we make friends, he won't, will he? We too have scolded him, haven't we?' Rabia said, trying to pacify Uma.

But Uma shot back, a little angrily, 'No, we can't. We can't ever make friends with him, and that's that. If you want to talk to him, then you needn't ever talk to us again.'

Madina had never imagined that Uma would say this. Nor had she expected that Uma would decide in this way for both of them. For Madina, Rabia's friendship was more important than anyone or anything else. She could never manage to live

through a single day without talking to her or seeing her. She
and Rabia had been inseparable, practically from their birth.
Madina walked on, very sadly, gazing down at the ground.
Ahmad had come between her and Rabia. She felt as if someone
had plucked away a precious object that had been hers alone.
She was also resentful towards Rabia, and felt as if a shadow
had been cast on her affection for her. This made her very sore
at heart. If Rabia truly returned Madina's affection, would she
have made friends with this Ahmad, knowing how much she,
Madina, disliked him? Couldn't she at least have warned her
about it? She didn't even do that.

She looked up for an instant, observed Rabia's look of
distress and quickly looked down again before Rabia could
meet her eyes. She brought the discussion to a close, saying,
'OK, then. If she wants to, let her speak to him. We don't have
to. But don't let us quarrel over this.' But all the same, she
didn't know how to wipe away that look of anxiety she saw in
Rabia's face. She felt deeply troubled as she walked on silently
towards their school.

☙ 18 ❧

Rabikka and Siddhikka were sitting along the passage
outside the kitchen. Siddhikka was squatting on her
haunches, while Rabikka sat cross-legged, her long skirt rolled
up to her lap. Sainu brought out some Gopal tooth-powder,
and poured a small quantity into the hollow of her hand. She
reached up and placed the packet on the window-sill outside
the kitchen, and leaned forward in front of the two girls. First
she asked Rabi to open her mouth. Rabi giggled in her odd way
and opened her mouth wide. Sainu dipped her forefinger in
the tooth-powder and rubbed hard at Rabi's teeth. When Rabi
tried to close her mouth, she gave a knock to her head.
'Saniyané, don't do that, it's nearly finished now.' Siddhikka,

who sat close by, began to cry, saying, 'Amma will be cross, Amma will be cross.'

Sainu felt weary. Every morning, by the time she had finished cleaning their teeth, taken them to the toilet and washed them afterwards, she was nearly dead. On the days when she had to bathe them, she almost broke her back. On top of all this, to wash their hair, get them dry and dress them? She muttered to herself that this Allah, who inscribed good things on a dog's forehead, and the Koran even on a hen's forehead, should surely have written a better fate on hers. She told the girls to gargle their mouths and brought them inside, to the kitchen.

Mumtaz was there, chopping vegetables. The expression on her face said, It might be a fast day, but we still have to cook in the mornings for these two wretches! Sainu said, 'Taju, make a couple of dosais for these two, will you?'

'I'll do it right now,' Mumtaz said, lighting the wood-fire, and placing the dosai griddle on top of the hearth. The firewood was green; the smoke made her eyes burn. She picked up the bottle of kerosene oil and tipped it gently, over the wood. The fire caught with a sudden burst. She stirred the batter and began to pour it out. Madina flew in from somewhere and sat down next to her sisters, saying, 'Anni, breakfast for me too, please. I have to go and do my exam.'

Sainu snapped at her. 'You've grown as big as a buffalo, but have you grown your brains? Do you take a plate and a tumbler of water and place it in front of you before you sit down, or do you sit down straight away, like a boy? Now bring a plate for each of your sisters, and place them in front of them as well. Are you a girl or what? Is this the way to behave?'

Madina ran to the almirah and brought three of the plates which were arranged there. She collected a chombu and a tumbler from the raised platform next to the kitchen hearth. Filling the chombu from the water pot, she poured out some water into the tumbler in front of Rabi, and then placed the chombu next to herself.

There was an unpleasant smell which seemed to emanate from Siddhi and Rabi. Madina stopped her nose and moved a little away from them. She knew that the smell was because their mouths were dribbling all the time. Saniyans, couldn't they swallow their saliva, at least? They knew well enough to swallow their food, didn't they, couldn't they learn this, too?

It was Mumtaz who had insisted they feed themselves. She wouldn't allow Sainu to do it. 'Leave them alone, Mammaani, let them feed themselves,' she would say. And sure enough, they had learnt to do it. Sometimes, Mumtaz was sharp with her mother-in-law, 'If you had only taught them to do each thing by themselves, it wouldn't have come to such a pass now. Things would be a little bit easier for you. You've given yourself all this unnecessary work, having to clean their teeth, wash their bottoms and give them their baths and everything.'

But Sainu didn't have the heart to agree. 'It's easy for you to say that. How could I teach them all this, when they told me their brains wouldn't ever develop? Besides, all this is only during my life-time. While I live, let me look after my children myself.' Her eyes would fill. Besides, even if Farida or Mumtaz tried to help her, there were times when these two wouldn't allow it. They could be very stubborn. The worst torture for Sainu was their monthly periods. Perhaps their brains didn't develop, but there was nothing wrong with their periods which came with regularity, each month. At such times, she would struggle away, four to five days at a stretch, providing them with the cloths and then washing and drying them. She would lose her appetite with all this going on. As soon as one finished, the other would begin, and then it would be her own turn. Half the month was given over to this business. And all that time, in her despair, she never ceased scolding Allah. 'Won't you take them away,' she would plead and pray. She took some comfort in the thought that her husband died without witnessing all this. What was the use of having any amount of money? What was the use, after all, of conveniences and choices?

There is no way of curing these two, and no way of finding any peace either, she would weep.

It was nearly time for Madina to set off for school. She pleaded with Mumtaz, 'Anni, give me my breakfast first. The bell will go soon.'

'Here, it's all ready.' Mumtaz put the first dosai on her plate, and poured her some chutney. Immediately Madina picked up her plate and ran with it to the hall, and sat down there, to eat. She was driven away by the smoke in the kitchen and the evil smell of her sisters.

Sainu, who was sitting on the bench in the courtyard, called out, 'Why are you going in there, di? You'll only spill your food everywhere. Remember that's where we pray.'

'No, Amma, I won't spill, I promise. The smoke there gets to my eyes.'

Of course, Madina felt sorry to see them. But there didn't seem a way of getting rid of this awful smell. Amma did her best; she bathed them in expensive Ceylon Lux soap every other day. But the smell never lessened. What to do? Madina never ever brought her school friends home, even by mistake. There was no problem about letting Rabia come. But what about the others? If they came and saw these two, sometime or other, when a quarrel arose, they would definitely refer to them, just to tease her. Besides, she felt that if her friends saw her sisters, they would no longer respect her.

Her mother, poor thing, loved them more than her life. She could never stand it if anyone breathed a word against them. Apparently Mumtaz's mother had teased her in front of someone, saying, 'Well, di, Mumtaz, is Sainu going to find husbands for those two crazy sisters-in-law of yours?' It seems another woman asked, 'So how is she going to get them married off, then?' At this, yet another had chimed in, 'What else, she's weighed them down with jewels around their arms and neck hasn't she? Are they going to understand what jewellery is about? Or is anyone at all prepared to marry them, even for the sake of jewellery?'

The very women who had been participating in all this gossip and mockery had come to tell Sainu everything that had been said. Sainu wept loud enough to shake the house to its foundations. Mumtaz didn't open her mouth. It was left to Farida to try and calm her down.

Mumtaz's mother was distressed, naturally, that she had given her daughter in marriage to this family, unaware of their problem. It seems someone had said to her, 'How could you have given your daughter to that family? Let us hope she too doesn't have children who are crazy. They say it's hereditary; carried from one generation to the other.' Sainu wept over this too. 'They are saying in the town, that my son's children too will be born like this. Oh Allah! Rabbi! Listen to that! Give those people the same fate as mine! Please show my children a better life.'

Of course she understood how things stood. She knew this was the reason why no one came seeking Farida as a bride. That young girl, Wahida, was to be married soon. Her daughter Farida would be eighteen when Ramzan was over. Was she any less gifted than Wahida? Didn't she have jewellery? Didn't she have money? Wasn't she as beautiful? No possibility of a bridegroom from their own kin group. As her son Suleiman said, they would have to look elsewhere. But how could she get into a car and go about? How could she leave these girls alone? She had told her son to give up the idea. We'll see what happens, she comforted herself; there must be a man for Farida somewhere already, he is not going to be born hereafter.

Sainu was exceptionally sad that day. The tears streamed down her eyes, involuntarily. She wiped them away with her sari. Madina had eaten, and left for school. The heat was getting worse. She rose to her feet and came inside. Her knees ached. She called out, 'Farida, Farida'.

Farida, who was combing her hair, came outside in answer to her mother. Her long skirt and davani showed off her height. She had her father's wide round face, and rose complexion.

This was the right age for her to be given away in marriage. Sainu fretted that it had to be put off. She said, 'Go to your akkas and comb and plait their hair, make sure to put enough oil. I'm going to lie down for a bit.'

'By the time I've combed out their hair, my arms ache, Amma. They always shake their head about, this way and that. They've got lice, besides. Why do they need such long hair? What if we cut it all short?' Farida spoke as if she was advising her mother. Tears appeared in Sainu's eyes, yet again. 'What thick hair they both have, falling in curls well below their waists. How can you have the heart to suggest we cut it off? How can I do it, di?'

'Why should you weep over such a thing? It is you who have to struggle every week when you wash their hair for them; you are practically fainting by the time you have finished. By the time you've towelled and dried it all, it is you who have aged.'

Sainu recognized the affection and concern which made Farida say this, and was silent. Had it been any one else, she would never have let it go. She agreed quietly. 'Very well, amma. Let it be until the festival is over, then we'll do it.'

Sainu went inside to lie down. The room was bright with sunlight. She drew the window curtains, and lay down on the bed. She wondered for a while why she was so overcome with sadness on that particular day. She realised that it wasn't just that day; she had been feeling like this for the past week. Since she heard about Wahida's wedding, her heart had been heavy with anxiety. Anxiety and regret that she had not been able to provide for Farida. A concern that Farida herself must be sore at heart. She thought, 'We hoped to give her to my sister-in-law's son, Salaam. But his mother, Zeenat, didn't like the idea, so he married Sherifa instead. But Allah's plans were different from hers, how could she prevent what was to come?'

She remembered with a shudder, how Zeenat had clutched at her and shed terrible tears when news came that Salaam had died in an accident in Dubai. Zeenat screamed with pain, 'What a mistake I made, Macchi, I was scared that if he married your daughter, my son would have mentally weak children, and got him married to my elder sister's daughter. Now she is left helpless and pregnant!'

Sainu had kept her resentment well hidden, and never betrayed it. People sometimes tried to take her side saying, 'Why should they look elsewhere for a bride when there's your daughter right here?' But Sainu only said, 'Well, so what? Zeenat looked for a bride who would suit them, and in the same way, I too must look for a boy who suits us. Besides, remember who Sherifa is. She's another niece. Zeenat has not gone outside the family, has she?' It was humiliating to reflect that everyone knew Farida had been rejected. It reflected badly on Farida! When Sainu remembered her husband, Latif Rowther, her throat choked. 'Had he been alive, would this ever have happened?' she thought.

Her grief over Salaam's death had prostrated her for many days. Her husband's sister's son. From the time he was a little boy, she had called him her son-in-law. That was how she always thought of him. The only consolation was that had Farida actually married him, she would have been left a widow by now. Allah had looked after her at least to that extent. Otherwise, a new vessel would have become an old one. When there was no way to find a lid for the new pot, how could she think of the old one? Was it possible to cover the old one now? But poor Sherifa, what use was her beauty and youth? She was left with her baby. What was her future to be, Sainu wondered, in confusion. They might get her married to Salaam's younger brother, Asik. But Sherifa was adamantly refusing to consider marriage again. What was to be done?

✑ 19 ✑

As soon as she heard the baby whimper, Sherifa rose and went into the bed room. The bed-clothes felt wet. She pulled them aside. The instant she saw her mother's face, Yasmin stopped crying and smiled. 'Catch hold of my precious,' Sherifa said, scooping up the baby and carrying her into the hall, where she sat down on a chair. Saura, lying on her bed, watched Sherifa and Yasmin. She held out her arms, saying, 'My precious little one, come to your Nanni.' The child slid down from her mother's lap and ran to her grandmother. Sherifa went into the kitchen, to prepare Yasmin's food. She lit the stove, and once it was burning brightly, said 'Bismillah' and put the milk on to heat. She pulled out the bench underneath the hearth, sat down and gazed through the window at the mango tree in the back yard.

The tree was covered in flowers and tiny mangoes. This tree fruited regularly, every year, ever since she could remember. As for her, she thought, she had fruited once, and then withered. These days she could neither stop nor prevent the restless state of her mind. A great sigh escaped her as she wondered for how long she must continue to exist in this way, like a withered tree. She could almost hear a voice speaking the truth in her ears: only until death. Overcome with self pity, she began to weep. Could she ever have supposed that her youth would turn into such a torment? She remembered, with a shock, that once she knew her youth to be a delight and happiness. But within a few years how great a change had come about. Nowadays, she could not sleep at night. However much she disregarded them, the desires of her body would not cease. This was causing her a continual pain.

It was now nearly two years since Salaam died. Although he lived for a few years after they were married, you could count the days they were actually together. After their nikah, he stayed with her for a whole month before going away. He returned two years later, for forty days. And that was it. He never came back.

In three years of marriage, they were together for only seventy days. At that time, when he was in Dubai, the belief that he would return soon was a great comfort, a means of disciplining her body and mind during sleepless nights. But now it was not like that. Hereafter there was nothing to hope for, nor expect. What hope or belief could bring her any peace now? A sob rose up inside her, and died down. Whenever she saw her reflection in the mirror, she wondered for how long her youth would continue to torture her. The thought of it was anguish.

Ever since the first anniversary of Salaam's death, her parents had pleaded with her to marry again. She was the one who stubbornly refused to consider it. Hereafter, her daughter Yasmin was enough for her, she said; she did not want any other life. Her father had quoted any number of Hadiths. Didn't the Holy Prophet marry Khadija? It is in our law alone that our Allah has given us the freedom to allow widows to re-marry, he said. Sherifa only replied, 'What you will do is to search for a husband for me. You won't look for a father for my child.'

After that, no one in the family pressed her any more. It was not that she objected to a second marriage as such. Her concern was that her child should not be damaged by it; she was absolutely firm about that. Could she be certain that he would love Yasmin? Would he treat her in exactly the same way as the children she would bear him? These were the worries that led to her decision. But all the same, it was hard. Although half the year was spent in fasting and chanting prayers, her desires and feelings were still there, and could not be ignored. What was she to do?

She came to herself with a start. Ché, how could she think such thoughts on a fast day! The fast itself will become worthless, she told herself. She remembered the milk she had placed on the fire. She rose to her feet with an 'Ayayyo!' The milk had boiled over, and put out the stove. The wick was wet through; the flames wouldn't catch. She undid the stove and began to wipe it clean.

Saura called out from the hall, 'Did the milk boil over and spill everywhere? I can smell it from here.'

'Yes, Amma,' she said irritably, as she finished wiping down the stove. She poured the milk into a wide mouthed pan, and picking it up with one hand, reached in the shelf for the milk bottle with the other, washed the bottle under the tap, and came into the hall vigorously shaking it dry.

Saura snapped out a rebuke as soon as she saw her. 'What are you doing, woman, shaking off your hand in that inauspicious way?' Then she noticed the bottle. 'Oh, I see, it's the bottle, is it,' she dragged, as if in apology.

Sherifa answered in a single word, 'Yes.' She sat down on the floor, under the fan, and set down the milk, to cool a little.

'How can you even think of sitting on the floor in your prayer sari. The whole house is wet with your daughter's urine,' Saura scolded. 'If you put milk on the fire, don't you have to watch it? Fine one you are!'

Sherifa, annoyed by her mothers complaints, answered back sharply. 'Did you say urine? Don't I clean it up at once? Why are you complaining?' But Sherifa also felt sad. It was her anxiety that made her mother complain so much. She shouldn't get so annoyed by it, she told herself. She went up to the bed, picked up Yasmin, and returned to her place. She felt the bottom of the pan to check whether the milk had cooled sufficiently, then, very carefully, with the forefinger and thumb of her right hand, picked up the skin that had formed on its surface, and draped it in one piece along the edge of the pan.

Saura watched the baby as she lay on her mother's lap, sucking her finger and said, 'The child is hungry, hurry up and cool the milk and give it to her.' She rose up from the bed, undid her sari, shook it out, and began to drape it again.

Sherifa poured the milk into the bottle and began to feed the child. She looked up and scrutinized her mother. Saura had a heavy frame, and was breathing hard. She was wearing a sari her husband had brought from abroad. It was made of very thin material, and every curve of her plump body was visible through it. Sherifa felt embarrassed by the sight of her. She had often spoken to her mother about it.

'What is this, Amma. You've been on the Haj and

everything, and yet you wear this kind of transparent sari.
They are selling such fine cotton saris in town. Why can't you
buy those and wear them?'

But Saura would never listen. She always put a stop to the
conversation, saying, 'You keep quiet. I find these convenient,
and that's it. After all, we are inside the house, most of the
time. When we go out, we wear purdah. So why worry?' This
was to pacify Sherifa.

Now she tied her sari tightly about her, making the front
pleats carefully. Then she asked eagerly, 'But tell me, what
happened the other day between Mumtaz and Nafiza?'

'Pach! They say all sorts of things. Who came and gave you
this gossip?' Sherifa was irritated. Why do they come and tell
Amma all this, she asked herself with disgust.

'Never mind who it was. Just tell me what they were saying
there.' Saura was even more eager to know.

Sherifa understood perfectly well that her mother wouldn't
leave her alone now. 'Why do you listen to all these stories,
and in the fasting month, too? Anyway, it was nothing.
Mariyayi came to do some work, so in the course of the
conversation, Mumtaz said that it was all very well for men to
sleep around, but she couldn't understand how women do it.
It looked as if she was insinuating something about Nafiza,
because Nafiza's expression went dead. That's all it was.' Sherifa
said all this with some embarrassment, and bent over her child.

'Oho, so that was what it was. And why should that slut's
expression go dead? She only said the truth; she didn't say
anything that isn't happening. Can she stare at her own sexual
parts the whole time?' Saura's voice, raised in anger and
mockery, disturbed Sherifa. She kept her head down, afraid
now that her mother might go and blurt this out to all and
sundry.

Saura understood that Sherifa was silent because she
disapproved of her mother's words, but she disregarded this
and carried on. 'By the way, does Nafiza get her monthly
periods?'

Sherifa didn't raise her head. 'Mm? I don't know,' she murmured.

'No, it's just that when I saw her yesterday, her breasts looked quite big, that's why I'm asking.'

'It can't be, Amma. And for goodness sake don't go and blurt out all this to anyone,' Sherifa spoke sharply. Wanting to bring the conversation to a full stop, she added, 'What do we care who is pregnant in this town and who isn't.'

Saura was left with nothing more to say, so she moved away, picked up a comb from the shelf, and stood in front of the window facing the street, combing her hair.

Sherifa couldn't help feeling very sorry for her mother but, wishing to turn her thoughts away from her, she bent over the child again. Yasmin's left leg kicked the air while she held the bottle in her right hand and drank her milk. She came into this world the spitting image of Salaam. Saura used frequently to lament, 'At least couldn't the child have had different features? Should she look so very much like her father? It's a constant torture for my daughter.'

In recent times, she had stopped saying this. She tried not to reveal her worries to Sherifa. Only when her daughter was not there, she would say these things to herself and weep. At least if Sherifa's father had been at home, she could have shared her concerns with him. But he came home from Singapore only once every two years. And within two months he tended to fly back saying that the shop must not be left unstaffed. As if he were only a visitor. But then, what was there at home which could bring him joy? The situation his daughters were in could only make him unhappy. She comforted herself that they had their son Razak at least, to console them. 'This was all that He ordained for us,' she told herself.

Someone pushed open the front door to the house that stood directly opposite Sherifa. As the outside light from the street fell on her, she looked up and called out to Raihaina who was just coming in, 'Shut the door at once! There might be men walking along the street right now.'

'And why do you sit facing the front door, anyhow,' Saura snapped, in her turn. Then, as Raihaina shut the door and locked it, she began shouting at her. 'Where have you been wandering about all this time like a wretched cow? Aren't you keeping the fast? Can't you stay in one place for just a bit?' The nerves in Saura's neck were standing out, swollen.

Raihaina was annoyed. 'Pach! You are always complaining about me. I was just here, nearby, Amma, at Sainu Mammaani's house. I was playing daayam with Farida, that's all.' She put her arms out to the baby and called her, 'Come here to Periamma.'

Sherifa looked at her sister, as if she were observing her for the first time. Her arms were like sticks; the skin hung loose on them. Her body was worn down; only her stomach stuck out, round as a pot. Her head looked too small in proportion to her body. She had combed back the thin tufts of reddish hair that sprouted on her head and had made a rat's tail of a plait, tied with a ribbon. Her sunken eyes and nose and mouth looked like tiny versions of themselves. She was four years older than Sherifa. Although she saw her sister every day, yet Sherifa felt pained to see that anaemic body and strange features. 'What can we do, that's her fate,' Sherifa told herself sadly, but she scolded her elder sister, all the same. 'You are the one who doesn't menstruate, so you must fast the whole month. Then why, when you are fasting, do you have to go and mind the whole town's business? Don't you feel faint or drowsy or anything?'

'Don't be silly; there's nothing like that. Nowadays no one gives me jobs to do or sends me on errands. They're scared of Amma. Yes, I did feel a bit drowsy, that's why Sainu, Farida and all of us were playing daayam. We were listening to songs from Radio Ceylon at the same time.' She loosened her davani and shook it out.

'Why must you go and play with them? Those two crazies always come and stand next to you. How can you stand the stench?' Saura grimaced.

'Pach! Quietly, Amma. You have to pity them, poor things. Besides, she's your brother's wife. If she hears you, she'll make a laughing-stock of you. She absolutely worships those two... what are you saying!' Sherifa rebuked her mother.

'What do I care for her, arrogant thing! Am I saying anything that isn't true?'

'Yes, yes, now leave this talk,' Sherifa said again.

The sunlight began to slant in the courtyard. Saura remembered that Razak was not yet home. She went into the street to look for him. Evil child, where had he vanished?

▶ 20 ◀

Firdaus opened the door of the chicken coop and took out the brooding hen. It sat within her hands, raising a loud kek-kekkek. Swiftly, she ran with it to the front of the house, opened the door and flung it out. It flew out of her hands and fell in a shuddering heap at the entrance of the house opposite.

Siva, sitting on the front thinnai, reading his paper, rose to his feet, startled, and tried to chase the hen away. Firdaus, meanwhile, called out from where she stood, 'Shoo... shoo...', in an effort to bring it back. She had hurried to throw the brooding hen into the street, afraid it would shed its dropping all over her as soon as it came out of the coop. She muttered to herself, 'The wretched creature has been there in the dark for all of four days, it seems it can't see a thing. Now it's going to shit all over the front yard of that house.' In her anxiety, she waved her hands wildly, calling out, 'Shoo...' Siva gave it a slap with the paper he was holding, drove it away, then looked up and smiled.

It was then that she came to herself. She became aware that she was standing right in front of him, close enough for him to see her clearly. Driven by fear and shame she turned round and hurried inside the house, as fast as she could. She was out of breath. Fortunately her mother was in the kitchen and she had escaped being seen. Even though she berated herself for it, she felt a spurt of joy because he had looked at her and smiled. She was not sure, herself, whether she had gone and stood there outside his front door deliberately, or by accident. It was a very long time since her heart had overflowed with happiness, like this.

There had been many occasions, since he first came to live in that house, when they had seen each other. But today was the first time they had been face to face, and at such close quarters. Each time she saw him, the attraction she felt towards him seemed to grow stronger. Even though he had a wife and child, she could not rid herself of this feeling. Every day, nowadays, Jaya left the child with Firdaus while she went about her chores. If a friendship had sprung up between the two families, it was because of Firdaus's loneliness, and the presence of baby Viji. Firdaus knew very well the impropriety of her love for Siva; yet the extent of her loneliness made her ignore it. The very sight of him made her heart beat fast. Her thoughts returned to him again and again, though she had no idea how he felt about her. She never thought of freeing herself from this state of mind. On the contrary, she didn't see why she need do that.

Each time she saw Siva, her yearning for a companion grew the greater. Every movement he made seemed to give out some sort of spark that seduced her. She had begun to realize the truth that no one could now put out the fire that had started to smoulder in her. At the same time, she understood only too well that none of this would bring her any good. She only smiled to herself.

Amina had seemed to be deep in thought during the past few days. Someone had brought her the news that Karim had spoken ill of her, Firdaus. From that moment, Amina had begun to show some urgency in getting her daughter married again. If her own son-in-law spoke so scandalously of her daughter, then what would not the world at large say, she thought, in pain. She began her search on the very day that Firdaus's prescribed period of idda following her divorce was over. All the same, she had to find a suitable place. These days, Amina never visited her son-in-law's house, and Zohra didn't come to her mother's house either. Amina didn't know whether this was because she was angry with Firdaus, or because she wanted to show solidarity with her husband.

Half the men who put themselves forward as prospective bridegrooms were over forty years old, whose first wives had died, and who therefore needed help in bringing up their children. Firdaus laughed at them. Were they wanting to marry just to acquire an ayah, she asked. Amina scolded her, 'Shut your mouth, di. In this entire town you are the only woman who actually insisted on getting a talaq! Who would have the courage to marry you? Will any decent man from a good family ask for you voluntarily? Won't they wonder what sort of impudent girl you must be to reject your own husband and leave him? You may be beautiful, you may be young; but you are still a used pot. Who would want to buy it?'

When Firdaus heard this, she shrank within herself. She asked herself again and again whether she had done something extremely foolish. Had she brought an everlasting shame on her family and on the entire lineage? She was tormented by guilt at the thought.

Nowadays, Amina didn't go to other people's houses all that much. She didn't attend any functions. Under their guise of concern for her, people tended to point out Firdaus's situation and vulnerability in a cruel way. Firdaus too was not unaware of how these women talked about her. Of course she could have accepted everything, told herself it was her fate, there was nothing she could do about it and got on with her married life somehow. But it had simply not been possible.

Her head ached with all these thoughts churning in confusion inside her head. She sat up, wanting to busy herself with something, at least to kill time and stop thinking. She

came and stood by the front yard. The heat was fierce. 'Before
this fasting month is over, it seems we will all be fried to a
crisp', she thought, opening the front door for the hen to come
in. Involuntarily her eyes looked across to the opposite house
and, seeing no one there, lowered in disappointment. She went
inside again, opened the big bronze anda and scooped up a
handful of broken rice. The hen had returned to the house,
and was standing in the courtyard. 'Poor thing, it must be
hungry,' she thought and scattered the rice in a shady corner.
The hen ran up and began to peck at it.

Someone tapped very softly at the front room window. She
opened it, wondering who it could be. It was Siva, standing
there. Drawing back against the wall, she asked, 'What is it?'

'I'm just off to school. Jaya will be back in a little while.
Please give her this key.' He held out the key to her, through
the window. Firdaus's heart beat fast. Trembling all over, she
held out her hand towards him. He caught her slender fingers
gently and pressed the key into the palm of her hand saying, 'I
must go.' Then he walked away.

Shocked on the one hand and delighted on the other, she
stared for a moment at the fingers he had held, then pressed
them hard against her face. She glanced at the oblong mirror
hanging on the wall, saw her face flushed red and glowing, and
realized that her beauty, suppressed for so long, had regained
its life. Suffused with joy, she hurried to her room and began
to relive what had just happened, over and over again.

It came to Firdaus as a shock and a torment that a man's
touch could give her such extreme delight. She felt as if her
body didn't touch the ground, but floated on air. She wondered
eagerly how it would be if he were to come to her that very
second and was immediately aware of a longing for his embrace.
In her imagination she brought him to herself, laid his arms
around her body and pressed her slender form against his chest.
She felt ashamed of her thoughts, and struggled hard to bring
her overwrought self under control.

She had never known a man's touch all this while, and had given up the hope of ever experiencing such a thing. The pity and love which she felt in the touch of those cool fingers brought out new and strange emotions in her. She could feel that love fall upon her frozen life, and put out roots which lengthened, branched and spread out all over her body. She wished time would stop at that instant.

She felt her body loosening and melting away into the air. She shook her head hard in both directions and came to herself. Overcome with shame, she buried her head in her knees. She thought how everything she did these days was entwined with him in her imagination. When she chose her clothes or combed her hair, when she did the cooking, even when her eyes were smarting with smoke, somehow it was as if she did it all for him. She understood very well the animation this gave her life, the happiness that sprouted within her; it had even pleased her that this should be so. But now, at this moment, it came to her with absolute certainty that he too was fully aware of this, and this gave her an immense and overwhelming joy.

☪ 21 ☪

It was time for Laylathul Qadr, the Night of Empower ment, the twenty-seventh day of Ramzan. Rabia was so excited, it was as if her feet wouldn't stay in one place. All the houses had been cleaned and washed down on the previous day itself. Looked at from the street, all the houses shone bright, newly white-washed. She loved the smell of white-wash. More than the smell itself, it was the associations it brought to mind of fast days and feast days that made her love it so much. She had become accustomed to associating the smell of white-wash with the month of Ramzan. This year every single house had been white-washed, without exception. She remembered that last year, and the year before that, there had been some houses which were left out. This year, they wouldn't be celebrating Ramzan at Nafiza Macchi's house. It was only three months since her mother had died. They had white-washed their house, all the same. Nafiza Macchi had not bought any new clothes. Neither had she made athirsam or any other fried snacks. She had told Rabia's mother that only Ahmad and Rafiq had been given new clothes. Because they had not made any special fried snacks in their house, Rahima Periamma had sent them a big platter full of athirsam and murukku. Rabia had gone and delivered it herself.

Nafiza said repeatedly, 'No, thank you, Rabia; please take it back.' Rabia answered in a very grown-up way, 'Let it be, Macchi,' and transferred everything into a big dish herself. Nafiza had told Rabia's mother about it the next day, adding, 'My daughter-in-law is a smart one.' Rabia's feet scarcely touched the ground after that. She often would try to do something clever, just to hear Nafiza address her as 'daughter-in-law'.

In the old days their street used to be bustling throughout the month of Ramzan. Each household would set off for Madurai to buy new clothes, which they would then display to every one else. On the night of Laylathul Qadr, they would wear their new clothes for the special prayers, and immediately after that adorn themselves liberally with ornaments and visit each other, enjoying themselves hugely. Later still, they would go in crowds to the mosque, filling the street with seemingly endless happiness. All the children would wear their new clothes and wander about between their houses and the mosque until their legs ached and ached.

The girls would show off their clothes and ornaments to each other, as they watched from outside while the men and boys went into the mosque for the night-long vigil and prayers. Ahmad would often challenge Rabia and Madina, 'Come on, let's see whether you are allowed to come in and pray like us.'

'Oh, go away,' they would say, ignoring him, playing about outside, and looking yearningly at the minaret of the mosque, decorated with serial lights. Often they would go on to Vadivel

Chéttiyar's house, right next to the mosque, and play on the indoor swing there. Rabia's father, Karim, traded in gram with Vadivel Chéttiyar, so the Chéttiyar family were very indulgent towards her. They allowed her to play on the swing, however many friends she brought with her. They stroked the children's clothes, looked at their ornaments, and asked affectionately where their parents had bought them.

The swing hung from the ceiling of the big hall of their house. It was a long and wide swing, big enough for a man to lie down on it. Four of the children would sit on it, side by side, while two pushed it back and forth. Vadivel Chéttiyar's wife, who spoke a language they didn't understand, would offer them snacks and press them to eat. The other women visiting there would speak to her affectionately too, saying, 'So you are Karim's girl, are you?' In her heart, she would feel very proud of her father.

But Zohra would scold her the next day. 'Well, di, you took your gang of friends and made a lot of noise there, did you? Every year you do this, and they don't get to sleep till one o'clock at night. Do you think it looks good?'

'But they never tell us to go away, Amma,' she would protest.

'As if they would say that, you silly thing, you. They allow you to play there for your father's sake. How will they tell you to clear off?' her mother would answer. The tone of her voice betrayed her pride, too.

Rabia would go on, 'Amma, why can't we have a swing in our house, too? Our hall is just as big as the one in Chéttiyar's house.'

'Oh, definitely! We'll definitely do it.' The note of mischief in her mother's voice as she repeated herself would incite Rabia to take to her heels immediately.

The day of the big feast was the same. But on that day, the men did not go to prayers at their own mosque. They said their prayers on the prayer grounds a little outside their town, where a special pandal was set up. On that day, the women and children wore their new silk clothes and jewellery, visited the mosque and their kinsfolk's houses, and returned home before the men came back.

But for the past two years there had not been the celebration and enthusiasm of former years. Last year, Madina's father had died in Singapore, so the family had not celebrated Id. The women from the other houses on their street were hesitant to go out in their new clothes, and slunk about, not wishing to be seen by Madina's family. On Id day, Madina's house was locked shut even in the morning. Nobody knew whether they wanted to shut out the town's enjoyment, or to prevent their own sorrow from embarrassing anyone outside. On that day, Rabia had felt very sorry that Madina had not seen her in her new dress.

Besides, on the Festival day she had gone with Uma, Ahmad, Rafiq and Razak to see a matinee show. It was a big disappointment to her that Madina had not been able to join them. Her mother and Rahima Periamma had muttered to themselves about Sainu. 'It's fine for the older people not to wear new clothes. But Madina is only a little girl. Why couldn't she allow her? Obstinate monkey!'

One year, Sherifa Akka's husband died. This year it was Nafiza Macchi's mother. Zohra had once complained to Rahima Periamma and Saura. 'Why is it, akka, that year by year the Feast Day gets less and less joyful? This has gone on for three years continuously, as if someone had cast an evil eye on us.'

Rahima Periamma laughed. 'Death comes to each of us when it is ordained. What does an evil eye have to do with it?'

'No, don't say that. Definitely, it has to do with someone casting an evil eye. It has to do with our labourers casting their evil eye. They come in their crowds, filling our streets and asking for alms on the morning of the big Feast Day, at the first cock crow. It's the jealousy they breathe out when they see our women in their best clothes and jewels, in all their beauty. It's that which has brought us so low. Giving alms to non-believers doesn't count as charity, you know. So why should we give them anything? It's because we give them alms that they come here. Would they come here otherwise? We should tell our Nattaamai, the town leader, to stop this first of all.' Saura spoke angrily, all in one breath.

Zohra stared intently at her, wondering why she was getting so heated. 'Poor things, they only ask for alms. How can we turn them away? They only come because they trust us.'

'So, does it have to come to this? It's the same story at Bakr-Id, too. Can we even walk along the streets, then? These people fall all over us when they come to get their share of meat. And now we are in this state,' Saura spoke without giving even an inch.

This time Rahima was clearly very angry indeed, but spoke without betraying it. 'O yes, you speak as if these people can fill their mouths and stomachs with the ten paisa we hand out, or the single scrap of meat we give them. No, it's not like that. They come to us because they have some rights as the labourers who work on our land. If it weren't for them, who would labour in our fields and gardens?' She spoke sharply, and walked away into the kitchen, as if she didn't wish to stay there any longer. Her face was flushed with emotion.

The conversation came to a close suddenly, and Saura had no choice but to go away. when she had left, Zohra asked Rahima, 'Why did you speak to her as if you were slapping her in the face, Akka?'

'What then? It's because of this woman and what she did that Sherifa is in such a state. Raihaina is left with nothing. What is the use of her wealth, her money? Low woman.' Rahima scolded Saura until her anger was appeased. Zohra joined in, in agreement, and even Rabia wanted to add her bit.

* * *

Rabia sat in the thinnai facing the street, absorbed in her own thoughts. The Sahar Muzafar was approaching, beating his little drum. She began to get excited as soon as she heard him,

at a distance. She ran inside and asked, 'Amma, the Sahar
Muzafar is coming; give me some rice.' Her mother scolded
her fondly and went off to the store-room, saying 'Why do
you have to run so fast and get out of breath? As if he is likely to
go away without accepting something from us!'

Rabia grabbed hold of the big silver salver which her mother
brought out, in which she had placed a measure of rice to one
side with a ten rupee note on top, and a heap of athirsam and
murukku on the other side. Zohra was shocked and called out,
'Adiyé adiyé, watch out! you're going to drop everything, di!'
But Rabia assured her, 'No Amma, I'll hand it all over very
carefully,' and carried the tray out into the street.

He was standing there beating his drum in front of their
threshold, wearing a green jibba and a white lungi, his paunch
thrust forward in front of him. As soon as she came towards
him, he stopped his drumming, took the tray from her with
one hand, and placed it on the thinnai. Smiling at her, he first
took the money and put it away in his pocket. Then he separated
all the things on the tray and put them away in the cloth bags
which he had slung from his shoulders, while, all the time, she
stared yearningly at his thamukkai drum. She wanted
desperately to touch it, just gently. He seemed to understand
her wish, for he held it out towards her, saying, 'Here, give it a
couple of taps and see. Go on.' But she felt too shy; she refused,
and ran inside.

Everyone had bathed early in the morning, and went about
their chores, their hair left loose to dry. It was a Friday, besides.
By ten in the morning, all the women would arrive, to say the
special daspih prayers. Before that, they would have to buy
the meat, cook it, and finish all the work. Because it was
Laylathul Qadr day, it would be the same in all the houses. The
aroma of cooking meat would float about everywhere and
pervade the street. In the afternoon the specially long Fatiha
prayers would need to be said. The Hazrat would come to
each of their houses to chant them.

Early in the morning, Rabia and Madina had gone to Yasin

Hazrat's house to invite him to come and chant the prayers at their houses. As soon as the meal was cooked, Zohra and Rahima would spread a mat in the hall, place on it a vessel full of rice, another of meat curry, and a platter full of athirsam, light some incense sticks, and wait for him. When the chanting was over, Rabia would deliver the rice and curry at his house. A good amount of rice and curry would have been delivered there already. They would collect the rice in a big silver anda, and the curry in yet another big aluminium vessel. These would be distributed to all their relations, later on. Any left-over rice would be made into vadagam the next day and laid out to dry in the terrace.

* * *

Rabia was waiting for the evening, sitting on the front thinnai. As early as three in the afternoon, Zohra had sent an errand boy with their nonbu card and tiffin carrier, to fetch the nonbu kanji. She had pleaded, 'I'll go myself, Amma.' But Zohra had sent her off to rest, saying, 'No, you go and sleep for a while. You're going to be awake the whole night, aren't you?' She had tried to do just that for a long time. Wahida, having watched her tossing about in her bed, desperately trying to pass the time, had chased her off, teasing, 'Look here, amma, you've slept long enough now, wake up!'

'What does Akka care, she can't leave the house even at night. She can't wander round the streets like me, having fun,' she told herself with pride, craning her neck to take a look at the clock. 'Watch out, di, you'll get a crick in your neck,' Wahida called out from inside the house, still teasing her.

The street was full of bangle and flower sellers. Zohra had already bought plenty of flowers for them. Earlier in the morning, she herself had bought enough bangles to fill both her forearms. Rabia lifted her right arm, and brought the bangles to her nose. They smelt sweet. Madina too had bought bangles this morning in the very same colour and design. Farida had watched them and laughed, 'There's no other way. We have to look for one husband for the two of you.'

The new golusu round her ankle and the gold chain round her neck filled her heart with happiness. Unknown to the others, she crept inside frequently, and looked at herself in the tall mirror, the height of a man.

Observing her excitement all this time, Wahida came up to her and gave her a gentle tap to her head. 'Come here, di, I'll comb your hair for you. You can put on your dress now, as well. See, it's nearly Asar time.' She took her by the hand and pulled her to the sofa, sat her down, and began to comb out her hair. Rabia realized that Wahida was murmuring some words to herself, and listened carefully, thinking she might be repeating some daspih prayers, as Zohra often did. But no, it was a cinema song that Wahida was singing very softly to herself.

Wahida was always like this. She always sang a cinema song as she went about her business. She always liked to listen to cinema songs on the radio. sometimes, Zohra would chide her, 'Wahida, you don't at all seem like a girl who has learnt to chant the Koran.'

'Why?' Wahida would ask, 'What's the harm in listening to cinema songs? Must you not listen to cinema songs once you've learnt to recite the Koran?'

But Rabia was anxious, all the same. Might she jeopardise her fast? She asked in some surprise, 'Akka, you are repeating a cinema song. Won't that break your fast?'

'Ché, ché. No, there's nothing wrong there. It's only when you've done your olu and you are ritually clean that you mustn't listen to cinema songs or sing them. Then you'll break your olu.' Wahida continued to sing softly as she combed Rabia's hair.

It was lovely to hear Wahida's voice. She sounded truly happy. Rabia thought to herself, 'With all her beauty, how would Akka look if she really were to act and sing in a cinema?'

She imagined her as a Lakshmi Sri Devi, and rejoiced in the vision. The shampoo had scented her hair; she lifted a handful and smelt it. She was allowed shampoo only on Ramzan and Laylathul Qadr days. On all other days, her mother would allow her only shiyakai, however much she craved for shampoo. 'Idiot, all this long, thick hair will start to drop if you use shampoo; and it will grow grey very soon.'

'Akka, please give me two plaits,' Rabia pleaded. Wahida did as she asked, and decorated her hair with flowers. 'Go now,' she said, chasing her away, 'Go and wash your face. I'll put powder on your face and mai in your eyes. But put on your new dress first.'

Zohra had placed her new clothes in her wardrobe, yesterday, all ready for her. Rabia ran to take her clothes out. She pressed her new paavaadai and blouse against her face, smelling them deeply. She always loved the smell of new clothes. She ran up to her mother in her under-skirt and asked, 'Amma, may I put on my new paavaadai now?' Zohra gave her permission, 'Yes, yes, do it now.' then she added, 'Give me that paavaadai, let me put it on you myself.' She held the new clothes in her hands, muttered a prayer, and urged Rabia, 'Mm, you say a 'Bismillah' too.' Then she dropped the skirt over Rabia's head, lowered it to her waist, and tied the waist strings tightly. 'Now go and put on your blouse yourself,' she added, returning to her work.

Rabia had been worried that her mother would tell her to put on a davani, and now she was delighted and unbelievably relieved. Realizing that she had forgotten about a davani in the press of work, Rabia ran to her room, removed her old blouse and began to put on the new one. Suddenly she wanted to bend down and look at her own breasts. She wanted to know whether they had grown big enough to be hidden under a davani? She felt shy, though. Deep within her, there was some kind of shame and repulsion which stopped her from looking at her own body with her own eyes. Even when she had her bath, she had never looked at herself entirely naked. Her mother had told her that she would surely go to hell if she bathed without any clothes. She had also told her that if she gazed at her own genitals, or at anyone else's, her face would darken. So how could she ever gaze at her own body? She looked at the rise of the blouse revealing her breasts and gently touched and stroked them. A thrill of excitement spread all over her body.

She thought of Ahmad, suddenly. One day, a year ago, also in the month of Ramzan, during the Tarawih prayers when everyone had gathered at her house, she had gone to play at Ahmad's. Rafiq was asleep already. Ahmad sat on the bed by his side, riffling through a book. She was surprised that he wasn't scared to be alone. If she were to ask him about it, he would definitely boast and show off. He would thrust out his chest, proclaiming, 'Scared? I? Ahmad isn't scared of anyone in this whole wide world, let me tell you.' That was why she didn't ask him about things like that, anymore. It was he who started the conversation, asking her whether she wanted to play.

'What should we play? There's just the two of us,' she said.

'We could play mothers and fathers,' he replied, eagerly. She agreed it was the best thing they could do.

He ran and brought a small basket woven out of palm-leaves, containing a whole set of pots and pans. Rabia too had baskets like this, bought at the craft exhibition in Madurai. He placed the basket in front of her and opened it. It contained tiny plates, spoons, tumblers, cooking pots and even a dosai-griddle. She was surprised that he had kept it all safely, without losing a single piece. As for her, she had lost half these things by now, she really did not know how. She felt both envy towards him and anger towards herself. How could he, a boy, be so careful while she, a girl, was so careless?

Ahmad ran to the store-room and brought some rice in one hand, and a couple of murukkus in the other. Meanwhile, she

arranged all the pots and pans in a corner of the hall, turning
it into a toy kitchen. She took the rice he had brought, and
pretended to cook it. He said in a loud voice, 'Here, dish up
the food quickly; I have to go to work.'

She answered very politely, 'Look, it's all ready; come and
sit down.' She placed a plate in front of him and filled a tumbler
with water. She put some of the rice into a dish, broke in a
piece of the murukku, and served him some of this on to his
plate. He finished eating silently. 'Very well, I'm going to the
shop now,' he said, and went off to stand in a corner for a
while. Then he came back. 'Appada,' he said. 'There was a lot
of trade today, in the shop. Serve the food quickly; sit down
and eat with me.'

In a minute he ran towards the wardrobe, lay down on the
floor, and putting his hand underneath it, pulled out a wooden
doll. He wiped off the dust with his shirt and handed it to her.
'Here, this is our baby. Give it some milk,' he said.

It was a beautiful boy doll, its body shining and smooth.
She took it from him very gently, as if it were a baby, gave it a
kiss and placed it on her lap. Anxiously, she said, 'We must
buy him a shirt and trousers, he's all naked, won't he be cold?'

'Yes, let's do that,' he said. Then he made as if to switch off
the light, and lay down saying, 'Switch off the lights now, lets
go to sleep.' She lay down next to him. Suddenly he sat up
again. 'The baby is crying; give him some milk,' he said. She sat
up too, picking up the doll and rocking it in her lap, saying,
'Don't cry, da, my treasure.' 'I told you to give him milk,' said
Ahmad, again. She looked at him, not quite understanding
what he meant. He touched her chest and said, 'Give him milk
from here.' She felt very shy, but he hurried her. 'Give it to
him, di, he's crying, isn't he?'

Although she felt shy, she also felt a needle of excitement
run all through her. She picked up the doll, and said to him,
'You turn away that side, da.' He nodded, turned around and
sat with his back towards her. Rabia lifted up her blouse a

little, placed the doll against her chest and held it there tightly. Ahmad turned round again and looked at her, asking eagerly. 'Is he drinking? Let me see too, di.'

She didn't say anything. He came up to her on all fours, lifted up her blouse and looked at her chest. In the gathering darkness, his face was like that of a baby. The eagerness of his search made his eyes glow. He took the doll from her and putting it away, gently stroked her nipples. He was greatly taken with the way they looked, like small, soft marbles. He gestured as if he were trying to pick them up with his fingers, then bent his head towards her and kissed them softly with his lips. Then he began to suck at them, like a baby. Touched by a kind of shock, her body began to tremble as she gathered him in her arms, holding him tightly as if eager and anxious to learn something.

After this happened, she didn't even go near his house for a whole week. She felt too shy even to look at him.

☙ 22 ❧

Zohra went up to the terrace, wanting to check whether the new moon had appeared as yet. In almost all the terraces of the houses round about, someone's head could be seen. She felt very weary. There were no stars in the sky. The darkness spread all along the street. Even as she watched, the darkness which lay on the street like a fine veil seemed to thicken into a blanket. Here and there, groups of children were still playing under the street lights. It looked like some kind of hopping game. It always astonished her that each game had its own season. If they played thellukkai for some time, then it would be only kabadi for the next few months. After that it would be spinning tops. Then pallaanguzhi with forty counters. So it went, turn by turn. But always, the game played along one street was the same throughout the town. They never ever changed it before its turn ran out.

Suddenly, she too wanted to be a child again. She wouldn't, then, have to bear all these burdens in her heart. It was only after they sighted the crescent moon that tomorrow would be declared the feast of Id. Even if they didn't sight it here, it would be enough if, on the eight o'clock news from Radio Ceylon it was announced that the new moon had been seen there. That would hold good here, too. Only after that could they soak the urad dal for tomorrow morning's vadais, and begin to chop onions. They must begin to prepare the kesari and paniyaram. The chicken that was tied in the yard must be sent to the mosque, to be cut in pieces by the Hazrat. Once it was cleaned, they must get all the vegetables ready for the afternoon's biriyani. But all this could happen only after the moon was seen. Although these were chores that the women were eagerly looking forward to in all the houses, Zohra only felt a great weariness. It is only when you feel happy about it that you engage with anything you do, she told herself. She, though, seemed to be burdened by her worries all the time.

Her mother's anxiety to get Firdaus married again distressed her greatly, even though she understood the reasons for it. Of course people in the village would gossip amongst themselves. But should they make haste and push her into a well a second time, because of that? Wasn't she a woman, after all? Shouldn't she be allowed her wishes and expectations? But Amma really tormented Firdaus, taunting her that a young girl should not be so daring, nor express her wishes so freely. If she refused to marry an old man who had lived out half his life, and who had children already, did that make her too daring, too hopeful? At the same time. Zohra knew she couldn't blame her mother either. It was best not to go against public opinion. The only good thing in all this, was that her husband, Karim, was not interfering in this business of a second marriage for Firdaus. It was because he intervened in the first place that this scandal came to her family. Would they ever be rid of it, in all the time to come? It seems that Sabia too had said to someone, mockingly, 'It's not as if what's happened in Amina's family is something new, is it? Her daughter is continuing in the same path as her sister. It's the way they are.' It had upset Zohra very much, when she heard this. Would this history follow them forever? In the future, would people asking for Rabia bring it all up again? Would they say the family wasn't altogether suitable? She began to worry about all this.

It was because of all this that she had started, from that very time, to be more strict with Rabia. The child had to fight with her for the few liberties that the other children of the town were allowed. Zohra comforted herself with the thought that there was nothing wrong in bringing up girl children strictly.

She thought about Wahida. She felt sad that within ten days she would be married. She wondered what such a vulnerable girl would have to suffer at the hands of that obstinate monkey, Sabia. Besides, Mumtaz had told her in secret that Sikander's behaviour and habits were very dubious. At the same time, though, Mumtaz had tried to keep out of it, saying, 'My husband and Sikander work in the same town, don't they? It's he who told me. Apparently he doesn't deny himself in the matter of women and drink. All the same, Zohrakka, don't tell Rahimakka, will you? Why should I get caught in all this? In the end it will be my head that rolls. If Sabia ever hears of it, she'll kill me. My mother-in-law will give me hell, besides.' But Nafiza had also said similar things to Zohra; her father, Kamal, also worked in Singapore. Zohra knew the two women must have talked about Sikander between themselves.

Zohra had raised the matter gently, with Karim. 'Have you heard that Sikander goes about with women in Singapore?' But he had been very casual about it. 'So what?' he said. 'How can we be bothering with all that? Men will be men. It's wrong only when women behave like that. As it is, he's marrying rather late. How can he control himself for so long?' And there the matter ended. What he said was true enough. Nobody worried about such things as far as men were concerned.

Karim then added, 'There's no need for you to go and tell Rahima all this. In any case, I'm sure she knows about it already.' Karim was in another kind of turmoil. They needed a lot of money for the wedding expenses, immediately following what they had spent on the festival, what with buying clothes and giving alms. He was worrying about how they would manage if they took such a big sum of money out of their profits. He was angry with his brother about this. Kader's father-in-law was hugely wealthy. Had they asked him, he would certainly have given them some financial help. Rahima was his only child, besides. Karim's wife, Zohra, on the other hand, had nothing.

Why was Kader like this? If they needed four or five lakhs for the wedding, then shouldn't he take two or three lakhs from his father-in-law? Just as Karim was worrying about how on earth he could get Kader to understand this, here was Zohra, muddling him about trivial matters. He was very firm with her because he believed that to share his own confusions with her would be making too much of her. Let the wedding be over first, he thought; we'll see about Sikander later. All the same, he tossed about in his bed all night. When Zohra asked him what the matter was, he shut her up sharply, saying, 'Nothing.'

Zohra heard footsteps coming up the stairs to the terrace. It was Rahima. She trod softly, hardly making a stir, and came up to Zohra asking, 'Well, have you seen the new moon yet?' Although Zohra could not quite make out her sister-in-law's serene face in the darkness, she heard the tone of weariness in her voice and realized that Rahima too was full of anxiety.

'No, I haven't seen it yet,' Zohra answered, and asked in her turn, 'Where are Rabia and Wahida?'

'Wahida is putting henna on Rabia. Your daughter has been pestering her for henna since this morning. She and Madina brought home a whole bunch of leaves from somewhere, and Fatima has just ground it for them. Straight after Maghrib prayers, Wahida began to put it on for Rabia. On top of everything she is insisting on flower designs all over her hand,' Rahima said. She went on, 'Anyway, Mumtaz told you something about Sikander, I heard. What was it about?'

Zohra was shocked that Rahima knew. She thought for a moment and then said, 'Oh, it wasn't anything like that.' She realized that she was in a terrible quandary. She guessed that, as Fatima was scouring the vessels, she had overheard what Mumtaz said. She must have gone and told Rahima everything, Zohra thought, her anger and irritation mounting. 'No, Mumtaz said nothing like that. She only said that her husband too was in Singapore, and that he and Sikander meet frequently.'

'Don't try to cover up, Zohra. I know what she said. Do you think she's only going to whisper it to you? By now she must have told half the town. And who knows how many people Nafiza has told, in her turn? If these women come to hear of something, they must let the whole town hear it too. And there is nobody like them to say one thing to your face and another when your back is turned. These same Mumtaz and Nafiza will come to you and speak meltingly of their concern for your sister Firdaus. But when you are not around they will tell me how bold she is, and how she deserves all she gets. They know perfectly well how close I am to you; they know that I will tell you what they said, but they are not worried. They take advantage because they are kinsfolk,' Rahima said. Zohra was sure her face was flushed with anger, but could see nothing in the darkness.

Zohra felt both anger and humiliation at the same time. How could they have spoken so affectionately to her, and then said something else to Rahima? Then she thought, that's human nature. Her anger turned towards Firdaus who was the cause of all this gossip. 'Let them say what they please. Let them have their fill of gossip. Who doesn't this town gossip about? It's a town full of jealousy and bad thoughts. But our girl didn't behave well, either. It's because of her wrong-doing that they all talk about her.' Zohra's voice grew hoarse, and tears began to stream from her eyes.

Rahima was embarrassed. She tried to comfort Zohra, saying, 'Idiot, why are you crying about all this?' She was remorseful that the conversation had taken this turn and ended in Zohra's tears. She muttered, 'Allah should grant women a good destiny. It seems that if He does not, then it could affect them for seven times seven generations to come.' Her voice sounded as if it were attempting to struggle out of a quagmire of frustration, Zohra thought. They both felt surrounded by the sorrow and helplessness of those words, and fell into a deep silence. At last they climbed down, as the chores still waiting be done pressed down upon them like binding chains.

23

Her mother and Periamma were up by three in the morning. They boiled water in a cauldron over a coal fire, had their baths first, and said the special Ramzan prayers. Then they began their work in the kitchen straight away, as it would be some time before the men were ready. Rabia too had got up with them. Periamma laughed as she said to Amma, 'You daughter is a real pleasure-loving imp. I think she didn't sleep a wink right through the night.' Her mother answered, 'Oh she, how will she sleep, she was playing with the other children in the street as late as ten or eleven at night.'

Rabia felt shy when her Periamma and Amma teased her. But it was always like that. She was always very excited on the day before the Feast day. Nobody along their street seemed to go to sleep. In every house, people came and went, bringing provisions for the next day's cooking; carrying chickens to be slaughtered. The whole street would bustle; flower sellers crowding around from early evening. Not only their street, but the entire town would be alive: groups of women gathering to collect water at the street tap, and crowds of visitors who had arrived for the celebrations walking up and down. All the children would be out, playing. Rabia would have had her hands hennaed by Maghrib time, and would sit on the thinnai watching the fun, her hands spread out lest the henna smudge.

She didn't like to have her hands hennaed when she went to sleep. She would not be able to scratch if mosquitoes bit. And it was just those days that the mosquitoes bit the most. So she usually had only her feet done before she went to sleep.

It had been the same the previous night. She had begged Wahida to fill her palms with all the flower designs she knew, and then sat on the thinnai as usual, watching the street.

It was really hard to sit quietly waiting until the henna dried up and fell away. She felt as if she had been tied up. It was for an hour, though. After that the games began. Once they were all gathered together – Ahmad, Rafiq, Razak, Iliaz, Madina and Rabia – they began to play Stone or Sand. Madina and Ahmad would not speak to each other; otherwise, they all played together. During an interval, Rabia boasted, 'Do you know, in our house, my Periattha has kept aside a thousand rupees in small change, to give out as alms tomorrow? I'll be the one to distribute it. Before that, and even before Bajar time, Amma and Periamma, will send me to give out the 'godumai panam'to four or so poor families. I'll go and give it out before daybreak, when it is still dark.'

Ahmad said, 'Why, we too have kept aside more than a thousand rupees in change. My Attha gave me the money and it was I who went to the Cinema theatre to change it into coins, counting it all out. Do you know that? Can any of you go and change a thousand rupees into coins and be sure you've got it right?' His face overflowed with pride at the thought of his own feat.

'Lies, lies! You could never go and count out the change correctly. All lies, lies!' Rabia shouted. She had no desire at all to get into a fight with him. On the contrary, she only wanted him to prove to the others his smartness at being able to turn a thousand rupees into the right number of coins – if indeed he had actually done that. She wanted to hear him do so, and to be proud of him. Everything he achieved made her feel intensely happy somewhere within.

'Ei, you believe me, do you, any of you? Come with me this

minute. We'll go and ask my mother. Or wait, I'll make a promise.' Suddenly he looked up at the sky and said fervently, 'I promise in the name of Allah, and on this Ramzan that what I say is true.' He struck the palm of his left hand with the palm of his right, making his promise. For a minute nobody said anything. But their faces registered their belief, and their eyes widened in surprise. Iliaz and Razak spoke together, 'How did you do it, da?

'Who do you think I am?' Ahmad said proudly, pulling up the collar of his shirt, smiling and glancing at Rabia and Madina from the corner of his eyes.

Iliaz remarked sadly, 'I've never seen all of a thousand rupees at any one time, appa.'

Razak felt ashamed. He muttered, 'We've got a thousand rupees in our house as well.' He thought of his mother and scolded her silently. 'As if that woman would ever give alms!'

Iliaz wanted to put down Ahmad somehow. He was irritated that the boy was showing off so much in front of Madina and Rabia. 'But all the same, you are not celebrating the Feast day tomorrow,' he said, and stopped short.

Rabia understood that Iliaz wanted to show up Ahmad. But Ahmad retorted, 'Not at all. Only Amma and Attha haven't ordered new clothes. But my brother and I have been given them. They're ready-mades.'

'But they won't make biriyani or fry vadais in your house. How about that?' Iliaz said.

Ahmad had no answer to that. Celebrating the Feast day meant wearing new clothes and feasting on biriyani and vadais. They could do only one of those things. If they were not allowed the other, then how could it be said that they observed the Feast day? He was confused. He had pleaded with his mother on the previous day. But she was adamant: she said it would be wrong; it was not even a whole year since Nanni died, they must not fry any foods in their house.

Rabia wanted to rescue Ahmad from his predicament. In a very adult way she said, 'What's the fuss? It happens in every family. Once there was no Feast at Madina's house. Another time there was no Feast in Razak's house. This year it happens to be Ahmad's house. If ever your Nanni died, your family mustn't observe the Feast either, you know that?'

At once Iliaz was furious. 'What did you say? Did you say that my Nanni must die? Just you wait till I tell my mother.' His whole body shook with anger.

Rabia was scared. 'Ché ché! That's not at all what I said. I was just giving an example. Isn't that right, Madina?' She invited Madina to come to her aid.

Madina was not at all happy that Rabia had taken Ahmad's side and spoken in his favour. All the same, she was bound to help Rabia. She tried to pacify Iliaz, saying, 'Yes, da, it's old people who die soon, that's why she just said that. Don't go and tell your mother all this.' All the same, he looked as if he were close to tears. They had to stop their game at once and go home.

Rabia was still fearful in the morning that Fatima might say something to Amma and start a quarrel. But Fatima wouldn't come to work on the Feast day. Instead, Mariyaayi would arrive from their estates to do the chores. She'd do all the work, wearing the new sari presented to her by Amma. So Fatima would be able to tell her tale only the next day. Worrying about it chased away all her earlier excitement and left her exhausted. Also her legs hurt from having gone to four or five houses to deliver the 'godumai panam', the money given before the fast officially ended, indicating that those who fasted understood the meaning of hunger. Why could they not have given it on the previous evening, she grumbled to herself, why must it be given first thing in the morning, only after Amma had her bath? Zohra called sharply from the kitchen, 'Rabia, haven't you had your bath yet?' Very well, she told herself, summoning up her courage, let what has to come, come; why should I die of fear, after all nobody is going to chop off my head.

As usual, she finished her morning meal by half past seven,

and went to her mother to put on her new clothes. Zohra said a prayer, put the clothes on her, and cautioned, 'You'll be a well-behaved girl, won't you, and not get your paavaadai dirty?' When she had said 'Yes, Amma,' nodding her head in a very responsible way, she came out of the room to find Periattha standing in the hall.

He looked very grand in a snow white lungi, white shirt and cap. Involuntarily she muttered, 'Ammadi, how very white his clothes are! How on earth does he manage to be so spotless!' The scent of the attar he was wearing seemed to fill the whole house. Periattha never made ready for prayers without wearing some attar. It was only Periamma who disliked the scent of it; she complained it gave her a headache. But Periattha always said to her, 'You know that it is sunnath – emulating the Holy Prophet himself – to wear attar when you pray.' Rabia thought to herself now that she must ask him to put some attar on her new clothes.

Kader called out, 'Rahima, it is time for prayers. Lay out the food.' Having hurried her, he shook out the prayer mat himself and spread it out in the hall. Rabia came and stood in front of him, saying eagerly, 'Periattha, does my dress look good?' Periattha looked up and gazed at her. '*Subahaan Allah*, Glory to God!' he said, 'How come you've grown up so suddenly?' His eyes widened as if in surprise. ' You want attar, do you? Come, I'll put it on you. But first, here take this for the Feast day.' He brought out a fifty rupee note from his pocket and pressed into the palm of her hand, saying, 'Say Bismillah and accept it.' She was so shocked when she saw the fifty rupee note that she thought her breath would stop, but she didn't want to show her surprise to him and struggled very hard to appear calm and unruffled.

Before Periattha left for the prayers, he drew out a chair into the front courtyard and made Rabia sit by his side. Crowds of their Hindu agricultural labourers lined up there. There were a few Muslim women and children amongst them, but they were mostly Hindu labourers. She felt very sorry to see them. They stood there very politely, arms neatly folded. Rabia had poured out the coins on to a big silver salver laid on top of a stool by her side. Periattha told her to give the little children twenty five paise, and the women fifty paise each. The men were to receive a rupee. She scooped up the coins in her hands and handed them out, one by one, very conscious of her silk paavaadai and her jewellery. When they all stared at her with yearning, she felt very happy but also excessively proud.

The men who worked on their estates asked, 'Mudalali, is this our master's daughter?' Periattha answered, 'Yes, da, she's my younger brother's girl.' For these people he took out ten rupee notes out of a bundle he kept in his pocket and asked her to give them out, one each.

The prayers would begin at eight, so when it was time, Rabia's uncle and father set off, with herself and Madina following as far as the mosque. From there, all the men of the town would walk together, chanting, and go to the kotbah stage, erected some distance out of the town, where the Ramzan prayers would be held. All the young boys accompanied them. Rabia and Madina stood under a tree with all the other little girls, watching them with envy. On that day too, Ahmad looked at them sarcastically, as if to say, You can't pray with us, can you? Rabia would ask her mother again and again, 'Why is it that we can't go to the mosque or the kotbah place and pray with the men?'

But Amma only said, 'No, absolutely not. Women can't go into the mosque.'

'But why?'

'No means no. That's all.'

In the town, the women put on all their finery and visited relations and neighbours. The whole street reverberated with wave upon wave of women's voices and laughter. But this would last only until the men returned to the town.

After the midday meal, Rabia planned to go to the cinema with Madina, Ahmad and Iliaz. But before that, she went up to her room by herself, and added up all the money that her relations had given her that morning. Before they set off for prayers, the men from each family would go and visit their relations, bid them goodbye and give the women and children gifts of money. Ahmad's father had come to Rabia's house and given them all money. In the same way, Attha and Periattha had gone to Ahmad's house, Madina's house, Sherifa Akka's house, and all the other relations. Rabia kept aside a ten-rupee note, and put all the rest of her money into a terracotta money box which she had bought specially from the market. Ten rupees would be enough to pay for the cinema, and to buy some snacks there.

Once, when the money box was full, her mother had asked her, 'Why don't you give me all the money you have saved up. Let's buy you a pair of gold-studs.' But Rabia hadn't cared for that. Who wanted more jewellery? She said, 'I really want to go somewhere on a train. Will you take me? Otherwise, buy me a cycle.'

Her mother said, 'Why would a girl want a cycle? No, you don't need one. And I haven't been on a train either. Why don't you go and ask your Attha?' She spread her hands.

How could Rabia ask her father, though? Better to keep quiet, she thought, and let it go. Wahida Akka had told her that once she was married, she would go to Singapore by plane. She had said she would take Rabia. There were lots of trains there. She told herself she would break her money-box and take the money with her then.

* * *

The cool early morning breeze fell on Firdaus as she sat on the parapet of the well, brushing her teeth. 'Ush – ah' she muttered as she pulled the end of her sari to cover both shoulders. From someone's house somewhere, a tape recorder was playing a song sung by Nagore Hanifa. For a moment she wondered from where it came, then concluded, 'Whose house can it be but Sabia's!' In his ringing voice, Hanifa sang, 'Extend your hands unto the Lord; he will never deny you anything.' Firdaus wanted to laugh cynically. She muttered to herself wearily, 'I too have asked Him for so many things; whatever did He give me?' She stood up and washed out her mouth.

It was the Feast day of Ramzan. Yet she felt parched and dry to the core of her heart; there wasn't a single drop of enthusiasm there. It was still a long while before sunrise. Darkness was spread all over the paved courtyard. She thought to herself, 'Such a huge courtyard can contain any amount of darkness.' What was the point of waking up so early? There was nothing to feel happy about, nothing to celebrate. She went and sat on the thinnai, her knees drawn up, her arms holding them tightly. The cool air was pleasurable; she breathed it in deeply, in long breaths. The coolness about her, the wide-spread sky and the companionable darkness touched her heart strangely. All the tensions she had felt deep within seemed to loosen, melt and dissolve into the air she breathed out, and disappear into the skies, while a child's innocence and happiness took root in her. She pressed the palms of her hands against her cheeks, closed her eyes and let herself experience that thrill. She felt as if the murungai tree in the garden rustled its leaves only for her. In spite of the loneliness that was always her experience nowadays came the sudden certainty that this sky, this breeze and this coolness were all there for her sake alone.

She knew too, without any doubt, why the cold and wind which had been tormenting her for so long had suddenly and strangely changed; the thought of Siva stroked her body like the cool breeze. He was there in everything, filling everything: in the wind which spread over the garden, in the sky, in the firmly treading darkness. Stroking her with his eyes full of compassion; preventing her from feeling guilt or fear with that gentle embrace.

'Haven't you had your bath yet?' Her mother's voice, sounding near her brought her back to herself with a rude shock. She turned to her mother, who has standing opposite her, her hand at her waist. 'No, Amma,' she said slowly, as she stood up, 'I was shivering with the cold, that's why…'

'So you wake up in the early morning, just to sit about, do you?' her mother complained. 'Why don't you get the hot water going? A fine thing you're doing, sitting huddled in the thinnai and dreaming away.' She walked towards the hot water cauldron, grumbling as she went.

Firdaus followed, went past her to where the sack of coal was kept, brought two handfuls of coal, shoved them into the grate of the stove under the cauldron, and dusted off her hands.

Her mother said, 'I'll pour some kerosene on the coals, and get the fire going. You go and soak a small measure of urad dal. We'll make some vadais.' She looked up at the silent Firdaus and added, 'Yes, it's true, we mustn't let such an auspicious day go by without putting the deep-fryer on the stove. If we miss it by accident one year, we'll be forced to go without for three years following. So why stand there as if some bad luck has fallen on you?' As she looked at her daughter and gave her reasons, there was a serenity in her voice Firdaus seldom heard.

'First I'll have my bath and say my prayers; after that, I have to distribute the 'godumai panam' before dawn breaks.' Without waiting for Firdaus to answer, Amina went inside the house to collect some fresh clothes. The way she walked off, her thin body like a dry leaf in the wind, pierced Firdaus and tore at her heart.

Obeying her mother's order, she set off without saying anything, climbed the kitchen steps, switched on the light and went in. In the sudden flood of light, lizards stumbled away, startled, while cockroaches froze, stuck together. She turned her gaze away, repulsed, and went towards the wooden almirah. Gritting her teeth, she prised open the tight lid of the aluminium container, measured out the urad dal, and placed it in a terracotta vessel. From the bronze container standing near the hearth, she poured some water over the dal and began washing the grains.

From the time she was a small child, Firdaus had never liked vadais. In those days, whenever her sister Zohra and her husband came to visit them, Amina would make vadais. And she never asked her why, when Firdaus stubbornly refused to eat them. She would just say, 'If you don't care for it, leave it. Go and buy yourself a couple of aappams from that beggarly aappakkaari who makes them.'

And today? Amina insists in a great fury that Firdaus submit a full list of reasons why she doesn't like a prospective bridegroom. And Amina won't accept any of Firdaus's reasons, anyway.

'Just yesterday I showed Zohra a photo, and told her that I am determined to negotiate with his family once the fast is over. He only has a couple of daughters. It's only to satisfy you that I asked for the photo. But I lied that I had to show your sister what an out-of-the-world wonder he is. He's good looking enough, even to please you.' The way she stressed those last few words made Firdaus cringe.

The grains of the urad rolled and slipped through Firdaus's long, rosy fingers, gleaming white. She washed them as if she were washing into them all her own burdens and pains. Because she had stayed for just two days with a stranger to whom they had married her, how did it make sense now for her to marry another man, twenty years older than her, and who had two daughters besides? From whatever perspective she considered it, however many times she went over it, she could not understand.

Her mother's emphatic words, 'even to please you' seemed to tangle in her mind, making her shrink into herself with shame. She wanted to fall at the feet of her mother, who had such a low estimation of her, and weep and scream to make her change her mind.

Amina came into the kitchen after her bath, asking in surprise, 'Still washing the urad dal? A good lot of time you're taking over it.'

'Here, I've finished, Amma,' she answered hastily, leaving the kitchen.

'I've left the petticoat in which I had my bath in the backyard; just rinse it out, will you?' Amina called after her, going into the front courtyard to pick up the prayer mat hanging on the line. She shook it out and went inside the house to say her prayers. From inside the house, she peered out, calling, 'I can't find the surma stick. Where did you put it?'

From the raised platform by the well, Firdaus called back, 'I've no idea. I left it there after I put it on for the Friday Luhur prayers. Look more carefully, Amma.'

She put her hand into the plastic vessel in which her mother had left a mixture of shiyakkai for her, and stirred. A chill went through her whole body, and she withdrew her hand quickly, shook it dry and began to remove her clothes. The sky lightened, warning her that she must finish her bath quickly; she took handfuls of the shiyakkai, placed it on the crown of her head and began to rub it in briskly. The tape recorder in Sabia's house had finished playing Nagore Hanifa's songs, and had moved on to a the ballad of Saithoon Bivi.

She wondered why they were playing this ballad at this time, even as it captured her attention completely. The sufferings of Saithoon Bivi were being sung and recited alternately by four or five voices, in tragic tones, melting the hearts of all who might listen. She too had heard this ballad many times; she too had wept. All that was before her own marriage. Now, when she considered her own life; all that seemed as nothing. The storyteller kept repeating, 'Listen! Listen to the sufferings of Saithoon Bivi!' An ill-mannered wind wilfully interrupted the flow of the song.

The grandeur of that voice and the melody of the song reminded Firdaus of Asirvadam Thattha who used to show bioscope pictures. She shut her eyes tightly and called him to mind. He had a round smiling face and bald head, rather like Gandhi. He wore no shirt on his dark-skinned upper body. A cross dangling from the black thread worn tightly round his neck, he would tap his fingers on his tin box and make magic; it used to be such fun to watch.

She'd peel off Rabia who was stuck to her waist like a lizard to the wall, set her down, screaming; bend down to the side of the tin box, attach her eye to it, and watch avidly. 'See, see! See the bioscope picture' he would begin to sing at the top of his voice, and Firdaus would watch with the closest of attention, not removing her eye, as pictures of Gandhi, Nehru and the Taj Mahal came and went. Even Rabia would be silenced, stunned by the loudness of his voice.

The minute she had finished, Firdaus would pick up the baby, put her on her hip again, and ask, 'What did you say was the name of the lady on the horse?'

'Mm. That's Jhansi Rani. Why do you ask? You like her a lot, do you?' he'd tease her.

Wanting to agree, yet sensitive to the mischief in his voice, she'd say, 'No, Thattha, I keep wanting to look at her because she seems to be such a daring lady, sitting on the horse and raising her huge sword.' She remembered a character called Jhansi Rani whom she had seen in a Raja-rani picture when a touring talkies had come to their town. Somehow, she hadn't liked that character at all. But she loved to look at the woman in the picture in the box.

As he poured the coins from his dirty blue drawstring purse into his palm and started to count them, she asked eagerly, 'And do you know any more stories about that queen?' She was overcome with shyness as she asked her question.

Stopping in the middle of his counting, he'd say, 'What more do I know? Have I been to school or what?' Sadly, he'd resume his counting.

Where was he now? Would he still be alive, or would he be dead by now? She pulled her thoughts away from those days. Sadness that life had been so happy at that time, and regret that she could not always have been a child gathered in her as she poured the warm water over herself again and again, driving away the shivering cold.

From the mosque, the call to prayers sounded, followed by

the Modinaar's chant, 'Prayer is better than sleep.' It brought
her back to herself in the present.

◦ 24 ◦

Kader sat on the bed next to Rahima, writing
something. Rahima had been feeling restless for the past
few days. Wahida's marriage would take place in less than ten
days. Because she wasn't entirely happy about the bridegroom,
she could not engage wholeheartedly in any of the tasks to do
with the wedding. The printed wedding invitations had arrived.
Now they would have to be delivered to all their kinsfolk and
acquaintances. Tomorrow morning, the agreed sum of money
for the bride and groom's wedding clothes must be handed
over to the groom's family. On the following day she must go
to Madurai and choose the clothes. It was customary for the
bride's and groom's families to go together for this. She must
go to each of the families in town and invite them to the wedding.
She must sift the rice for the wedding feast. She must go and
invite each of their close relations herself. That was the custom
of the town. The very thought of it all made her head spin.
Once the material was selected for the clothes, she must have
them tailored. She must buy all the vessels and household goods
which were part of the marriage dowry, and see that they were
delivered to the groom's house. Sabia had already warned her
brother, 'She's your only daughter, keep that in mind.' The
jewellery, worth over a hundred sovereigns, was all ready.
Although it was certain that it would all be done in grand
style, yet she was not happy in her heart. She felt a deep
resentment against her husband. Were it not for his obstinacy,
they might have chosen a suitable boy for Wahida, without
making such haste, she felt. However, to talk about it or even
to think about it hereafter would be like forgetting Allah, she
decided, casting away such thoughts.

Kader stopped writing, looked up and asked, 'When are you going to be distributing the invitations to our townsfolk?'

She left off her thoughts and answered, 'This very day. We can go to the people who live elsewhere, tomorrow, by car.'

He asked, a little anxiously, 'But you are keeping the six day fast following the Feast, aren't you? Won't you get tired if you wander about the town?'

'So what? It's got to be done, hasn't it?' she said.

There didn't appear to be the slightest indication of happiness in her expression. 'What is the matter? You don't at all look happy,' he said.

'It's nothing. But I hear that the bridegroom's behaviour in those places isn't quite right. I don't feel happy in my mind.'

Kader looked up and observed her closely. His face revealed a moment's anger and confusion, and then cleared. He composed himself somewhat. He said, 'Listen here. If he's a man, he will be like that. It isn't right for you to make a big deal out of it. Is there a man in all this world who can truly be called excellent? If you have decided you'll give your daughter only to such a man, let me tell you it's not going to happen in your lifetime. Keep that in mind! It isn't such a big thing if a man does wrong things; once he is married, inshah Allah, he'll reform himself. Go now, go and see to your work. And don't put on a long face in front of that child. I am more concerned about her than you are.' His tone was both stern and serene.

He added, 'Somehow, this makes me doubt the extent of your faith in God. Tell me, can even a speck of dust move, if He doesn't wish it? Whether it is good or bad, give thanks to Him and be at peace.' Now Kader sounded sad; anxious that by going over and over the same thing, Rahima was committing the sin of questioning what was ordained.

Rahima was distressed. She could not understand why Kader, who had always listened to whatever she had to say so far, was so stubborn in this matter alone. She wondered whether he thought she, Rahima, was trying to break up his close relationship with his sister. And there was some truth in

what he said. She understood that no man can be perfect. All
the same, knowing what they did, why should they make a
mistake? She couldn't understand it. Her head ached. Nothing
would be gained by confusing herself in this way. She must cast
her burdens on Allah and just go about her business. Who
could change the destiny He ordained?

'Rahima,' Kader called after her. 'Look here, when you are
delivering the invitations, please go to Current Officer
Balakrishnan's house and tell them they must definitely come.
If you don't know their address, ask the driver, Mutthu. Or
ask Rabia: Balakrishanan's son Ramesh is her classmate.'
Having issued his command he bent over his accounts once
again.

Rahima came out of the room without saying anything.
From Zohra's room, Karim's voice could be heard, raised in
anger. She stopped for a moment to hear what he was saying,
but he was shouting so angrily that she could make out nothing.
Zohra kept intervening and trying to calm him down, saying,
'Very well, leave it alone, now, Someone might hear. If she says
anything again, we'll deal with it.' But when Karim was angry,
he altered into some kind of animal. Nobody was able to stop
him then. Rahima couldn't understand how Zohra was able
to live with his temper. Each time she served him a meal, it was
with fear and trembling. The food had to be all ready exactly
in time, when he entered the house. If there was the slightest
delay, he would shout at her rudely and leave at once.

'He's a real saithaan,' Rahima muttered to herself, seeing
him thrust open the door and hurry out of the house. Zohra,
following him out of the room, saw Rahima and gave a slight
smile. In answer to the question on her sister-in-law's face, she
said, 'It's nothing, Akka. He was eating quietly a little while
ago. I was making dosais for him. Nafiza came in, asking for a
little chutney for the children. Instead of going home quietly,
she said to him, "Well, Maamu, it seems your daughter is going
to be married?" He said, "Yes. Be sure to come." She took the
chutney and said to him, "Of course I'll come. But you are

giving one daughter to your Akka's family. In the same way, please give your other daughter to us. Although she wasn't your sibling, my mother too was like a sister to you. Don't forget that. I've always thought of Rabia as my daughter-in-law. Don't go and disappoint me." And off she went, having said this. He didn't say anything to her then. I was deeply embarrassed. The minute she left, he started to shout, "This is a woman who gads about as she pleases. Am I likely to give my girl to her?" She was only making conversation; are we going to have a wedding straight away? He gets so worked up, so angry. How upset Bashir would be if he were to hear of it!'

Zohra said all this in a single breath; her expression betraying her embarrassment. 'Shouldn't you consider who's around you, when you speak aloud at daytime?' she went on, mortified. Rahima felt as if her heart had missed a beat. She didn't want to say anything. Some kind of confusion rose from within and enveloped her as if in a cloud of smoke. 'Why should your husband bother about what she does? If he doesn't want his daughter to marry into her family, let him say so and stop at that. There's no need to say anything else.' Rahima's face was dark with distress. 'Why cause unnecessary problems and incite hostilities? Tomorrow we'll be holding a wedding at our house. Won't they be our guests then? But get ready now! You and I have to go into town and invite everyone.' It was very obvious she didn't want to continue this conversation.

They dressed up, put on a discreet amount of jewellery and prepared to go. When they had each draped a dupatta over their saris, drawing it well over the head and tucking it in, they called Wahida. 'We're off to deliver the wedding invitations. Make sure that Rabia is here to keep you company. Lock the door behind us.' And so they left. The words that Karim had used about Nafiza went round and round in Rahima's head. A heavy ache gathered together and pressed down on her.

When they returned, it was with the comforting feeling that they had invited almost all the households in the town. Because they were keeping the six day fast, they felt very tired and dizzy.

In each house they had been scolded fondly. 'How can you do this, you women! You are wandering about like this on a day when you are fasting. You could have come round with the invitations later, couldn't you? A fine thing, going about in this heat! You won't even drink a mouthful of water in our house!' Rahima answered all of them tactfully. 'No, Akka, we have any amount of jobs to do. Because it was the month of Ramzan, we couldn't do any of this at that time. Now there's only a week, isn't there, for the wedding. I can't even sleep when I think of all the work.'

They had agreed. 'Of course, that's how it has to be. It's the wedding of the eldest child. And it will be the first big event in your family. The whole town has been waiting for it to happen, expecting a grand feast. Of course it will be a grand wedding.' They had said to Zohra, smiling, 'After this, we'll expect you to announce the coming of age ritual for your daughter! You must arrange a feast for that too.'

As they walked along in the street, Rahima was scathing. 'A single mention of food is enough for these people. They'll be the first to arrive at our door. As if we won't have a feast for Rabia. Why should they keep on reminding us about it?'

Zohra agreed. 'True, Akka; in my hometown I've not seen people making such a rush after rice and meat. It's peculiar to this place.'

Exhausted by their trip to town, they went to bed early that night and were soon asleep. But everyone in the house woke up when the front door was struck, well past midnight. It was Karim who opened the door. Their farm labourer, Paraman, stood outside, torch in hand. Behind him there was a crowd of ten or fifteen; both men and women. Karim was confused; he didn't know what to make of the situation. He raised his voice. 'What is this, da, at this hour?'

Paraman tried to speak. He began, 'Ayya, look at this. Listen to this scandal...'

Karim stood aside. 'Come in first, all of you,' he said. They all followed him into the big courtyard and stood to one side, their arms folded. That was when he noticed the pretty young woman, possibly from the big town, who stood a little apart from the rest.

By that time, Kader had woken up and come out to the courtyard. He came and sat down on the rope-strung bedstead there, still half asleep and with half shut eyes. With some annoyance, he asked, 'What is it, Parama? Whatever the matter is, you could come in the morning, couldn't you? Do you have to wake us up at this hour?' His long, light-complexioned face looked tired and weary. Opening his eyes wide, he looked closely at the people who had gathered there. Suddenly becoming aware that he had come out only in his lungi and banian, he called out to Karim, 'Hand me the cloth that is hanging on the line.' He draped the cloth over his body. Rahima and Zohra peered out of their respective windows observing eagerly what was going on. Rahima began to comprehend the situation.

'No, yejamaan, if we don't talk about this and decide on something immediately, I'll lose my reputation completely. I'll just have to hang myself and die; there will be no other way. For us Konar, our honour is more important than our lives.' He thumped his chest with fervour. Then he covered his mouth with the cloth he held in his hand and began to sob and cry aloud. His wife, Ramaayi, stood quietly in a corner, watching him.

'Well, Ramaayi, you tell us what happened,' asked Kader, without much enthusiasm. Karim was silent, unable to say anything, before his elder brother did. But he was clearly irritated.

But Paraman ran towards her in a fury, drawing out a knife from his side and shouting, 'What is she going to tell you, the whore?' His companions pulled him back forcibly, but he growled, ' Wait, di. I'll see to you later, di.'

Kader repressed him. 'What is the matter with you, shouting like this at this early hour? Can't you shut up?' And suddenly he noticed that Paraman's son, Thangayya, who lived in

Coimbatore was present there, along with a young woman
who was new to the town. Kader began to understand what
had happened. 'Now you tell me, Parama, what has actually
happened? And when did he arrive?' He indicated Thangayya.

'It's all because of this wretched fellow, Ayya, I stand
dishonoured. How hard I toiled, strapping my mouth and my
stomach, denying myself everything in order to put him
through SSLC, and bring him up as a man. I didn't want him
to be an agricultural labourer like me, but in a good
employment. Now we know, Ayya, what employment he has
actually been up to. Here, this is the young girl that he's
brought with him. What will happen to my honour, my
reputation? You must protect me now, Ayya. I can only be at
peace if you drive her away right now, this very minute.
Otherwise I'll just hang myself, Ayya.' Having said this, he was
just about to prostrate himself at Kader's feet.

Shocked, Kader drew his feet up to the bed, saying, 'Dé, get
up; don't fall at my feet and make me carry a burden of sin.'
Then he looked up at Karim, as if to ask him, What shall we do
now? Karim returned that glance for an instant and turned
away.

Kader summoned Thangayya to come close to him. 'Who's
that girl, da? Tell me, what's the problem?' he asked. There
was a sharpness about his tone. Thangayya drew near to Kader,
hesitantly. Was this the son of a labourer on his estate? Kader
was astonished at how stylish and urban he looked. His clothes,
the way his hair was cut were all suited to the town. His
middling brown colour suited his attractive looks. He had
grown quite tall.

'Mudalali, I pay my respects to you. Ayya, I was working in
a shop there. This girl lived in a house nearby. Her father is a
taxi driver. We fell in love with each other. That's why I ran
away here with her. I've put a tali around her neck, and married
her in the temple. But Appa has pretty nearly flogged me to
death. You've got to protect me now.' Now he too was in tears.
There was a humility in his voice. He was very scared because

he knew that if Kader were to make up his mind he could separate him from his wife.

Kader was silent for a while, his head bowed. He too must have been unclear as to what to do. Rahima watched him from where she was. The young woman was very beautiful. In the yellow light of the courtyard lamp, Rahima could see how frightened she was.

Kader looked up at the girl and said, 'Come here, amma.' Very slowly she walked up and stood next to him. She was wearing an expensive sari. Unlike Thangayya, she must belong to a somewhat better off family.

'What is your name, amma,' Kader asked.

'My name is Gomati,' she answered, in a soft voice, speaking in Malayalam.

Realizing immediately that she was a Malayali, Kader and Karim were shocked. They said together, 'Oh, you are a Malayali, then?'

Paraman jumped in at once, seeing that they were shocked; not willing to let the opportunity go. 'See this, yejaman. What is our caste and our community? Without considering any of that, he brings this Malayalcchi here.' His companions were hard put to restrain him.

Karim scolded, 'So we are enquiring into it aren't we? Why can't you shut up for a while?'

'Tell me,' Kader asked the girl. 'Can you speak Tamil?'

She was quiet for a while, her head bent low. Then she said, stammering over the words. 'I don't know how I'm going to live here. There isn't even a bathroom in their house.'

Paraman leaped in once more. 'Yes, of course my home is only a hut made of palmyra-fronds. So now you know. Run home to your father, then.' He was infuriated and humiliated by her words.

Kader scolded him, 'Ss. Be quiet, da.' Then he turned to Karim with a look that meant, 'What do we do now?' Kader knew from the expression he saw on Karim's face that he had determined already that whatever the efforts of those present there, he would not consent to sending the girl away.

Karim said, in measured tones, 'See here, Parama, take it that she is your daughter-in-law from now on. The tali has been tied on her. You cannot, with a clear conscience, send her away. It isn't right for you to sing this dirge about the end of your caste and community. Just think what that girl's fate will be if you send her back. Who will marry her? Besides, these two love each other. So just leave off jumping up and down between heaven and earth, and shut up. Otherwise, you can threaten to hang yourself, or even go and do it; it's as you please.' Having said this, Karim turned to his brother. It seemed to Kader his brother's words were absolutely right, so he nodded his head, in silent agreement.

When Karim spoke up so suddenly, giving his verdict, Paraman was totally overcome and unable to say a single word. It was clear, from her expression, that his wife Ramaayi, on the other hand was in absolute agreement with the outcome.

Now all the kinsfolk who had accompanied Paraman had long faces. They had come there in a fury, eager to drive the girl away; but Karim had silenced them. Besides, they were bitterly disappointed that they could not even say a few words in vindication of the honour of their caste.

Kader spoke a word or two to each of them, enquiring after their fields and the progress of their lives. Then he said, 'Very well, time for all of you to return. What has happened has happened. That girl has come here, putting her trust in our boy. It is up to us to look after her now. Get up, Parama. It's going to take a couple of days for you to cool down. Let this girl stay here in our house until then. Do you hear me? De, Thangayya, go with your father and make your peace with him.' And so he insisted that they all leave. It was very clear that he was both irritated and distressed.

When they had all left, Rahima took the girl to a room upstairs, spread a mat, found a pillow, and told her to sleep.

She looked extremely sorrowful, her face pale with disappointment and shame. Rahima touched her shoulder and asked her with gentle concern, 'Why did you do this, amma? How distressed your parents must be! If a man dresses well and tells you a few lies, should you run away with him on the strength of that?

The girl began to sob and weep. She could just understand what people around her were saying, but because she could not speak Tamil properly, she was making a great effort to express her feelings through her tears. Hearing her weeping, Kader came upstairs, and stood outside the door, quietly. He was overwhelmed by the vulnerability her voice betrayed. It sounded like a voice at a funeral raised again and again; expressing grief, loss, uncertainty and utter helplessness. Deeply distressed, he raised his head and gazed at her.

It wrung his heart to see the still childish contours of her face, the terror in her staring eyes, the trembling of her slender form. Was Thangayya capable of ridding her of her fear and grief, and of giving her complete protection, he wondered, anxiously. With a father's sympathy and sense of responsibility he said to her, 'Now don't weep any more, amma. I am here. I will look after you; it's no problem at all.' He himself had not known all this time that he could speak with such tenderness. The girl quickly pulled away her right hand from Rahima's clasp, brought them together in a gesture of thanks, and stopped weeping.

Rahima had watched it all silently all this while. Now, an expression of pride filled her face as she reflected on her husband's compassion, and for some reason, tears streamed from her eyes.

During the next two days, all the women of the town came to inspect the girl, as if she were some strange commodity. Each had her questions, probing and pestering Rahima, Zohra and the girl, leaving Rahima totally disgusted. 'If they must gossip, should it be to this extent? Why can't they concentrate on what's going on in their own homes? Can we tell any of them not to come here? They are all people of our community, after all,' she scolded, pouring it all out to Zohra.

Rabia though, floated in happiness for those two days. She brought all her friends, and showed off Gomati with great pride. News of the girl's beauty had spread around town like wildfire. Within the next two days, Thangayya had made peace with his father, and came to the Mudalali's house to bring his bride away. Rahima let her go, advising her, 'Of course it is only a hut. But don't make too much of it. Thangayya will look after you well.'

◈ 25 ◈

It was their own special town-festival. The sound of a radio playing in the distance pierced through the heavy darkness and flowed down the street. Amina was asleep. She had not been well for some days. The doctor had given her some pills for high blood pressure. She complained of pain in her knees, besides. She had gone to the estate that morning, because they were cutting down the coconuts, and that had also tired her out. The pain-killers she had taken put her to sleep very early. Firdaus, however, found it impossible to sleep. She rose up, opened the door, and went to sit on the front thinnai. The sky was bright and clear. Not a cloud in sight. A play, 'Valli's wedding', was going on, just a street away. Without a single exception, all the women of the town had set off to see it at ten o'clock, their saris pulled tightly over their heads. They had to go right past this house to get there. She had lain in bed, listening to their hesitant footsteps going past. In earlier times, Rabia would come to their town every year at the festival time. She loved to go on the roundabouts, to buy toys, and to go to the plays. But this year she hadn't come. Hereafter, neither her sister Zohra, nor her brother-in-law was going to send her. Firdaus longed to see her. To seat her on her lap, and pet her. She smiled to herself. There was an ache in that smile. She too would have loved to go to the play. But her mother would never allow her. Besides, who would keep her company? The whole town had shoved her aside, looked at her with repulsion!

The entire sky was filled with stars, sparkling in clusters; so beautiful to look at. A meteor burst into flame and fell. It struck her that it was herself. She believed it to be herself, most definitely. Wasn't she like that one meteor that burnt and fell while crores of stars went on sparkling in the sky? When she was little, if ever she saw a star fall, she would look at a tree in leaf immediately, just as her mother had instructed her. If not, she had been told, she would lose her memory. Now she longed that the meteor she saw would make her forget the past and create some kind of amnesia. But if she alone were to forget what had happened, would everything come out right, then? If the entire town were to forget it all, that would be good, of course. Particularly, if at least her mother and sister were to forget, how good that would be. They could be at peace, without their perpetual concern over Firdaus.

How many beliefs and superstitions there were, concerning these skies! When she was small, her mother would say that if she saw three storks flying together, she was bound to study well. She did indeed study well. But would they allow her to carry on with it? She could hear someone singing in the play, 'Unyielding forest…' A breeze blew. She trembled a little in the slight chill, and tightened her arms about her knees. She could hear the sound of the door opening in the house opposite. Must be Siva. He must have come away half way through the play. Of course, Jaya wasn't in town, either. The baby was ill; she had taken her home to her mother's house. Firdaus remembered that Jaya was not in this town most days, and longed, all of a sudden to see Siva. She stepped forward quietly, very gently opened the outside gate and put her head out. The creaking of the tin gate made him turn his head with a quick movement. When he saw her standing there, he was stunned for an instant. For a second they stood there silently, looking at each other. His look pinned her feet – which wanted to run away and hide, in spite of herself – to the ground.

In the dim street light, his glance fell on her, brimming with love. The breeze embraced her trembling form and then blew away. Her heart was troubled, but she never thought to disappear. He stretched out his arms, standing where he was, and as if she had been waiting for that moment she floated up to him without hesitation, like a feather scattered from a bird's wing, looking directly at him all the while. She nestled within his arms. Emotions that had been held stagnant within her for years together broke free and began to flood through her, and Siva was overwhelmed for a moment by her intensity and ardour. The passion that arose from her young body, trembling like a little chicken, almost frightened him. She entwined her body with his, as if in a frenzy to sink into his loving embrace and dissolve in him. The sacred thread hanging down his wet and dripping back caught in her hands, shocking her and bringing her to her senses for a moment. In that instant she thought of her mother, who would be heart-broken if she knew; who might even die. Resolutely she pushed away that thought. She realized that, more than anything that surrounded her, more than her mother, it was her own happiness that mattered to her now. She clung to Siva with greater ardour. The distant sound of songs and recitals from the play faded away against her deep breaths.

When she returned home, a cock was crowing somewhere. She walked into the house with footsteps as quiet as a cat's, and went and lay down next to her mother, not able to decide whether what had happened was a dream or not. A dream could not have made so deep an impression in her mind. When it came to her that it was indeed real, she felt a thrill go through her which was at once fear and joy. She could touch and feel the hair standing on end all over her body. But if it was real, how was it possible that it happened? What was it that had incited her do such a big thing? What was it that flung away in an instant her fear of Allah, her belief in her religion, all her mistrust and suspicion of the town, and over and above all this, her love and attachment to her family? What identified her as so daring a woman? Just this body and its needs? Can one give up everything for the sake of an instant's happiness? In her confusion she felt as if her skull might burst open.

She thought of Siva. She knew that what he felt for her was not just bodily lust. When he was with her that night, he was able to let her know by his hands and their touch that he loved her. Remembering this she overflowed with joy.

But what if someone had seen them? The thought rose inevitably, making her heart tremble. Had that been the case, she knew that he and she would be made to stand in the mosque, facing the entire congregation, shamed in front of them all, and subjected to the severest punishment. She was seized with a terror greater than the fear of death. Did nobody see them, really? Might they have been seen, after all? But were that so, the whole town would have heard by now. No, it certainly can't be, she told herself. Her mind tossed about and she fell asleep at last, still in a turmoil.

* * *

Amina woke up with a start, feeling a rush of warmth against her. She saw Firdaus tossing about in bed, in the cold air, her body feverishly hot, and rose to her feet, frightened. 'She was fine when she went to sleep last night, how is it that she is shivering with fever now,' she muttered to herself, bringing a wet cloth which wrung out and pressed to Firdaus's forehead and neck. 'Firdaus! Firdaus!' she called, trying to shake her awake. But Firdaus seemed completely unconscious of her. There was no way of taking her to the doctor; there wasn't a bus. And she didn't know who to send, to bring a doctor home. Amina felt a stab of pain in her chest. She panicked at the thought that she had become so very helpless. Deciding to go to Sabia's house and ask Sikander to help her, she hurried next door.

Sabia herself was sitting on the outside thinnai of her house, rolling her prayer beads between her fingers. The anxiety she saw on Amina's face made her rise to her feet immediately. She was worried that it might be bad news, that something had happened to someone at this crucial stage in the wedding arrangements. 'What's the matter, Amina?' she asked.

'Nothing, Sabia, it's just that Firdaus has a high fever; I need someone to fetch the doctor. If Sikander is at home, please tell him to take his bike and go.'

Sabia's anxiety ebbed away and left her at peace. 'Oh but he was up all night because of the festival and is fast asleep now, Amina. He won't wake up just yet. What shall we do?' She went on, 'Why don't you give her a decoction to drink and see what happens? Has she a cold as well?'

'Nothing like that. She was fine last night. This has happened very suddenly,' Amina told her.

'You could do one thing if you liked. I have some pills from abroad, to bring down a fever. If you give her that, it will work at once.' Sabia went inside the house. Amina couldn't bear to wait there. She hurried away to her own house before Sabia's return.

Having gone inside the house to fetch the pills, Sabia gazed at her son fast asleep on his bed, lost to the world. If she were only to say to him that Firdaus was ill and needed a doctor, he would definitely fly off on that errand. Sabia knew he had an eye on Firdaus's beauty. He stood in the terrace, often, gazing towards the entrance of her house, in the hope of catching sight of her head. It irritated Sabia to see this. All the same, there was nothing she could say. Firdaus kept herself away from the threshold, taking care not to be seen by Sikander. In any case, had she done so, Amina would have killed her. What was the good of all that she once had, she just let it all slip away, Sabia said to herself. For a moment she asked herself whether she should actually wake up Sikander. It was a family without the support of a man. Also, Zohra would be really distressed if she knew. She might even ask Sabia, 'Didn't it occur

to you to help them?' Yes, Zohra was her brother's wife. Sabia
needed to stand well in their relationship. All this ran through
her mind as she tapped him awake, after all. 'Here, wake up,
Sikander, wake up. It seems Firdaus has a fever. Please will you
go and fetch the doctor?' She almost expected him to say No.

More aware that she was saying something about Firdaus
than that she was waking him up, Sikander sat up half asleep
and asked with some eagerness, 'What is it, amma, what has
happened?' His mouth split open into a yawn. He had gone to
bed only at four o'clock in the morning so he could have slept
for a lot longer. Had his mother woken him for any other
work, he would only have rolled over and gone to sleep again;
he would not have got up so easily. Sabia laughed to herself.
'It's just that Firdaus is burning with fever, apparently. They
want to send for the doctor from the next town. Amina asked
if you could go for them, that's all,' she said.

He got to his feet swiftly and said, trying to hide his
excitement from his mother, 'I'll go straight off.'

'You get ready, then. I'll go across and take a look at her,'
said Sabia, setting off for the house next door.

Her knees were painful, so she climbed the front steps slowly.
Amina was in the kitchen, preparing a decoction. The house
was full of the smell of roasting coriander seeds. Sabia stood at
the door and called, 'What's happened? How is Firdaus now?'

From the hearth, Amina called to her, 'Oh, come in Sabia.
She's just the same, actually. I've just sent Siva for the doctor.'

'Adadaa! So you've sent him already! And I've asked
Sikander to get ready, as well. So you don't need him then?'
Sabia returned to the front steps and called across to her own
house, 'Listen son, Sikander!'

By this time he had come out of the house and was kicking
the motor-bike to get it started. He called back, 'What is it,
Amma?' Then leaving the motor-bike on its stand, he walked
up to Amina's house.

'You don't have to go after all. It seems Siva has gone,' Sabia
told her son.

Sikander was severely disappointed. Siva had knocked off the prize and glory owing to him. His regret showed in his face. He was also frustrated that he had missed this opportunity to earn Firdaus's regard. He directed his anger at his mother. He guessed that she had chased Amina away earlier, saying he was asleep. Without a word he turned round and went inside the house. Having his sleep ruined made him even more irritable. He took his shirt off, hung it up and lay down once more.

He remembered that his father, Sayyed, was arriving from Sri Lanka the next day. There was no need to go to the airport to fetch him. He would come home on his own. He had become used to doing this, over several years. There was nothing left for his father to do, by way of the wedding arrangements. Sikander and his mother had done most of it themselves. His mother complained frequently, 'Look at this man! He hasn't arrived here yet. And here I am, hard at it, all by myself!'

She carried on as if the groom's family had a lot of work to do. That was her nature. She turned even trivial matters into a big deal. After all, the most important thing they had to do was to visit the families in the town and hand out the wedding invitations. She had paid for all her expenses from the money his uncle, Kader, had given her. Since they usually white-washed their house at Ramzan time, they didn't even have to do that again. He looked up at the cross-beam, as he lay in bed. The wall shone bright, with white-wash. He had pleaded with his mother to have the house colour-painted on the outside. She had refused, obstinately, saying, 'You and your father will go abroad shortly. It will only be us women, staying on here. Why waste money painting the house, just for the wedding? Besides we are going to celebrate the nikah at the bride's house, not here.'

He was annoyed at her miserliness. And then, his father always nodded his head in agreement, whatever she said. 'What's the use of all their wealth? They are creatures who have no idea of how to live, he muttered to himself. The wedding would be held in four or five days. But there was no spirit of celebration in the house. Well, how could there be, if she refused to spend even a few coins? She refused to allow her own cousins to approach her. So how was she likely to welcome her husband's kinsfolk?

His father's sister, Nurnisha had visited them on the previous day. Sabia, as usual, would not talk to her directly. It was Nurnisha who came out with it, as if it were her prerogative. 'Well, sister-in-law, my nephew's wedding is approaching; don't I get a new sari?' Sikander was in the same room at the time, but pretended that he hadn't overheard.

Sabia snapped at Nurnisha, 'Did you bring up my son, by any chance? You are quick enough to claim your rights!'

Nurnisha would not give in. 'Why, do I have a right as an aunt only if I have brought him up personally? Whatever it is, he is my nephew, isn't he? And he is your only son. If you make a splash over his wedding, then we would all have a chance to congratulate him and you!'

She knew Sabia's character very well; her sister-in-law was not going to give in. All the same, Nurnisha said her say, at least for the sake of it. Even though Sabia spoke so sharply to her, she wasn't riled. Once she had gone, Sabia shouted abuse, loud and long. 'Shameless whore! Harlot woman! I don't even want to look at her because of her bad ways. How brazen she must be to come here to claim her rights, the cheap broomstick!'

Nurnisha had been married to a man who lived in a neighbouring town. He worked elsewhere in India, and owned a pavement stall selling ready-made clothes. He came home for festival seasons such as Onam, Deepavali and so on. They had a baby boy, followed by twin girls. They were reasonably well off at that time. Then suddenly her husband fell ill and died. According to the gossip, he had picked up a sexually transmitted disease. After that, Nurnisha had returned to her home town with her three children. Because Sabia would give her no support or help, Sikander's father, Sayyed rented a small house and moved her into it before leaving for Sri Lanka. He fully intended to help her, and sent her money every now and then. But Sabia put a stop to it. It was a common saying in town that Sayyed Rowther couldn't even piss without his wife's permission, he was so crazy about her.

Nurnisha struggled along with her three children, hard put even to get enough to eat. Then she began to take up with various men. Now, anywhere else, if a woman were caught doing wrong, the whole town would bring her before the panchayat. Here, though, that problem didn't arise, because the lay leaders of the community, the naattaamai and the mutthavalli, were both her clients.

In the midst of all this, her husband's younger brother heard about what was going on, and arrived post haste, to pluck away the heir belonging to his family. It still distressed Sikander to remember the scene: his aunt weeping wildly as her son was taken away from her by force. After that, something came over her, and she gave away even the girl children for adoption. Perhaps she thought, since she struggled even to put food in their mouths, there was no way she could bring them up properly and arrange marriages for them; perhaps she decided that they would have no future if they were to stay with her. Or perhaps, as Sabia said, she was afraid they would stand in the way of the life she had chosen. Only Allah knew.

Whatever it was, Sikander felt a lot of pity and compassion towards his Nurnisha Kuppi. In general, he always tended to help anyone who faced hardship. He normally kept aside half that he earned in Singapore, for charity. Mostly, he gave financial help to those who had come from India to Malaysia seeking employment, and who were struggling to find something. His friends teased him, saying, 'Dé, our Sikander is Karna's heir.' He even sent money to Nurnisha Kuppi every month through his friend Sahul, who kept a grocery store. Nurnisha would say to him, ' Listen, nephew, your mother would kill me, if she knew'. And he would answer, 'As if she's going to know, Kuppi!' He thought to himself, I must somehow contrive to give her a new sari tomorrow; poor thing, she asked Amma so hopefully.

He couldn't get back to sleep. His thought had begun in one place and taken him elsewhere. He thought of Wahida. She was far too young for him, he considered. He was not in the least happy about marrying her. From the start, he had wanted to marry only Firdaus. She was just old enough for him; they were related, too. At first he had tried to indicate his wish, obliquely. Then he left aside his shyness and asked openly. He even argued with his mother, but she absolutely refused to agree. 'What have they got there that makes you hanker after them? Am I so crazy that I will give my only son to a family who can't scrape together so much as ten sovereigns? Can Amina match our status with her wedding gifts? Can she even give a feast appropriate to a bridegroom? What has she got by way of a mother-in-law's house where you can visit and be fed and clothed? A fine wish you've got.' Besides, she was adamant that they should not break her kinship ties; he must marry only her brother's daughter.

Even now, he had no objection to marrying Firdaus. Finally he had raised the question of age. But even that had not made an impression on Sabia. Now he was tired of it all. He was also very weary, having stayed up all night to watch the play.

He could see his mother coming into the house. She was muttering a complaint, loud enough for him to hear, 'What sort of strange fever was that supposed to be? Sure, she was in a hurry, but need she have asked for help from a Hindu man?' He too felt deeply annoyed by this Siva. As soon an opportunity presented itself, he decided, they should drive him away from this street, particularly from that house. If a Kafir came to live in a Muslim street, anything might happen, he thought. And if any such thing happened it would be such a terrible disgrace. Let the wedding be over in good order, he decided, then we'll see about him. It was only after coming to this conclusion that he felt calm. Gradually he fell asleep, thinking of the previous night and the way the girl who played Valli danced.

Sabia, aware that he would not be needing any breakfast, finished her bath and adorned herself plentifully with her jewellery. At five o'clock that day it would be an auspicious time; she could have the black beads strung for the tali. She would have to invite some important people for that. Tomorrow morning, the posts for the wedding pandal would need to be fixed. There would be lots more to do, she told herself, taking up her dupatta and putting it on in readiness to go on her visits.

⊂ 26 ⊃

Rabia ran home to tell Zohra the news: Yasin Hazrat's mother, Ayishamma, had died. Instantly Zohra and Rahima covered their heads and said the prayers for the dead together, aloud, 'Inna illahi va innu ilaihi rajihœn : Peace be on your soul; you have gone ahead, we follow'. They looked at each other, wondering how soon they should go to the Hazrat's house. She was a very old lady. In recent times she had been ill and confined to bed. Zohra thought her death had been merciful. 'Poor thing, she was a good woman; her life was such a struggle,' she said to Rahima. She went on, realizing that it was time for the Luhur prayers, 'Should we go and see the family right away? If we go now, there won't be any men in the front pandal; they will all be at the prayers.' Rahima agreed it would be the best plan. 'Yes, get ready; we'll come back and say our prayers.' They picked up a dupatta each, wrapped it about themselves and set off.

Mumtaz and Nafiza were already walking along the street. 'You're going to the funeral house, aren't you? We'll go with you and keep you company,' Mumtaz said.

'Where's your mother-in-law, Sainu? Isn't she going too?' asked Rahima.

'She? Oh, she set off ages ago.' Mumtaz laughed mischievously.

Rahima re-entered the house, removed her chappals and came out again, calling to Wahida, 'If your Attha comes home, serve him his lunch, amma.' The surface of the road was so hot, it burnt her feet.

Nafiza remarked, 'Well, Akka, it looks as if you've left your chappals behind.'

'Yes, because whether it's a wedding or a funeral, people are out to pinch your chappals, aren't they? Thieving wretches!' Rahima said resentfully.

'Just wear them and come, Akka,' advised Zohra, 'We can leave them at a neighbouring house.'

'That's right; and if you visit a house nearby on your way to a funeral, they'll flay you alive,' Nafiza laughed.

What she said was true enough. Everybody knew it was very wrong to do that. Rahima smiled to herself, thinking that Zohra came out with some foolish ideas sometimes. She walked on, saying to the others, 'Good, let's carry on and not stand here wasting time.'

The house of the bereaved was only one street away; they could get there easily by going through a narrow lane. Fatima's house was just adjoining the lane. Zohra drew aside the sacking screen that covered the front door, and called out from the street, 'Is Fatima there?'

Nuramma hurried out from within. 'Who is it? Oh, it's Zohra, is it? Where are you off to? Is it to the funeral? Fatima has gone out somewhere; probably she's gone there too. Why, did you want me to give her a message?'

Rahima and Zohra said, 'Please tell her as soon as she returns, to go to our house and sweep and swab it. We'll be on our way.'

They had gone just yesterday to Madurai, to buy the wedding saris. It was a hectic time for Rahima and Zohra. Sabia had gone with them They had already given her a sum of thirty thousand rupees as the wedding dowry. Now, if the bride's family gave thirty thousand rupees, it was customary for the bridegroom's people – in this case, Sabia – to give a commission to the mosque at the rate of fifty rupees for every thousand they received. Out of the rest, setting aside the cost of the bridegroom's clothes, she had to choose three saris for the bride: a kuurai sari, for the tali tying ceremony, the muhurtam sari that she would change into, and the one she would wear when the wedding was finalized. Rahima and Zohra were greatly irritated by her firm decision to finish all her purchases within ten thousand rupees. She had one son; how could she insist on counting her pennies even in the matter of his wedding! That ten thousand was made to cover all the details of the wedding: the bride's bangles, comb, mirror, face-powder, hair-pins, chappals, and mai for her eyes. Kader, who had accompanied them throughout, had to put a stop to Zohra's and Rahima's muttered complaints.

Now, Nafiza asked eagerly, 'Did you find that the shops in Madurai had all the designs you wanted?'

'Mm. They weren't bad. They are just the usual – the ones that people from our town would choose, as a matter of course. What new things would we buy? But do come to our house at Asar time, both of you, and look at the saris.' It was the custom in their town to invite friends and kinsfolk to view a bride's trousseau, and Mumtaz and Nafiza accepted with alacrity.

They walked on silently. An oppressive heat seemed to fill the street. Hating the burning air, all four women walked on silently, with an instinctive sense that any conversation would only serve to slow them up. Although they walked together, each was wracked by her own thoughts.

A big pandal had been erected in front of Yasin Hazrat's house. They were no men about, so they did not have to cover their faces. Inside, the corpse had been laid out on a bench in the hall, the legs stretched out in a northerly direction. Hereafter they could not mention her name. The smell from the incense sticks assailed them as soon as they entered. Because she was an old woman, there was no sound of weeping; the

house was silent. Only from Ayishamma's daughter's room,
an occasional sob sounded. All four women looked at the face
of the dead woman and spoke the appropriate words from the
Koran. Because she had been ill, there was a stench from the
body. The face was fleshless and had fallen in; it had darkened.
Mumtaz and Nafiza avoided looking at it, and went straight
into the room inside.

It was a very small room, but at least ten people were sitting
there. Ayisha's daughter wept in a corner, softly, almost silently.
She had pulled her sari well over her head and covered her face
as she wept. They squeezed themselves in and sat down with
the others.

Someone tapped Rahima on her shoulder, and she turned
round. A distant relation of Kader's smiled at her and asked,
'Are you well, Rahima?' Rahima nodded. 'Is your daughter
well? It's a long time since I've seen her; I hear she's getting
married. We haven't had an invitation, though.'

Rahima was deeply embarrassed. What would Ayisha's
daughter think? She answered briefly, 'Yes, I must come and
invite you.' Quickly she turned her face away.

It seemed that someone had just arrived at the house from
elsewhere. The newcomer raised her lament in a loud wail, 'Oh
my mother, you who gave me birth, have you left me and gone
away?' All the women who were seated near the door craned
their necks to the best of their ability, trying to make out who
had come. Nafiza and Mumtaz exchanged glances. Zohra
noticed a sly smile flicker on their faces for an instant and then
disappear. It meant, 'Does an old woman who died of illness
merit all this mourning?' But the loud weeping obviously
reawakened Ayishamma's daughter's worn-out feelings. She
began to raise her voice once more, crying out, 'Amma, you've
forsaken me now.'

Nafiza whispered to Mumtaz, 'Where did you buy this sari?
It looks very good on you. I meant to ask you ages ago, but
forgot.' Zohra and all the other women could hear what she
said, quite clearly. Rahima suddenly noticed something.

Mumtaz and Nafiza had both powdered their faces lightly, and applied mai to their eyes.

Someone sitting behind Mumtaz, pulled at her dupatta, making her turn around. The woman began to tease her, 'Well, amma, I hear the bridegroom is coming home! Be ready for an energy boosting injection. Take good care of your health, now.'

She was a woman from their own town, but Rahima couldn't recognize her. She was the same age as Mumtaz. A tall woman. Although her colour was a mid-brown, her features were lively. Her large eyes revealed a certain audacity. Rahima tried her best to remember who she could be.

Mumtaz answered the woman in a low voice, 'Yes, my husband is on his way here; you, of course, have yours always by your side, so you want to make fun of me.' Her face revealed her obvious happiness at the imminent arrival of her husband. Rahima observed them closely.

Nafiza cut in, 'Better get pregnant as soon as he returns. Otherwise he'll take it out on you after such a long abstention.'

Mumtaz enjoyed all this teasing. 'Oh yes, he's abstained for all this time, did you say? You can say that about me, and I'll agree. But who knows how many hayricks are available there for men to graze upon? It's only we women…'

Zohra was deeply embarrassed by their chatter. Was this the place for all that? Annoyed, she gave a slight pinch to Nafiza's thigh which was pressed close against hers, as if to say 'Shut up.' Mumtaz saw all this from the corner of her eye, and instantly turned away. But Nafiza made it clear that she would not be repressed. She whispered into Zohra's ear as if to pacify her, 'You be quiet, Akka. What are we saying that is so strange? It's only what everyone knows.'

Rahima, who had noted the conversation between these women, as well as Zohra's attempt to intervene, said softly to her sister-in-law, 'They are irrepressible, these saithaans. Leave it, now.' But Zohra, in her turn, was aware that Nafiza and Mumtaz had overheard Rahima's words, and had assumed –

with relief – that they were spoken from generosity rather than through censure.

The woman who had teased Mumtaz, now leaned over Nafiza's shoulder and whispered, 'You stopped with two, very cleverly. Look at me, in seven years all my time has been taken up with carrying and bearing four children.' Having complained bitterly, she then went on with a smile and a wink, 'Tell me, did you rear your children on mother's milk or not? The state of your milk-machine tells me somehow, you didn't!'

Nafiza turned sideways and asked archly, 'Well? How does it seem to you? As if I did or didn't?' She carried an expression of overflowing pride.

The woman repeated, 'It definitely looks as if you didn't. Just see the state of me. If I undo my blouse, they are all over the place, like calves which have been let loose.' Rahima could hear the regret in her voice, over and above the teasing.

'Too true… I didn't breast feed… my children,' Nafiza dragged out. 'But as for you, if you had only breast fed your children, would you be in this state? You must have fed your husband as well. Machaan must have rolled his daspih beads all night. That's why yours have dropped like that.'

Rahima noticed that all the women there were enjoying the banter between these two. All of them were watching. Ayisha's daughter had stopped weeping. She lay with her head on the lap of an older woman, her face covered with the end of her sari. For a little while there was complete silence. It was a small room, in which they were all sitting together, tightly packed. Rahima was drenched in sweat. She wiped her face and the back of her neck with her dupatta, muttering to herself, 'April is over, and yet it's still fiercely hot.'

Nafiza continued her conversation with the other woman. She liked having an appreciative audience. Nafiza, Mumtaz and the other woman, all three were clearly proud of having caught the attention of those around them. Rahima was astonished and repulsed by their utter lack of fear or self-consciousness at talking in this way in a house where a funeral was taking place.

Suddenly Mumtaz asked, as if it had just struck her, 'But what is this, Najima? I hear you are quarrelling with your husband?'

It was then that Rahima realized who the woman was. She was the daughter of Davud, the butcher. When Rahima last saw her, she was plump and glowing. Now she had grown so thin, one could scarcely recognize her. Both her face and body looked pale and bloodless. Now she spoke in a low voice. 'I came here just before Ramzan, intending to stay a few days with my mother. There seems to be some problem between him and my brother, so he's refusing to come and join me. Where can he go, after all? Let him come if he wants to, otherwise not. If he does come, in the end it will only be harmful to me. He'll surely turn up of his own accord when the urge is on him. He's only in the next street. Does he even have to catch a bus to get here? If he doesn't sleep with me for a week, his 'thing' will throb with pain like a whitlow; then there's no other way, he's got to come.' Having said all this, Najima turned and looked towards Rahima.

Instantly, Rahima turned her face away with an expression of indifference. Zohra, sitting opposite her, dropped a crafty smile.

'Just listen to her telling us what she believes!' Mumtaz put her hand up to her mouth as if to contain her laughter. 'So tell me, if he gets the urge, does he have to come only to you? As of there is no one else about! How many women are there all along the countryside? Don't deceive yourself; I'm warning you.' She put on a hectoring tone, and then laughed. She laughed until the tears flowed from her eyes, and taking care not to smudge her mai, she flicked off the tears neatly, with her forefingers.

Najima, however, was not put out in the slightest. Shrugging her shoulders, she said, 'How you carry on, as if you are telling me something special! Let him do whatever he likes. If he comes, we'll take it as income; if not, we'll consider it as outgoings. That's all.' Her tone was indifferent, as if she didn't wish to pursue the subject.

Their conversation ended abruptly, as if by agreement. The room felt as if it were boiling over with the heat and the uniform breathing of all the people gathered there. Tahira's sobs still sounded, between tiny intervals. Her heavily veiled face seemed to declare firmly that she needed nobody's words of comfort, nobody's looks of sympathy.

Najima's gaze fell on one face after another, flickered, slipped and moved on. Suddenly she remembered something. 'By the way, Mumtaz, who stitches your jackets for you? I've been meaning to ask you for a long time. He does them really well. Come on, let's have a look.' She pulled off Mumtaz's head cover, and then peeled off the dupatta, and looked at Mumtaz's back and neck. Suddenly she pulled away the sari covering her chest so that the front of her blouse was displayed.

Shocked, Mumtaz burst out, 'Adiyé!' and dragged back her sari to cover herself. 'A fine thing you are doing,' she said, laughing modestly. Her face was flushed bright red. All the same, Rahima noted, she showed no signs of anger.

Najima took it all casually. 'Oh, yes! As if you possess something that nobody else has. Or do you think they will grow smaller if we look at them? I'm just asking you, who stitches your jackets for you?'

It was Nafiza who answered in place of Mumtaz. 'It's that Battani Bai, don't you know him? That's the fellow. Who makes yours? Aren't they any good?'

'I give mine to a wretched worthless fellow, who ruins the jackets and wastes the cloth. Just see how it all hangs in folds in front.' For an instant she moved her sari to show them her blouse, and then replaced it. 'But what does it matter whether we have blouses made or go without? As if any husband appreciates his wife! They only stumble and fall on you in the darkness, like goats or bulls; then they are up and off.' Her words were full of disappointment, but ended with a cackle of laughter. 'If you wear a nice sari they won't look at you; if you stand there naked they won't even notice. Isn't that so?'

It was embarrassing for Rahima to stay there. When she considered how Ayisha's daughter would react to all this, she was full of concern. She also noticed how Zohra's face was tightening more and more, with disgust. Nafiza and Mumtaz, however, seemed to be agreeing with Najima, nodding their heads. Nafiza muttered, 'There are a few who appreciate their wives, but you only see them in the cinema.'

The oppressiveness in the room, and the conversation that went on there, made Rahima gasp for breath. She felt like getting out that very instant. But she gritted her teeth and continued to sit there out of necessity, knowing that it would be impolite to leave so soon after their arrival. She remembered that they would have to say their prayers after they went home, and this added to her worries.

Yasin Hazrat's wife Saitthoon entered the room, and gazed about her, looking for a space to sit down. Rahima beckoned to her and called, 'Come here,' and moved to make some space. Saitthoon was out of breath. She was pregnant, and nearly full term. The voile sari she was wearing was twisted around her, revealing her big stomach and backside.

She had crossed the crowd and reached them in a couple of steps. She gave a great sigh, saying 'Uss ... Allah!', leaned her hands on the floor and sat down. Hearing the intermittent sobs, she asked Rahima, 'Is Tahira still weeping?'

Rahima nodded her head. Saitthoon said to Tahira soothingly, 'How will it help if a woman in your condition weeps and frets all the time?' Then she asked Rahima one question after another: 'When are you holding your daughter's nikah? How far have you got on with all the wedding jobs? Have you handed over the dowry money?'

'Yes, we've done all that. Thirty thousand rupees.' Rahima's voice betrayed her depression.

'Thirty thousand, was it?' Saitthoon's voice lingered over the amount, in astonishment. Then she changed the subject.

'Ammadi, how oppressive it is here. I didn't realize how it would be, and now I'm trapped! Please, ammas, turn the fan this way towards me, a little.' Someone found the table fan which was working in the corner of the room and turned it in Saitthoon's direction. Her whole body was wet through. Apart from her stomach, there was no flesh on her body: she was all skin and bones. Rahima felt desperately sorry for her. She already had six children. This would be the seventh. With great pity she asked, 'Why do you ruin your health like this, Saitthoon, getting pregnant every year?'

Rahima noticed that with Saitthoon's arrival, the younger women's banter had come to an end. Nor did the women sitting round about them show much interest in what the older women were saying.

'What did you ask me? Why do I get pregnant? Well, what do you suggest I do? He says I shouldn't use any kind of contraception. He says that would bring about Allah's anger upon us. You tell me now, how many more children can my body bear? What strength do I possess? You can't take hold of a pinch of flesh anywhere from my body. If I go to see the Doctoramma, she gives me a terrible scolding, saying I'm anaemic. With this one, it will have been seven children in ten years. What is the rest of my life going to be like? As for him, he quotes the Shariat and the Hadiths that children are our wealth and that it is a sin to prevent them. But who is it that bears the brunt of it all? Is it the man? Not at all; it's the woman, of course.'

'Yes, but do we do everything in life according to Allah's word? Who on earth behaves exactly as He wishes? If that were the case, this world would be a heaven. Allah has said that the giving and taking of dowry is a sin, but who listens to that? It just goes on. Even the Jamaat take no notice; they take their share and keep quiet. Those of us who have the money give it, those who don't have anything struggle hard to give what they can. We might do this in the matter of bridegrooms, but who can deliver a child every year? You just go off to the Hospital in

Gandhigram without his knowledge, and have a sterilization done. How can it be that he refuses contraception and so you just have to go on bearing children?' Rahima rebuked Saitthoon firmly.

'You can say what you like, amma, it is I who have to live with him. He'll carry on about what will happen to the whole town if the Hazrat himself breaks the rules, and sew up my mouth. Let it all go. I'll bear these children as long as I can, and go and die when I can't.' Saitthoon's voice betrayed her absolute helplessness.

Her lack of freedom and its tragic consequences touched Rahima. Once again she asked hotly, 'So if you carry on like this, how is it all going to end? Why don't you at least ask your husband that?'

'What end? We mustn't have sex. How can that be?' she gave a small smile.

Nafiza intervened at this point. 'Why don't you hang a "balloon" on him?' she cackled with laughter.

Saitthoon was shocked, and raised both hands to cover her ears. 'Allah! Allah!' she said, 'how can you talk like this, di, it's obscene.'

'What's obscene? What I said is obscene, is it? Maybe, but I think nothing is more obscene that getting pregnant and going about with a big stomach every year.'

The banter that had come to a stop with Saitthoon's arrival now looked as if it were reviving with Nafiza's intervention. One or two women agreed with Nafiza, nodding vigorously.

How could they carry on like this in a funeral house? It occurred to Rahima that because the dead woman was so old, there was nobody to make too much of a fuss.

Saitthoon repeated, 'These women have really gone too far. Just listen to their speech.'

Unwilling to lose the opportunity Zohra cut in, 'Those two would happily marry an eighteen year old lad, each.' She laughed, satisfied that she had provoked them.

But Nafiza was determined to take it as a joke. 'Zohra Akka, you always find the right occasion to say what you want. Say what you like, then.'

Now Saitthoon asked, full of concern, 'Well, Mumtaz, I hear your husband is coming home. In the name of Allah, let there be a child following his visit this time.'

Nafiza said quickly, with double meaning, 'Oh yes, he's coming soon. Mumtaz is going to unlock her box of presents. Two boxes, in fact!'

'Oh yes,' said Mumtaz resentfully. 'As if my mother-in-law will sit me down, unlock the boxes and hand me all the goodies in heaps! She even hides the fish curry she has cooked, and gives it to me one piece at a time.'

'Never mind your mother-in-law, your husband will hide a golden biscuit for you in his banyan or his underwear and give it to you secretly. He'll know you won't sleep with him otherwise,' Nafiza said.

'Ché! There's nothing like that. He's scared of his mother.' Mumtaz was vehement; she seemed to want to establish this in front of everyone.

'Why do you tell lies? Of course he must have given you presents secretly on previous occasions. He'll do it again,' Nafiza repeated.

Mumtaz was getting angry. 'Akka, I'm telling you. He has never ever hidden things away and given them to me secretly. If he had done that, it would be wrong, haraam.'

Saitthoon calmed her down and put an end to the argument. 'Ada, it's only your husband who gives you gifts, it isn't anyone else, is it? Of course, you won't admit to taking them. But why do you get so cross about it?'

Nafiza had not expected that Mumtaz would get so annoyed at her teasing. She had only spoken about what happened normally; why should Mumtaz take offence? She couldn't understand it. Her face fell with disappointment. What an actress, she thought to herself, and refused to speak after that.

A surprisingly long silence fell amidst them. It seemed to

Rahima that Death had lost its meaning and sat above Ayisha like a caricature of itself. Although the old woman had met it so naturally, yet Death retained an impenetrable strangeness. It seemed to look at the silent faces roundabout, seeking a way to make them fear it.

Rahima looked at Zohra as if to say, 'Let's go.' Zohra indicated she too wished the same, and so they prepared to leave, saying 'Asallaam aleikum' to everyone there. Nafiza and Mumtaz rose to their feet to go with them.

The hall outside was full of women, all of them past their middle-age. Mumtaz's mother-in-law was there too, seated in a corner. As soon as she saw them, she pulled her sari over her head and joined them in one leap. They covered their faces as the crossed the pandal outside, now full of men, and came out into the street.

'I've been wanting to leave for a long time,' Sainu said to Rahima, 'but I felt too embarrassed to go on my own; I knew there would be all those men outside.'

Rahima said, 'You must have come here quite a while ago. Did you have to wait all this time?'

Sainu didn't like her daughter-in-law to talk to any one. She was afraid that others would fill her with bad advice and cause conflict within the family. Her sudden haste now suggested that she had waited all this time only to pounce on Mumtaz and take her away. Rahima often said to Zohra, 'As if Mumtaz needs anyone to teach her anything. Poor thing, she's so innocent, isn't she!'

Sainu was annoyed and cross. 'We should have gone back ages ago. Who knows how Farida managed with those two. If both of us leave the house at the same time, who will keep her company? Farida is left all alone!'

Mumtaz muttered, out of her hearing, 'As if someone is going to carry off this woman's daughter!'

Rahima felt comforted as they came out into the light after having been trapped indoors for so long. The fresh air falling on her face felt good. She enjoyed a sense of liberation, as if freed from a severe repression. Her tongue was dry. She thought to herself she would have a bath as soon as she reached home, and rid herself of the sultriness they had experienced. Her mind felt restless, leaping from one thought to another. As she walked, she remembered the banter that had gone on in a house of bereavement. The way these women had talked wasn't anything new. Whenever four women got together, the conversation would be the same. It wasn't just these two; most of the women in this town laughed and joked in the same way. She knew it well. But it astonished her that they could speak like that wherever they wanted. How was it that they could not feel any fear in the presence of death, nor recognize the truth it spoke? She pitied them for their incapacity to think at any length about death. Zohra tended to get angry with them, but Rahima felt sorry. When they reached home, it was Zohra who scolded them roundly, as if she alone were the guardian of good behaviour among all women, and these two were born for the sole purpose of ruining it. Rahima was exhausted by the time she had calmed her down by repeating, 'Leave it Zohra; let them say what they please and go their way.'

❧ 27 ❧

Sainu and her daughter-in-law returned to their home just as Mutthu came out. Sainu gave him a sharp look as if to ask, 'What are you doing here?' Immediately, he said, 'Ayya asked me to look for Rabia here and bring her home, that's all.' His wide face seemed to Mumtaz careworn and ridden with anxiety. She stopped short at the threshold, observing him closely.

Sainu spoke with annoyance, 'If that's the case, you could stand outside and call out, couldn't you, why must you go into the house?' Mumtaz kept quiet and hurried into the house, smiling to herself as if to say, 'Today this fellow is a dead man.'

'Amma, I did stand here and try calling out, but no one at all answered, that's why…' he said.

'Everything has to keep to its own place, da. Mm… What good does it do talking to you. The times are such. In the old days our servants and labourers would only approach their masters with their shoulder-cloths tied around their waist. But nowadays…' she complained. 'Yes, yes, just go away now,' she told him, and went inside. She dipped a small vessel into the water trough just by the entrance to the house and washed her arms and legs three times, up to her elbows and knees. Then she washed her face three times before entering the house.

Farida sat on a chair reading a book, with her legs up, laid across the sofa. Her davani had slipped, baring her breast sideways. Sainu was furious. 'Look at the way the she-donkey sits, without any notion of seemliness or decency,' she thought to herself. Aloud, she said angrily, 'Amma, you're a girl; cover yourself decently and put your legs down when you are seated. Don't act as if you are a boy.'

Immediately Farida put her legs down and wrapped the davani carefully about her. Mumtaz was aware that her mother-in-law was annoyed about something that day, and that because of that everyone in the household was bound to get a scolding. She took cover in her own room hoping to escape her share by spending the whole day out of Sainu's sight. Besides, because Suleiman was expected home shortly, she had, in any case, to clean her room and decorate it as best she could. She thought of him and felt a sudden thrill run through her body. She took out the bunch of keys that were tucked in at her waist, opened her wardrobe, and took out the letter he had written her most recently. She locked the door, lay down on her bed and began to read it. By now, she had read and reread it about ten times. Indeed, she almost knew it by heart. In her last letter to him, she had written out for him the entire song that Sheikh Muhammad had sung, beginning:

My Macchaan who took ship and went away,
who fills my dreams,

my longed for Macchaan,
when will you return to me?
I wait for you.

After he had read it, he had written this reply, teasing her mercilessly. She had decided that this time she would not allow him to go away again. She had written this to him, most clearly. For how long was she to spend her youth in solitude?

Let him tease her as much as he liked; after all, he was her husband. Besides – insha Allah! – she hoped that this year at least, she would conceive. It worried her that if he kept on coming and going in this fashion, it might take many years for her to bear a child. When consulted, the doctor-amma had declared, make your husband stay with you for a year at the very least. She had told him all this in her letter, as well. So far, he seemed to be in agreement with this.

Sainu, sitting down in the hall, called out to Madina, intending to send her to fetch her betel-box. It was Farida who answered. 'Madina has gone out, I don't know where.'

'Where is she holding court, in all this heat?' her mother demanded. She thought for an instant. 'So were you alone all this time?' Sainu's voice sounded agitated, bursting out of swirling thoughts.

'Why? Rabbi and Siddhi were here all the time, weren't they? They went off to sleep just now. I gave them their food and put them to bed. She didn't turn up even to eat her meal.' Farida spoke casually.

Sainu was uneasy. She trembled to think what it could mean for Mutthu to be coming out of the house at a time when Farida had no company. If this wretched daughter of hers were to get into some kind of trouble, what was Sainu to do? If any one had seen him, they would definitely make up all kinds of stories. And why wait for that when within the house itself there was enough mischief in the shape of Mumtaz! It was enough for her, wasn't it? How she would twist the truth and spread it about! Oh Allah, Sainu said to herself, cringing at the thought.

At the same time she tried to calculate what could have been the real reason for his coming inside the house. Although she believed her daughter, she could not find it in her heart to trust her youth. Supposing something disastrous happened! Her stomach quaked. Let Suleiman come. The very next month they should get hold of a man and hand this girl over to him. It was only after she had made this decision that she felt a little at peace.

She fetched her betel-box herself, leaned against a pillar and stretched out her legs. Her whole body ached sorely. Siddhikka woke up and staggered out. The spittle which had dribbled out of her mouth while she slept had dried into white lines at the side of her mouth. 'Amma, Amma,' she said as she squatted by her mother, spreading out her skirt. Sainu scolded, 'Roll your skirt up when you sit down, di.'

'Amma, Amma, where did you go? Where did you go?' Siddhikka asked repeatedly. 'Farida hit me. She hit me.' She pointed towards Farida. Her eyes would not stay still, but rolled around everywhere.

'Where would I go? I was just visiting close by. Farida, why did you hit the child, di?' Sainu asked, pretending to be cross.

Whenever Sainu returned home from an outing, Siddhikka had to claim her privilege. She would make the same complaint over and over again until Farida had been reprimanded. So Sainu scolded Farida, then lifted up Siddhikka's long skirt and wiped her mouth. 'Did you eat properly,' she began. Then realizing the skirt was damp, she started. 'Have you gone and wet yourself? And in broad daylight too! What's the matter with you, stupid! It's all my fate!' Sainu hit herself on head, calling out, 'Farida, just look at this one!'

Farida had been observing all this, even as she continued to read. 'Go on, Amma. You clean her up yourself. I can't do it,' she said resentfully. She returned to her book.

'Of course, di. Of course I have to accept the fate that has been dished out to me. If I want to fall down on my bed for just an instant to ease this stitch at my waist, can I do it? What use is this daughter-in-law I brought home? She's shut up in her own room, cosy as a brooding hen. That's the boon she brought with her. And I just have to accept it.' Sainu turned all her fury on to Mumtaz, and began to shout loudly. But Mumtaz never emerged from her room, although she heard it all.

Calling Siddhikka a crazy idiot a thousand times over, Sainu changed her clothes, and began to clean the room where she had been sleeping. Fortunately Rabbi had slept turned to one side, and so had not been soaked. Siddhi, totally unaware of all the confusion about her, was happily pulling lice out of her hair.

Madina came running into the house. Immediately she screwed up her nose, saying, 'What is it? What a stink!' She asked her mother, 'Did Siddhi wet herself?'

Sainu had not been able to vent her fury on anyone so far, and had been lamenting aloud, all alone. Now she had the satisfaction of having found a victim. 'You slut, you vagabond, where the hell have you been? Why does a she-donkey have to have legs? I'll break them off and stick them in the fire, see if I don't. You think you are a small child, do you, to wander about as you please? Look at your chest, all swollen like that! You've grown up into a woman, shouldn't you have some idea of decent conduct? How dare you leave the house and go away, when your sister is alone in the house?' Sainu was shouting in a fury, the words flooding out of her, without a break. Her heavy body heaved and she gasped for breath.

Farida was incensed. She couldn't bear to see Madina standing there shocked, holding on to the pillar. She spoke up for herself loudly. 'Why have you been shouting and scolding like this from the time you came home, as if something terrible had happened? So what if I was alone in the house? Did anyone carry me off?' A note of anxiety crept into her voice. 'The doctor has warned you of high blood pressure. Shouldn't you have some patience? You grow older but you don't seem to be any the wiser.'

Sainu calmed down at last and sat down quietly. Madina and Farida felt a stab of pity to see her like that. Nobody said anything more. Farida grabbed Madina by the hand and dragged her into the kitchen. She scolded her, 'Well, di? When you are with Rabia, don't you even remember to eat? I'm asking because I really don't understand it.' Then she put a plate of rice next to her sister, and poured some kuzhambu over. Madina began to eat without saying anything. 'Look at your skirt,' Farida went on, 'it's all covered in dust and leaves. Have you been playing in the mud? If Amma had noticed, you would have got another shouting. And by the way, there was a tin of almonds here. Did you make off with it?'

Madina gave her a stealthy look and admitted it. 'Yes, I took it to Rabia.'

'You know what will happen to you, don't you, if Amma knows that? Now listen carefully to what I tell you. Annan is coming home tomorrow, you know that don't you? He totally disapproves of all this loafing around and playing about. Just be careful. Don't get punished within an inch of your life.' Having given this advice out of her anxiety for her little sister, Farida went off to her own room.

Just as soon as she had finished eating, Madina ran up to her mother. Sainu was deep in thought, her forehead wrinkled. Madina went to her sister instead and said, 'Akka, Zohrakka has invited Amma and Mumtazanni to go there this evening to look at the wedding saris and things.' She ran off again into the street.

* * *

Rahima had asked Madina to go with Rabia to fetch the tailor in order to make some of the wedding clothes. When Madina arrived there, she found Rabia all ready, her face washed and powdered. It was then she realized her own unkempt state. Thinking that her own house was in too much of an uproar, she said to Rabia. 'Just wait a moment, let me wash my face as well.' She borrowed a towel to wipe her face, and tidied herself. Wahida powdered her face for her.

As they set off on their way, Ahmad turned up. As soon as he saw them, he ran up and said, 'Ei, will you come with me? I'll teach you to ride a bike. Here's the money, to hire one.' He opened his hand to show them. Rabia looked at Madina uncertainly. Madina would not look directly at Ahmad, but addressed herself to Rabia alone. 'My brother is coming home tomorrow. He doesn't approve of all that,' she said.

Rabia really did want to learn to cycle, but she didn't have the time just then. She was needed at home to run errands all the time. She said, 'Not just now, Ahmad. Let the wedding be over. I'll come after that.' Her face had shrunk in disappointment.

He must have felt badly, too. But hiding his feelings, he walked along with them, asking, 'Very well then; but where are you off to, now?' When they told him, he said, 'Very good; off you go,' as if he were giving them permission. Then he ran away, calling out, 'Rabia, come to our house later on. I'll show you all the new toys that my Attha has bought.' Rabia noticed that his words and actions were all meant to make Madina feel excluded.

The tailor's house was two streets away. On the way there, Madina asked, 'Will you be accompanying the bride when she leaves for the groom's house, after the wedding?'

'Yes, I'm going with her. Periamma has asked me to. And I'll see my Chitthi there.'

' How long will you be away?'

'I don't know. They were saying at home, they will bring her back for the seventh day feast.'

'I'll find it hard, not having anyone to play with,' said Madina. 'But in any case, hereafter I won't be allowed to play about. My brother hates it if I even step into the street. He scolds me saying girls shouldn't play. He is always telling me to read the Koran and to pray. Just like your mother.' Madina sounded worried.

'But your brother is here only for two months, isn't he? It won't be too bad,' Rabia consoled her friend.

'No, no, ' Madina contradicted Rabia hastily. 'It seems he's going to stay for a year this time. It seems he'll go away again only after Anni has had a baby. They were saying so at home. But Rabia, don't you get a baby anyway, once you are married? So why does he have to stay here? Do you understand it?' But Rabia was quiet for a while, making no answer, and then twisted her lips and shrugged, as if to say, 'I don't know.'

By this time they had reached the tailor's house. The front doors to the house were closed, though, and a heavy lock held them together. 'It looks as if nobody's at home,' Madina said. They looked at each other, wondering what they should do next.

It was a small tiled house. They both knew that there was a back entrance leading to a backyard with a cowshed and a lime tree. They decided to find out whether it was open. And indeed, it was, when they made their way there. It usually was left open for the cow to be brought home in the evenings. They went in. It was a small door-frame and they had to bend low in order to go through. There was cow dung spread about everywhere in the backyard. Feeling repulsed by this, they trod carefully on tiptoes and reached the back door to the house. It was bolted from within. But Rabia was charmed by the chattering of birds from the lime tree and its cool shade which spread all over the backyard. Gesturing to Madina to be quiet, she craned her neck and gazed upwards, searching for a bird's nest. Seeing the clusters of lime fruit which hung within reach, she reached up and plucked a couple of lime leaves, rubbed them between her fingers, then breathed in their scent deeply. When Madina saw this, she too reached up in her turn and plucked a couple of fruit. Rabia was distressed by this. 'Please don't, di,' she said, 'let's go home; someone might see.'

'I tell you no one will see. Wait, let's take just four fruit. It's so tempting.' Madina plucked a few more.

'Ammadi, it's wrong to steal. I don't want any part in this. And don't think that no one will see. Have you forgotten about the malaks who sit on your two shoulders and keep watch all the time?' Rabia made a last attempt to stop Madina, by reminding her of the recording angels.

Madina stopped for a moment. There were six fruit in her hands now. Deciding to keep just those, she turned to go, calling out, 'Very well, come then, let's go.'

Rabia stared at the fruit in Madina's hands, as if to ask, 'But what about those?'

Madina tried to pacify Rabia. 'What's done is done. We'll take these with us now. We'll pay for them when we come back tomorrow.' It was after this that Rabia was satisfied. Her expression of distress and confusion cleared away. She came outside with Madina. They looked at both sides of the street to make sure they had not been seen, and set off at a quick pace.

The oppressive heat seemed to enclose the street as if in a pandal; the light dazzled their eyes. The burning rays of the sun seemed to follow them even as they hastened to cross it. Its hot hand seemed to hold them in a tight embrace. As she heard the call for the Asar prayers sounding from a distance, Madina clasped Rabia's hand and walked on silently. She too knew about the malaks who kept watch from her shoulders. The Hazrat had told them a lot about it, in the madrasa. The malaks on the right shoulder would count up her good deeds, while the malaks on the left would record her bad deeds. Everything would be added up at Judgement day. Allah would send her to hell if the bad deeds were more and to heaven if the good deeds won. If she wanted to go to the highest heaven, the seventh one called Jannath-ul Firdaus, she would have to do very many good deeds. She felt deeply remorseful for having stolen the fruit, knowing all this.

Rabia broke into her thoughts. 'Why do you keep on worrying about it? We've decided to pay for them tomorrow.'

Madina came round. 'No, its not that. I was thinking about my brother. It seems I must wear a davani all the time, from tomorrow. Amma has told me not to be seen without it, hereafter. It seems Annan will scold me otherwise. Hereafter he won't even allow me to go to the cinema.' The memories of her brother, etched in her mind, were all to do with fear and dread. His very visit felt like a terrible nuisance.

'If you are definitely going to wear a davani from tomorrow, then I'll do it too,' Rabia offered gladly. 'We'll do it together, shall we?' she repeated, consolingly.

Madina's face brightened immediately. 'Truly?' she asked. 'I felt shy to appear in a davani all at once. I was afraid that all the women would tease me and say something embarrassing. Now at last I feel alright about it.' She held Rabia's fingers even more tightly. The tightness of that clasp indicated her assumption that Rabia would do anything for her, she belonged to her.

⟡ 28 ⟡

The women had gathered in a crowd in Rabia's house and filled it with noise and bustle. Four or five mats had been scattered around in the hall, on which Mumtaz, Nafiza, Sainu, Saura, Fatima and the rest sat. They were examining the silk saris which had been laid out in the middle. Zohra was pouring out tea for all the visitors. Wahida sat on a chair in one corner, her head covered and bowed down. Rabia ran up and sat at her feet, and began to watch the fun. As soon as Rahima saw her, she asked, 'Did you fetch the tailor?' She didn't wait for an answer, but walked on, towards the kitchen.

'No, Periamma; the house is locked. I'll go there later,' Rabia called after her, loudly. At the same time, Nafiza asked eagerly, 'Macchi, how much did this kuurai sari cost?'

Rahima scolded Rabia, 'Adiyé, don't shout like that, you'll tear my ear-drums'. Still in the kitchen, she turned towards

Nafiza and said, 'The bill is right there. Check for yourself.'
She came out of the kitchen and sat down with the others.

'No, I just wanted to know if you managed to get a discount.
But they are all very beautiful, all the saris,' Nafiza said.

'It's all pure silk. We bought all these at the Co-optex shop.
It has to be good zari, doesn't it, which won't blacken. These
are saris must last a long time and wear well.' Rahima spoke
with pride, but those words, 'last a long time and wear well'
seemed to press upon her heart painfully.

'This onion-skin coloured sari will really suit Wahida's
complexion,' said Mumtaz, 'and the material is really soft and
fine, isn't it?' Nafiza nodded in agreement.

Fatima asked, 'Well, Akka, how many thousands did it come
to altogether, for all the saris?

'It came to a lot, certainly. Then there's the expenses for all
the jackets and petticoats, on top of that.'

Sainu appeared concerned. 'Why on earth did you spend so
much money on a single sari? With her slim build, will your
daughter be able to carry all this zari? You could have bought
two or three, each costing less.'

Mumtaz's face flushed with anger when she heard this. She
whispered to Nafiza, 'Just listen to the wretched woman! When
my family gave her my dowry money, she handed the mosque
what was due, and kept the rest for herself. She chose a sari for
me in the worst possible taste.'

Zohra gestured to her to keep quiet. Mumtaz was an
audacious one. She was prepared to say the worst things about
the person sitting right next to her. Zohra said softly, 'It's quite
usual in this world to say one thing to people's faces and quite
another behind their backs. But you'll say a thousand things,
looking them right in the eye.'

Saura turned the saris over in her hands and said, 'They are
all beautiful. Your daughter will live like a queen. May she
have a long life and bear many children.' She raised her hands
and blessed Wahida from a distance.

Rahima was much moved by the emphatic words with which

Saura blessed her daughter; tears gathered in her eyes involuntarily. Wiping them away, she said, 'Go up to her, Akka, touch her and bless her.'

'This wretched pain in my knee stops me from getting to my feet. I'll touch and bless the child as I leave,' Saura assured her, sipping her tea.

Rahima asked Sainu with interest, 'Is Suleiman due to arrive tomorrow morning?' She was too scared to ask Mumtaz. If she were to do that, she knew, Sainu would fall on her in a devilish fury saying, 'How dare you ignore his own mother and ask that woman?'

Now Mumtaz turned her face away with a little smile. Sainu said, 'Yes, he'll be here in time for the morning Bajar prayers. And you know something, Rahima? Do you remember his business associate in Singapore, Abdulla?'

'Yes, I remember him. Isn't he the old man who married three times?' Rahima was startled. 'Why, has something happened to him?' she asked.

'Don't be silly. What can be wrong with him, he's as firm as stone; he must have drunk some elixir. No, the fellow is coming home to get married for the fourth time, it seems. How do you like it?' She clapped her hands and laughed.

Shocked, everyone there raised their hands to their chins exclaiming, 'Is that true? What a man!'

Zohra couldn't believe it. 'Go on, Akka, you're joking!' she said.

'Adi, I'm telling you it's true. You just ask her.' Sainu pointed to Mumtaz.

'Yes, Zohrakka. "He" wrote to us to say so.'

Nafiza said to Mumtaz, 'But how is it possible? Can he even get it up? Isn't it surprising?' She made a face of extreme astonishment.

'Why else is he getting married? You don't have to be so surprised,' Mumtaz assured her.

Wahida was squirming with embarrassment. Rahima realized this and sent her away from there, saying, 'You go to your room now, amma. if you sit up like that for such a long time, your waist will ache.'

'Look at this Rahimakka! Her daughter feels embarrassed, so she sends her away. She's going to know all about it in four or five days. Let her know right away. What is she going to lose?' Mumtaz cut in, and said to Wahida, 'You just stay, amma.' But Wahida had been desperate for her mother's permission, and took to her heels.

Nafiza shouted after her, 'Adiyé, don't fall down, be careful. The bride shouldn't break an arm or a leg.'

Just then one of the men putting up the pandal outside the house called very politely from the threshold, 'Amma, please may I have some water to drink?'

It was then that Zohra noticed Rabia sitting there, in the room. 'So here you are, watching people's mouths,' she said crossly, chasing her away. 'A fine thing! Get up, don't stay here listening to other people's conversations. Go and fetch some water in a chombu and take it to the men outside.' Rabia had no wish to leave. Reluctantly she got to her feet and went.

'Your daughter is a serious one. Smart at all she does. Did you notice how keenly she was listening?' Sainu's praise of Rabia was tongue-in-cheek.

Nafiza was anxious not to break off the conversation, and returned to the same subject as before. 'When that man came home last time, didn't he get married, and even bring his bride round to your house? It must have been only two years ago. Is he going to marry another girl so soon after that?' Her long lashes fluttered, mimicking an excessive surprise.

Mumtaz said, 'I tell you, yes. None of the three he married has died. They live right here, in the town. He has built each one a separate house, and set up a separate household. He's got lots of money; he enjoys life. Who knows how long this one will last. And they are all young girls. There's no lack of young virgins in poor families, of course. But one thing: the girls all have to be fair-skinned and pretty. Ayya makes up his mind only after seeing their photos.' Her words poured out in uncontrolled anger and contempt.

'That's exactly why I asked whether that man has the stamina to sleep with a young girl,' Nafiza stressed. 'Poor girls! Who knows how they suffer, married to an old man!' She put on an expression of concern, and laughed.

'Don't you worry, Nafizakka. He'll eat almonds and pistachios to build up his virility,' Fatima teased.

'Why are you getting at me di? I'm only speaking the truth. If a man who is about to retire marries a young girl, you have to feel sorry for the girl, don't you?'

Rahima agreed. 'These fellows make these marriages and speed off on their own. The poor girls lose their way and find themselves doing wrong things.'

'That's ... not possible... in this case.' Sainu dragged out the words in emphasis. 'When he's not in town, they aren't allowed to step out past the threshold. He's employed watchmen to guard them. He's warned them he'll shoot them if anything happens. All the household servants are women. It seems the wives must stay indoors as if they were prisoners.'

Shocked, Rahima remarked, 'If he goes on like this, where will it end?'

Zohra had an answer to this. 'Maybe this old man thinks that he'll do the same as the Holy Prophet, who married eleven times.'

Rahima murmured, 'But how long ago was that? The circumstances were different then. What is the need for this wretched man to do this now?'

'All right, so he gets married. But immediately after that he brings his wife and shows her off shamelessly, to each and everyone. When he comes on this visit, the moment the marriage is over, he'll bring her, to our house and to Saurakka's, expecting a feast.' Mumtaz laughed, but her voice betrayed her worry about preparing a feast for the wretched man.

Rabia sat on the outside thinnai, eavesdropping on the conversation. Her fear that her mother would scold her if she went inside kept her itching feet well shackled. She stayed outside, but listened avidly.

Nuramma stumbling along the street unsteadily, came up to their front door. Seeing Rabia there, she said to her, 'Well, woman, what are you doing here all by yourself?' She went inside hesitantly. Rahima, sitting inside the room, observed Nuramma approaching, and instantly felt sorry for her. A small and trembling body. White hair. A stained voile sari. She approached them with a scowl upon her face, gesturing as if she were cracking her knuckles. As she came near, both Rahima and Zohra greeted her very hospitably. 'Come, come, Nuramma, come and sit down.'

Nuramma replied, 'I'm coming.' But when she drew near, she had her complaint to make. 'Well, ladies, didn't you think that I too was anxious to see the wedding trousseau and dowry? Nobody sent for me!' Then she made everyone move aside, 'Make room for me, please, let me sit down.' She chose to sit at the centre, as if it were her right.

Fatima complained in her turn. 'I didn't tell you because you can neither see anything properly, nor get about easily. I thought let her just fall on her bed and stay there. But of course you caught scent of what was going on, and turned up, didn't you.' She muttered to herself, 'The old hag will insist on doing what she likes.'

Rahima calmed her down. 'Let her be. She's an old lady, she has her whims and wishes. Let her see everything and give her blessings.'

Nuramma went on, 'That Sridevi of our house, what's it to her? I'll come and go as I please in my Mudalali's house. Why should she mind? Now where are they? Which ones are for what occasions? Show me, let me see.'

With great care, Rahima took out each sari one by one, and described them to Nuramma. Seeing her explaining everything so patiently Saura laughed and said, 'Its like talking to four dumb idiots at the same time.' But Rahima stopped her with a look, and went on, 'Look at this one, it the kuurai sari. This one is for the tali tying. And this one will be for the seventh day feast.'

'Wait a minute, you haven't told me the prices.'

'Oh the prices? Wait, I will check them for you,' Rahima looked out the bills and gave out all the prices. She did it all very seriously and intently, paying no heed to the glances which Mumtaz and Nafiza exchanged. Finally she asked, 'Well, Nuramma, are they all right?'

'Whatever my darling daughter wears must look good on her. But these are wonderful. May she wear them like a queen.' Nuramma gave her heart-felt blessings. But she added, 'They are very expensive, that's the only thing. But good zari is like that these days. In those days, you'd get this same sari, with exactly the same zari, at a moderate price. How much it costs now!'

Enjoying watching all this, Saura finished her tea with relish and leaned across to put the tumbler away to one side. Then she said to Sainu, with a show of much concern, 'Ele, Sister-in-law, you must get Farida married as soon as Suleiman comes home this time. Don't postpone it any more.'

Sainu smouldered with anger at the sudden concern for Farida that her sister-in-law appeared to show. Wasn't she the one who refused to give her daughter Sherifa to Suleiman, her own brother's son? Didn't she choose to make an alliance with her sister's family instead? What did she care for Farida, she thought, resentfully. She didn't show it outwardly however, saying instead briefly, 'Yes. Insha Allah! It's with that intention that my son is coming home.' Saura understood that Sainu did not wish to hear anything more about the matter. She kept silent, not wishing to provoke Sainu's displeasure.

Zohra invited all of them to go and see the dowry which had been laid out in one of the inner rooms. 'Here we come,' said Saura, getting to her feet first. But it was a difficult business for her to heave up her heavy body, or to walk about; all the rest had arrived in the room ahead of her. Fatima teased her mother, 'Just look at my Amma, she pushed in front of everyone else. There's no stopping her when she's so keen.'

Nuramma, for her part, scolded her daughter fondly. 'Why don't you shut up? Why should you start burning up if I come here first? May your bad thoughts all be foiled!'

Mats covered the floors of the large room, on which silver vessels had been carefully arranged all round. Water-pots, ranging in size. Shallow serving vessels, the same. Tiffin boxes, from three compartments to five. Everything in brightly shining silver. In one corner stood a wardrobe. Next to it one large suitcase and two smaller ones. A Koran laid on a cauldron. Hurricane lamps. There were objects displayed all over the room. Saura asked, after inspecting everything, 'But where's the chinaware?'

'That's all been packed into the card-board box you see there, in the corner. They mustn't break, must they?' Zohra pointed. The card-board box stood next to the cooker, also in its box.

Rahima asked, out of courtesy, 'Well, Akka, is all this sufficient, or need we provide anything more? Please let us know if anything is lacking. The bed and its mattress have already been ordered, and will be delivered directly to the bridegroom's house.'

Sainu said, giving a big sigh, 'You only have one daughter. Who will you give gifts to, if not to her? Your sister-in-law Sabia is a fortunate one. She gained a bride with a beautiful face and beautiful wealth. I know perfectly well what a self-willed lady she is. She set her heart on making this alliance with her younger brother's daughter, and she succeeded. It was destined for her that she should get a daughter-in-law with such a dowry.' Everyone there understood that she intended to denigrate Mumtaz in front of them.

Mumtaz gritted her teeth and whispered to Nafiza, 'The slut! Given the position she's in, it's a wonder she got a daughter-in-law at all! On top of that she makes these innuendos.'

Rahima hastened to change the course of the conversation. She said to Sainu, 'But you haven't seen the everyday saris yet, have you? Look they are all in the wardrobe here.' She took a key from the bunch at her waist and unlocked the wardrobe. Two of the shelves were full of saris, all of them of textiles from abroad.

Zohra said proudly, 'There are a hundred in all. All of them are made of foreign textiles. Not a single local-made sari.'

'Where did you pick these up, Akka?' Mumtaz asked.

Nafiza answered her. 'Don't worry, your lord and master will bring you saris like these from Singapore. But where will we people pick them up? In our own Burma Bazaar, of course.' She looked at Rahima for confirmation.

Rahima nodded. 'Of course it costs more if you buy them here. But what to do? They speak badly of us if there are local saris in the trousseau.'

'You do your utmost, but your in-laws will never be satisfied. No, never, never, never...' Nuramma lingered over the words, turning them into a song while she waved her hands and began to dance.

Her antics made everyone laugh. Nobody could match her at her jokes and her teasing, her prancing and dancing. There were always a few women surrounding her and enjoying her goings-on. Fatima was afraid that she would get into trouble some day, and warned her about it. She also worried because Nuramma was also given to spreading gossip.

Nuramma, encouraged by the women's laughter, begin to sing to a tune rather like a song of MGR's, 'You sister-in-law is a disgrace... Such a woman I've never seen, such a woman I've never heard...Such a woman is she.' She went on, turning towards Saura and Sainu, 'They say, "The cash stays in her hand, but the dosai has gone into her mouth." Such a woman is she. Well, what am I saying? Isn't that *kirik* ?'

The two women agreed, and egged her on.

Although Rahima had known beforehand that no one had a good opinion of Sabia, she was troubled by what was being said now. She was afraid, too of how Sabia might treat Wahida. It struck her that there was very little to rejoice in this wedding over which they were spending so much effort and money. Still, she continued to look her usual serene self, knowing that the slightest expression of anxiety on her face would distress and upset her daughter. She had to struggle very hard to achieve this.

They all returned to the hall and settled down. Wahida came down from her room and joined them. Saura alone seated herself on the sofa rather than the floor, saying, 'I can't sit down on the floor anymore, amma, I won't ever be able to get up again.' When she sank down, the sofa creaked, causing Nafiza and Mumtaz to exchange an amused glance. Fatima rose to her feet and left, saying, 'I must be going now. I have to cook the evening meal.'

Nafiza, who had been waiting for her to go away, started on Nuramma immediately, 'Come on, Nuramma, tell us all about your wedding and what happened on your first night.'

Nuramma's voice was bubbling over with enthusiasm as she began. 'Come, come, my princess, you want to hear my story? Listen, I'll tell you.' She stretched out her legs pleasurably. 'Ele, Saura, push the betel tray this way.' She took the tray, plucked the stem off a leaf, rolled it round some chopped betel nuts and popped it into her mouth. Instantly her mouth took on a blood-red hue.

'Just see this, my women!' Nuramma opened her toothless mouth which looked like the shell of an empty gourd, and stuck her tongue out. 'Look how red it is even now, at this age, and imagine how red it must have been in my youth! My Macchaan used to be so delighted by it. My beloved Macchaan who has left me and gone.' Lingering over her words, she was carried away, and wept a little. Then calling to mind she was at a bridal ritual, she quickly smiled instead.

'Listen, all you women, do you know how pretty I was when I was young? So pretty I was. They talk of the fourteenth day moon. I was as bright as that. Don't judge my looks as they are now and think I'm telling lies. There are women here who are as old as I am. They know how fair-skinned and beautiful I used to be.' She raised her stick-like arms and pointed to Saura and Sainu.

Those two tried to suppress their laughter, and encouraged her, 'Yes, yes, carry on.'

'And who do you think my husband was? Don't imagine he was any old ordinary lad. No, no, he was a wealthy man of Singapore. He was doing business and having a great time in Singapore until this wretched war came along. The world war, that is. That was when he left everything, shook out his shoulder cloth, threw it over his shoulder and fled, fearing for his life. He never returned to Singapore. Here he was desperate to earn his livelihood, he wandered everywhere, he struggled and struggled, and finally turned up at my Attha's.' She looked about, to see where she could spit the betel juice that had gathered in her mouth.

'Ayyayyo, don't spit anywhere here,' Zohra called out anxiously. She ran and fetched the spittoon that was under the thinnai in front of the house and placed it next to Nuramma. 'Here, use this.'

Nuramma pursed her lips, gathered her spittle and spat it in a stream. 'Where was I?' she asked, trying to get back to her story.

Zohra's face betrayed her disgust. She had begun to worry about cleaning out the spittoon, it was clear from her expression. The spittoon was never needed by anyone in their house. Very occasionally, when they cooked fish, or made a biriyani, Karim would chew betel. The spittoon came into use on that day, and was washed and put away at once. Were Karim to see that it had been used by Nuramma, he would certainly ask to have it flung away. Zohra told herself that she would ask Fatima to see to it. She was at peace once she had made this decision. 'You were just saying he came to your father,' she said, picking up the thread for Nuramma.

Nuramma took it up eagerly, 'Yes, yes. And then...'

The Modinaar's call to prayers sounded from the mosque, 'Allahu Akbar...'

Zohra immediately admonished everyone there. 'Sh! There's the call to prayers. No one must talk. Everyone keep silent, please.' Hastily she pulled her sari over her head. Swiftly, the rest of the women did the same. Fearing Zohra's anger, Nuramma stopped chewing. This made Nafiza want to giggle, and she struggled to control herself.

Once the call for prayers was over, they all raised their hands, each praying silently. Nuramma waited until this was over, but then began again in haste, lest they all disperse to finish their prayers at their own homes. 'And then what happened was this. You know my father kept a butcher's shop. Well, he turned up there to run errands for my father. And then you know what happened? One day my father left his butcher's knife at home. When he was just about to slaughter a calf, he looked for it in the shop. It wasn't there, of course, so he called out to "him", "You there, hurry, run home and fetch my knife." So he came running at top speed to our house. He could draw breath only when he reached there.'

Nafiza broke in at this point, deliberately. 'You haven't told us his name though. What was it?'

'How can I pronounce it di?' Nuramma was coy. Then, giving in, she said. 'All right. It's two fifties plus another of the Holy Prophet's names.'

'What does that mean?' Nafiza pretended not to understand.

'Work it out, amma. What does two fifties make? That's his name.'

'Oh ho, it's a hundred, isn't it? *Nur*, no? *Nur Muhammad.* Very good.'

'That's it. You've got it. Where was I? Oh yes, he came running to our house. He called out from outside, Akka, Akka. I had come of age by that time, and was staying at home. Standing behind the closed door, I asked him what he wanted. "Your father needs his knife immediately. The Hazrat is waiting to slaughter a calf." I ran and fetched the knife which was tucked into the roof, and waited behind the door, wondering how to hand it to him. Meanwhile he was hurrying me, and calling out, "Where is it? Where is it?"

'So I decided there was no way but to hand it to him myself. I opened the door a crack and held it out with two fingers. He took it and hurried off. But it seems that very day he decided that the owner of the two fingers must become his bride. It seems he thought, if her fingers are so beautiful how beautiful her face must be, like the fourteenth day's moon.' Her face was full of pride, lost to her memories.

'Leave that now. Go on and tell us about your first night,' asked Mumtaz, eager to hear more. The time for the Maghrib prayers was passing by. Darkness began to gather in the courtyard. Mumtaz gazed at the darkening courtyard and Nuramma by turns, partly annoyed that she was taking so long to tell her tale, but reluctant, all the same, to leave in the middle of it.

'What's the great rush, di, with you?' Nuramma scolded her fondly. She had no wish to lose this opportunity to relive her old memories and to talk about them. Besides, who was going to bother about an old woman's stories, these days? These people, for some reason, were willing to listen to her; she wasn't likely to forego the chance.

'What was that you were asking me about? Pust nite or gist nut? Leave that, whatever it is! I'll tell you something much more interesting. You listen to this.' She spread some lime on a betel leaf, folded it over and tucked it into her mouth. Although it troubled the minds of all those present there that the time allocated for the evening prayers was being wasted away, they stayed where they were, eager to listen, gazing at Nuramma. As for Wahida, she was astonished that the old lady could talk so easily and humorously.

'Yes, so what was I saying? I didn't even begin? All right, so once I sprained a leg, and was laid up, unable to walk or do anything for myself. Why, Saura, you'll remember this.' She called in Saura as a witness, and was satisfied when she nodded in confirmation. 'And then, you know what happened? I just lay in bed. My younger sister had to come and look after me. She would come in the morning, feed me, take me to the toilet, comb my hair, cook all the food, serve my husband his meal, and go home only at night to her own husband and children, having finished everything at my house. Poor child, she had to suffer so much hardship.' For a moment she wiped her eyes, remembering her sister's sacrifices for her. The next moment her face brightened. 'My husband used to say to her, "Why, Gulshan, what will you lose if you look after me for a bit during the night as well? Doesn't a man have that appetite too?" She never got cross with him for asking. She would just go off, saying, "Oh, go on with you, Macchaan!" Among all these women who are more than willing to go for it if a husband offers himself for free, my sister was true as pure gold. How would it even occur to her to betray me? Think about it.' She stopped for a moment, looking to see if her audience was relishing what she said. Her voice was as merry as her words. It slipped and slid, melted and dissolved. Wahida moved aside a little, to avoid the spittle that sprayed from her mouth as she spoke.

The darkness covering the courtyard made it quite clear that the Maghrib period was now definitely over. Nafiza and Mumtaz had decided that now there was no other way but to say the Maghrib prayers later, together with the Isha ones. They were quiet now, making no attempt to interrupt Nuramma in her flow.

'Then the next thing that happened was this. I shouldn't say anything about my husband, you know. He was pure gold. He was only teasing my sister; he would never ever look at another woman. How could I bear to see him suffer so during the nights? And it wasn't just one or two days; the doctor had me in plaster for three months. Which man would be prepared to be patient for so long? He just doted on me. As for me, my mother left us forever when we were just babies. A pisaasu took her and pushed her under water. Who was there for me besides him?'

Once again Nuramma was overcome with emotion.

'How does the pisaasu come into it?' Wahida asked eagerly.

'That's quite another story. One evening, my mother and two other women, neighbours, arranged to go together to a certain pond to bathe, early the next morning. A pisaasu, hiding there, had overheard all this. It came and knocked at our door and called my mother by name; but it was at midnight, not early morning as they had planned. It sounded exactly like the next door neighbour, so my mother thought it must be early morning, bundled up the clothes to be washed and put them on her head, and followed it out. As soon as they got into the water, it tried to push my mother in and drown her. By this time, all the others gathered there, having looked for her in her house, and found her missing. When they arrived at the pond, there was my mother, lying alone on the shores, having fainted away. There was no one else there; not a single soul. At the time her soul departed from her body, apparently she said, "The baby girl is in her cradle; the jewellery is all in a box; look after them." And then she died. How could she have consented to leave us two little girls? How that life must have suffered at its moment of departure!' Nuramma came to an end, and gave a long sigh.

A silence descended on all of them, like heavy rains coming to a stop. Saura alone turned her face with a look of slight contempt, as if to say, 'Don't I know the state of your family? Look at the airs the slut assumes!'

But Nuramma took no notice of that. Her one concern was to make her story ever more pleasurable, and to hold her audience's attention. 'And then, and then, where did I leave off? I'm getting so old, I forget easily.' She came back to the story she was telling, before this diversion. 'Oh yes, and he too, poor man, for how long could he control his desires? One day, this is what he did. One day he brought me a string of flowers, and wanted me to wear it in my hair. In fact, he placed them in my hair himself. Then he picked me up as gently as if I were a flower and took me to his bed. And then, what can I say, my

raja, came to me so carefully so that my leg felt no pain at all.'
Her face flushed shyly, either because she was actually
remembering something that happened long ago, or because
she was sharing these stories with others. For some time she
seemed sunk in the happiness of that memory, then she went
on. 'Then, the next day, my sister came to our house. She looked
at me, she saw that my hair was washed and spread out, she
saw the happiness in my face. She hesitated a bit and then asked
"What is all this, Akka, what's going on?" I didn't say anything
to her. I only sang a song to her. She didn't say anything more.
And guess what that song was?' She addressed the question to
Mumtaz, grinning widely so that her reddened gums were
bared.

'However would I know what it was. You tell us now.'
Mumtaz's voice bubbled over with eagerness.

'It was the song that Saroja sings to Sivaji in the film
Raagapirivinai . It goes, "Didn't the moon come tumbling to
me across the skies, without feet? Didn't I embrace it without
hands and give it my love?" That was the song I sang. She
understood at once. How she fell about laughing! When
Macchaan came home, she kept singing this song and teasing
us a lot. The teasing went on for many days; don't ask me for
how long.' She joined in heartily with the laughter surrounding
her.

When they all laughed together, they made a sound as if a
money-box full of silver coins was being shaken. The whole
house rippled with the sound of their laughter. The laughter
seemed to fall and scatter against the newly coloured walls,
and the whole house began to gain an air of wedding festivity.

They all rose to their feet, satisfied and pleased that the
storytelling was over, but still unwilling to leave, and began to
say goodbye.

'Stay and eat with us,' Rahima invited. But Nafiza said she
must go. 'We've been here since the Asar prayers. Heaven
knows what has happened at home, and where the boys have
gone. Let me go now, amma.' Mumtaz left with her.

When they got into the street, Mumtaz said enviously, 'Big dowry, isn't it?'

'They have the one daughter. And they have no shortage of money,' Nafiza answered her. 'She showed us all of it, but they never showed us the jewellery. They never do that, for fear someone will cast an evil eye. But who amongst us doesn't have her own jewellery?' Mumtaz was irritated as well as disappointed at not having had a glimpse of the bridal jewellery.

'But we knew, didn't we, that they would never display that. That's the custom of the town. They'll display the furniture and the vessels. They'll deck her in jewellery for the day before the of the wedding, when the Fatiha is said over her. We'll see everything else on the wedding day itself, that's all,' Mumtaz assured her 'But what's the good of doing all this? The bridegroom isn't quite right. And the mother-in-law is a wicked old lady. It's like rearing a parrot and then giving it into the paws of a cat.' Mumtaz laughed. There was both envy and satisfaction in her laughter. Nafiza nodded and smiled in agreement.

☞ 29 ☜

When everyone had gone, Zohra said to Rahima. 'This morning, at the funeral, Nafiza said something to tease Mumtaz, who got quite cross with her. But now, look, they seem to be laughing and chatting together merrily.' She seemed quite surprised by this.

'Well, yes. They are neighbours, after all. They really can't manage without each other. If they gave up on their friendship, who would either of them have to gossip and joke with? For one donkey, another donkey is a blessing. Let's get on with our work.' Rahima busied herself with what she needed to do.

But Zohra went on, 'Of course they talked nicely to us all this time, but who knows what they said to each other afterwards? It's like a chronic infection with them.'

Kader had told them he would be late back from the town that day. Rahima shut the door of the room where Rabia and Wahida were asleep and went to her own bedroom, but didn't want to sleep. She switched off the lights and slid down on her bed. The faint light of the night lamp dispersed the darkness in the room, which in turn seemed to disperse and fling away her few certainties. Without the bustle and brightness of daytime, the darkness of the night proved that the courage she believed herself to possess didn't exist, after all. She was overcome with fear. A fear she never known at any time, for whatever reason. A fear that she might be about to make a very great mistake shook her to the depths of her being. Unable to understand how she could have been brought so low, she sat up in bed and, as if afraid to give way to the darkness within her, she stepped very softly out of the room, went down to the hall, switched on the TV, and sat down on the sofa opposite it. The thought that she would have to part from Wahida in a very few days pressed upon her heart. A few days ago, her father had spoken to her very anxiously.

'She's an innocent child; she doesn't know what is good and what is bad. It is our responsibility to make sure she has a good life. In our community we don't make a marriage based on the girl's wishes. So, it falls to us to decide upon a bridegroom about whom we are happy in every way. Once we have that certainty, there won't be a problem.' There was a certain emphasis in the way he said, 'falls to *us*', even though he had many reservations about his son-in-law's stubbornness. He had comforted his daughter, in the end, saying, 'In the end, it's His wish. It's not what we want, but what He thinks that will come to be; can we change that?'

Rahima could say nothing. Who was going worry about Wahida's wishes? Was she able to understand what she wanted, anyway? Was she even of an age to make such decisions? Knowledgeable as Rahima herself was, her opinions were not being valued, so who would pay heed to Wahida? During the marriage ceremony, when the Haji-amma waited with the black beads in her hand, and the Hazrat came with his witnesses to ask the bride for the 'Sayyedu', her acceptance, what sense did it make? Once the invitations had been printed, the guests invited, and all the arrangements made, would any bride dare to come out with her true opinion?

Rahima felt very tired. The Sinhala play which was showing on the TV came to an end, and the presenter's voice saying 'Ayubovan' brought Rahima to herself. It was then that she noticed Rabia standing next to her, scratching her head. Surprised, she stood up and switched off the TV, saying, 'Aren't you asleep yet?'

'Let me sleep with you, I'm feeling very scared.'

Rahima raised her eyebrows in surprise.

'It's that story about the pisaasu that Nuramma told. It scares me, Periamma. If I tell amma she'll scold me for listening to the grown-ups talk. May I get into your bed?' Her expression was piteous as she asked for this permission. She also looked pale with fear.

'Idiot!' said Rahima fondly, hugging her and taking her into her bedroom. When she made her lie down, Rabia held on to her tightly, saying, 'You come too.' She felt comforted by the smell of marikozhundu in her aunt's hair mingled with a faint smell of sweat.

'Tell me, Periamma. Is it true, what Nuramma said? Are there jinns, really and truly? They say they fly between the heaven and earth.'

'You say it scares you. Then why talk about it? No, you just go to sleep now. Just say a prayer and go to sleep, you won't have bad dreams.'

'No, Periamma, I'm not afraid anymore. Please tell me.'

'Yes, there are jinns. But they are good creatures. They won't hurt anyone. It's just that when they are out and about at night time, you shouldn't cross their paths. They say that if you do, they will beat you and kill you. Many people claim to have seen jinns. They say they fly between the sky and the earth.

Is that enough for you? Now go to sleep.' Rahima rattled off all this information and then closed her eyes.

For some time Rabia was quiet, closing her long lashes in the vain hope of ignoring the darkness looming in the room, then she said softly, 'Periamma.'

'Mm? What's it now?'

'That is, I want to ask you something, but Amma mustn't know,' she said. Rahima wondered what was coming.

'Very well. Ask me. I won't tell your Amma.'

'That is, how many husbands can a woman have?' Rahima was aghast at the question. But Rabia went on, 'That is, you know Ramesh who is in my school, his mother has two husbands, it seems. Uma told us. And I saw them as well. That's why I asked. If a woman marries two men, isn't she being bad?'

Rahima understood who she was talking about. But why should she ask this? She said, 'Yes, it is wrong. A woman should have only one husband. If she marries two men, then yes, she is doing a bad thing.'

'So is that why Firdaus Chitthi and Sherifakka didn't marry another husband?' Rabia asked eagerly. Wondering how to deal with her doubts, Rahima said, 'Why, of course they can marry. It's only if their first husbands are still there that they shouldn't marry another. Neither your Chitthi nor Sherifakka have a husband now. They will certainly marry again.' She was embarrassed by these questions, but also anxious because the child was asking questions which were beyond her years.

'You were saying this evening, weren't you, about this man called Abdulla. You said he had four wives. What about that?' Realising that the child was very confused, Rahima struggled to give her an appropriate answer. Meanwhile, Rabia pressed her. 'Tell me, Periamma. He is marrying again and again, even when his wives are there. Isn't that wrong as well?' Rabia shook Rahima by the shoulder and held her hand. She loved the feel of her aunt's hands; the palms were as soft as cotton wool.

Rahima started as if she had been thinking something else. 'What did you ask me? About men marrying again? According to the Shariat, men can marry four wives, it isn't wrong. If women do it, it is wrong. Right, are you going to sleep now or not,' she scolded gently, putting a stop to the conversation.

Rabia was frightened for a moment. Was Periamma angry with her? She leaned against Rahima's back more closely, in an effort to placate her. After being quiet for a little while, she whispered again, 'Periamma.'

'What now?'

'That is, I've decided to wear a davani from tomorrow. Is there a new one at home, for me to wear for the first time?'

'Why this sudden wish? Whenever your mother asks you to, you always refuse stubbornly!' Rahima smiled sweetly.

Like a cracked record she started again, 'That is, it seems Madina is going to wear a davani from tomorrow. I decided to do it at the same time, along with her.'

'Oho, so that's what it's about. I was wondering why the rat was running scared, for no reason. Of course, take what you like. All your akka's davanis, new and old, are yours now. She's going to be married, isn't she? Hereafter she'll wear only saris.'

'But she doesn't know how to wear a sari. How will she manage?' Rabia was astonished.

'A woman has to get used to that. Of course she'll manage. As for you, you just wait. See if I don't find the same bridegroom for the two of you and see you both married.' Rahima teased Rabia.

'Go on, Periamma,' said, covering her face shyly. She was always embarrassed if the very word 'marriage' was mentioned. If, on top of that they kept talking of a single bridegroom for the two of them... ? Suddenly she thought of Ahmad. With all the wedding festivities going on, she hadn't seen him properly for many days. She fell asleep deciding she would go and see him at least on the next day. She dreamt that Ahmad had married her as well as Madina. But she didn't like it one bit that he married both of them, not her alone.

* * *

The next day, Rahima and Zohra were up early, ready to set off after their baths to invite Amina to the wedding. They only had to go to the neighbouring town. The return journey would take just an hour by car. Besides, Sabia's husband, Sayyed, had just come home from Sri Lanka. It was proper that they visit him as well.

Rabia came and stood next to Rahima. She held in her hands a fairly new davani of Wahida's which she wanted her Periamma to drape on her. It was obvious, from her expression, that she longed to go with them, to see her Firdaus Chitthi. Zohra noticed it, but chose to ignore it as she went about her chores. Rahima took the davani, chanted something under her breath, and put it on Rabia. 'Come on, you must say Bismillah too. Now you look very grown up.' Rahima touched Rabia's cheek to ward off the evil eye. She went on, consolingly, 'Look, we are making a very quick visit; we'll be returning almost immediately. You know you are accompanying Wahida after the wedding when she goes to her mother-in-law's house. You'll stay there all of four days before you return.'

Rabia was surprised that her aunt could discern what she was thinking. She also realized that her mother knew it too, but pretended that she did not.

Zohra saw that her daughter was wearing a davani all of a sudden. She asked in surprise, 'Amma, how is it you changed your mind about wearing a davani? Well, you look a real girl, at last; you look beautiful like this.' She turned to Rahima and said, 'Come, Akka, it seems that Suleiman has arrived home. We ought to make a quick visit to them.'

'Oh yes; it's a good thing you reminded me. Sainu will kill us if we are late with our visit,' Rahima pretended to be terrified.

When they arrived at Sainu's house, Zohra caught a glimpse of Madina and realized at once why Rabia had decided to wear a davani. She wanted to laugh. Then Suleiman appeared, looking like a Sufi, with his beard and fez cap. After they had exchanged greetings, Rahima said, teasing him, 'Well, well, what has happened to you? You seem to have converted to Islam all of a sudden?'

He smiled in return. 'Do you know that it is very wrong to be born a Muslim man and not have a beard? Out there our people are very meticulous, you know that? If we compare ourselves to them...' Suleiman stopped short, shaking his head in despair.

Sainu teased him, saying, 'Very good. You are here now, aren't you, to reform us.'

He didn't take in his mother's pleasantry. 'I heard you are celebrating Wahida's nikah,' he said to Rahima. 'I'm very very happy to hear that. I'm fortunate to be able to attend the marriage.'

'Yes, appa. We thought of sending you a separate invitation by post. Then, since you were coming here anyway, we decided to invite you in person. Be sure to come. Wahida's father will also come and invite you,' Rahima assured him.

Sainu intervened to say, 'Your husband came to visit, directly after the Bajar prayers. He's already invited him. It's Karim who hasn't appeared yet.'

They were sitting in the hall. But there was no sign of Mumtaz anywhere. Rahima looked around for her, in the hope of teasing her a bit before leaving. They heard the pressure cooker's whistle, coming from the kitchen, past the courtyard. Immediately after that their noses were assailed by the aroma of meat curry. She was cooking something special for Suleiman, Rahima thought to herself. 'Sainakka, why is there no sign of either Farida or Mumtaz?' she asked.

'Farida is standing in the backyard, giving those two poor things their bath. Where will Mumtaz go? She's getting her husband's meal ready, that's all.' Rahima nodded, noticing that Sainu was not embarrassed to refer to Mumtaz in so off-hand a manner, even though her son was sitting right next to her.

'Have some coffee,' Sainu offered and raised her voice. 'Ele, Mumtaz! Come and show your face here for a bit.'

As if they had already agreed on their response, Rahima and Zohra protested together as they rose to their feet, 'Ayyayyo, don't go to the trouble of coffee and all that, please, Akka. We really must go.'

'Oh, of course, a cow that is going off to graze in the meadow is unlikely to carry its own load of hay, is it? You'll be given a feast at your in-laws, won't you. I wasn't thinking,' Sainu joked.

Rahima returned, 'Go on with you, Akka. You know what my in-laws are like.' Then noticing five or six people, men and women, on the street, just approaching the front door, she said, 'Well, we must go. It looks as if there are people coming to see Suleiman. You'll need to look after your guests.'

Rahima crossed the courtyard and peeped into the kitchen. She said to Mumtaz, 'Well, well, is the new bride cooking something special for the groom?'

Mumtaz was bent over a coconut scraper. She looked up startled, and said, 'Rahimakka, come in. When did you arrive?'

'Oh, we came quite a while ago. You, of course, are so happy, you didn't even hear us arrive!' Rahima said playfully. She observed the joy in Mumtaz's face, and the keenness in her voice. 'We are going now,' she told her, 'we'll talk later.'

When she returned to the hall, she saw that Nafiza, Karim, and some others had also arrived. The men were seated on the sofa, while Nafiza sat on a mat spread out on the floor, next to Sainu. She said, 'Right, Akka, I must go now. We are actually on our way to the bridegroom's hometown. We'll see you all later on.'

Suleiman said eagerly, 'You'll see Sikander, won't you? Please be sure to give him my salaam.'

'Certainly,' Rahima assured him. She give Nafiza a little smile and teased her, too, saying, 'You've just arrived from next door, I take it, to greet your friend's husband.'

Finally the two women set off, having asked Fatima to keep Wahida company at home. As Mutthu drove the car along the street, Zohra grew very silent and Rahima, unwilling to disturb her, sank back into her seat and shut her eyes. Zohra's silence suggested that she was preparing herself mentally, to meet her mother and sister. The journey would have felt less tedious had they been able to converse, and Rahima felt sad that Zohra's state of mind clearly did not allow that.

The car left the main road and was going more slowly, through village roads. Rahima was happy to see the little hamlets, coconut groves and fields they passed. She lifted her face to the cool breeze as she gazed outside. A couple of village children called out 'Hi, Car!' and waved as they sped past. She felt sorry that they wore nothing other than their shirts. She was astonished that they smiled so spontaneously and innocently, in spite of their piteous state. Why is it that we are not able to smile like that, she asked herself, troubled.

Rahima looked up at the mountains in the distance, and noticed that by ten in the morning, they were already glowing in the sunlight. Zohra was still silent, gazing out of her window. Rahima sighed. How many memories these village scenes must bring her sister-in-law, she wondered. She spoke up at last. 'We have almost arrived at your hometown. Bundle up all your thoughts, put them away, and look a little more lively. You don't want to upset your mother and sister even more than they are already.' Zohra nodded vehemently in agreement.

Firdaus heard the sound of the car, ran up to the front door and peeped out into the street. Her face brightened at the sight of Rahima and Zohra alighting from the car. Firdaus looked beyond them to see if there was anyone else with them, and disappointed, turned her gaze on the two women once more.

She threw both arms around the two women as soon as they entered the house, embracing them and laughing with delight. 'I've been thinking of you and looking forward to your arrival since yesterday,' she said. She ran past them in eight leaps, to fetch a finely woven mat from the corner of the hall which she spread for them, first shaking it out. 'Sit down, Akka,' she invited them.

Rahima sat down on the mat, and gazed at Firdaus. In spite

of all her worries, the girl's face had a sparkling beauty. She suddenly felt as if it dazzled her eyes. She forced herself to turn her eyes away and, looking about her, asked, 'Are you well? Where's your mother gone?'

'I'm very well, Akka. Amma has gone to the little shop to buy some kerosene oil. She'll be back very soon.' She rattled on, 'Why didn't you bring Rabia? How is Wahida? Are Macchaan and everyone else well?' She came to a sudden stop.

Zohra answered her. 'Everyone is well, Rabia will come with Wahida; she'll accompany her when she comes here after the wedding. But tell me, how are you?'

Zohra looked closely at her sister's face. She noticed a change such as she had not seen all this time. The look of emptiness she had noticed when she visited some time ago seemed to have gone without a trace. Had she reconciled herself to her situation so soon? The question rose in her mind, but remained unanswered. How often Firdaus had tried to commit suicide! How many times she had refused to eat and had locked herself inside her room! How did this sudden clarity of expression come about? What sudden happiness caused such brightness? All paths to happiness had been closed off to her, ages ago. Zohra was both confused and scared.

Rahima, remembering suddenly, tapped Zohra's thigh and shook her. 'Get up, my sister-in-law will have a fit if she knows we visited here first. Let's go and show our faces there, and come back later.'

Firdaus giggled. 'What Akka is saying is true. If she knows you came here first, there will be no end of trouble...' Rahima noticed that Zohra was not pleased at Firdaus's laughter.

When they arrived at Sabia's house, they found Sayyed sitting on a chair, leaning back. He was thinking fondly and proudly of his wife. What a clever woman! She had waited patiently and made a marriage for her son with her brother's daughter. This was no small matter. She had refused stubbornly to look elsewhere for a bride for Sikander, although he was getting on in years; she had stood her ground, and succeeded. He was hugely proud of this. He took his fez off, placed it on the sofa next to himself, and stroked his own head. It was at that instant that Rahima and Zohra entered the house, and walked up to him saying, 'Asalaam aleikum, Anna. Are you well?'

He folded back his legs which had been stretched out, and greeted them, saying, 'Aleikum salaam, come amma, welcome, welcome. Have you just arrived? Is everyone well at home?' He twisted round to call, 'Look here, Sabia, come quickly.' He sounded delighted.

'Who is it?' Sabia called back, and came out slowly, swaying from side to side. When she saw them, she greeted them, and turned towards her husband to say, 'I was wondering why Rowther's voice was pealing out with joy. Now I see that it was at the sight of his brothers-in-law's wives! I don't know what it is, but he's so very fond of you both, amma.' She too sounded pleased and proud.

Her words made Sayyed congratulate himself; his expression was ecstatic. Sabia spread a mat for them, asked them to sit down, and went inside. Sayyed asked eagerly, 'How is my daughter-in-law? I was intending to come and visit her today.'

'First tell us how you are,' asked Rahima. 'How long are you going struggle all by yourself, so far away? Shouldn't you come back now and decide to stay with your wife and children?' She very nearly added 'in the last years of your life', and was greatly relieved that she stopped herself, just in time, from uttering such inauspicious words. The very thought that she might have uttered them made her stomach churn.

Sabia coming out with a plate of biscuits, said, 'Yes, please tell this man. What good did I get by marrying him? We've hardly lived together. He comes home once in two years, and then runs away as if he's had enough of the sight of us.' She wiped her nose with her sari. Sabia was always reproaching Sayyed for his absence. Anyone she talked to about this was subjected to a downpour of complaints. Rahima often thought that Allah had given her just one son to match her constant lament.

'Amma, amma, don't cry now,' Sayyed said to her, and scolded the visitors playfully. 'What is this, amma, as soon as you came you made Sabia weep. Poor thing! Look at my wife, her whole face is flushed.'

Zohra was irritated by their fond games. They are carrying on as if they are little ones, she told herself.

Sayyed stopped being playful and turned to them. 'What did you ask me? It was about my coming home forever, wasn't it? I was thinking about staying here from now on, actually. Because Sri Lanka is no longer as it used to be. The situation is very bad now. They think of all Tamil people as their enemies, there. In two or three places, there has been rioting, as well. They are not so hostile towards Muslims just yet. I've left the shop in the hands of a friend. Insha Allah, let us see. I must return one last time, tie up everything and come back for good.' He spoke quite anxiously. For a while they were all quiet.

Zohra broke into the silence. 'It looks as if you have erected the pandal and everything.'

'Yes, it is all done. Even the black beads have been threaded.' Sabia went in once more and returned with a small jewel-box. She handed it to Rahima, saying, 'Here, have a look at this. This is the presentation jewellery. This is what he has brought as our wedding present.' She sat down beside them saying, 'Allahu.'

'Thank you, we'll take a look.' Rahima accepted the box, examining Sabia's face at the same time to see if she could detect a look of regret. She must surely be feeling frustrated, Rahima knew. But because it was Sayyed's wish, she had to agree to giving it away. Besides, the man could never keep things to himself. He was sure to prattle the very next day to Kader and tell him about the jewellery he had brought Wahida. And Kader would be very angry if it did not reach the right person.

There was a chain, from abroad. It sparkled and shone. Both Rahima and Zohra took it in their hands and admired it. Then

Rahima returned it saying, 'We've admired it. Please put it away now. We'll just go and invite some of your neighbours, mothers and children.' They rose to their feet and wrapped their dupattas about them.

'Have a mouthful of coffee before you go,' invited Sabia. But Rahima refused firmly. 'No, thank you. We'll be given coffee in all these places. Even if we refuse, they'll force it on us. So we'll just set off.'

'Very well then. Come back soon. Come and have your midday meal here. I'll cook for you, and have it all ready.' Sabia's tone was insistent.

They agreed, rose from their mats and set off across the courtyard, glancing at the simple, white-washed walls of the hall with a slight smile. Zohra asked, 'Where's the bridegroom?'

'He's gone to invite his friends. He'll be back very soon.' Sayyed told them

They said goodbye to him and left the house. Angrily, Zohra muttered, 'She's getting her only son married. Can't she be bothered to paint the house even? How can she be so miserly!'

But Rahima silenced her. 'Pshu! Be quiet; we know what she's like. Then what's the use of lamenting, as if we are seeing it all for the first time.'

* * *

Rahima handed Amina an invitation, saying very affectionately, 'You are the first person I'm inviting in this town. You must come, most definitely.' Firdaus squatted next to the doorframe. There was a look of disinclination on her face, which made Rahima wondered whether she disapproved of Sikander.

Amina, accepting the wedding invitation, caught hold of Rahima's hands and said, 'I would love to accept and attend the wedding. But I don't know how to manage it.' She stopped short. Her brown eyes rested on Firdaus for moment, and then returned to Rahima.

Rahima understood what she wished to say and, in order to stop her words, she pressed Amina's dry and withered hands between hers. 'That is no problem at all. You must have no hesitation or worries about anything; you must come, I insist. What has happened in your family is nothing so unusual in this world. Because of that one thing, how long will you confine yourself to your house, without joining in with the community, its celebrations and sorrows? If people want to gossip, let them. Allah will look after us. You mustn't worry like this and ruin your health.' Rahima spoke very gently, consoling Amina.

Firdaus bowed her head even lower than before. She looked closely at herself for a moment, at the faded blouse and sari that she was wearing. She felt ashamed. Every time Rahima glanced at her, she lowered her eyes and gazed at her own hands. She twisted the border of her sari around her finger. She could see from Zohra's expression that she felt humiliated by the state of her sister. However close she was to Rahima, Zohra would not like her sister-in-law to assume that Amina's family was close to poverty.

Zohra now intervened before Amina could reply to Rahima. She needed to establish to Rahima that the family was not in such dire straits. She burst out angrily, 'Amma, why are you keeping her in this beggarly state? As if she comes from a poor family and has nothing of her own?'

Rahima was quiet, she understood from Zohra's look of discomfort why she was so angry. But it struck her as foolish of Zohra to reprimand her mother in this way, and to try and insist on her family's honour. Rahima was embarrassed by it.

Amina's wrinkled face became even more wizened when she heard Zohra's question. She turned to Firdaus and drove her away from there, ordering her sharply, 'You go into the kitchen. There's plenty of work for you there.' Firdaus said nothing, but rose quietly and went. It was not a new experience for her to be humiliated by her mother, but for her to do it in front of Rahima made her deeply resentful.

After Firdaus went away, Amina gripped Rahima's hands

once more, and spoke in vindication of her position. 'Rahima, you tell me yourself. Have you seen how beautiful she is? She's like the fourteenth day's moon. Has the light left her face, in spite of all she has suffered? Does this one understand what a struggle it is for me to safeguard her all the time? She scolds me for keeping her in a beggarly condition; but what would she look like if I allowed her to dress well? As it is, do you know how many fellows there are, who hang about this house? Does this one have a clue how hard it is for me to look after the girl all by myself, without a man in the house?' She spoke fervently, and her eyes filled with tears as she said, 'Just get up, open that wardrobe and take a look. Every single sari there was bought for her. The entire wardrobe is full.'

She went on, 'When my child is in this condition, how can I dress well and go about? I don't know what sin we committed. Allah has thought it fit to place the two of us in this condition. If that is his pleasure, then so be it.' Amina lifted the end of her sari and wiped her eyes. Her light skin had reddened. Zohra said nothing but pulled at the woven straw of the mat on which they sat, breaking the pieces. An atmosphere of helplessness and oppression surrounded them.

Rahima felt too exhausted to make an effort to end the silence. She struggled to swim across it. It seemed to her that this family was fighting for breath, caught in a situation from which it could not be rescued. She greatly feared that these two might be dragged under and be lost forever. She felt that terror pressing on her heart, making her gasp for breath. She wanted to get away from there by herself, and escape.

Over and above all this, she discerned a change in Zohra after all their time together. It seemed as if the closeness they had experienced for so long was broken; that a gap had appeared between them. Zohra's anxiety to establish her family's honour in front of Rahima also established that in her heart she considered Rahima an outsider. She could not imagine that such a thought would come to Zohra suddenly, out of the blue. As she wondered for how long Zohra might have been

nursing the thought, a great sadness came over her. The two
women made no attempt to talk to each other on the return
journey.

❧ 30 ☙

When there were just two days before the wedding,
Fatima disappeared suddenly. In fact she had not been
seen since the early hours of the night even before that. When
Nuramma woke up in the middle of the night to listen to the
jinns' antics, she noticed that her daughter was not in the
bedroom; only Iliaz was there, asleep. She was scared that the
girl might have gone to the backyard. How often she had
warned the wicked girl that if she crossed the path of a jinn, she
might be struck down and killed. She hurried to the backyard
and searched for her. When she was not to be found there,
Nuramma panicked. Muttering repeated to herself, what has
happened, what has happened, she raised the wick of the
hurricane lamp and set out to look for her. For a moment she
wondered whether Fatima might have gone to the Asaari well
for drinking water. But drinking water at this hour? No, she
told herself, shaking her head.

She sank down at the threshold of the house, leaning against
the door frame, her head in her hands. Her head was spinning.
A confusion of thoughts came to her, filling her with dread. In
her panic, she could decide nothing. She thought she must
wait until daybreak, and then go to Rahima. Suddenly she
started to feel a great sense of self-pity. Memories of all the
tragedies in her life came back to her mind, one by one. Why
did the Lord create some people, only to make them suffer?
The overwhelming sorrow she felt broke out of her in a
lamentation. The daybreak established for her, finally, that
Fatima was not going to return home. She began to abuse Allah
roundly and very loudly, as if she had the right to do so; justice
was on her side. In front of her house, the neighbouring women

began to foregather, some to laugh at her, some to offer their consolation.

Rahima arrived and took the bewildered Iliaz home with her, left him with Zohra, and returned to comfort Nuramma. 'Why do you shout like this and invite the whole town to crowd around? She's not a small child; she must be somewhere near here,' she said, knowing it probably wasn't true.

Sherifa and Saura turned up for a while and quickly went away again. Only Sherifa knew in her heart that Fatima had almost certainly run away with Murugan. She had no wish to come forward and announce this to everyone. In a little while it would become apparent, anyway. Let them know it then, she told herself. If she were to broadcast the news now, for the sake of a moment's sensation, the townsfolk would turn round and accuse her. 'She knew about it all the time, but she kept quiet and let the community be shamed,' they would say. When she thought of this, the disdain in her heart showed just for an instant in the corner of her mouth.

'It's a terrible world,' she told herself. Fatima's husband left her and disappeared. Many people said he lived somewhere nearby, had married another woman and set up a household with her. Nobody had the wit to ask him any questions. Neither had they the commonsense to understand Fatima's poverty, her position. Now she had eloped with a man she loved. This one deed of hers was going to bring shame and dishonour on the whole town. In an obscure way, Sherifa felt proud of her.

Saura sat on the thinnai, her legs stretched out. She was thinking hard, her eyes half closed, as she dug into her ears with a hairpin. She was in a state of high excitement. Sherifa was quite likely to know of Fatima's whereabouts. The two women lay on the same pillow during the day, after all. Besides, they were of the same age. But if she asked Sherifa, her daughter wouldn't give anything away.

She did know, in a vague way, about the Murugan affair. 'She must have run off with that fellow, the wicked slut,' she told herself. She would keep her mouth shut for the time being, until rather more evidence came to hand. All the same, she wished she could talk to someone about it. She felt a gathering anger against Fatima. 'Very well, she took to her heels, the harlot, but couldn't she at least make off with a Muslim?' Having said this out aloud, involuntarily, she opened her eyes, startled, and looked around. No one about. She gave a sigh of relief. There was another worry in her mind. 'If Fatima made a kuzhambu, how delicious it was; how much one relished it! And you just had to say it was good; just as soon as it was cooked and off the stove, she'd pour out a dish full, and bring it round. So proudly!' More than anything else, this would be, for Saura, the greatest loss and disappointment.

From her bedroom window Sherifa watched her mother sitting on the courtyard thinnai: she could guess everything, more or less, that was running through Saura's mind. Poor woman, hereafter who was she going to cajole into making a special kuzhambu for her? Fatima was always immensely flattered and pleased that a rich woman like Saura took food from a poor person like her. Saura would begin like this: 'Why, Fatima, at one time you used to make a kuzhambu using the heads of salted fish. Don't you do it anymore?' Sherifa was always irritated by her mother's low cunning. But Fatima answered willingly. 'Why, of course I'd make it. Only, these days I can never get hold of salt fish heads.'

'I've eaten salt fish kuzhambu in so many places and so many houses, but no one can make it like you, you are really gifted,' Saura would say. Fatima would be as thrilled as if Saura had held pieces of ice against her head. The very next day, she would beg or borrow some money to buy what she needed to cook a salt fish curry, and bring round a whole pot full of it.

Sherifa spent all her time taking her mother to task for this. But Saura only said, 'How you carry on, endlessly, like a machine chugging away! Just shut up.'

Yes, poor Amma, she'd feel it very badly. It certainly was going to be big loss for her, Sherifa muttered to herself as she tossed on her bed.

The room, closed since the morning, felt heavy with heat, making her feel weary. However many times she tried to get up, her heart seemed to droop with weariness. Her body lay heaped on the bed, like old clothes. Although a long time had passed since she lost everything, on that day her heart felt a keen sorrow as if at a new loss. She lay there, unwilling even to wipe away the tears that streamed down her cheeks, unable to understand why she was being reminded of all that she had lost. The hot tears turned cold and wet on her cheeks.

Fatima had spoken to her boldly and openly, very often. She had never hidden her thoughts. Sherifa was surprised by that, but also embarrassed by her explicit language. At the same time she realized that although Fatima's words repulsed her at times, what she spoke about was natural enough.

There was a day when Fatima asked her directly, 'Don't you feel sexually frustrated?' Sherifa was taken aback and shaken by the question, but answered, 'No, it's not a big deal with me. I've never felt frustrated.' She couldn't entirely control the tremor in her voice, and lowered her eyes immediately because of that.

Fatima asked, 'Here, let's see, look me in the eye and say that again.'

Sherifa knew she did not have the strength to face the consequences following her admission of defeat. 'Very well, it's true,' she said. 'I do find it hard. Sometimes I can't sleep at nights. But, so what?'

'See, you've admitted it.' Fatima's eyes glittered with delight at her victory. She raised her small body a foot off the ground before touching the earth again. The scent of jasmine, drifting to them from its frame, seemed to match their mood at that hour. Fatima watched, with pleasure, the bees sitting on the flowers and drinking nectar.

Sherifa was astonished at her friend. Fatima had far fewer advantages than herself, yet she spoke up without hesitancy. At the same time, Sherifa was frightened too. For example, when Fatima said, 'Look at these men; they go where they like and take their pleasure. Why shouldn't women do it?'

How could she say such a thing? Sherifa looked at Fatima anxiously. 'I don't know, amma. I don't think it's right for you to say such things. Is that all our lives are meant to be? If we can't control ourselves even in that, how are we to manage? We have our children. We have the great joy of bringing them up. If we forget that and…' She hesitated, and then went on, 'I'm going to ask you something; will you answer me truly?'

Fatima looked at her closely. 'I can tell what you want to ask me! It's about Murugan, isn't it?' She laughed as she gave a wink. Her laugh was exultant.

'So you're admitting it's true?'

'Suppose it is?' Fatima sounded indifferent.

'You wretch! What are you saying? We and our community as a whole possess such a thing as our honour! You have a small child! Don't you think about all this?'

Fatima stared at Sherifa for a moment. 'So? Let it be. Let it all be. Why do I have to safeguard their honour? The elders of this worthless town, what have they ever done for me so far? Nothing whatsoever. So why should I bother about all that unnecessarily? If something gives me pleasure, I'll go for it. Besides, I'm not a wealthy woman like you, amma, to renounce everything and sit in a corner for the sake of the family's honour.'

Sherifa didn't say a word, after that.

* * *

'Muslim whore! She went and seduced my poor son and carried him off. May you be ruined! May you fall into a hell-hole!' In broad daylight, Murugan's mother stood in the street in front Nuramma's house, screaming in anger, scooping up the dust and flinging it about. Sherifa watched from her window. In reply, Nuramma shouted from within, in her weak voice, 'Idle slut, was a low caste Palla boy's prick all she could get? She couldn't even get a Muslim?'

The neighbouring women had all gathered round watching the fun, full of excitement about it all.

There was one thing that continued to puzzle Sherifa. Why did Fatima abandon Iliaz, leaving him orphaned? How could a mother do that? When she thought of how Fatima had run away, leaving Iliaz behind, while she herself refused to marry a second time because of her child, she could not comprehend it at all. She was profoundly repulsed by Fatima's action, but at the same time was aware of her own helplessness and weariness of spirit. Somewhere in the corner of her mind a slight envy of Fatima's independence sprouted, and then began to take root quickly.

She began to ready herself, with great sadness, to face the other events that would happen that day.

∽ 31 ∽

After the Asar prayers, the Jamaat assembled in the mosque excitedly, ready to discuss the situation. The important elders were all there: the lay leaders, the naattaamai and the mutthavalli as well as the imam. These people were seated in front, their heads lowered, faces tight with shame. Wave upon wave of anger swept over the crowds filling the mosque. Some of the younger men could scarcely contain their fury. Had they been able to get hold of Fatima or Murugan, who had subjected them to this unending humiliation, they would have torn them apart, limb from limb. An upsurge of emotion seemed to unite them: a fierce need to safeguard the honour of their religion and community.

Nuramma looked shrunken and bent as she cowered next to the madrasa pillar. She felt as if a thousand eyes were gazing at her, piercing through the white dupatta which enshrouded her. Tears still filled the dim eyes in her wizened and dark face. From the badam tree, a cool breeze blew. Within the water trough, the fish slid through the water weeds, leaping and playing.

Suleiman was the first to raise his voice in the assembly. He shouted, 'Why is everyone silent? How are we going to recover from the humiliation we have suffered today? Because of this wicked whore none of us can walk with our heads held high anymore! What are we going to do about it?'

The naattaamai stretched his hand towards him, trying to calm him down. 'Why do you shout so loudly in the mosque? Be a bit patient.' The naattaamai turned to the mutthavalli.

'How can we keep from shouting, Maamu? Our honour has gone. What else can we do, tell me? My blood is boiling. If this had happened in Saudi, by now the woman would have been dragged into the street and stoned to death. You know that, don't you?' Suleiman breathed hard. Some of the men next to him quietened him and made him sit down.

The mutthavalli stretched his hand towards him saying, 'Be quiet for a while, appa. We are all here to discuss this very thing. Listen, what has happened has happened. Who knows where that donkey has disappeared! Now let us talk about what has to be done here.'

The naattaamai nodded his head in agreement, cleared his throat lightly and began. 'We are all agreed that a forbidden thing has happened in this town. The honour and respect which we have protected so carefully and for so long has gone in a stroke. She has run off with a Kafir boy. Hereafter she will not be allowed to enter this town. This is all we can do for the time being. At the same time, the Jamaat considers it necessary to ban Nuramma from the community. Hereafter we will not accept any contribution to the mosque from her. No Hazrat must go to her house on any occasion to say the Fatiha. She must not participate in any of our events, and she will not be eligible for the nombu kanji, or any of the communal feasts. Do you understand what I'm saying?' As he finished speaking, his eyes swept over the congregation and turned to Nuramma.

The congregation assembled there understood quite clearly

that the elders had decided together what they would say before coming to the meeting. The naattaamai had made his statement abruptly in order to avoid an endless and ugly discussion inside the mosque. The people there realized this, and were quiet. As for Nuramma, when she heard the naattaamai's words, it was as if her life had left her. Already broken by shame and anger, she was stunned by this further punishment.

There was no sound from the congregation, except for a slight rustle. Nuramma looked around desperately, but was disappointed in the hope that someone would speak up for her. 'Ayya, what my girl did was wrong. But please don't take revenge on me. I have... never committed... a sin. At my time of life... what can I do... where will I go... Oh, Allah!' The words dropped from her in fragments, while sobs broke into her old and tired voice.

Once again Suleiman leapt to his feet and shouted. 'You didn't have the wit to bring up a female child with the necessary discipline. Your punishment is because of that.' Waves of sound rose and fell from the crowd, in agreement with him.

Nuramma wouldn't leave it alone, like a child she repeated herself, weeping, 'Just because she did wrong, don't take it out on me.'

'Elé, Nuramma, you know what the honour of our community is about. If we don't safeguard it ourselves, who will do it for us? Think about it yourself. If we let you off today, tomorrow no one will have any sense of fear, will they? Unless we take this decision today, tomorrow anyone will dare to do anything. Do you understand?' The naattaamai combed and stroked his long beard with two fingers. He felt satisfied that he had been able to explain it all to Nuramma so reasonably.

Nuramma realized at last that it was no use whatever to beg and plead with these people. Suddenly a feeling of freedom overcame her. It was now certain that she was to be banned from the community. She knew she could do nothing to prevent it; yet she was in a sudden frenzy to say something after all. Liberated from all the controls she had known, as if she were bursting out of her chains, she spoke, stretching her arm out, 'Ayya, all you elders and big men, so you are going to ban me from the community! Very well, let it be so. You say it was a sin for my daughter to elope with a Kafir. Is there a single man who hasn't slept with one of our Hindu worker women? Speak out, let me hear. Let just one of you stand up; I'll agree my daughter did wrong.' Her finger pointed all the way round the assembled crowd, leaving out no one.

For a moment everyone there was stunned and speechless. Nuramma began to shout again, 'It's because I am helpless that you do this to me. Allah will pay you back for making me suffer. You are not going to get away with this wrong-doing. Ye Rahman! Rabbé! My stomach is on fire!' She stooped down and gathered the dust off the ground with both hands and threw it upwards, towards the sky.

Enraged by all this, Suleiman and some other young men, leapt up from the midst of the crowd and came running towards her, shouting, 'Strike her down and kill her, the old slut!' The naattaamai and mutthavalli stood up, shocked and confused.

Kader ran ahead of all of them, and stood in front of Nuramma shielding her. He pushed the young men away and shouted, 'Ei, move back, all of you. Just remember where you are. This is a mosque. Aren't you ashamed to start this kind of scuffle in this place? Of course what this woman said was wrong. But I also know that she is not always in full possession of her wits. Just leave this business alone now, and let us go on with what we have to do.' He was anxious to put an end to the affair immediately.

Suleiman called out, 'How can we allow her to oppose the Jamaat? You are an elder of the community, how can you talk like this? Are we men at all, to listen to a female? Or are we effeminate boys?' He was not prepared to lose this opportunity to display his fervour for his religion and community. His obstinacy irritated Kader, who appealed to the naattaamai.

'See here, you speak to these lads and control them. Otherwise there's going to be an ugly scene here, right inside the mosque. The whole community will stink!'

The naattaamai agreed. He stretched both arms out, and silenced everyone. amidst the rustling of the crowd, Suleiman alone spoke loudly. 'Somehow you have all joined together and brought this town to rack and ruin. Do whatever you like, why should I waste my breath and shout myself hoarse?' He went and sat in a corner.

Kader spoke to Nuramma who cowered by the pillar, trembling, 'Go home now.' She made no reply, but stumbled out of there, conscious of escaping with her life. That frail form, moving away, gave him a feeling of acute discomfort.

The skies had begun their preparations for the night. The badam tree sat quietly, as if it knew it would be wrong even to rustle its leaves. In the widespread hall of the mosque which had no doors whatsoever, crowds of bats crashed against the walls and scattered. The gentle lapping of water in the water-trough suddenly sounded as loud as a roar which spread over the crowd. The Modinaar Bawa, unaffected by all that had happened, finished his olu ablutions and stood ready by the nagara, looking at his watch and calculating the exact time when he should sound the call for prayers.

The naattaamai was both angry and resentful that Kader had sent Nuramma away, of his own accord. How could he do that when the discussion was still going on? The naattaamai looked at the mutthavalli, and saw the imprint of the same thought on his face. Neither of them said anything, however: to cross an important man of the town such as Kader, would just bring problems. Besides, this mosque had been built for the community by Kader's father. Kader was held in special regard in the town, because of this.

Kader looked about him and said in a strict tone, 'Right, now let us leave aside what has happened, and decide on what we should do next. We must never have this kind of trouble again in this town. That's what we've got to ensure.' He went to sit in his place, listening to the rest. Suleiman said, loudly enough to be overheard by everyone, 'Terrific things they are going to do!' His face was bright red with anger and humiliation. Kader took no notice of him.

Naattaamai Moosa cleared his throat. 'Good, let us all think about it. Let me hear your thoughts on how we may prevent this kind of obscenity from ever happening here again. We'll act accordingly.'

Besh Imam spoke up and gave his opinion. 'What need is there to think so hard about it? It's the responsibility of men to keep their women well under control. Do not allow your women folk to go about alone either in our streets or to other towns elsewhere. Not during the day, nor at night. Tell the women of our community they must never go to the cinema. Forbid it. Make this an absolute rule.' Besh Imam spoke up very rarely. But what he said was usually considered wise. Most of the people gathered there agreed with him. The naattaamai realized that by their expression.

'What Besh Imam says is very true. Hereafter, our women should never go outside their homes unnecessarily. In particular, they must not go to the cinema.' He stopped for a moment. Satisfied that there was no opposition from the crowd, he got up saying, 'Very good; the meeting is ended.' He was pleased with himself for having concluded the meeting promptly.

Suleiman followed Kader who was leaving the Mosque briskly. 'Why did you do that, Maamu? You let her go in spite of all she said!' He could not let go his resentment. 'You'll see. Hereafter these Hindu fellows will never respect us. They'll look upon us with contempt.' Suleiman looked highly agitated.

Kader looked at his red face and his sharp twitching nose, and felt sorry for him. 'What can we do, Suleiman? In this world, bad things will happen now and then. But it isn't right for us to be provoked into acting without control.' He touched Suleiman's shoulder and pressed it as if he were comforting him. 'Be patient,' he said as he went on his way, full of his own sorrow and confusion.

Kader wondered at Suleiman's extreme anger, while at the

same time agreeing that there was some justification for it, perhaps. However much one tried to accept it, it could not be denied that what Fatima did was disgraceful. One could not help asking again and again what had impelled her. Rahima was the one who was most upset about it. All her anxiety was for Iliaz and Nuramma who had been abandoned and left to struggle on their own.

Kader felt a surge of respect for his wife and her special character. Who else would feel such a responsibility and concern for Fatima's family? He worried that he might have hurt her sensitive nature very badly over Wahida's wedding. His feelings of guilt for having totally ignored Rahima's opinion had troubled him for some days, and he had struggled to get over them. Even if he did nurse a complaint against her, how was he justified in ignoring her so completely? He walked towards his home, his heart very heavy.

He remembered what happened on the previous night. Rahima had come limping into their bedroom. When he asked, 'What has happened?' she answered, 'It's nothing. Fatima isn't here, so I've had to do everything myself; my legs ache.'

Slowly she came and sat down on the bed, pulled open a drawer from the chest nearby, took out the jar containing an ointment and began to apply it, lifting her sari up to the knee. Kader watched her for awhile, and then took the jar from her, saying affectionately, 'You lie down; let me do it.'

'Oh, please don't worry. I'll do it myself. You don't need to make your hands messy.' She was firm in her refusal; her face was very still and that made him sad in a strange way. Her face was very visible even in the faint light of the night lamp, but he was confused because he could not comprehend what she was thinking. He lay down on his side of the bed, trying to work out why she seemed so tense. How was it, he wondered, that she could harbour within herself so huge a hurt, yet never speak a single hard word to him? The room filled with the smell of the ointment. She applied it all along her leg, from the knee to the heel of her foot, rubbing it in firmly. Softly she rose to her feet,

placed the jar back into its drawer and shut it. She limped up
to the door and went outside. When she returned, she carried
a chombu of water in the palm of her hand, the hand held flat.
She went up to him and said, 'Take the chombu, please, and
put it on the table.'

He didn't understand why she was asking him to do this,
but reached across, took the chombu and put it on the table,
covered it with a the lid that was lying there, and lay down
again.

'I did wash my hands. All the same the smell does linger. I
asked you to take it because I didn't want my fingers to touch
the mouth of the chombu.' She gave her explanation coolly,
and lay down beside him. He waited until he was certain she
was asleep, rose up, went to her side, lifted her right leg on to
his lap and began to press it gently to relieve the pain. He was
stricken to the heart, aware of having done her a very great
harm.

Had he not been in such a hurry, had he gently and gradually
explained to her his responsibilities, this situation between
them need not have risen. In a great confusion, he kept on
pressing her leg gently until he found his own hands being held
tightly. Rahima had sat up, had caught hold of his hands.
'Don't,' she said. 'It doesn't hurt any more.'

Gently he said, 'Go back to sleep.' She dropped her head on
his shoulder then, and began to weep, holding on to him tightly.
He comforted her silently, unable to endure the helplessness
that her tears revealed.

* * *

'Well, Kader, what brings you here?' The voice brought him
back into this world. When he looked up, he realized that he
had walked past his own shop and reached the outskirts of the
town where Yunnus kept his stall. Yunnus was talking to him
as he made up a package. 'Nothing at all, Anna, I just wanted
to exercise my legs,' he said, turning back towards his shop. He

realized it was very nearly time for the Maghrib prayers and turned instead into the side street leading to the mosque. The evening light was fading away as darkness began to fall.

✑ 32 ✑

Firdaus realized, from the expression on Amina's face, that her mother was overwhelmed by a terrible fear. News had reached her of Zohra's maid servant Fatima's elopement, and all that had happened at the mosque following that. Firdaus herself was in a fine state of confusion. She could guess what her mother's reaction to all these events would be. It was certain that Amina was never going to leave Firdaus on her own, hereafter, even by mistake. She was overcome with anguish because of this.

When she thought of Siva, happiness streamed through her. Who was it who had sent him to her at a moment when she was convinced that there was no future for her; that hereafter she must live out the rest of her life as a mere corpse? Who could it be, other than Allah? Without his doing, how could anything happen in this universe? If what she was doing was a sin, why would Allah Himself have sent Siva to her, she had consoled herself. But now a terrible fear which she could not fathom, began to take root in her. She thought, helplessly, that the relationship between her and Siva was no more certain than a bubble of water. The shadow of fear that the bubble might burst at any moment, had been with her all the time. But since yesterday, it was stronger, and she could scarcely bear it. Supposing she had to part from him… ? She found herself incapable of deciding anything. There was one thing she knew for certain, though. She would never commit suicide. She was determined to live in this world. She was determined to enjoy all the happiness that was destined for her. She would not give up this world for anyone or anything. But she wanted Siva too. She could not contemplate a life without him. He felt the same. He had told her so himself, several times. But neither of them knew how that could be.

Once, leaning against his shoulder, she asked him, 'Siva, you will never leave me and go away, will you?' He asked, in his turn, cupping her face in his hand, 'Are you afraid?' She could see the fear and the questioning lurk in his eyes too. 'Yes,' she admitted, the tears spilling from her eyes and filling his hands. He gathered her to himself, her face pressed hard against his chest, and said, 'There is nothing at all to fear.' At the time his words seemed only to deceive both of them. 'How can that be?' she asked him. But he could not answer that.

At another time he said, 'Why could I not have been born a Muslim?' When she asked him why, he said, 'Nothing would have stopped me then from making you my second wife.' She could only smile in disbelief, meaning, 'What is there to say?'

Why was the world like this? If two people loved each other, why should it matter to anyone else? Had Siva been a Muslim, he could have made a second marriage; being a Hindu, he could not. Firdaus was too confused to comprehend anything. Siva loved Jaya; he loved Firdaus too. Why shouldn't it be possible for one man to love two women? If he was able to give his love generously to both women, why should anyone else be bothered? She saw no difficulty here at all. But she knew too that Jaya would not accept the situation that easily. Nor was Firdaus herself willing to embrace the idea out of a true generosity of spirit. It just seemed to her that it was possible to accept that he loved two women, and to go along with it. But what end could there be to all this? The thoughts churned inside her head, undermining her head and heart. She wished with all her heart that time could stand stock-still at that moment. The passing of the day, filled as it was with memories and dreams, was hateful to her. She was certain of one thing only: no fear or confusion was going to take away her thoughts of him.

* * *

Preparations were in full swing for the mid-day feast given on the day before the wedding, when prayers for the ancestors would be said. All the chores which Fatima would have done with great care, had now fallen to Rahima and Zohra. Busy about her work, Zohra muttered, 'The Palla slut could at least have seen the wedding through before she made her exit!' But Rahima came up to her and hushed her. 'Sh! The house is full of hired Hindu workers; don't speak contemptuously about their caste!' Zohra immediately bit her tongue and looked about her.

From eleven in the morning, the women of their town began to make their visits. Rabia and Madina had been given the job of greeting all of them, and serving them sherbet and betel leaves. Wahida had been dressed and adorned very beautifully, and made to sit in a chair. She looked a princess in her silk sari and the jewellery which covered her. Rabia delighted in her, and compared her to one of the princesses in the story books she had read, of Vikramadityan, and other kings and queens. She felt an overwhelming pride in Wahida's beauty.

Rabia had packed her own clothes the previous day, in readiness to accompany Wahida to the bridegroom's house on the day after the wedding. Besides, she would see her Firdaus Chitthi. She could scarcely contain her happiness at the thought of it. Madina longed to go with them too, but knew perfectly well that Suleiman would never allow it. Rabia complained, 'Why did your brother have to return home just at this particular time?' She was irritated at the very thought of Suleiman. Since his homecoming, Madina was never allowed out. He kept scolding her, 'You've grown as big as a buffalo; why do you want to roam around the town?'

The aroma of ghee rice wafted to her from the kitchen, tickling her palate. She pushed aside a desire to eat, thinking to herself she would see to it later, and went to sit in the pandal. Women were coming and going in crowds, each wearing a silk sari and jewellery under her dupatta. The house was full of the noise of chattering and laughter, making her feel festive.

She pulled her davani more securely. It would insist on slipping off from her chest. Her mother would scold her, if she saw. Whenever she thought of her mother, her hand adjusted the davani automatically. My mother is to me as Suleiman is to Madina, she thought, and suddenly remembered Ahmad. Where had he gone? She had not caught sight of him. Someone came and sat beside her, relieving her from her thoughts. 'Well, are you dreaming of your grandmother's village already?' Madina smiled, throwing her arm around Rabia's neck, and leaning against her fondly. Rabia felt a bit shy when Madina pressed up so closely against her, but liked it all the same. She felt even more affectionately towards her friend, that day.

She came to herself when she heard Zohra's voice calling out, 'Rabia, Rabia!' She ran inside, calling out, 'Here I am, Amma'. Madina followed swiftly, after her. Zohra grumbled at them, 'Will the two of you give us a hand with the wedding chores, or would you prefer to tell each other stories? Here we are, killing ourselves without even Fatima to help, don't you girls have any sense of responsibility? All right now, run and get the sherbet from the kitchen, and serve all the guests.' Having assigned them their jobs, she hastened away. Wahida caught their eyes and smiled. They smiled in return and ran into the kitchen.

Nafiza and Mumtaz had arrived early in the morning, all dressed up, to help Rahima and Zohra. At mid-day, the Hazrats and other important men had arrived, chanted the Fatiha, and eaten the feast. After that, the ten married women whom Wahida had invited, to honour the memory of her mother Tahira, sat down to eat. Rahima attended to them herself, serving them, and distributing flowers and betel leaves amongst them.

It was three in the afternoon, by the time all this was done. Crowds of women began to fill the house, taking no account of the Vaikasi month's heat, still unabated. Mariyayi and two other hired coolie women were busy scouring all the cooking vessels heaped up in the courtyard. When they saw Mariyayi, every woman there registered an oddly knowing look for just a moment. Neither Mariyayi nor Zohra was unaware of this, but took no account of it. Most of the women were close friends and relations; besides, what they were signalling was true, after all.

That day too, the chief topic of conversation continued to be Fatima's flight. It was Mumtaz who began. 'Well, Akka, Fatima's absence must make you feel as if your arm was broken. I don't know how you are going to manage everything by yourselves.'

'Of course. But what do you suggest we do? Of course we feel it badly. How could this wretched woman go and do this? How did she have the heart to abandon her own child and run away?' Zohra lamented. She could not get over it.

Saura said, hand on her cheek, 'How could she lust after a man like that, mad creature! Ammadi, Ammadi, there are two men in your family; how on earth did she leave them alone?'

Rahima cut in immediately, stopping her from saying anything further, 'Ché ché! Never say such a thing, Saurakka. The men of this household have always known their responsibilities towards her, and acted accordingly.' She was distressed that Saura's thoughts had taken such a turn.

But Saura would not be stopped. 'You be quiet, now! Why are you taking her side? How impudent must a woman be, to do such a thing, in spite of being born a Muslim? The very thought of such a deed makes one tremble. How could she go after a man, like that? Thuutheri!' She mimed spitting into the courtyard. 'But if the monkey dies, is all life to end? Let us get on with our work!'

All the women there agreed with what she said, each adding her bit. Sainu, who had been silent all this while, now chipped in. 'And does is it finish there, di? Besides bringing this whore into the world, her mother Nurumma went and dishonoured all our men when the congregation met. My son, Suleiman, is absolutely stunned. He hasn't slept or eaten for two days, he's so upset that the town has gone to the bad so completely.' Her face looked flushed and burning with anger and shame.

'I absolutely agree. Hereafter, who is going to show any respect towards our men in our shops and our streets? It's celebration time for these Hindu labourers, isn't it? We women at least stay inside our houses. How are our men to walk outdoors with any pride? How could she have shamed the whole community?' Saura said. She went on, wondering whether Nafiza might have had previous knowledge of the affair, 'Why, Nafiza, wasn't that fellow working in your husband's shop? Didn't you get an inkling of what was going on between those two?'

Instantly Nafiza spoke up, in great agitation, 'What are you trying to insinuate? Fatima worked in this house, so can you say that these people knew what she was up to?' She really was very angry, and had to grit her teeth. She told herself that if she let it go, these people might even say that she had instigated the elopement.

Saura went on, turning to Rahima, 'By the way, it seems it was your husband who said they weren't to punish that impudent woman. Mustn't you show some discretion when you ask people to be merciful? Are we to let off a woman who said such dreadful things? Shouldn't she have been beaten to death?'

Rahima didn't say a word in reply. She didn't care to say anything at all. She was shocked that these women who had shown such solidarity with Nuramma and Fatima until yesterday, had now turned into their bitter enemies. How could this be? Why should the whole town show such extreme hatred towards her because she ran away with a man? From where did such cruelty and hostility towards an old woman turn up? What instigated this anger which each of them was now revealing, even if it didn't actually affect anyone? Rahima could only be astonished by it all.

Sainu said in her turn, bitterly, 'Very well, she went looking for a man; couldn't she find a Muslim boy? The impudent girl had to go with a Hindu!'

Nafiza said nothing. She was always thrown off balance when they discussed matters such as this, sadly aware of her own embarrassing position. She was plagued by her conscience which told her that everything that was being said might apply to her too; she could neither say anything nor sit still. She was on tenterhooks that if this conversation went on any longer, soon somebody would accuse her too, obliquely. Mumtaz saw the alarm and confusion in her expression, and guessed accurately what was going on in Nafiza's mind; she began to enjoy the situation. For her part, she wanted the conversation to carry on, and not come to a stop. Nafiza was aware of this, too.

Just as Nafiza was opening her mouth, determined to change the subject, Rahima spoke up. 'The bride has to be decorated with henna. Who is going to do it?' She too felt the need to change the thrust of the conversation. Nafiza took a deep breath, saying to herself, 'Allahu.'

'Is the henna ground already?' asked Sainu.

'No, it still hasn't been done. We usually put it on in the evening. Why should it be ground so soon?' Zohra answered.

'I too was wondering why there was such haste about that. We only do it in the late evening. I'll do it for the bride, myself,' Mumtaz offered.

'No thank you, amma. Your husband has just come home from abroad. If you come and settle here for the evening, who's going to answer to him?' Zohra teased.

Mumtaz demurred. 'You talk as if we are fussing over each other every day. Who wants to sleep with their husband every night?'

Zohra laughed mischievously, 'What is this, di? You were waiting for him to come home all this while and now you say this! Are you tired of him already?'

'Who knows how many times they do it every night? It must happen each day before dawn. Of course she's tired of it.' Nafiza gave a conspiratorial smile. She wanted her words to remind everyone how much Mumtaz had been yearning for her husband; she derived a mean pleasure from doing this. She stopped short, as if to impress on everyone that she wasn't just teasing her friend.

But Mumtaz didn't appear to be put out. 'So what am I to say? Did Fatima have to time her elopement just now, to coincide with his return? The man is distressed to death about it, as if the whole community has gone to ruin! He thinks the whole town has gone to the bad, with her running away, and he blames all of us women.'

What she said was true enough. Suleiman was making his complaints everyday. He kept saying that the community had to be thoroughly reformed, that the women had been spoilt and ruined. He couldn't accept what had happened, one bit. He was troubled all the time by the humiliation to the town, and wondering how the stigma could be removed. His mind was swirling with plans. Mumtaz often thought to herself that if he were to know about Nafiza's affair, he would just about destroy her. Sometimes Mumtaz thought, with an evil delight, well, what if she were to tell him about it? But the next minute she would remind herself that it could blow up into something huge and divide their two families, and decide to keep quiet. 'The wretches! Let them go their way. Allah watches everything that goes on, anyway, why should I get mixed up in it?'

Zohra sent Rabia away from there. 'Get up, get up. Leave off listening to the older women's talk and go and mind your own business', she said. Rabia rose to her feet and left unwillingly, looking at Wahida the whole time. Wahida gave her little cousin a sweet smile.

Madina had gone home for a while. Rabia came to the front of the house and stood looking at the pandal, once again. Four or five men were standing on stools, sticking tinsel paper decorations to the edges of the pandal. She loved the rustling and the colour of the pretty paper. The pandal was very attractive, with all its floral designs. The paper chains seemed to preen themselves as if they were aware that it was because of them that the pandal, which had looked so sleepy and listless in the morning, was now so very beautiful.

Mariyayi came out of the house, carrying a box made of woven palm leaves, heaped with rubbish. She was setting off to the river to dump the lot. When she saw Rabia standing beside the pandal, she started as if she had suddenly remembered something. 'Rabia, come here,' she called, affectionately.

Rabia came to herself, and went up to Mariyayi, asking, 'What is it?'

'There's a doll in this basket. Your Amma said it wasn't needed and asked me to throw it away. Just take a look and see if it is yours?' She put her hand into the basket, and groped about. Pieces of paper fell out and scattered about. Rabia looked away into the distance, anxiously. The smell of sweat from Mariyayi's body reached her nose. Although she disliked it, she waited, wondering what it could be, and stopping herself from grimacing. 'How on earth can Attha bear to stay in Mariyayi's house when she stinks so,' she asked herself.

'Here, I've found it.' Mariyayi found the wooden doll and handed it to her. Had Amma actually told her to throw it away? Rabia died for an instant and returned to life. It was the doll that Ahmad had given her. She gathered it into her hands and looked at it closely for an instant. It stood tall like a magnificent man. Its long arms and legs! The mound between its legs, left unmoulded lest its male genitals were exposed! She felt a great affection for this doll which she could not explain. There were many nights when she had slept with it, tightly held in her arms.

Her mother had often complained, 'Look at this creature, with its bare bottom. You wretch, couldn't you at least find a female doll to play with?' But, as far as Rabia was concerned, it wasn't a mere doll. She certainly wasn't going to listen to her mother. She continued to feel love and closeness towards it. Nowadays, she often kept it by her side without anyone's – particularly her mother's – knowing. Sometimes it was under her covering at night, or inside her pillow. She would fall asleep, lost in the sweetness of its touch. Sometimes she would wonder whether the doll stood for Ahmad in her heart. It would lay its head on her breast and embrace her at night, as if it took over the right that belonged to Ahmad alone. The tender warmth of her own body would leap into it, so that it came to life and protected her through the night.

⌒ 33 ⌒

The smell of the henna being ground on the grindstone seized hold of Rabia and dragged her to the kitchen. Mariyayi was hard at work. Rabia ran up and stood next to her for a while, watching the softening henna, as she pulled the grindstone over it, again and again. To the right of Mariyayi, there was a silver dish on which she had place the henna she had already ground, rolled into a ball. To her left was a palm leaf winnowing-tray half full of henna leaves, still waiting to be ground. Mariyayi paused to sprinkle some water on to the grindstone, and then continued.

Rabia asked her, 'Do you have to grind all this? Won't your arms ache?'

Mariyayi was pleased by Rabia's concern. 'Yes! I'll do all this. There has to be enough for all of you.'

Rabia went on eagerly, 'By the way, where did you find all this henna? They tell me you brought it with you? Will it go a good red?'

Mariyayi stopped grinding for a moment and said with pride, 'I've planted a tree in our garden, did you know that?'

Rabia was breathless with delight. 'Why didn't you tell me all this while? Please will you bring some with you very often from now on?'

'Of course. Why not? Would I ever deny my thangam?' Mariyayi lifted her hands, touched the sides of Rabia's face, and then cracked her knuckles against her temples.

'Ay! Look how red your hand has got!' Rabia took Mariyayi's hand in both hers, and admired the redness of the henna against the dark skin. Then she turned her own hands over and contemplated the outspread palms.

Mariyayi freed her own hand before asking, 'What's happened? You seem sunk in some thought, suddenly?'

'No, it's just that the henna they put on me for the Festival, has not disappeared at all. It's still all there. So I'm wondering how to have a fresh lot done now.'

Mariyayi was casual. 'So what? Tell them to go over the same designs exactly, this time too,' she advised. This struck Rabia as being very sound. She stood there considering who she could ask to apply the henna on her.

Zohra arrived there, barked at her daughter and chased her away, saying, 'What is your business here, please? You keep going round and round, getting in the way of anyone who is trying to get some work done. Go away now, the henna is not going to run away, is it?'

Scared of her mother, she left the kitchen and went to gaze at the preparations that were going on underneath the pandal in the inner courtyard, for the feast for the wedding day. A palm leaf mat was spread there, with all the ingredients for the next day's biriyani laid out in separate heaps: onions, green chillies, all kinds of vegetables. Two of the coolie women who had been hired to help were seated there, peeling and chopping. One of them watched Rabia running along and jumping between the heaped vegetables and called out, 'Ammadi, master's daughter! Watch out, don't fall down and hurt yourself!'

Rabia did not pay her any heed. She was so proud of her new long skirt and davani. She could hardly contain her delight in the new danglers in her ears, the new ankle-chains decorating her feet.

In the hall, they were getting everything ready for Wahida's betrothal nalangu. On silver salvers, all the materials were laid ready: rice smeared with turmeric, betel leaves and nuts, powdered fenugreek, oil, coconut, bananas, sugar. A lantern had been lit, and placed ready, in a corner. There were crowds of women, seated on mats, whispering and rustling.

Zohra muttered to herself, 'As soon as the nalangu ritual is over, we must see that the henna decorations are done, and bring everything to a close.'

Sainu complained, 'In the old days, it was the custom to do the nalangu ritual in the early morning of the betrothal day. Nowadays, they seem to finish it off on the evening of the day before the wedding. How times have changed.'

Saura chimed in, agreeing with her, 'Yes, that's so. If the elder brother's wife and the new bridegroom's family were all from the same town, all this nalangu material was made ready and taken first from the bride's house to the bridegroom. We did the nalangu there first, then everyone returned to the bride's place to do the nalangu here. It was all finished in time for the Bajar prayers. Nowadays, the bridegroom is often from out of town; we do the nalangu to the bride ourselves.'

Listening to her regretful tones, Mumtaz muttered to Nafiza, 'Why does she have to feel so sorry about that?'

Nafiza said, in her turn, 'Let these old ladies say what they like. Who is going to get up so early in the morning to do all this before the Bajar prayers? Don't we have our lives to live?' Then, seeing that all the women were now standing ready, with the money in their hands, ready for the nalangu, Nafiza called out to Rabia who stood at a distance, watching everything, Madina at her side.

As soon as Rabia came to her, Nafiza made her stand behind Wahida, who had been seated on a stool facing west, the nalangu materials in front of her. 'Come here, stand behind your Akka like this. Now hold out the upper end of your davani like this, ready to catch the coins that people will circulate around Wahida's face and then throw towards you.'

Sainu was quick off the mark, however. 'What's this? You can't have the younger sister standing behind the bride. That only happens when we do the nalangu for the bridegroom.

Madina, you come instead. Come and stand here, behind Wahidakka.' She summoned Madina sharply. Madina stepped forward with great embarrassment, too afraid to go against her mother.

Mumtaz and Nafiza, observing all this, exchanged glances and smiles. Zohra whispered to Rahima, 'Whatever it is, you have to say Sainu is a smart one.'

One by one the women there touched the oil with their fingers three times, then picked up a little of the rice and powdered fenugreek, encircled Wahida's veiled head, and tossed the rice, along with some coins. Madina, catching these in her davani, squirmed with embarrassment and shyness. Rabia stood by her, trying to make her feel comfortable, signalling with her eyes, 'It's all right; don't feel shy.' Most of the women handed the money, wrapped in a betel leaf, to Wahida directly, circling her head only with the rice. Nafiza and a few others smeared Wahida's face with oil and sandalwood paste for a joke, laughing as she blushed.

Rahima asked the women there, 'Come on, ammas, won't someone sing a nalangu song now?'

Nafiza and Mumtaz refused vociferously, claiming they were too shy. Saura scolded them fondly, 'Such modesty! But you are never shy to say the most outrageous things, are you? Silly idiots!' She began to sing in a shrill voice, *Nalangida vaarum amma*, the invitation to all the women to participate in the nalangu ritual, a few women singing along with her.

As soon as all the women had finished the ritual, seven women arranged themselves in front of Wahida, and seven behind her. The seven in front lifted up the trays standing on the floor beside them, one by one, and handed them over Wahida's head, to the women standing behind her. Those seven laid the trays down on the floor for a moment, and then returned them to the women in front. This exchange happened three times, durng which, Rabia, terrified that they might drop the lantern on Wahida's head, muttered to herself noiselessly, 'Careful, careful, slowly.' She looked at Madina who had been catching the nalangu rice all this time, still squirming with embarrassment, and gave her an encouraging smile. Madina, realizing that her friend was mischievously trying to make her laugh, gave her a shy smile.

Saura continued to sing her song, without stopping. She didn't know the whole song, and so had to keep on repeating the first four lines of it. Rabia, listening to the repeated tune, was reminded of the way a single line of an old cinema song would be repeated sometimes, in their cinema theatre, before a showing. Ahmad would say, 'The wretched fellows, they have put on a cracked record.'

Rabia wanted to giggle. Saura had lost a front tooth, besides, and a couple of words came out sounding very muddled. She was very amusing, both to watch and listen to. All the women enjoyed her rendition of the song, teasing her and laughing. The whole house assumed an air of fun and enjoyment.

Nafiza touched Wahida on the shoulder, made her get up from her stool and brought her to sit on one of the mats spread out in the middle of the hall. Zohra was distressed to see the oil pooling on top of the girl's head and complained, 'Ché, why couldn't they have given her just a token trace of oil instead of making her hair all sticky!' She brought a piece of old cloth and tried to blot off Wahida's face and the top of her head.

'Leave it! We must have the chance to tease a new bride, mustn't we? All these games and playing about will only be for day; don't take it so seriously,' Nafiza was playful, but there was a touch of irritation in her voice.

'Very well, it's starting to get dark; please all of you touch the girl with henna,' Rahima hurried everyone sitting there. The more distant relations who had come from afar, now rose to their feet, and began to say their goodbyes. Rahima invited them, courteously, to stay and add their touch of henna before leaving. She knew it was getting dark and they would not wish to delay any longer, but gave the invitation, all the same.

'No, no,' they all protested, 'it is getting dark; we have to go past four streets. We will be here tomorrow morning for the tali-tying.' And so they left, with their bags of betel leaves and nuts.

When they had gone, Rahima and Zohra said a 'Bismillah', and put the first touches of henna on Wahida's hands. After that, Nafiza and Mumtaz sat down on either side of her, and each taking one of her hands on her lap, began to cover it with designs. Rabia sat down next to them, eager to watch it all. She looked up to see Madina leaning against the wall, and summoned her with a nod of her head to come and join them.

Madina picked out the coins that lay mixed up with the rice in her davani, and took them to Rahima, saying, 'Please take this'. Rahima looked her up and down and smiled, 'How grown up you've become, as soon as you decided to wear a davani!' She gave a fond tap to Madina's head and said, 'Go on, keep it!' She went away into the kitchen. Rabia gave a sigh of relief. Thank heavens Periamma didn't take the money; how humiliating it would have been otherwise! She knew her Periamma wouldn't accept it, but she had worried about it all the same.

'Very well, Rabia, shall I go now?' Madina said, preparing to leave. She felt too bad to stay there. She repeated to herself crossly, 'When I go home, I'll give it to Amma.' Rabia came up to her, put her hand on her shoulder and hugged her affectionately, saying, 'What's the hurry, now?' Her touch was comforting, reassuring Madina not to feel embarrassed.

'Wait, let me give you some henna; put it on when you go home.' Rabia ran inside, scooped up some henna in a betel leaf, and brought it to Madina.

Madina went home, saying, 'Good; I'll come round in the morning. My brother will be back around now.'

Rabia heard Nafiza's voice calling out her name. 'Coming,' she returned, and went to her side. Nafiza said to her, 'There's a wooden box with compartments, in the top drawer of the almirah in my kitchen. The wooden press for henna hand-designs is inside it. Will you fetch it for me?'

Rabia said she would, and began to run. Outside, tube-lights

had been fixed to the pandal, to chase away the darkness. It
was dazzlingly bright there. The workmen were placing chairs
inside; row upon row. Ahmad must be at home now, she
thought, as she set off.

Ahmad was sitting in the hall of his house, making a kite.
Pieces of paper and broomsticks were scattered on the floor
beside him. When he saw her, he called out, 'What is it, Rabia?'
She was surprised by the unusual note of affection in his voice.

'That is, your mother wanted me to bring her something
from here.' Her voice was trembling, and she had broken out
in a sweat before she could finish.

He got up from his seat and came to stand very close beside
her. 'Why are you so scared?' he asked, taking her hand and
prising open her fingers so that he could see her palm. 'Haven't
they put any henna on you as yet?'

She was taken aback, filled with delight and shyness at the
same time. She didn't know whether she should pluck her hand
away from him or not as she stood there, stock-still. He pulled
at her fingers and shook them, bringing her to herself. 'Ei,
Rabia, what is it?' At that moment she plucked her hand away.

He spoke sharply. 'Why, do you think you will lose
something if you are touched?' he returned to his place and sat
down again.

Her face was aflame with remorse. Why did I pluck my hand
away so foolishly, she asked herself reproachfully, what a fool
I am. I liked it, didn't I? Then why did I pull my hand away?

Since the morning, she had yearned to show Ahmad her
new skirt and davani, and full of disappointment that she could
not. So why, when she was with him at last, was she behaving
so badly? She was annoyed with herself. She looked down at
her satin skirt, the colour of vadaamalligai, and the black
davani draped about herself; she remembered that Wahidakka
and Amma had remarked to each other how pretty she looked
in them. She recalled the new silk skirt waiting to be worn the
next day, and suddenly felt very happy.

There was a moment's silence. She began to wonder why he

gave no indication at all whether he had even noticed her new clothes, and determined that she would leave only after she was sure he had looked at her properly. She flopped down on the floor next to him, eagerly. She ran her fingers down from her knee to her foot very deliberately, smoothing down her skirt. She brought one of her two long plaits over her shoulder, to the front, and began to re-do it. She played with the new bangles on her wrists, making them tinkle. He took no notice of any of these manoeuvres, concentrating instead on trimming the tail of his kite, and getting it exactly right. This upset her, and set her wondering helplessly whether it had been very wrong of her to pluck her hand away from him. Wanting to pacify him, she drew nearer, and asked, 'Why haven't we seen you for so many days?'

He noticed the ache in her voice, and said, 'Who, me? I've been here all this time.' He gazed at her for a while, and said, 'I'm going away to town tomorrow, with my Maama. He'll be here to attend the wedding at your house. I'll return only when the vacation is over.'

He saw her face cloud over with disappointment, and her eyes, which were always so bright and eager, tighten. He liked very much the single hair that curled at her temple, and swung up and down when the breeze blew. He had first begun to like her because he imagined that she resembled his mother. He could both understand – and could not – why she, in her turn, liked him so much. He thought to himself that his going away would hurt not only her, but himself, too.

She asked, longingly, 'Do you have to go?' She couldn't find any more words.

'It's my mother... ' he began. Suddenly his throat choked painfully. The words came out, brokenly. He didn't wish to go away, either. But would his mother listen? Who could he play with there? He would not be allowed out into the streets, but would have to pass the time imprisoned inside the house. That was why he had decided to make a kite and take it with him. Here, he could climb the mountain. Or catch bees and butterflies. Tie strings to the tails of dragonflies and play with them. Bury dragonflies and dig them up after fifteen days to see if they had turned into coins. Iliaz had said he had done it. He could ride a cycle. Teach Rabia to cycle. Fight with Madina. His mind brimmed over with all these hopes which would not be fulfilled.

Rabia asked again, 'So you won't be back until the holidays are over, will you?'

He made out easily from her tone that it was actually a demand that he should return straight away, and not stay on at his uncle's house. He answered casually, in a very grown up manner, 'That's what they are saying. Let's see.'

She, for her part intuited that his answer was only meant to provoke her, so she tried again. 'But why won't you say what you want?'

With a mischievous smile at the corner of his mouth, he asked, 'When should I return? Immediately, or only when the holidays are over?' He repeated his question as if he were waiting for her command. She was sure he asked her that out of a desire to please her, and that made her very happy. She dropped her head, saying to herself, 'Ammadi, how wicked he is!' Her lips must have moved slightly, because he scolded her fondly, 'What are you muttering to yourself now?'

'Nothing,' she assured him. She seized his hand and gave it a light pinch, then ran away to pick up the henna presses from the kitchen.

* * *

When she entered the house with the henna presses, she encountered her mother, who plucked them from her hands. 'Do you have to take so long to go two houses down the road,' she scolded, hurrying away inside. It was then that Rabia noticed that Wahida's grandfather had arrived from town. She ran to sit by his side, saying, 'Welcome, Nanna! Have you just arrived?' She was very fond of him.

He took her hand affectionately, between both of his, and teased her fondly, 'What is this di? How grown-up you are, in your davani and everything.'

'Go on, Nanna,' she said, dropping her head and squirming shyly.

But he went on, addressing Zohra, 'Yemma, why didn't you find a bridegroom for this little one too? We could have finished both nikahs together, couldn't we? We could have saved ourselves the expense, too!' He smiled widely, showing his betel-stained teeth.

Not willing to lose the opportunity, Nafiza cut in proudly. 'Why do you have to seek elsewhere for a new bridegroom, Maamu? Here's my son, all ready. All you have to do is to get them together and have a tali-tying. You just ask her. She's so very fond of him.'

'Oh, ho, is that how it is? Then let's get on with it and finish it all smartly,' he said, playfully, laughing.

Although she knew that it was all in play, Rabia liked what they said, and enjoyed it all, deep down. She imagined it really happening, and felt good about it. She could not understand why she felt a thrill go through her entire self at the mere mention of Ahmad's name. At the same time she was distressed that he seemed not even to have noticed her new dress that day.

Zohra brought the conversation to a close swiftly. Smiling, she said, 'First let your granddaughter come of age. The you can look for a bridegroom to suit her.'

Wahida's grandfather had brought her a kasumalai necklace, made of twenty sovereigns worth of gold. He took it out of a jewel case, handed it to Rahima, saying with pride, 'Show this to everyone, amma.'

Zohra thought of her own family's circumstances. Had her father been alive, would he not do the same for her own daughter? For a moment the thought that she and her daughter were deprived of that generosity pressed heavily on her heart.

Rahima noticed the changing expression on Zohra's face

and was distressed. These changes in Zohra, in recent times, made Rahima profoundly anxious. It was after the preparations for Wahida's wedding had begun that something had changed in Zohra. Rahima was suddenly aware of her anger towards the women who filled her house. There was no single one she could point at; they were saithaans, all of them, she told herself, trying to calm down. She understood clearly that some irresponsible gossip had succeeded in dividing her family, but did not know who to blame. Nafiza and Mumtaz, who at this very moment were joking and laughing and making merry, for instance: what part did they play in achieving Zohra's change of heart? Rahima's own heart felt weary and empty.

She handed the kasumalai to Zohra, saying, 'Here, you show this round, yourself.' She went to sit next to her father. She had been on her feet all day, and her legs ached. Hanifa leaned his head against the sofa, saying in a tired voice, 'It is still burning hot!' Rahima looked at him affectionately. Time had weakened him. His wizened and dark body and his balding head had taken away from his former magnificence. He was beset with illnesses, besides. Rahima reached for his hands and placed them between her own. The warmth of his trembling fingers seemed to communicate many things to her directly. A sadness grew in her, shattering her peace even more, as she wondered how much he suffered from the inevitable loneliness that old age brings.

'The necklace is very beautiful,' she told him. 'Where did you buy it?' It was clear that her words were sincerely meant, and not spoken from mere politeness; she really did think it was a beautiful piece. Even Mumtaz was heard to praise its beauty. Rahima was stabbed with a sudden fear that they might cast an evil eye upon the necklace, and upon her father who brought it. Inwardly, she prayed to Allah to deliver them from the evil eye of envy, and to keep her father from all harm even until his hundredth year. It was only after this, that she was restored to a state of calm.

'You are very tired; please come and lie down for a little

while.' Zohra came and insisted on taking him inside for a rest.

Nafiza and Mumtaz, who had been waiting for him to retire, now felt comfortable enough to chatter in their usual way. Both of them immediately pulled away their saris from their heads and tucked the end into their waists, saying, 'It's a good thing Zohrakka took Maamu away inside. How long could we have sat here, pulling our saris over our heads and not daring to open our mouths!'

Zohra came out again, and teased them. 'Don't I know you both? Now you can sing and dance to your heart's content.'

Rahima leaned over from where she was seated, on the sofa, and gave them a playful tap on their heads. 'Sit quietly for a while like modest and well-brought up women! You won't lose anything.'

Mumtaz spoke up, loudly enough for Zohra, who was now in the kitchen, to hear. 'Why, Rahimakka, is this kasumalai such a big thing, after all? Don't you think the ring that our Mariyayi brought her daughter is just as valuable, even if it is worth only one sovereign?'

'Say so,' agreed Nafiza.

Zohra peeped out from the kitchen, scolding them fondly. 'You've started your work, have you?'

'We speak the truth; does it hurt you, or what? Whatever it is, it won't be equal to Mariyayi's love and affection, that's all.' They laughed together. Rahima went inside to her father, defeated by the two women's banter.

Nafiza said, applying the henna to Wahida's fingers, 'Tonight is the last night that you will sleep by yourself, what about that?' She gave a knowing smile. 'Besides, tomorrow is going to be your first night with your husband! Hm, do we need to teach you anything?'

Wahida blushed a bright red with shame. Her head drooped down, even lower.

'What are you saying? Why do we have to give Wahida any lessons? As if her husband doesn't know anything! All these years as a bachelor, he's been busy learning it all. What are you going to teach her that he doesn't know?' Mumtaz teased.

Wahida understood their banter only in part. Deeply embarrassed, she wanted to get up and run away. How could she, though, when they held her hands and were applying henna to them? She was shocked and repulsed at the same time.

꒰ 34 ꒱

Once all the preparations for the evening meal were over, Kader came out of the house, and sat on one of the chairs in the pandal. A faint breeze glanced past the leaves of the banana tree tied to the pandal. By this time, on the next day, all the hustle and bustle of the wedding would be over; Wahida would have gone to her husband's house. The very thought of it troubled Kader. From where he sat, outside the house, he could see, through the open doors, the wide corridor set with rows of iron pillars, and the rooms leading off it. Vegetables were heaped in the courtyard, and the hired women were hard at work. It was Mariyayi who was supervising them. He pitied her. Crazy woman! She tended to take responsibility for all the chores, as if by doing so she could convince herself of her rights in this family, and demonstrate them to everyone, besides.

He realized that from the next day, after Wahida had gone, this huge house would be empty and bereft. Although she had not spent most of her years here, her departure this time would be unbearable. Yet, what was to be done? All of a sudden he wondered whether Sikander was the right man for his daughter. The doubt was not an entirely new one. Without ever giving an outward sign of it, he had been nursing this doubt for many days. Had he betrayed it, he would have played into Rahima's hands. He would never allow that, he told himself sternly.

Kader was always surprised to see fathers – many of them his own kinsfolk – play with their baby daughters in their laps, freely revealing their love. He himself was too reticent by nature, to do it. Although he wanted to show Wahida all the love he had for her, he could only speak to her from a distance. His own father doted on Sabia Akka, yet he always kept her at arm's length. Kader didn't know whether his father thought one should always be reticent in showing one's love towards one's daughter; or that it was wrong to touch them once they were grown up. Kader was the same, though. Many of his ways were a continuation of his father's. Sometimes, when he looked at Wahida, he was reminded of his mother. Her serenity and beauty – the very likeness of his mother – filled him with pride. But he never, ever, expressed his love for her openly. Rahima sometimes asked him, 'So what are you going to do with all this love that you keep hidden away?'

He was distressed by his memories of his mother. What was the use of his father being so wealthy, when he insisted on his wife being cooked alive in the kitchen, on most days? He'd leave his shop and turn up at home suddenly to make his demand: 'Fifty men have come to the mosque on tabligh work Jamila, to check that all religious duties are being performed correctly. I want you to cook enough idiaappam and iddlis for all of them, and send them at once to the mosque, in readiness for their evening meal.' Off he would go, not bothering to wait for an answer. In a little while a labourer would arrive with ten to twenty chickens. In those days, the butcher did not slaughter a calf everyday and sell the meat. It only happened on Saturdays. On those days, the whole town was fragrant with the aroma of meat curry. It was almost as if an invisible form traversed all the streets, spreading the aroma. The children rejoiced greatly in it, too. It astonished him that even today, if a sudden aroma of meat curry hit his nose, he would think it was a Saturday.

His mother never spoke a word of complaint. He had never even known her to wince, or pull a face. And it was because she undertook it all silently that his father heaped all these duties on her. At least once a week he commanded her to cook a feast for the tabligh visitors. Kader sometimes asked her, 'Why do

you struggle like this, Amma? Why don't you refuse to do it?'
She'd answer, with a very beautiful smile on her serene face, 'Is
he ever cruel to me? He is only asking me to appease the hunger
of the visitors to our mosque. Don't you know that that's a
good thing to do, Kader?' Her words would seem to imply
that he was worrying far too much about a very simple matter.

In the last days of her life, his mother told him, 'You must
give your daughter only to your Sabia Akka's son.' She spoke
out of a fear that these kinship ties might be lost. 'Sabia must
not lose her tie with this family because she has married and
left this house. Her relationship with this community and her
tie with this family must be long-lasting. That is why I tell you
this. If you don't agree to it, all her ties her will be lost.' His
mother had gazed at him as if she were demanding a promise.
He felt certain at that moment that nothing and nobody in the
world was more important to him than his mother; he said,
'Insha Allah.' Now, he was troubled every day by the thought
that the tight bond between him and his mother had prevented
him from making the right decision regarding his daughter's
entire life. He couldn't say for certain that it was because of his
one promise to his mother that he made this decision in spite
of his poor opinion of Sikander, and the disparity in age
between him and Wahida. There was also a matter
outstanding, between him and Rahima. He knew that he would
not get another opportunity to pay her back if he missed this
one. But he was wracked by the thought that he could never be
justified in sacrificing his daughter's entire life in order to score
a point off his wife. What did his deep love for his daughter
mean, in that case? Was it a lie, after all? He could not work it
out. Full of confused thoughts, he laid his head back against
the chair as if suffering from a headache. Tears, for some reason,
seeped from his closed eyes.

He heard Suleiman's voice, saying, 'Well? Are you drowsy,
Maamu?' and came to himself with a start and opened his eyes.
'Nothing like that. Come, sit down,' he said, indicating a chair
next to him.

'Has the cooking not started yet? I thought I might come and keep you company for awhile,' Suleiman said. 'It's been such a long time since I participated in a nikah in our town. What does it matter where you travel, Maamu, you never get the same joy as when you are in your own home town, on your own land, among your own people. Never elsewhere; not in Malaysia. Not in Singapore.'

Kader was astonished by the look of fervour on Suleiman's face when he said this. He understood at last, the extent of Suleiman's love for his homeland in spite of all his travels, but something told him that Suleiman was a frog in the well, all the same. He nodded his head in agreement, however, and said, 'No, the cooking hasn't started yet. The calf is being slaughtered in the shed; once Latif Bai washes the meat and hands it over, then the cook can start his work.'

'So how much meat and how much rice altogether have you asked them to cook?'

At that moment, Kader's father-in-law and Karim were walking towards the pandal. Kader stood up briefly in respect, and sat down again nearby, once his father-in-law was comfortably seated. Suleiman, who had also stood up, greeted the older man, saying, 'Asalaam aleikum'. Hanifa greeted him in his turn, and asked Suleiman when he had returned.

'Just a week ago,' Suleiman answered very politely. It was many days since he had seen the old man, who looked much weakened. 'How is your health?' he asked.

'I am as you see me,' Hanifa answered, smiling wearily, 'I am ready to go when the angel Israel summons me.'

Suleiman was distressed. For a moment everyone was quiet. Anxious to break the silence, he picked up the conversation which had been broken off. 'Well, Maamu, how many measures of rice are you planning to cook?' Karim was the only one who continued to stand, leaning against the palm-leaf thattis surrounding the pandal, his arms crossed.

'They usually reckon that a measure of rice will feed eight. We've calculated for six. There won't be less than a hundred in the bridegroom's party. So let's say twenty measures for them. In our town, we must send some to at least fifty families who are our kin. If we say a measure for each family, that comes to fifty. Then there are all the outsiders; business friends, but also all our estate workers, labourers and coolies, who will expect their share of the feast. So in all, we decided on a hundred measures of rice,' Kader said.

'A hundred measures!' Suleiman was astounded for a moment. 'And the meat?'

'Oh, the meat? We thought a kilo of meat for each measure wasn't quite right, so we've made it one and a half kilos. It will taste good then,' said Kader. He added by way of concluding the conversation, 'Yes, it has been a lot of expense.'

Hanifa interrupted Suleiman at this point, saying, 'We have one child. Who else will we do all this for? Let people eat well and give her their blessing.'

'Oh yes, indeed!' Suleiman nodded his head in agreement.

Hanifa was always embarrassed to address his son-in-law directly, so he asked Karim, 'In this town, how much commission do you give to the mosque, from the money given to the bridegroom?'

'Here the custom is to give fifty out of every thousand. What do you do in your town?'

'It's exactly the same,' said Hanifa, 'I just wanted to know. You do also have the mihr money, don't you?'

'Oh yes, we have that too. It's something like one out of every thousand. When there's the tali-tying in the morning, they'll write it in a book and get it signed.' Karim spoke as if it were a joke. He stretched out his hand, pulled out a piece of the woven thatti, and began to pick his teeth.

'In Saudi and other countries they only have the mihr. Here they accept a dowry from the girl's family. Isn't that haraam?' Suleiman was censorious. 'Nothing is done according to the law. Nothing. It's all unorthodox. We've lived among these Tamil people and turned into them.' His voice was full of anger and resentment because of the deterioration of his community, and his helplessness either to prevent the situation or to change it.

'What do you want us to do, Suleiman? Things must change with the passage of time. Tell me, who can prevent that?' Kader said, trying to pacify Suleiman. He tried not to show his annoyance at Suleiman's assumption that he alone cared to safeguard the community's honour.

'All you elders of this community, what have you done for it? Here, just yesterday, a woman made off with a Kafir boy. And what did you people do? Can you give me a guarantee that another woman will not take her for a role model and do the same, hereafter? You cannot. Did you decide on any disciplinary measures to prevent the same thing from happening again? Of course not. If you continue to take no notice, what is going to happen? You tell me, sir!' He spoke heatedly, counting on Hanifa to take his side. Kader was annoyed in the extreme. He turned to Karim and gave him a look as if to say, 'Who asked this fellow to come here?' Then he turned away.

Hanifa was not at peace over this matter, either. 'Whatever it is, this obscenity should never have happened, it's true. In our mosque too, and among all my business acquaintances, all righteous men have asked me about this matter. Those who are not bothered are sinners. This news is something that no Muslim man can stomach.' Even his old and tired form was shaking with anger, Kader noted.

Kader sat with his head bowed, not wishing to make any reply, in the hope that his father-in-law would control himself. He knew that whatever he said would be construed as condoning the affair, and so he kept quiet.

Fortunately, at that moment, Latif Bhai appeared and summoned them saying, 'Who is coming to check that the meat is weighed out properly?' Karim stepped forward, but Kader stopped him with a look, rose up and went with Latif Bhai. Karim understood that his brother wished to leave the place because of Suleiman's presence there, and stood aside for him.

Suleiman realized that Kader intended to slip away from the company, and was angry. Such a big man, he told himself, sneeringly. Hanifa, meanwhile rose to his feet, saying, 'Well, let me go and get some sleep.' He said goodbye to Suleiman, and retired into the house. Now there were only Karim and Suleiman left in the pandal. The smell of the spices frying for the biriyani drifted towards them from the cooking yard. The cooking had begun. 'Would it be midnight now?' Suleiman asked Karim.

'Yes indeed, and even later than that,' Karim answered.

'Why is it you never give your opinion?' Suleiman asked again. He really wanted to know where Karim stood.

Karim told him, 'You know my brother; he will never speak out until the situation is really bad. Of course one must show mercy, but I don' see how one can feel sorry for that awful woman. Anyway, let it go. I can't say anything because it isn't right for me to intervene when my elder brother says something, and contradict him. It wouldn't be respectful. Do you understand what I'm saying?'

Suleiman felt a sudden sense of relief. The relief of having found a person to whom he could speak his mind and be understood. He felt greatly encouraged, believing he was not alone anymore. In his eyes, Karim appeared as a Jihadi. There would be at least one or two men like Karim left in this town, even after Suleiman himself had gone away, who would be prepared to fight to the death in order to safeguard the honour of the community. They would ensure that the women were well disciplined.

They began to talk about the preparations for the next day. Suleiman asked how many buses had been arranged to transport the bridegroom's party. Then he said to Karim, 'I need an ambassador car like the one your family has, Maamu. Where can I buy one? How much will it cost?'

'Why do want to buy a car? You will be going abroad again, soon, won't you? So why do you need one?'

'It's not just for me. Of course it will be useful for me as long as I am here. And I've got used to having a car; I can't go here, there, and everywhere by bus. Besides, it will be useful for the mosque's business. It will be particularly useful for the tabligh's business of reminding Muslims of their obligations. It will be really handy for me and for a few other tabligh men to visit the neighbouring towns. And then, after I've gone back, the car can be at my house. It can be there for the use of the mosque.'

Karim controlled a smile and said, 'Will the car be for you or for the mosque?'

'Why should you smile? Let us say it is for the mosque. So what? Don't we have to do what good we can in our lives?'

Karim clapped his hands and gave a provocative laugh. 'Do you know what this reminds me of? It reminds me of the Hindu custom of buying a bull and dedicating it to the temple.'

Suleiman didn't quite comprehend what Karim was getting at. He smiled proudly and said, 'Let it be like that. I don't see that it's a joke if I provide transport facilities for the mosque.' He exuded the self-satisfaction of a man who was putting into effect some sort of new law.

He's truly a crazy fellow, Karim said to himself. All the same, he had to admire him for his zeal at so young an age.

Mariyayi emerged from the cooking quarters, balancing a basket on her head. She had arrived at their house in the early morning, but had not yet finished her chores and returned home. Her gait revealed her weariness; her face showed her absolute exhaustion. 'What's in your basket, Mammaani?' Suleiman asked, teasing.

Karim showed no reaction at all to Suleiman's mode of address, but Mariyayi's face bloomed with shy delight. All trace of her weariness disappeared instantly. She was overwhelmed that Suleiman had addressed her using a kinship term, and that too, in Karim's very presence. 'It's just that the older Sir has asked me to deliver the sheep's head, intestines and trotters at your house; that's all,' she said politely, swaying and sliding away modestly towards Suleiman's house. She carried away the smell of the sheep's offal which had come floating in with her.

'See how modest she is,' Suleiman said, laughing. Karim's laughter joined his, oddly, at that hour.

A great yawn split Suleiman's face as he rose to his feet saying, 'I'll go now, Maamu, I'm really sleepy. *A'udu billahi minsh saitaan-ir-rajim.* I seek refuge in Allah against the evils of *Saitaan*.'

Having sent him off, Karim settled down in his chair, leaning well back. His right knee hurt. He pulled up another chair in front of him and stretched out his legs. For the past week he had been bothered by this ache in his knee. Besides, he had travelled to Madurai that morning to buy the laddus for the bridal presentation. His wandering about there had increased the pain. He thought the pain would be eased if he were to rub in some ointment, but knew that he could not go and ask for it at this time of night, as the entire household was asleep.

On the day Rahima and Zohra had gone to Sabia Akka's house in order to hand out the invitations, he had been lying down with severe pain. He heard someone opening the closed door very gently, and turned his head to see. It was Rabia, standing there. He was very surprised. She had never approached him in this way. Suddenly aware that he had never allowed her near him, and distressed by the thought, he asked in an affectionate tone, 'What is it, amma?'

'That is, Akka told me your leg was hurting. She gave me this ointment, and told me to rub it in for you. Shall I do it?' She spoke eagerly, and came to stand next to him.

Karim looked at his daughter and wanted to smile. 'You are going to practise medicine like a grown up lady, are you?' he teased. His heart swelled with pride. 'She's a very smart girl,' he told himself, feeling proud of her as he had never done before.

Without waiting for his permission, she folded back his veshti to the knee, poured the eucalyptus ointment on his leg. 'Is it here that it hurts?' she asked, rubbing it in firmly. He smiled to himself as she lost all the nervousness she had displayed as she stood by the door, and plunged into her work in all earnestness.

He thought of the way she had stood at the door a little while ago, so meekly, her tail between her legs. He tried to remember a single occasion when he had been loving and close towards her, and was filled with distress. He wondered why he found it impossible to have a loving relationship with a girl child. He did not believe that he had ever disliked her. He remembered that he had always bought whatever she had asked for, since she was a child, and made her happy in that way. His lack of enthusiasm towards her was nothing other than his excessive desire for a son. Besides, when was he at home, after all? Apart from when he ate and slept, there were never occasions when he sat down and talked with his wife and child. He was certain that the reason he had kept Rabia at a distance was not because he lacked any affection for her, but because of his nature, his character. 'That's enough, amma; Attha's ache has all gone,' he said, taking her hand and drawing her close to him.

She came up to him, anxious to know whether she had rubbed in the medicine properly. Her father looked at her, realizing with a surprise, how much she had grown. This was the first time he had looked at her so closely, since she took to wearing a davani all the time. He felt a sudden affection for her fill his heart. There was a moment's silence while she stood there waiting for permission to go. 'Attha has to go to Madurai tomorrow. What shall I bring you?' he asked.

She was astonished that he was offering her such a big reward just because she had rubbed the medicine on his legs for a few moments, and stood stock still. Then she said, 'I would like some gold hoops for my ears, to wear at Akka's wedding. Will you buy them for me?' Her tone betrayed her fear that she might have asked for something too big; her uncertainty that she might be given it. Her large eyes had widened even more with surprise.

Anxious to dispel her fear and to encourage her, he asked, 'Just the hoops? What else?'

'That's enough, Attha,' she hastened to assure him. 'The electricity is off now. Shall I fan you with the hand fan?' she asked, full of concern. He knew that her concern for his comfort was another way of showing him how grown up she was.

The next day he boasted, in Rabia's presence, 'Do you remember my telling you, when we were praying, about the ache in my knee? My daughter applied some ointment to it, and it just flew away like cotton wool.'

He remembered, sitting in the pandal, how Rabia had run away from there, overwhelmed with shyness and delight at the same time. He smiled to himself and felt in his pocket to assure himself that the hoops he had bought in Madurai were safe. Rabia was fast asleep before his return. He would give them to her in the morning.

He also remembered how, when he was standing in the market in Madurai, buying vegetables, he had heard a voice calling out to him, 'Anné!' Turning round, he was shocked to see Fatima standing there.

Not caring that they were standing in a public street, she ran up to him, and fell at his feet, weeping. Embarrassed, he lifted her up and asked, 'What now?' Trying not to show his anger, he went on, 'So what do you want to do now? Weeping in the street in this ugly way... What use is it to think of your son and weep now? We can't do anything about it now, so just go away.' He spoke sharply, trying to get away from there at once. He couldn't bear to look at her, and the spectacle she was making of herself. He was deeply distressed to find everyone in the market turning their eyes on him and Fatima.

'Anné, please if you somehow bring my son to me and return him to my care, you'll be blessed. My mother will never consent to come away. Please just bring him to me.' He was sorry to see the state of her as she pressed her sari end against her mouth and sobbed so that her entire body was wrung. It was unbearable to see how thin and dark she had become. Hiding his annoyance at seeing her, he asked, 'Where's that fellow?'

'He has found a job here, selling vegetables in the market. I work with him.' Her tongue could barely say the words.

Hearing her weeping, a couple of men had left their work, and come very close to them, staring at them with inquisitive eyes popping out of their heads. They were drawn by Fatima's sobs which rose up, without caring a jot for the midday heat pooling in the street. 'Ché, what sort of obscenity is this', Karim thought to himself. Anxious to get away from there as fast as possible, he said to her, 'It's time for me to go. I have to arrange for the boy to be brought here without anyone's knowledge. It's going to be quite a problem. Be patient for a while; I'll send Iliaz through one of our errand boys.' He was distressed by the state of her, all the same, and said, with an effort at patience, 'You'd better show me your stall, so that I can identify it.'

She had been terrified to approach him in the first place and was shocked and surprised that he had not been furious, but had actually agreed to bring Iliaz to her. She pulled herself together and said, 'There, that's the one. Please do this one favour for me, Anné. Don't punish me for the sin I committed.' Again she wept, sobbing her heart out.

Feeling desperately sorry for her, and thinking to himself, 'Crazy slut!', he put his hand in his pocket and drew out a hundred rupee note. 'Here,' he said, handing it to her, and walking away as fast as he could, from there.

The sound of cauldrons being rolled along, brought Karim to the present. He looked in the direction of the noise. The professional cook was bringing the cauldron for the biriyani's talisa, the sauce that would accompany it. Karim was very tired. He wondered whether he should go and sleep. He knew, though, it was difficult for his brother to supervise everything himself, and so he lifted his legs off the chair where they had been resting, rose to his feet and stretched himself. His hands reached up and brushed the tinsel hangings; he looked up at them, and brought his hands down. He stood there for awhile, listening to the hangings rustling sweetly in the nights breeze.

Perhaps they should have added some serial lights by way of decoration, he thought.

He walked towards the cooking area, questioning himself suddenly whether there had been a tali around Fatima's neck. Why did he not look carefully, he chided himself. He smiled to himself as he wondered how Suleiman would have reacted had he known Karim had given Fatima the money. Still smiling, he doubled up his lungi and began supervising the cooking. The cook, Sahul Bhai, was stirring something in an anda. Karim said to him by way of encouragement, 'You know how everyone always spoke of the food cooked at Mohammad Ali Rowther's house! How famous it was! Tomorrow's feast must match that, Sahul Bhai!'

35

Wahida could not sleep for the discomfort caused by the henna abrading her hands. She itched all over, as if mosquitoes were biting her in various places. She scratched herself, without worrying about destroying the henna. The dim light from the night light filled the room. From the bed where she lay, she looked out of the window, and out into the street. A single tree belonging to the ORAS family could be seen overhanging the shadowy street; the darkness lying dense within its branches.

The branches were lost in that darkness; she could not make out a single leaf. From the dark nests deep within those branches, a few birds gave a slight twitter. She was filled with a longing to hide herself away with them, somewhere far away. She was aware that on the next day she would be in another house, in an unknown man's bed. What was she feeling now? Happiness or fear? Unable to understand what it was, she looked at Rabia, sleeping by her side. Rabia was in a deep sleep, lying absolutely still in her bed. Wahida was overcome with grief, suddenly. Would she herself be able to sleep so soundly ever again, without a single care? No, she certainly would not. She was going to leave her home forever. She could not bear to think that she was leaving her home, her family, her mother and aunt and cousin. After her hands had been covered with henna, the previous evening, her mother had fed her herself. How could she be parted from such a mother and her love?

Leaving this house where she was born would be an unbearable loss. The long corridor where she had run about and played as a child; the courtyard with its large paving stones; the iron pillar around which she had twirled as a child until she was dizzy – she could not imagine being separated from all this. She had never felt such a sense of loss whenever she went away to her Nanna's house, for the school terms. It was strange that she should feel it so strongly now. In the old days, very often in the evenings, the electricity would be cut off. At such times her Amma and Chitthi – joined by Nafiza, Mumtaz and others – would sit in the front thinnai chatting and joking together, enjoying the fresh air, waiting for the men folk to shut up their shops and return home. She alone would stay in the courtyard, lying on a rope bed, gazing at the sky. She would listen to her Chitthi's battery-operated transistor radio playing songs from Radio Ceylon. Sometimes Mumtaz peeped inside and teased, 'Your daughter will never be part of a crowd, Rahimakka; there's no one quite like her when it comes to savouring the joys of solitude!'

Wahida was never bothered by any of this. She was always filled with wonder by the night sky. What was there above the sky? Where did the sky end? She could not begin to understand any of it. She knew many stories about the skies. Her mother always got very cross with her if she stayed alone in the terrace when it was darkening. Come down now, she would say, the birds are flying across the sky! If Allah created the seven hells, the seven heavens, the seven seas and the seven mountains, then who was it who created Allah? If there had to be an Allah to create all this, then did there not have to be someone to create that Allah in the first place? She was confused by all these questions which she asked herself.

She dared to ask her mother, one day. Rahima's face reddened and furrowed. 'If ever you ask such questions, the very next moment you become a Kafir. Don't ever do it again,' she said. Even now, she trembled, remembering the sternness that sounded in her mother's voice. She had been very frightened when she realized that her mother, who could control everyone without actually speaking a single word, was capable of such a terrible anger. Wahida had never approached anyone, after that, in an attempt to clear up her doubts.

She heard Rabia mutter something in her sleep. She sat up, and gazed at her, trying to make out what she said. The aroma of biriyani came floating into the room. She could hear people moving about in front of the house.

She thought of Sikander. How would he behave towards her? Would he be loving, or would he be like Karim Chaccha, a hot tempered man? Would he act like the husbands she had seen in the occasional movie, who on the first night of their wedding, touched their wives gently and embraced them? Or would he be different? She was full of doubts. Why did Nafiza and Mumtaz speak in such an ugly way? They were women too, weren't they? Did you become like this if you only ate your fill and stayed within the house, without thinking any other thoughts, she chided them silently. But Amma and Chitthi are here in this house all the time, she thought; did they ever speak a single salacious word? Again and again she scolded those others silently. She was herself surprised by the adult manner in which she wanted to admonish them. She thought again of Sikander. What would she do if he did not act like a cinema hero, but in some other way? Could she speak up and say she did not like his behaviour? She did not think she could. What would he say when he saw her pretty looks? Surely he would rejoice.

Suddenly she felt both fear and self-pity. Supposing he wasn't at all as she imagined; suppose he were a bad man? What could she do then? The thought pressed hard on her. Her head ached. Before she had gone to bed, her mother had said to her, 'Sleep well; don't think of anything. That way your face will be beautiful in the morning.' But however hard she tried, she could not sleep one wink.

* * *

Various images appeared in her dreams, and vanished. She was a small child, running along Kakkaali street, where she used to play as a child. Her mother came chasing after her. The street stank because of its open drains. Her mother had warned her many times, not to go and play there. In front of each of the huts there were low barriers which were meant to contain the drain; you had to cross those, in order to enter the hut. Hens scratched at the drains, making the whole street dirty. All the women belonging to the street usually gathered in one of the thinnais, laughing happily, betel leaves filling their mouths. Her mother didn't have a good feeling about that street, however.

The street seemed to grow longer and longer, endlessly. Suddenly, she couldn't see her mother anymore. She began to look for her, searching desperately. Now she was in a forest all by herself, calling out, Amma, Amma. She thought she would die of fear. Someone was shaking her awake. 'Wahida, wake up!' She opened her eyes, startled. It was Chitthi, standing there. 'Wake up; you should have your bath before dawn,' she said, helping her up and taking her into the bathroom.

As she brushed her teeth, Zohra hastened her, 'Hurry up and wash off the henna on your hands; then you must have your bath.' Wahida squatted down next to the water heater and peeled off the henna, and was delighted to see her hands covered in designs. She stood up and removed her clothes except for her underskirt, which she tied across her chest, then opened the tap which allowed the hot water to fall into the waiting bucket. Steam rose from the boiling water and touched her face, so she began to pour in cold water from the water trough, chombu after chombu. Zohra called out from outside, 'Wahida, open the door!

'I'll have my bath myself,' Wahida begged. But Zohra was peremptory. 'No, that won't do at all. I will bathe you.' So Wahida shyly opened the door for her.

'Why must you feel shy? We are both women,' Zohra soothed her, pouring the shiyakai on Wahida's head, and beginning to rub it in.

The tali-tying was arranged for ten, and so Nafiza and Mumtaz had arrived by eight in the morning. Rahima had invited them the previous evening, 'Make sure you come early; I'm depending on the two of you to dress the bride.'

Nafiza entered the room, and asked Wahida to get up from the bed, saying, 'Well, blushing bride, have you had your breakfast?' Wahida muttered a 'Yes'. Nafiza began to comb out her hair.

Mumtaz teased, winking, 'I don't suppose you slept all night, did you?'

Nafiza admonished the squirming Wahida, 'Don't move your head; I'm combing your hair, aren't I?' Then she spoke sharply to Mumtaz, 'Must you go and start your teasing at this one, of all people?'

Wahida's bed had been spread entirely with the ornaments for her hair; lipstick, powder, scent and other make-up from abroad in a makeup box; flowers, and the silk sari she was to wear. Nafiza asked for all the things she needed to do Wahida's hair, one by one: the forehead jewel, tassels, ribbon, hairpins.

Mumtaz, besides handing these to Nafiza, seated herself in front of Wahida, poured some cream into the palm of her hand, rubbed her hands together, sniffed at them, and began smoothing the cream on to Wahida's face. 'Smells lovely, doesn't it?' she commented, making a mental note that she must ask Suleiman to buy her just such a lotion, one way or another.

Wahida was silent, watching them decorate her. The two women, Nafiza and Mumtaz had dressed and made themselves up very carefully, before they arrived. Nafiza wore a maroon-coloured silk sari, with a blouse of the same colour. Long jimikki ear-drops and a necklace studded with stones made her look very attractive. Mumtaz wore a parrot-green silk sari, with a red blouse matching the sari-border. With this she wore dangling earrings and a kasumalai necklace; her arms were covered in gold bangles. She looked beautiful too, though she did not quite match up to Nafiza.

'Akka, aren't you wearing rather a lot of mai? Won't it smudge?' Wahida asked.

Mumtaz stopped her work for a moment, picked up the mirror lying on the bed and examined her face. 'Why, do you think it's too much?' she asked the other two. Then she reassured herself, 'It doesn't seem so to me.' She went on with what she was doing. Wahida had never seen Mumtaz without eye make-up. She was even known to say, 'If I don't wear mai, I'll die, won't I?'

'Have you finished with her make-up?' Rahima asked, entering the room. Without expecting a reply, she opened an inner drawer of the wardrobe, and took out the jewel boxes it held.

'It's all done except for putting on her sari. But the bridegroom's family have to bring that. Give us the sari she must wear until then,' Nafiza said.

'First let me put this jewellery on her. You can do the sari after that. I have plenty more to do.' Rahima blotted the sweat which stood out in pearls on her forehead with the end of her sari, and sat down on the bed with the jewel boxes in her hands. Nafiza and Mumtaz were excessively eager to see the jewellery, as the expression on their faces openly betrayed. Rahima had shown them only half of all the jewellery she had ordered for her daughter. They were just about to see the rest. Rahima would have ordered earrings in the very best designs, they knew. The two women had determined to have similar earrings made for themselves, were Wahida's new ones to their liking.

Rahima said 'Bismillah' and opened the boxes. First she opened a tiny box and took out a nose-ring which she handed to Wahida, as she began to unscrew her old ones.

Nafiza saw the nose-ring with its eight stones sparkling in Wahida's hand and asked eagerly, 'Why, Akka, it's a Sridevi nose-ring, isn't it? Are those diamonds?'

'As if only diamonds sparkle,' Rahima teased. 'No it's only gold. Wahida's Attha says that only gold is traditional in this family; he didn't want us to buy vairam.' Rahima spoke quietly, as she fixed the nose-ring on her daughter. She took each piece of jewellery one by one, showed it to Nafiza and Mumtaz, and then put it on Wahida.

Wahida felt a spurt of happiness. She thought how Rabia would jump about with delight were she here at this moment. She asked, 'Where's Rabia, Amma?'

'Who, she? I don't know; she's probably watching the fun, standing about somewhere in the pandal. If she were to see all this jewellery and ornaments, she'd demand that we arrange for her wedding as well, this very minute.' Rahima laughed.

Nafiza agreed, proudly, 'Well, what else? She's not someone to be slighted, is she, my future daughter-in-law. She's a clever little thing.' But Rahima suddenly thought of Karim, and wondered what he would have done, had he overheard this.

Rahima had made six pairs of ear-drops for Wahida. The one with green stones caught the eye with its exquisite beauty. Mumtaz picked it up and asked eagerly, 'How many sovereigns worth was this one?'

'It's only a sovereign's worth. Do you think it's pretty?' Rahima sounded pleased.

Mumtaz said, a little hesitantly, 'I too would like to have a pair made just like this.' It was clear that she not at all certain Rahima would lend her this pair to show her goldsmith.

'Go ahead and do it; who's objecting?' Rahima said proudly. She seemed delighted and pleased that everyone there liked and approved the designs she had chosen for her daughter.

Nafiza laughed, but said a little anxiously, 'Just wait; every woman in this town will be wearing exactly the same danglers like this. It's like one woman planting a seed, and the roots reaching everyone else.'

Wahida wanted to laugh. It was true: if a woman in this town wore a sari with a good design, or someone was seen wearing a new piece of jewellery, the very next day every other family would want one of the same kind. Saurakka used to say, 'It's enough for one woman to become pregnant; enough for one woman to buy a new sari; why it's even enough for one woman to take a piss – everyone else will follow.'

As soon as she had put all the jewellery on her daughter, Rahima made Wahida stand up so that she could admire her. Then she told her, 'Now listen carefully to what I tell you. Whenever you put on your jewellery, make sure you are sitting in the centre of your bed. Never stand up and do it. You don't want the ornaments to fall down and the stones to drop off. You hear me?' Then she turned to Mumtaz and asked, 'Please, will you call Zohra here, amma? Let her come and see.'

Nafiza began to drape the silk sari on Wahida meanwhile. Rahima stood for awhile, lost in her daughter's beauty. Then she stroked the sides of Wahida's face with both hands, and cracked her knuckles against her temples to ward off the evil eye. Seeing the tears of pride in her mother's eyes made Wahida's own eyes fill, and she hastily looked downwards hoping no one would notice.

Nafiza finished draping the sari on Wahida, saying, 'Ammadi, now at least will you pull off the davani you have been clutching to yourself? Very well; it won't be time for the muhurtam until ten, but we could take the bride into the hall right away. What do you think, Rahimakka?' She sought Rahima's permission to do this.

'Just wait a moment. Let us send for her Attha to come and see his daughter.' Rahima went out quickly.

Wahida wanted to see her entire self in a full-length mirror. She was eager to know what she looked like now, adorned as she had never ever been, before this. She controlled this desire, though, knowing how Mumtaz and Nafiza would tease her, if she should ask for a mirror.

In a little while Kader came in, but seeing the other two women there, made to leave, in embarrassment. They, in their turn left at once, excusing themselves.

Kader's heart filled and brimmed over with joy as he gazed at his daughter, standing in front of him. He was astonished to see how tall and grown up she seemed, in her sari. He felt even more proud because she was the very image of his own mother. His knowledge of her gentle character added to his pride in her. He came close to her, lifted her lowered face with both his hands and said affectionately, 'Why be shy in front of your Attha?' He realized, suddenly, that in all these years, he was touching his daughter for the first time. Quickly he suppressed the thought.

He placed both hands on her shoulders and pressed them gently, trying to communicate his love towards her. 'Well, amma, have you got enough jewellery do you think, or would you like more?'

Wahida felt sorry to see her father struggling to express himself and his love. She smiled gently, to try and put him at his ease, and nodded to indicate, 'I have quite enough.'

'Wahida, little one, you've changed into a woman, it seems!' Karim came in, but stood behind his elder brother. Kader immediately removed his hands from his daughter's shoulders, waved his hand as if saying goodbye, and went out hastily.

Karim Chaccha's appearance had a calming effect on Wahida. She thought his entry effectively released her father who seemed to be stumbling about, not knowing what to say.

'What is this? How have you changed so suddenly?' Karim came up to her, and placed a hand affectionately on her back.

'Go on, Chaccha,' she said, blushing furiously.

'I'm going, I'm going. By the way, where's that little sister of yours? I haven't seen her anywhere!' He went out again, quickly, having said this, leaving Wahida astonished that her uncle could talk to her so lovingly.

* * *

Looking beautiful in all her finery, Wahida was now made to sit on a sofa, placed against the wall and facing west, right in the middle of the hall, while all the women of the town seated themselves on the rows of mats laid out on the long and wide verandas. She sat with her head well lowered, holding tightly with both hands, the red veil spangled with gold which covered her face, lest it fall off. With difficulty she had controlled her wish to see who were the women sitting in front of her. Even though her neck was hurting, she sat with her head bent low, afraid that were she to sit up straight she would earn a bad reputation for lack of modesty. Rahima had warned her, the day before, that the way a bride held herself on her wedding day would be remembered and spoken about to the end of her life.

Every five minutes, Rabia ran up from somewhere or the other, fell on her cousin's lap, rolled over, and ran off again. In her silk skirt and davani, she too, was unrecognizable. Rahima and Zohra, meanwhile, were receiving all the women guests and showing them their seats. Both wore saris of the same design and colour.

When a woman unknown to Wahida arrived, Rabia stood at the side of Rahima and Zohra, greeting her in a very grown-up way, and as soon as she was seated, rushed up to her cousin, leaned across her to whisper in her ear, 'That's Ramesh's mother.' Wahida noticed that at the lady's entry, a rustle of whispers rose from the women gathered there, but could not understand why. Rahima, however, understood, and was much distressed by the attention the newcomer was receiving. It embarrassed her greatly that people were staring at the woman so unashamedly. She felt belittled that a guest she had invited personally was humiliated in this way and she was unable to

prevent it. It added to the sadness she felt already, at parting
from her daughter. When the bridegroom's party arrived, the
attention of all the women here would be diverted to them;
until such time she could not stop them from gazing at
Ramesh's mother.

Zohra too, had noticed the attention the woman was raising.
She too had been suffering from a similar problem. When
Mariyayi went about in her new sari, and when Paraman's
daughter-in-law arrived at their house, many of the women
there followed them about with their inquisitive eyes, probing
them with interest.

Suddenly it seemed to Zohra as if the house was filled and
surrounded by gossip and intrigue, and as if these two women,
their guests, were in a kind of thicket from which they could
not find their way out. Rahima and Zohra were embarrassed
that these women had been trapped inside, caught unaware.

Rabia and other children came running up to announce the
arrival of the bridegroom's party, and everyone's attention
was caught up in the excitement of it. Greatly relieved, Rahima
and Zohra hastened to the front door, ready to greet the
newcomers. Wahida heard her mother welcoming them all
with a tray of auspicious objects in her hands, and bent her
head even lower. Her anxiety made her drip with perspiration.
The women from their own town moved further back, making
room for the visitors as trays of gifts from the bridegroom
were brought and laid in front of her.

Sabia spoke up with authority: 'Make room for the
bridegroom's party, amma'. Nafiza and Mumtaz, sitting at
Wahida's feet smiled at each other, and turned to gaze at the
bride.

'Come and see, everyone; I have brought fifty-one platters
holding the bridegroom's gifts,' Sabia announced proudly,
looking around her. She touched Wahida's shoulder, and said,
'Sh... Allahu'. She called to Nafiza and Mumtaz, 'Come on,
you women, get up, let us dress the bride in the sari in which
the tali-tying is to take place!'

Immediately the two women touched Wahida, made her stand, embraced her and took her inside. Sabia, going in with them said, 'The bridegroom has gone to the mosque already, in the car; hurry up and dress her. And put this garland and sera of flowers on her afterwards.' She hurried out again,

Nafiza shook out the bridal sari of red silk and began draping it on Wahida. Mumtaz muttered, meanwhile, 'What's all this? Fifty-one platters of gifts? It all sounds miraculous!'

'What else did you expect? She took wads of money in dowry, didn't she?' Nafiza answered sharply.

Dressed now in her bridal sari, Wahida had been made to sit on the sofa once again, in the middle of the hall. Two men arrived to receive the bride's word in acceptance, along with the Hazrat who held a notebook. A silence fell on all the women gathered there.

The Hazrat's voice rose loudly as he asked, 'In the presence of the first witness Janaab A.M. Hanifa Rowther and second witness Janaab S. Suleiman Rowther, are you agreed that a nikah is to take place between Sultan Rowther's grandson and Sayyed Rowther's son Sikander, and Kader Rowther's daughter and Muhammad Ali Rowther's granddaughter, Wahida Begum, for a mihr of one thousand and one rupees?'

Sabia, who was sitting very closely in front of Wahida, leaned across and whispered in her ear, 'What do you say?' Wahida, in utter confusion, didn't know what she must do. Sabia herself looked up at the Hazrat, and said, 'Asalaamu aleikum', took the notebook from his hands, and got Wahida to sign it. After a while, Sabia took out the string of black beads and tied them around Wahida's neck, asking the girl to say the five kalimas in testimony of her faith. As if she were certain that she alone could pray to the Lord to make her only son's life prosper, Sabia took that responsibility upon herself.

Wahida yearned for her mother at that moment. The garland pressed heavily on her neck, and the sera with its hanging flowers fell over her face covering it.

Sabia said to someone, 'Take all these gifts and put them

away inside.' Then, breaking open packets of sweets, she flung them towards the wedding guests, by the handfuls.

The bridegroom was about to arrive: Rabia and Madina stood ready at the front door of the house, ready with the arati with which they would circle him, to cast away the evil eye. Meanwhile, Mumtaz hurried into the kitchen, poured milk into a dish, sweetened it with sugar, mashed a banana into it, and brought it into the hall with a new silver spoon, ready to feed the bride and groom. By this time, Rabia and Madina had done an arati to Sikander, and were pestering him for money. Smiling, he handed Rabia a hundred rupee note, and entered the house, followed by some of his friends as well as the photographer. The girls rushed off to stand by Wahida, and to edge into the frame of each photograph.

As soon as the nikah was over, Zohra took upon herself the responsibility of ensuring that Paraman's daughter and Ramesh's mother were given a vegetarian meal, and sent home with bags of auspicious betel leaves and coconut. Karim took charge of serving out portions of biriyani which would be sent to all their friends and relations. Meanwhile, Kader supervised the meal which was served to the guests seated in the pandal which had been erected on the terrace.

Each was absorbed in what they were doing, but all were aware, with a great sadness, that the time for Wahida's departure was drawing closer and closer. Rabia alone was overwhelmed with joy at the thought of seeing her Chitthi, Firdaus, very soon.

᎒ 36 ᎒

As soon as she climbed down from the car, Rabia ran off to find Firdaus. Wahida smiled to herself, not wishing to stop her. Poor child, for how long she had been waiting! Sabia's house wasn't new to Wahida; she had visited here very often as a small girl. Yet on that day it felt very strange. Sikander chose to stay with his friends and did not display any special feeling towards her. She felt very disappointed at this. She had wept in the car, all the way here; but he had not said a word to comfort her. She had stopped at last when he touched her, giving her a measure of courage and even pleasure. For the first time in her life, a man was sitting close to her. All of a sudden it became clear to her that she would gain nothing by weeping. She thanked God for this insight.

Upstairs, the room she was taken to was filled with the scent of roses. She loved the smell of it. The new bed that had been constructed specially for her stood ready in the room; the wardrobe was still in its straw and paper wrappings. She told herself that hereafter this room alone would be her space. Hereafter, all her joys and sorrows, the good things in her life and the bad would take place within these four walls. Nothing was going to happen to her that these walls didn't know. This was all that was to be, until the end of her life. Suddenly she was filled with shame. Everyone experienced this, she thought; why do I imagine that it is unique to me, and distress myself? Stubbornly she freed herself from morbid thoughts and turned her attention to the noises outside her room.

She could hear Sabia's voice sounding continuously. She was ordering the servants to set about cleaning the house. No one else's voice seemed to intervene. A slender thread of fear began to take root in Wahida's mind, and to spread. A fear that hereafter she too must bend her will to Sabia's. At the same time, she remembered her father-in-law, Sayyed. His endless affection for her gave her some courage. He had never failed to bring her some gift, every time he returned from abroad. Whenever he visited them, he spoke to her with affection and tenderness. Her mother's great happiness was that Wahida could not have chosen a better father-in-law. Her father too had that belief.

Time passed by, and she began to feel the tedium of sitting there all alone. Just as she was wondering why Rabia, who had been sent specifically to keep her company, had left her alone so long, she heard the rustling of the silk skirt as the little girl came running up to her. Rabia came to a stop, breathing hard. Sabia followed her in, scolding, 'Why must a girl child run about like this, instead of being quiet and modest?' She went out again, her big body swaying.

Rabia and Wahida were both struck dumb. They only exchanged glances without saying a word. Rabia came to her cousin's side and flopped down on the bed. All her happiness had fled in a second. How on earth was her Akka going to cope with this woman?

Now Sayyed came into their room, saying 'Allahu.' He seated himself very close to Wahida asking, 'Well, amma, what are you up to?'

Rabia answered for both of them, 'Nothing, Maamu!'

'Up to nothing? But here you are, fully clothed!' he said, cackling with laughter, as if he had cracked a joke. Shocked, Rabia hung her head. Wahida pulled her sari well over her head and bent down, as well. Rabia thought to herself that with his shrunken and thin body, his paunch and his weedy beard, this man looked like the Ji Bhumba demon in the Jeyashankar film.

He touched Wahida's neck and made her look up. 'For how long are you going to sit with your head lowered? Doesn't your neck hurt? There's no one here who shouldn't see you.' He spoke affectionately.

Wahida, for her part, was desperate to go to the bathroom. Who could she ask? How was she to manage it? She was in a state of confusion.

As if it was his responsibility to make sure she was not too shy in his house, he asked, in an effort to put her at her ease, 'Tell me if there is anything you need. Hereafter this is your own house. Take courage in that thought. You mustn't sit here, staring at nothing. Very well, I'm off. I'll come back after I've said my prayers. We'll eat then.' He had a word for Rabia, as well, in jest. 'Well, woman? You look after your Akka and make sure nobody carries her off, won't you?' He got off the bed and walked off, swaying from side to side.

Rabia watching him, giggled, and whispered into Wahida's ears, 'Doesn't he walk like a duck?'

Wahida put a finger to her lips and scolded, 'Sh! You shouldn't make fun of your elders like this.' She was afraid that someone might have overheard. Then she sent Rabia away, saying, 'Please go and fetch Sabia Kuppi. I need to go to the bathroom.' She felt hot and humid in her silk sari and flowers. It was very hot; humid even though it was evening time. The fan was full on, yet she was perspiring and exhausted. She was also bothered because she had begun her period. Getting up quietly, she lifted the suitcase she had brought with her, placed it on the bed and opened it. Amma had placed a Koran right on top. Remembering she must not touch it when she had her period, she probed carefully for her napkins. Amma had packed all that she needed by way of make up, as well as her clothes. Tucked away among her clothes was the packet of sanitary napkins. Zohra had laughed as she had hidden it away among her clothes, 'You are taking this too, aren't you, as bridal gifts?' She pulled one out now, hid it in the folds of her sari and put the suitcase away. If Rabia saw her she would pester the life out of her asking, 'What's that?' and 'What's it for?'

When Sikander and Wahida sat down to their evening meal, Sayyed placed himself next to Wahida, and, with a great show of concern, poured a spoonful of chutney on to the dosai on her plate. Then he said, 'Why, Sabia, there are only the four of us eating; why did you make so much chutney? Won't it go to waste?' He muttered to himself, 'She doesn't understand the value of money, does she?' But Sabia shut him up smartly, saying, 'Oh, why don't you keep quiet.'

After dinner, Sayyed continued to pester Sabia, saying, 'Why haven't you made any arrangements for the night?' At last she shouted back at him, annoyed beyond endurance, 'Why won't you shut up? The girl is in the wrong time of the month.' Even then, he came up to the room where Wahida was seated, and said with a woebegone expression, but speaking quite familiarly, 'Well, amma, I hear that you are in the wrong time of the month?' Wahida was shocked that he could ask such an intimate question without any shame, as if he were asking her if she had a headache! But Sabia followed him, scolded him and drove him off. 'How can you talk to your daughter-in-law without any shame, like this? How can you come up to her room and ask her questions like this, you shameless man!' Once he had gone, with a silly smile on his face, Sabia said to Wahida, 'All right, amma, why don't you change your clothes and go to sleep now? You must be tired. I'll speak to Sikander and tell him to come up now.'

Rabia came upstairs, her eyes closing, her whole self dropping with sleep. Her voice was cajoling, as she asked, 'Akka, where should I go to sleep?' Wahida didn't know what to answer. If only she could ask her to sleep by her side! But they would not allow that. Knowing she would be frightened to sleep by herself, Wahida said to Rabia, 'You go and sleep with your Firdaus Chitthi.' Rabia was delighted to be told this. 'Very well, I'll tell Kuppi, and then go. I'll come first thing in the morning.'

Just as she rose to her feet, Sikander entered the room. 'Where are you off to di,' he asked, taking her by the hand, drawing her to him and giving her a close hug. Feeling terribly shy, trying to free herself, she stuttered, 'Let me go, Macchaan.'

'I won't do anything of the sort,' he said, holding her more tightly. A smell of cigarettes came from him. Rabia struggled to free herself. Wahida didn't like his teasing one bit. She asked herself, 'Why is he doing this? Can't he see how awful she feels?'

Sabia called out, 'Leave her alone, now; no need to be so playful with your sister-in-law. I've told Wahida to get to bed because she's tired. Hurry up now, and go to bed too.' Just as soon as his arms loosened a little, Rabia pulled away his hands and flew off like a sparrow.

Sikander took the cup of milk that his mother had brought,

placed it on the bedside table, and came towards Wahida. She had removed her silk sari, and sat cowering like a chicken, wearing one of her ordinary saris. She still didn't know how to drape a sari properly; Sabia had to help her earlier. It had been one more cause for complaint. 'If only I had a daughter, she would have been such a help to me; now I even have to change your clothes myself. What to do!'

Sabia had been grousing since the morning. Had she had girl children, she could have claimed the special money, gifts and sweets which were offered, customarily, to the bride's sister-in-law. She felt deeply resentful about this. From the moment of the tali-tying, until they returned home, she had grumbled about how lucky her brother and his wife were. At last, Nafiza whispered to Zohra, 'Who asked this woman not to have girl children? If she really was so desperate, she could have gone and adopted a girl from an orphanage, just to be able to demand the 'nattanaar' gifts.' Rahima and Zohra, hearing this, had laughed silently.

Sikander took off his silk veshti and shirt and hung them up. He seemed to feel no qualms at all about standing about, wearing only his underwear. Ignoring the fact that Wahida was in the room, he casually took out a lungi from his almirah and tucked it around his waist. Unable to watch, Wahida buried her face against her knees. It seemed to her that he didn't consider her presence there in the room, in the very least.

Aware that the moment had come for him to draw near and sit beside her, her whole body began to shudder. Somewhere at a distance, a dog began to howl fiercely. The noise seemed to enfold the night in a violent clasp. A strange mixture of fear and anticipation made her gasp for breath. Being alone with a man for the first time in her life filled her with a very new sensation of shyness. Her whole body shrank at the thought of what others outside the room might be saying.

He came and sat down by her, lifted up her face from her knees and gazed at her for a moment. 'Well, di, are you sleepy? Amma told me what's the matter. So you've escaped from me tonight. We'll see to all that later.' He spoke as if he had a right over her. 'Very well, drink this milk and go to sleep then.'

The way he spoke, as if he were very familiar with her, lessened her fear a little. She took the milk, drank it, and curled up in a corner of the bed. She was aware of a slight smell of sweat, mingled with that of cigarettes, emanating from him. Because the entire day had been so tiring, it wasn't too difficult to drop off asleep, even in her new surroundings. She was only aware of an anxiety that she had arrived into a world which she could not begin to comprehend.

* * *

Rabia came to Wahida quite late in the morning, having had her bath at Firdaus's house, and her hair plaited for her by her Chitthi. She did not like being at Sabia's house at all. It felt like a stranger's house. She had spoken to Firdaus about her anxiety on her Akka's behalf. How on earth would poor Wahida stand it? Firdaus had said firmly, 'This is her house from now on. She can't just go away, saying she doesn't like it. Your sister has to stay here from now on, until she dies.'

Rabia went into the house very uncertainly. Wahida had already had her bath, and was drying her hair with a towel. She was wearing a silk sari. Her long hair tumbled down and fell below her waist, looking very beautiful.

'Have you eaten?' Rabia asked.

'Mm,' Wahida murmured, meaning, 'Yes'. It seemed to Rabia that she was a little bit happier than she was yesterday. 'Have you eaten, as well?' Wahida asked in her turn. 'There are vadais here. Go and eat.' She sounded anxious about her little sister.

'I don't need anything more; I've breakfasted,' Rabia assured her, climbing on to the bed and lying down. 'Akka, do you like Macchaan?' she asked directly.

But Wahida would not reply, asking eagerly instead, 'Do you like him, though? Tell me that first.'

Rabia, for some reason, had not liked Sikander. But how could she tell her Akka this? She gave a token agreement, for the sake of it. 'Mm, I like him.' Wahida noticed her lack of enthusiasm. For Wahida's part, even though Sikander had chosen to ignore her, she respected him for having left her alone. At the same time, she was saddened by Rabia's expression of disinterest.

At that moment Sabia looked into the room. 'Well, di, my little niece, we haven't even seen you all this while; you didn't even turn up to eat here. If I don't look after you, your father will kill me, do you know that?' Having joked with her, she invited her affectionately, to go down and eat. Both girls, Wahida and Rabia, were surprised to hear her loving tone. Rabia felt uncomfortable, however, and refused to eat, saying, 'No thank you, I've eaten already.'

'Very well then, come down with me. Take this tea to your Macchaan.' having summoned her, Sabia went down into the kitchen. Wahida smiled at Rabia, hearing the emphasis in 'your Macchaan', and realizing why Sabia sounded so loving all of a sudden. Rabia noticed the adult nature of Wahida's smile. It seemed to her that Wahida had changed, but she couldn't comprehend why, although she thought quite hard about it. The fear, so apparent in Wahida yesterday, seemed to have disappeared, leaving her face clear. The sari she wore seemed to make her look more grown up, too.

She remembered that she had to take Sikander his tea, and felt nervous about it immediately. She didn't like to do it, one bit. But knowing there was no way of avoiding this chore, she went into the kitchen half-heartedly. Sabia was hard at work with the cooking, helped by two servant women. As soon as she saw Rabia, she handed her a tumbler saying, 'Here you are, amma, take this up to him.' Not content with this, she went on crossly, 'Why are you acting so coy and shy as if you yourself are the bride? Don't stand there blinking; go and give him the tea before it cools.'

Rabia felt humiliated. The two servant women turned to

look at her, gave a small, knowing smile and went on with their work. Rabia hastened towards the stairs, cursing Sabia under her breath, 'Fatty, mundé, saniyan.' She hated having to listen to Sabia. How could this saniyan speak like this to her, when she had only been there for one day! How was Wahida, poor thing, going to stand it? Rabia felt for her.

She went up the stairs, and walked into the large front room. She guessed that he would most probably be in the balcony, and looked for him there. She was shocked to see him standing in a corner there, smoking a cigarette and gazing into the street. A question began to shape itself in her mind, 'Have they got Akka married to a bad man who smokes?'

He heard the tinkle of her anklets and turned, asking, 'Come, Rabia; it looks as if you've brought me something?' He walked towards her.

Thinking to make good her escape before he reached her, she put the tea down on a table that stood there, saying, 'I've put it here. Goodbye.'

Before she could run off he had reached her and held her tight, saying, 'Where are rushing off? Why are you so scared, tell me? Have I grown horns or what?' He was laughing. This made her even more frightened. Trying desperately to free herself from his grasp, overcome with shame and humiliation, she kept on saying, 'Let me go, please let me go.'

For some reason, he suddenly loosened his hold about her waist a little, held only her right hand tightly in his, and began to speak again. ' Why Rabia, are you scared to look at me?'

Her head lowered, she answered, 'No, of course not,' Her throat was dry before she could finish. Her whole body began to perspire. A mixed smell of cigarette and scent emanating from him made her feel queasy.

'Oh, so you aren't scared! Then why are you struggling to get away? Am I going to eat you up or what?'

'I'm off. The tea will get cold. Please drink it now,' she said again, trying to free herself once more. She had to get away somehow. Trying with all her strength to pull her hand away from his grasp, she broke one of her glass bangles. It scratched her, drawing a few drops of blood, and she called softly, 'Amma', wiping at it with her davani.

He scolded her fondly, 'Why did you pull so hard and hurt yourself?' Pulling out his handkerchief, he wiped away the blood.

She began to whine like a child, 'Let me go. It stings so; I must go and put some medicine on.' This was her chance to escape from him, so she made much of it, grimacing as if with pain, and moaning, 'Oh, it hurts so much… '

She didn't like his rough hands at all. Once again she thought of Wahida. She, after all, would get away from there in a couple of days; Wahida was going to be here for the rest of her days with these two, Sabia Kuppi and Macchaan. The very thought of it made her shudder. She stopped muttering and mumbling and was still for a moment. At that instant, Sabia called from downstairs, 'Rabia! Rabia!'

His hands fell away from her immediately. She took advantage of that moment at once, and ran as fast as she could, leaping headlong down the stairs. She ran all the way into the garden, stood under the murunga tree and drew long breaths. She thought once again, and with extreme anxiety that her poor Wahidakka must spend the rest of her life with a bad man who smoked. She calmed herself down at last, determined that she would never again go anywhere near him.

~ 37 ~

It was midnight, and Wahida was surrounded by the silence in the room. It seemed as if that silence poured out of the dimly glowing night light. Sikander lay at her right side, his face registering the peace of a deep sleep. Half his bare body leaned on her, pressing hard against her. Full of irritation, she used all her strength to push him away. The satisfaction of sexual union had calmed him and put him to sleep, while her mind was tossing about unendurably. She was troubled by a terrible pain below her waist and belly. She had never expected he would behave to her in such a casually violent way. The trust she had placed in him on that first night vanished like smoke by the third night of their marriage. All the dreams and hopes she had invested in a marriage relationship had shattered in an instant, leaving only a wasteland. This realization was more unbearable to her than the bodily pain. He had treated her as if she were an object; he had acted as if he only had a job of work to finish. She could not remember any hero of cinema or story, who had been so offhand. So, was this all there was, she wondered. She shut her eyes tightly and immediately felt an emptiness, as if the whole world had grown dark.

The tears coursed down from the ends of her eyes. She wiped them away with the end of her sari. She felt trapped, as if she were caught in a net, struggling, something having been forcibly taken away from her. Desperate that such a night of weariness and sorrow should end, she looked at the clock. In the pervasive darkness of the room, she couldn't make it out. She gazed at it a little more carefully. It was nearly two o'clock. Over and above Sabia's character and Sikander's rough ways, the thought of her father-in-law's love consoled her and gave her hope. The belief that his affection would somehow help her to live out her days in this house without experiencing too much distress gave her a little courage. Once again she thought of Sikander's behaviour, and her throat choked with a kind of grief; a grief she could neither swallow, nor spit out.

Indeed, this grief was such a new experience to her, that she was helpless to deal with it. So new and so violent it was. How could she make it go away? She had a notion that it might help a little if she could cry out in aloud in her pain. But how on earth could she cry here, in this place? The question only pained her the more. Very quietly she rose from her bed and pressed her feet against the floor. A throbbing pain stabbed her between her legs. She gritted her teeth and swallowed.

Somehow she twisted the sari which had come undone, about her, opened the bedroom door and went towards the bathroom, treading softly. She noticed, sadly, that the loud noise of the bolt being drawn, didn't make the slightest dent in his sleep.

The bathroom stood at the end of the long hall adjacent to her room. She thought that she could easily reach it, lit as it was by the night-lights, and began walking towards it carefully, her legs still aching. It was then that she noticed someone sitting in the chair in the hall, eyes fixed on her door. Shocked, she stepped back and gazed carefully. She was trembling with fear. It was Sayyed who stood up and came towards her, stroking his silky beard. 'Where are you off to, amma? Is it to the bathroom?' he asked.

Although she came to life again, after dying of fear, shame made her whole self cringe. Why on earth was this man sitting opposite her room at this time of night? And he was asking her, without any idea of discretion, where she was going! She felt deeply humiliated. He touched her back and pointed to the bathroom, saying, 'Yes, you go, amma.' She was aware of the fingers pressing on her. As she covered her head and began to hurry away from there, he whispered, 'Did it hurt a lot?'

She was stunned. She looked up at him, not quite sure what he meant. Her stomach turned at the look of eagerness she discerned on his face, even in that dim light, and the gaze which crawled, like a horrible worm, all over her body. As she tried once again, to walk away from there, he asked again, 'What happened?' His face appeared to her, like that of an aged wolf. Fearfully, she hurried away from there, went into the bathroom and locked it behind her.

Her whole body was shuddering. Her fingers were trembling too much to take hold of the chombu. The pain in her lower abdomen was so great she could hardly stand; she sank down on the washing stone. She felt a stickiness between her thighs; she didn't dare check whether it was blood, or something else. She pulled the plastic bucket under the tap, and turned the tap on at full. The loud, howling sound of the water falling, chased away the silence there. She believed she could dissolve her grief in the comfort of that sound. She was tormented by the question, what am I going to do now? Together with that, there was her fear that this was all her life was going to be. Her tears rose at last, loudly, as if they would break the night apart, and throw away the pieces. Weeping, she began to pour the water over her head and bathe; to wash away the pollution from her body. Even at that moment, she remembered very well what Zohra told her: that immediately after sex she must have a bath and wash her sheets and pillowcase.

⌁ 38 ⌁

Sherifa was cleaning and putting to rights her untidy room. The keys to the inner compartments of her wardrobe were lost. She had searched everywhere for them. In the end she opened the wardrobe, took out all her clothes and laid them on the bed. She went through each stack of clothes. She had emptied the entire wardrobe, but the keys were still not to be found. She was deeply annoyed. Now what was she to do? The entire wardrobe was in disorder! She decided to call Raihaina so that the two of them could fold all the saris again and put them away, and so she picked out all the silk saris and piled them to one side. They were all hers, chosen for all her rites of passage: when she came of age, for the wedding, the tali-tying, for the fortieth day bangle ceremony, the fortieth day after her baby was born. She picked up the sari she was given for the first Ramzan festival, after she was married. It stood out, it seemed to her, even among all those new saris. Salaam had gone and bought that sari for her, himself. She felt a stab of grief as she realized that she would never again wear all these saris. She always took a great delight in dressing well, and adorning herself. Fatima often teased her, saying, 'What is this di, as it is, you are as beautiful as a piece of sculpture; why do you need to dress up and look at yourself in the mirror all the time? Look at me, here I am as dark as coal, looking like a piece of burnt firewood!'

People would talk badly about her, hereafter, were she to dress herself in silk saris, or put on make-up. Could she not, just once, put on a good sari, fill her hair with flowers, wear all her jewellery, and admire herself in the mirror? But there were Amma and Raihaina in the house. If Amma knew, she would begin all that talk about re-marriage, once again. There would be no respite from it. Besides, Amma would start weeping again about Sherifa's position as a widow. Sherifa would only have stirred up a sorrow from which there was no relief. Sherifa felt badly. Because she was left without a husband, could she not dress well, anymore? Did she have to be a vavarasi, a woman with a husband who was alive, even to adorn herself? This town was a terrible place, she thought to herself. Why should she go to the length of getting married, just to dress well? She felt resentful and sad at the same time.

As she was arranging the silk saris, two letters fell out. She bent down, picked them up, and turned them over. One was a letter that Salaam had sent her from abroad. The other was one she had written to him. He had brought that letter with him on his last visit, and teased her about it.

A shadow fell into the room. Sherifa looked up to see Saura standing there, her mouth full, munching. Saura's eyes swept over the room, and then fell on her daughter, not sure what was going on. They seemed to ask Sherifa, What are you up to? Sherifa met her gaze steadily, annoyed with Saura. Did she have to eat all the time? Did she have nothing else to do? Saura's cheek bulged with whatever she held in her mouth, while her jaws moved mechanically, like a machine. Sherifa wanted to laugh, but controlled herself; Saura was her mother, after all.

Since Saura continued to stand there blinking, Sherifa said briefly, 'I've lost a particular key; I'm just looking for it.' She was desperate to get her mother away from there, before she started to examine all the silk saris heaped up there.

Saura didn't understand why her daughter was so tense. she said, rather crossly, 'Did you offer to send some food to Nuramma?'

'Yes, I did, so what?' She had decided to give the food without her mother's knowledge. How did she find out? She asked, 'Why, has anyone come for it, or what?'

'Yes, Iliaz is here, standing in front of the house. Why do you get involved in all this? It will be a case of the stray hen you allowed into your patch, the stray dog you allowed to lick up your dishes. A fine one you are! Is the money lying about in heaps here, or what?' Saura went away, grumbling. Sherifa went on with her work, anxious to forget her annoyance with her mother's mean-mindedness. Had Saura noticed all the silk saris heaped there, she would have sat down at once and raised a lamentation. She had been so upset by Nuramma's request that she hadn't paid any attention to what Sherifa was doing. Very good, Sherifa told herself, smiling quietly. Raihaina had taken the baby out. She decided to finish it all, herself.

She laid the letter in her hand on to her lap and unfolded it gently. It was stuck together and difficult to open, since it had not been unfolded for a long time. As soon as she saw Salaam's beautiful writing, neat as a string of pearls, her heart filled, and tears began to seep from her eyes. She pulled at the end of her sari and wiped them away. The letter was witness to a relationship so tightly bound up with her feelings and passions. It was a small attempt to reveal all love, all affection towards her. But he was gone, leaving only this token with her. He had changed into something invisible to her. There was only this evidence of his having been there; himself being nowhere. In this world, in this life, no one would see him any more. They must wait for an afterlife to see him. Her whole self quaked. Where had he gone? Was she never, ever to see him in this world? How could that be? How could it be right for a life, a

form which had lived and moved before her eyes, to vanish so
suddenly! He wasn't of an age to die. Why did Allah need his
life alone, when there were so many old people about, leading
only half lives? Then the truth must be that Allah has no eyes.
Or should one not say that there is no Allah? But no one was
prepared to say that. How was it that people justified his early
death by claiming that it was his destiny, or that the days
ordained for him in this world had come to an end. Her head
felt as if it were splitting. For a minute she leaned against the
wall and shut her eyes.

Steadying her heart, she spread out the letter and began to
read. It seemed to her that it was not a letter, but his voice
speaking.

Dearest Sherifa,

*Asalaamu aleikum. How are you? I received your letter and was much
pained to read it. You have written about how much you suffer because
of our separation, and made me share in your pain. What you say is
true. Youth doesn't last for ever. At an age when we should live together
and share all our hopes and dreams, circumstances have driven us to
spend our time in different directions and different places. Of course it
is a painful situation. It seems that it is the need to make money that
drives a man all over the world. Of course I am sad and sorry to have
left you there and come away, as if I have no other means of livelihood.
I know hundreds of people here, who have left their wives and children,
and live here for years together. I, at least, have decided firmly to
return after one or two more of these periods abroad. But what about
these others, who have no other alternative but to continue here for
the rest of their lives? When we think of their terrible situation, ours
doesn't seem so bad, after all. Men who are always in search of money
and wealth, don't seem to consider that they are throwing away their
youth and the best days of their lives. It seems that their need for
wealth traps them to the extent that they cannot even reflect about
these things. Do you know how hard the friends who share my room*

struggle to cope with their frustrations? (I too.) But I feel that I can
look forward to a great freedom. Be patient for a few more months. I
will return soon. I am sending, with this letter, two saris as my birthday
present to you. More later. Please give my salaams to my family and to
yours.

with much love,
your
Abdul Salaam.

Grief overcame her again, when she finished reading. He had
wanted to share her unhappiness, and to comfort her so much
in her loneliness. But today, that loneliness stretched away in
front of her, like an endless and solitary footpath. Could he
ever have thought he would leave her abandoned for ever? She
had begun to lament and complain just as soon as he went
away, abroad. She had said, she could not manage at all,
without him. He used to bring those letters back with him, to
tease her. Now she opened the letter she once wrote to him.

My dear Macchan,

Asalaamu aleikum. How are you? Today makes it 32 days since you left
me and went away. Each day feels like a hole year to me. Every day I
stay awake when I should be asleep, thinking of you it is very difficlut
at such times I think of my mother and feel sorry. I don't know how she
manged like this for 30 years. Perhaps she was so busy looking after her
children she had no time to think maybe if I had a baby I may not have
time to think about you. Last night when I opened the wardrobe I saw
our wedding photograp and thought about you imediately. Because
you went away within 40 days of our nikah I feel as if I have forgotten
your face. Somehow, I have gritted my teeth and lived through one
month out of 24. I don't know how I'm going to live through the other
23. The very thought of it gives me a fright. please look after your
health. Here, if I eat any nice food, I think of you. Everyone in my

family and yours is well. No other news here. Telepone me when you
can. It will be a comfort to me to here your voice at least.

with kisses,
Sherifa

When she finished reading the letter, her eyes were blinded
with tears. He had shown this letter to her, on his return, and
teased her so much, saying, 'Well, di, did you ever go to school
or not? Little idiot!' How could his soul bear to leave him
when he loved her so much? What did he think of, in those last
moments? Dim with tears, her eyes probed among the saris
piled on the bed and stopped at the yellow georgette silk and
the red rubyqueen saris. The saris he had chosen with such
love, for his wife. She remembered the commotion in Salaam's
parent's house, when the parcel arrived: it was a veritable
earthquake.

Sherifa's mother-in-law practically wiped the house with
her. She could not bear it that her son had sent a present to his
new bride, hoping it would comfort her during their
separation. Her father-in-law was even worse, leaping in fury
between earth and sky.

'The wastrel! How could he forget his own mother! Just
because he has clapped eyes on his new bride!' It sounded so
ugly to Sherifa. Had her mother-in-law been a stranger to her,
she might have borne it. But she was her own aunt; Saura's
own sister. Shocked that even within so close a relationship,
there could be such jealousy by her mother-in-law, Sherifa
wept for a whole day. She had been wondering whether she
should confide in her mother, but when Saura dropped in to
see her, that evening, Sherifa's heart broke in sorrow and
shame.

There was no need for her to say anything. Saura went
directly to her sister, and spoke, face to face. 'I hear your son
sent some saris? Do you imagine my daughter hasn't seen the

like of them? You know it yourself. How many boxes of presents has she unlocked, which her father has sent her? Is there a sari or object from abroad that she doesn't possess? I felt reassured that I had given her to my own sister's family; is this cruelty all she gets in return? You haughty beggar-woman!' Having said all this in a single loud shout, Saura then turned to her daughter and said, 'Let me tell you this: listen well. If you ever wear those two saris, you will end my life.'

The saris that had caused so much contention lay as they were, still unfolded. Sherifa had put them away in an almirah in her mother-in-law's house. They had lain there, untouched. She had written about all this to Salaam, adding, 'If only you had sent a sari to your mother at the same time, all these troubles need never have come about.'

He had replied, in his turn, 'Of course I have no problem in sending her a sari, too. But it was in my mind to impress on you that it is you I am thinking of, while I am here. I had planned to send Amma a sari separately, a few days later. But there has been all this fuss meanwhile. Please don't touch those saris again.' Remembering this, too, Sherifa grief welled up once more.

When she left her marital home after her husband's death, the bridal gifts had all been returned. These saris must have came back with them; she was only noticing them now. A great sigh burst out from her. She felt very tired. So that was it. There was nothing left. Everything was over and done. Hereafter she would never again wear a pretty sari, leave alone these ones.

She left the bed, came to the window and gazed outside. The street was silent; the usual noises of the village absent. The sun shone brightly. She could feel the heat slipping in through the window. The heat made her weary of heart. She was aware that more than any other season, the high summer increased her sense of loneliness and brought about an emptiness; but she didn't know why. The rainy season heightened the body's sensual awareness, inducing such a yearning that it distressed her. But the hot season reminded her of her loneliness, and hurt her in another way. Such a feeling of emptiness was very difficult to bear.

Sherifa wondered why the street was so silent. Then she remembered that it was the day Wahida's in-laws had invited the whole town for a feast. A bus had arrived that morning, to transport at least two representatives from each family, to Sabia's home town. Saura had refused to go, however. She didn't have a good relationship with Sabia. Rahimakka had come to invite her personally, but to no avail. Poor Amma, Sherifa thought. She just loved to eat biriyani, yet refused to go to the feast through sheer obstinacy. Sherifa felt disappointed, too. She hadn't gone anywhere near Wahida's house, from the day of the wedding. Why should she go and spoil such an auspicious event? Rahima and Zohra had tried to cajole her, saying, 'You are like our child, you are one of the family.' Of course they would invite her. But it did not feel right to her to attend.

How much she used to enjoy wearing her silks and her jewellery, and to participate in weddings! Now she was forced to pluck away and fling off all the little yearnings and desires that pulled at her, calling her to join in: the conversation of the women as they walked about, their adornments, the children's play, the scent of sandalwood pervading the very air, and above all the feeling of joyousness splashing and spraying everywhere.

A little girl was playing kittipul all by herself in the street. There was no one to play with her, apparently. Sherifa smiled, thinking to herself she would like to join the little one. She shut her eyes for a moment, recalling images of the times when she was just as old as that: when she and Fatima and other children played kittipul, when they went to see the cinema show at the touring talkies, when they cooked food and picnicked by the Satthaani lake, when they swung from the trees on makeshift swings, after their picnic. Desolately she wished she could have stayed a child forever.

⌒ 39 ⌒

Madina stood waiting in the street. She was so excited by the thought that Rabia was coming home that day, she could scarcely stay still. It was five whole days since she had seen Rabia. It had been a struggle for her even to pass the time. Uma's house was three streets away, and her brother would not allow her to go there unnecessarily. So she could not even play with Uma. They had put a stop to visits to the cinema, as well. Hereafter, no woman from this town was allowed to go anywhere near a cinema theatre. All this made her very cross. All his rules impinged on her the most, she felt. Since his arrival home, he had been thwarting her from going out anywhere. Even her mother had taken him to task, finally, saying, 'Why are you being so very repressive towards her, da? If she can't go out at her age, when will she ever get the chance?' Madina had been astonished that her mother had spoken up on her behalf. Of course she was right, though! Once she came of age, she would have to stay within four walls until her dying day. How would she ever experience such liberty again? The thought that she was being deprived of it already filled her with self-pity. Madina also wondered whether her mother's sudden concern for her had something to do with the annoyance she felt towards her son and daughter-in-law. Madina partly understood, but mostly did not.

She grew agitated the instant she heard the car at a distance. Her legs twitched to run at once and stand at the threshold of Rabia's house, but she struggled hard and stopped herself. No, she wouldn't do that; she'd wait and see if Rabia would come looking for her, she decided, and went back to the front steps of her own house. As the sound of the car approached, people emerged from each of the houses along the street, and stood on their front steps looking out eagerly.

Farida too placed herself at the window strategically, so that she could view the street without being seen. Her eyes seemed sad, somehow. Seeing her little sister at the door, she asked, surprised, 'Why are you standing here, di? Don't you want to go to go to their house?' But Madina said nothing. Sainu and Mumtaz had gone to Wahida's in-laws' house for the feast. The bus had not returned yet. It might be late returning, Farida thought to herself. The sound of the car made her feel both excited and hopeful. Wahida and the bridegroom descended from the car. Saura greeted them with an arati and took them inside. Madina watched intently. Rabia took her time to climb out, her hands full of something. She didn't go home straight away, but came running towards Madina's house. Before she could enter, Madina rushed out into the street, and the two girls hugged each other tightly. Still at the window, Farida burst into laughter. As they came in, she teased, 'Well, how many years is it since you saw each other?'

Rabia feigned anger. 'Go on, Akka,' she scolded fondly. Then, handing a packet covered in plastic to Madina, she said, 'Look! See what I've brought you!'

Madina looked enquiringly at her friend. Rabia's face had gained in beauty, suddenly. The new skirt and davani suited her, and showed her off to her best advantage. She said to Madina, who stood there watching her, 'Come, let's go up to the terrace. I'll show it to you there.' She came right into the house, ran across the courtyard, and began to climb up the wooden staircase leading upstairs. Madina hurried after her. 'Here, go carefully,' Farida called after them. 'Don't let it break down!' Then she went swiftly and placed herself by the door, so that she could be seen by Mutthu, who had got off the car, and was leaning against the wall of Rabia's house. She smiled at him briefly, and went inside.

Upstairs, there was a gentle, golden evening light. Rabia opened the packet, and spread it out in the palm of her hand. Madina stared, not sure what it was all about.

'These are aerial roots from a banyan tree. These are sampangi flower seeds.' Rabia separated them out with the fingers of her other hand. The banyan roots had fallen apart and were thread-like; white, long and thin. The sampangi seeds were coffee coloured and round. Madina looked at Rabia again, wondering what they could be used for. Rabia pulled one of her plaits over her shoulder and stroked it with pride. Madina had always loved her friend's long hair and gazed at it now. Rabia looked at Madina with her wide eyes and said, 'Yes, look at my hair. It's grown so long just because of this. Say you dry these out a bit, soak them in coconut oil, and then massage your head with the oil. Your hair will grow just like mine. My Chitthi told me. Every time I go there, I put this oil on my head. I bring some with me when I come home. The banyan tree is just next to my Nanni's house. I play with the hanging roots all the time. I thought I'd pluck a handful for you this time. Here, put these out to dry.' Rabia rattled all this off in a single breath, and handed the packet to Madina.

Madina was delighted. She imagined that her own rough, short hair had grown out instantly, and loved Rabia for having thought of her, and bringing this gift for her with such affection.

The two girls went to their usual secret place beneath the water tank. This was an enclosed space, open only on one side. This was where they always exchanged stories and secrets. They felt very safe and protected there, as if they were in a small room, away from the heat and the rain. Sometimes, when it rained, they would squat there on their haunches, eating the snacks they had brought with them. The rain water lapping at their feet gave them a lot of pleasure.

Now Madina sat down, cross-legged, eager to ask Rabia many things. Rabia, understood this, and sat down next to her, ready to talk. Madina waited for a moment as if that were obligatory. Then she asked in a rush, 'Do you like your Macchaan?' She was a bit jealous of Rabia's new relationship, yet she wanted to hear all about it.

Rabia's expression changed strangely when she heard Madina's question. She didn't like her Macchaan at all. But how could she say this openly, she wondered. Madina looked at Rabia with surprise, and waited. At last Rabia admitted, 'I don't like him, di, somehow.'

'Why not?'

'That is...' She felt shy to speak about it. Besides, she didn't know how to explain it. Still, she didn't want to hide anything from Madina. So she said, 'He isn't a nice man, Madina. He smokes. He's a bad man.' Realizing that she would have to explain a bit more, she went on, 'He won't leave me alone. Grabs my hand, keeps on pinching my cheek. It's awful.' She gave a shrug of disgust.

'Why does he act like that to you? He's got your Akka, hasn't he? Why can't he fondle her, if he wants?' Madina's sudden vehemence confused Rabia even more. Madina then asked, 'Well then, did he give you any presents?'

'Chi... No, nothing like that. Of course, after that I didn't go anywhere near him, did I?' Rabia was proud to report. But Madina apparently lost interest. Rabia too wanted to change the subject.

Madina then asked, 'How is your Akka? Does she like your Macchaan?'

'I don't know; I can't make it out. But she never seems to smile. She kept a serious face all the time we were there. Sabia Kuppi was saying that her daughter-in-law had not yet got over being home-sick. But I don't really understand why Akka is like that.' Rabia lowered her head, thinking hard.

There was still a lot that Madina wanted to know. She also thought it was her responsibility to explain things to Rabia, and clear away her doubts and anxieties. She asked, 'Tell me, what did Wahida do at early morning Bajar time? Did she always have a bath or not?'

Rabia didn't know what Madina was getting at. 'What do you mean?' she asked.

'That is, if she and your Macchaan were happy together during the night, she must have a bath and wash her hair before five in the morning. Don't you know that much? Idiot!' Madina scolded Rabia fondly.

Rabia was just about to ask, 'What do you mean by "happy"', but remained silent. She thought she half understood, and half did not. Madina, on the other hand, felt proud of herself in relation to Rabia's ignorance. There was something she knew, and could explain to Rabia. She said, 'My brother and Anni lock themselves into their room every night. My Anni has a bath and washes her hair first thing every morning, before she does anything else. Its been like this, ever since Annan came home. My mother grumbles all the time, saying it's as if they are just married.'

'What on earth do they do, behind locked doors? Do you know?' Rabia asked. She asked her question more because of Madina's eagerness to tell, than out of her own interest to know. Madina was both irritated by Rabia's ignorance, and filled with pity. In one way, Rabia's ignorance was a rare opportunity for Madina to show her own superiority.

Madina stared for a moment at Rabia's innocent, child-like face. Suddenly, she gathered Rabia in her arms and kissed her face ardently. Rabia, uncomprehending, was even more startled when Madina ran her fingers all over her body. She half sank uncomfortably against the rough, cemented floor of the terrace, still shocked and fearful, while Madina held her tightly. Suddenly Rabia remembered a time, long ago, when she was with Ahmad, and felt herself being roused. Her fear fell away as she lifted her arms and clung to Madina.

⇚ 40 ⇛

Half-way through the night, Nuramma woke up, hungry. On the previous evening, Iliaz had come home weeping, having dropped the food Rahima had sent right into the street, by accident. Not knowing who else to ask, Nuramma sent the boy to eat at Sherifa's, and went to bed without having eaten anything herself. Now she was famished. Iliaz lay next to her, fast asleep. Hunger turned into grief, pressing down on her, and then was transformed into a fierce anger against the boy. 'The boy has bad blood! As soon as he was born, he chased his father away. Now he's driven off his mother as well, and stands alone, an orphan. When Allah has written such a fate on his forehead, who can do anything?' She sat up and stared at the cooking hearth in the corner of the room. In the light of the lantern, she could see that there really was a cat curled up there. For how long could she exist by begging meals from other people, she wondered, with a great sense of weariness. The sudden weakness she felt throughout her body, besides a severe pain in her knee, frightened her. Was she going to die soon, perhaps? Did it please Allah if those who were already struggling, continued to suffer until the moment of death?

Suddenly she remembered her childhood days. Perhaps Allah would never forgive all her sins. When she was fourteen or fifteen, she had been very lively. Her mother Kairunissa had a reputation as a haughty and flaunting woman. Of all the huts in their locality, hers was the only one from where loud and audacious speech was heard. Although no one in that street was less than forthright, Kairunissa was in a class by herself; well known as a quarrelsome loud-mouth. She never seemed to consider Nuramma's father as her husband, leave alone as even a human being deserving respect. She always belittled him, saying, 'Eat what you are given, and just go!'

When they were young, when Nuramma and her little sister came home from their play, and knocked at their door, they would frequently see a stranger opening the door and walking away. Perhaps the lack of any other income was the reason for Kairunissa's choice of life. Once Nuramma came of age, Kairunissa herself began to arrange and invite clients for her daughter. Soon, Nuramma became used to her means of livelihood. She even liked it, and welcomed her clients warmly. On most days, Kairunissa and her younger daughter slept on the thinnai outside the hut, keeping guard, while Nuramma was inside, with a man. Her father Kaja Mohiuddin, hating all this, had become a walking corpse; at last he refused to come home, and stayed away in the mosque, most of the time.

She had grown completely used to her life; delighted with

the two rupees and blouse-piece her clients gave her. Not only had she entered into prostitution without being compelled into it; she also invited her younger sister to join her. But at last, there came a day when she grew tired of it all, and said to her mother. 'I am fed up with all this. Hereafter, please don't let anyone come here.'

Alarmed by the utter boredom that sounded in Nuramma's voice, Kairunissa asked, 'So what do you propose to do, hereafter?' Scared at the thought of how she was to survive for the rest of her days, she sagged down on to the front steps. Nuramma, too, worried about this, but was convinced that nothing was worse than the senselessness of her present life. She said resolutely, 'We'll think about that later. First let's be rid of this life and this town, and take ourselves off, elsewhere.' By now she felt a responsibility not only to free herself, but her sister too, from their current circumstances.

In a care-worn voice, Kairunissa asked, 'So, are you thinking of getting married, then?' Her question was clearly meant to impress on her daughter that such a dream was never going to come true. It was also meant to point out to her they would have no other means of livelihood, if she chose to abandon this one.

Nuramma answered, 'That's all I need, when I've got someone's child growing in my stomach!' The cynicism and bitterness at the heart of her words, spoken with such an air of helplessness, effectively shut Kairunissa's mouth. She never opened it again.

The terrible memory of those days as she wandered about seeking a means of livelihood, the baby having grown too big to abort safely, was still etched in Nuramma's mind.

Overcome by feelings of sadness and guilt following her memories, Nuramma was also seized by a terror that it was now time for her to be punished for her earlier sins, perhaps. She thought of all the lies she had told just a few days ago, in Wahida's house. She herself was amused now, by her attempt to present her family as an honourable and wealthy one by embroidering the truth and lying. These stories were not the

cause of profound guilt, however: after all, when she made up
that strange fiction about her mother's death, and the gold
and wealth she left behind, she had also just wanted to entertain
her audience. Besides, if she were truly such a sinner, why was
the jinn waiting to grant her that treasure? After all, the jinn
was not so foolish as to give it all to a sinner! And she was
absolutely certain that the jinn meant her alone to have it some
day. Nuramma was very confused by all this.

* * *

When she was a little girl, she and other children of the
neighbourhood used to spend their day taking their cow to
the fields. Having drunk their kanji, first thing in the morning,
they would set off with palmyra boxes on their heads. Inside
the boxes were their sickles. They followed a footpath past the
village, and walked across the irrigation tank. Once they
climbed on to its further shore, they could see green fields
spreading out in front of them. They tied up the cow to a tree,
so that it could graze along the ridges separating the fields,
and then shook out their skirts which had become wet and
muddy while crossing the irrigation tank. Flinging their skirts
high in the wind, they would allow the mud to fall off and the
clothes to dry.

Later, they would turn the palmyra boxes upside down on
their heads, like sun hats, and squat down in rows to cut the
grass growing there, chatting all the time. Loudly they would
call out the names of all the wild shrubs and bushes growing
there: aavaram, arali, touch-me-not, wild basil. Avoiding
these, they would gather a bunch of grass in their left hands
and scythe it off neatly with the sickle. The bunches of grass
would be laid out neatly in a row on the ground. When there
was enough to fill the boxes more or less, they would do so and
go back to their play. There was a little pipal tree by the side of
the tank, which they loved to climb and sit on... They had
such fun together, then. It was bliss to watch the mountains in

the distance, the fields spreading out everywhere, wave upon wave of the crops swaying in the wind, the water in the tank reaching as far as the eye could see; to smell the grain, newly ripening.

One day, as she was bent over the grass, busy at her work, Nuramma saw, hanging from her hands, a plant which she had pulled up; clusters of bright gold coins clinging to its roots. For a moment she was frozen with the shock of it, unable to move her limbs. How to explain this treasure which hung miraculously from the plant she held in her hands, when she had heard such gold only belonged to big houses and kings' palaces! And then it all vanished the moment she called out, 'Come here and see this, all of you.'

After that she plunged into a state of shock, unable to convince anyone of what she had seen. For the treasure had disappeared magically. That was the first time that the jinn showed her the treasure. It had certainly shown it to her a second time. What prevented the jinn from giving the treasure to her on both those occasions? She had an unshakeable belief that it would not disappoint her a third time, and was determined not to upset herself about it. Now that she had grown so old, surely the jinn was not going to delay much longer? It was not going to get many more opportunities now. Besides, it would be really useful to have that treasure at that moment. 'I'll give the men of this town a good shake up; let them just see! After that they will never ban me from the community, the wastrels!'

She was out of breath. Hunger tore at her entrails. She laid her head down, and tried to go back to sleep. How much longer would it be, until daybreak? She would send the boy for puttu to Katthaan's house, at dawn. She had set aside a tidy sum of money out of the Ramzan alms she had been given, and this gave her some courage. With a sudden tenderness born out of that courage, she turned to Iliaz. He was fast asleep. He had tried to reassure her, the previous day, saying, 'Nanni, from tomorrow, I'm going to help pack the goods in Rahimakka's family's grocery shop.' Once again sorrow and pity filled her, and the tears streamed from her eyes. She scolded Fatima, silently. 'You obscene whore! In a frenzy of lust for that man you went off, leaving this little child to go to ruin! Evil wretch! It doesn't matter where you go, you won't prosper, you won't have a life.' She tried by her curses to lessen her hunger, sorrow and despair. The night and its sadness only extended, endless.

ᖇ 41 ᖆ

Mumtaz was taking down the clothes drying on the line in the courtyard, one by one, gathering them together in her arms. As she pulled down Farida's davani, she felt a stab of annoyance. These days Farida acted as if she were in competition with Mumtaz, whether in the matter of cooking, or chores around the house. Then there was the backbiting. The minute Sainu re-entered the house after going out anywhere, Farida was whispering to her. After that, Sainu had nothing better to do than to raise her voice and shout.

To Mumtaz it seemed that Farida was jealous that her brother and sister-in-law were able to be together; that it irked her so much, she had to keep complaining to her mother about them. She was never so bad as this at earlier times. In fact, there had been occasions when Farida spoke up for Mumtaz, and even earned her mother's wrath because of it. Why had she changed so much? Was it only because Mumtaz and Suleiman were so happy together? Mumtaz could not make it out. Sometimes she would tell herself that Farida was of an age to get married; of course she must have her hopes and desires. For some days she had been noticing something else. Farida's expression changed when she heard the car belonging to Rabia's family; she ran to the window facing the street, and stood behind the curtain, looking out at someone. Mumtaz's reflection was quickly followed by the thought of Suleiman and she shuddered. She could not begin to imagine what he would do if he knew about this. She had absolutely no doubt that he would be prepared to kill.

Although her annoyance with Farida prompted her to betray the girl, she remembered Suleiman's terrible temper, and let it go.

Even last night, when they were in bed together, Suleiman asked her, 'I came home this time, determined not to leave until I've arranged a marriage for Farida. But it looks as if a satisfactory bridegroom won't turn up. Shall I get her married to that boy Aziz, arrange a visa for him, and take him away with me?'

Mumtaz understood immediately why he planned not only to give Farida away to Aziz, but also to take him away from this town. She said nothing for a while, quietly touching his hands and playing with his fingers. If this marriage happened, the relationship between Nafiza and Aziz would be broken for ever: that would please her. She was furious that while she herself lived an irreproachable life, never going within sight of a man for years together when Suleiman was away, Nafiza should be living with a man when her own husband was in town. Sometimes, Mumtaz would even wonder whether she was actually envious of Nafiza. But the very next moment she would tell herself, in a congratulatory manner, 'Ché, am I a woman with such low standards?'

Yet, she found herself unable to agree to the arrangement immediately. If Aziz were to go abroad with Suleiman, and work with him as his partner, he would have a share in the business which was now solely Suleiman's. She didn't like this at all. She could not agree to sharing the profits, which were now solely theirs, with her sister-in-law's husband. But if she were to say this, Suleiman would be very angry. Tormented by all these thoughts, she remained quiet, deciding to wait for the right opportunity to speak.

Suleiman was holding her tightly at that moment, but she appeared unaware of his embrace. He bit her ear gently and whispered, 'What's the matter with you? You are lying there like a corpse! Are you fed up with it already?'

'Oh, it's nothing at all,' she said, coming to herself, and putting her arms about him.

⟨ 42 ⟩

Suleiman came out of the mosque, having attended the Luhur prayers. It annoyed him to see the badam tree leaves which lay all over the pavements of the mosque. He found it unendurable that all this rubbish had not been swept away. He stood there awhile, looking about him for the Modinaar. It irritated him even more that the Modinaar was nowhere to be seen. Suleiman himself paid the Modinaar's monthly salary, besides taking care of the mosque's electricity charges. In spite of all this, he had not felt satisfied that he was doing enough for the good of the community. This was the reason why he had bought the car, mainly for tabligh duties, but also for the family's use. He felt proud, now, of what he had achieved. The car stayed at his home, because there was no space in the mosque's premises.

He was just about to go home, when Karim called out to him, 'Come here, and talk to me for awhile.'

Suleiman went up to him, asking, 'What is it, Maamu?'

'Are you hungry already, at a quarter past one? Sit here for a little while.'

Suleiman stood there, unable to refuse Karim. He really was very hungry. He had bought viral fish that morning, and asked for it to be cooked. He wanted to go home and eat it before it cooled. Suleiman doted on fish. His visits home from Singapore were always made in the summer. True, he didn't care to leave the pleasant climate there, and come here when it was so hot. But it was in the hot summer season that viral fish was plentiful. His friends would tease him, saying he would be burnt dry in the sun. He never said anything in return. The very thought of the fish made his mouth water, now.

Karim sat in the madrasa, just by the water troughs. Suleiman went up to him, lightly dusted off the floor next to him with his handkerchief, and sat down saying, 'Allahu'. Karim looked as if he was going to question him, Suleiman realized.

Karim began with a long preamble. 'Well, nephew, it looks as if you really are doing any number of good things!'

Suleiman was impervious to the mockery in Karim's voice. He stared at the older man, not quite sure what exactly he referred to. 'What exactly are you talking about, Maamu?' he asked.

'You're acting as if you don't understand! And after making such a contribution to the mosque!'

'Oho, is that what you meant?' Suleiman was overcome with pride, not for once realizing that Karim was teasing him. He continued, full of self-praise, 'What do you think of my project? It's going to be really useful for all the tabligh work, won't it? How hard it is now, to go to all the little towns and villages when there is no bus or any other transport! That's why I wanted to buy a car for the mosque. I've wanted to do this for a long time.' His expression revealed his satisfaction at having achieved something important.

Karim watched him with a certain kind of enjoyment. He asked with an innocent expression, 'Isn't it rather like the way people donate bulls to temples, in these parts?'

Suleiman agreed, nodding his head proudly in agreement, totally unaware of the joke.

Karim went on, 'Whatever one might say, nephew, no one will ever match what you have done, nor gain so much merit.'

Suleiman was so happy, he was even prepared to forget his hunger. They were both silent for a while. The breeze blew strongly, suddenly. Suleiman took his fez off, lest it fly off, and held it in his hands. The water in the hauz rippled in the wind. The fish sliding about among the long water weeds reminded him once again of the meal waiting at home. Courtesy stopped him from walking off in the middle of a conversation, however, so he asked, 'Well, Maamu, have you heard any news about that whore who eloped?' His voice took on a stern note.

Karim, annoyed, made his displeasure plain. 'I really don't understand why you get so worked up about that silly slut.'

Suleiman, in his turn, was angered by Karim's lack of interest or concern, but he gritted his teeth. His face reddened behind his sparse beard. He stared at Karim for a moment through narrowed eyes, before lowering them. His thin lips trembled as he asked, 'Tell me, what am I to make of it if the elders of this town, such as you, speak in such an irresponsible fashion?'

'What can we do now, appa? The donkey has bolted. How are we to punish it now? We must wash our hands off it, that's all. I still can't understand why you are so upset. In any town something more or less like this will happen once or twice. Who can put everything right?' Karim was tired of it. He was also getting quite angry with Suleiman. The fellow was getting quite above himself.

Suleiman began again. He could not accept Karim's irresponsibility, as he considered it. 'How can you say that, in such an irresponsible way? If you take that attitude, what can we expect of others? Sometime ago, I heard that these Kafir boys were beating their drums and making a racket in front of the mosque, at prayer time. I was horrified, do you know that? Men like me go abroad without fear, because we trust elders such as you who stay here. But what will happen to our community if you refuse to watch out? Don't you realize that it is your duty to prevent the community from going to ruin?' It was very clear from his expression that he was burning with emotion.

Karim disliked what he saw in Suleiman as well as finding him tedious. He had intended to tease Suleiman a bit because of his folly in buying a car, but the man was working himself up into a frenzy. He was quiet for a little while, as if he didn't think it right to get equally angry. Then he tapped Suleiman lightly on the shoulder, and said, intending to provoke rather than calm him down, 'Don't get so heated, nephew! It isn't possible for any of us to safeguard another person. It is Allah alone who must safeguard all of us. Only that which he has written on our foreheads is going to happen.'

Suleiman stared at Karim's wide face, unable to understand the emotion he saw there, and feeling helpless. Having lived abroad for so long, he struggled to understand what people who continued to live here meant by their words and their facial expressions. All of a sudden, his anger ebbed away. 'Born a Muslim, how can you bring yourself to speak in this way?' His voice was full of despair, almost as if he were pleading for help, or asking for a little mercy.

Now Karim almost felt sorry for him. It struck him suddenly that it was wrong to mock at him; it embarrassed him that he had done it. He wanted to bring the conversation to an end. He said, 'Right, Suleiman, forget what has happened so far. It is our duty to make sure that our community isn't humiliated in this way again. This kind of thing will never happen hereafter. Come, let's go home; we'll talk on the way.' He helped the younger man to stand up, and brought him out of the mosque.

But Suleiman told himself, 'All these people care about is to eat their fill, and then to go about the town. If they possessed a drop of the faith that is mine, would such a thing have happened here?'

He heard his name being called out and came to himself. It was Rashid, who kept the stall just outside the mosque. Suleiman heard him say, 'Anna, a man in a huge car asked the way to your house just now. Go back quickly.'

Suleiman said goodbye to Karim hurriedly and hastened homewards, wondering who his visitor might be. When he saw the car standing at the corner of the street, he knew at once that it was Abdulla bhai who had arrived. He went in eagerly and made his salaam to the man seated in the hall, welcomed him and embraced him. When they were both sitting together on the sofa, Suleiman asked, 'Well, is the nikah over? Have you brought Maami with you, now?'

'Would I come by myself, without her? No, no, we've both come. Jasima is inside.' Abdulla spoke with great pride, blushing as he pronounced his new wife's name.

Mumtaz observed Abdulla through the narrow gap where the door joined the wall. He was very slim and tall. Although he was definitely more than sixty years old, there wasn't a grey hair on his head. An aristocratic complexion. Not a spare inch of extra flesh on him. A fine nose and a chiselled mouth. He must have been extremely handsome in his prime, she told herself. But why should he, at his age, marry a young woman? That young woman was in Mumtaz's room, at that very moment, with Farida. She reminded herself of the girl's form. She would be just about twenty-five years old. She was very beautiful. Because she was born so beautiful, but in a poverty-stricken family, she ended up with this old man. It's all one's fate, Mumtaz thought as she began frying the fish. They would be invited to stay to the meal; she had to hurry to get everything done.

After they had eaten, Suleiman took Abdulla and his wife to meet all his relations, and introduced them with great pride.

↫ 43 ↬

The sunlight lay thickly scattered all over the street. Its burning heat stopped people from any movement. Rabia stayed close to Wahida since their return home. In a couple of days, Wahida would leave them. After that she would return only for the fortieth day feast. So Rabia had no great inclination to go away and play. She felt an even greater affection towards Wahida, a greater desire to cling to her. And she knew the reason why.

That day was the day after Wahida's return, and since

morning the bridegroom was receiving a lot of ceremonious attention. Rabia was annoyed by this and guessed, from Wahida's expression, that she felt the same. More than that, Rabia was sad and resentful. When she herself could understand that her cousin was not happy, how could Amma and Periamma not realize it? She gazed at their faces, trying to make out whether they realized the true state of affairs but pretended they did not; she remained baffled. It looked as if they were genuinely happy as they bustled about. Rabia seemed to be the only one who cared. All the same, she still could enjoy the vattalappam which was the special sweet prepared for the bridegroom.

Just as soon as they had finished their midday meal, all the women who lived in their street arrived, one by one, to visit the new bride. From each house, they brought bags of sugar and flowers. There was talk and laughter everywhere. Even Sherifa came, to visit Wahida. Their hall was crowded with women: Saura, Nafiza, Mumtaz and Mariyaayi were all there. Kader, who always had a nap after lunch, insisted on returning to the shop. Sikander was lying down upstairs, protesting that he could not sleep with all the noise about him. Apparently, a new bridegroom could not leave the house!

It was Nafiza who started off the conversation with Wahida. 'Well, new bride,' she teased, 'how do you find your mother-in-law, then?' Sayyed was related to her in some way; she looked upon him as an uncle.

Wahida looked down and gave a gentle nod, letting it be understood that Sabia was well.

'Of course she is well; why shouldn't she be? I asked how she treats you,' Nafiza said.

Mumtaz intervened. 'What will she do in five days? Even my mother-in-law was nice to me for a week after I was married, getting me to lie down and plying me with food!' she said mockingly. Everyone there laughed as she lingered suggestively over the words 'getting me to lie down'.

Rahima cautioned them, 'Lower your voice, amma. Sainu Akka might turn up at any time!'

'Let her come! Is she going to chop off my head or what? I only said what's true,' Mumtaz shook her head contemptuously.

Nafiza winked and laughed, 'See, she can speak out like this nowadays: it's all because of the courage that she gains from sitting on her husband's lap.'

'Of course,' Zohra agreed, adding fuel to the fire.

Rahima changed the topic, calling to mind something else. 'By the way, Mumtaz, your husband was accompanying that new bridegroom and showing him off all over the place, wasn't he? That poor girl! How can that man marry a girl who could be his daughter, and be so shameless about it? I can't accept it, somehow.'

'Who can accept such a thing? If it's an eyesore to see that man flaunting himself and his wife; what can I say about this one who takes them round everywhere!' Mumtaz held her chin in surprise. She certainly didn't approve of her husband's part in all this. She went on, 'After the old man left, my mother-in-law cursed him roundly. Just because a man has the money, should he act in such a high-handed way, she asked.'

'Your husband was prepared to pull out his tongue because Fatima ran after a man, but here he is sticking by this fellow! You should put him wise about that old man, who already has three wives, but goes and marries a fourth, ruining a young woman's life,' Zohra remarked. Even Rahima had never seen her so angry and frustrated, before this. She never stopped talking about it, since Abdulla's visit.

Mumtaz was quiet for a while, unable to counter Zohra's anger, or to find an adequate answer. Then she said, 'It's not that I haven't taken it up with him, Akka. But do you know what he said to me? "What is the matter with you," he said, "the man is acting in perfect accordance with Shariat. He is allowed to marry four wives, isn't he? If he had gone against

Shariat, it would be wrong. But now he is acting absolutely correctly." But of course, I didn't let it go at that. I asked him, "Does that justify this terrible thing he has done? Ask your conscience and then tell me."'

'These old men marry very young women, and then take themselves off abroad. The girls are left to pick and eat here and there, where and when they can; if the fellow then goes and dies, of course they go astray totally. After that the whole world will laugh at us, calling this Rowther's daughter and that Rowther's wife a slut and a whore. This old man won't think of all that.' Saurakka put in her complaint.

'Why, even when he is actually here, it's not as if he can give her any pleasure, is it? It would surprise me if he is able to do it even occasionally. And what can she think of him, when she sleeps with him? He's like her father! Are we to say it's disgusting or pathetic?' Nafiza slapped herself on the head. Her face reddened for a moment.

'But the girl looked very cheerful and serene, didn't she? Not the least sign of anxiety on her face. And she was smiling the whole time,' Rahima sounded surprised.

'It's all because of the money. He's stacked the jewellery on her neck and ears and arms, hasn't he? She's pleased and delighted because of that,' Mumtaz remarked.

Just then, a couple of new visitors arrived at the house, and Zohra and Rahima went up to welcome them and find them seats.

Immediately, Nafiza and Mumtaz homed in on Wahida, sat close beside her on either side, and bent over, as if to exchange secrets. Mumtaz whispered, 'Well, has it all happened?' She and Nafiza could hardly contain their eagerness for all the details. They had to ask, though they knew that Wahida would tell them nothing.

Rahima came and sat by them. 'What are you asking her?' she wanted to know.

'Oh, nothing. It's just your daughter is so shy, we wanted to know whether she is quite familiar with the bridegroom, now. What has happened, tell us? It must be done by now. Nearly a week has gone by,' Mumtaz said.

The three of them made a separate little group, while the rest of the women were engaged in a conversation about someone's jewellery. Rahima's face wrinkled with worry, when she heard Mumtaz's question. She said, 'What can I say? The girl is still too shy to go anywhere near him. Who knows whether she talks to him, even at night?'

Rahima was gnawed by the anxiety that she might have done something wrong. Was Wahida keeping away from her husband because she disliked him, or was it her natural shyness that made her act that way? She could not make it out. Besides, she knew that even if Wahida disliked her husband, she would never distress her mother by telling her that. Rahima didn't know what to think. Her heart was filled with a pain she could not fathom.

Mumtaz tried to console her. 'You don't worry about anything! Of course she'll feel shy. Leave it with me; I'll rid her of her shyness in a single day.' she turned eagerly to Nafiza. 'What do you say, Nafiza? Shall we show her a cassette? What about this evening?'

'I don't have a single cassette of that kind. But you, surely, have something? Suleiman must have brought one or two? Bring it; we'll get her to look at it.' Nafiza said in reply.

Rahima, distressed, hastened to intervene. 'Ayyayyé, don't do anything of that sort; she won't like it.'

But Mumtaz would not have it. 'You be quiet, Akka; leave it to us. Let this crowd go home. I'll bring the cassette late in the evening. We'll put it on then. I have a cassette from abroad.' She rose to her feet saying, 'Well then, where is the bridegroom? I should congratulate him, and go.'

Nafiza joined her, saying, 'True, we haven't seen him at all. I must also go, after congratulating him.'

As soon as they asked to see Sikander, Rahima panicked.

'Listen, girls, don't go and exchange dirty jokes with him! It will be really shameful!'

Saura butted in, 'But they are off for that particular purpose, don't you know that?' She shook with laughter. Rabia was hugely amused to see Saura's heavy breasts heaving up and down.

Mumtaz called to her, 'Rabia, you come along with us.'

Rabia, not sure why she was being summoned, stared blankly. Mumtaz explained to Rahima and the others, 'He's a new bridegroom; he wouldn't have slept all night. What if he's fast asleep, and his veshti has slipped off? So it's best if she goes first and wakes him up.'

Rabia, who had half risen, now sat down again, saying, 'Chi, how horrible! I'm not going.' Scared that they might drag her off bodily, she held on to the end of Wahida's silk sari, and clung to her cousin.

'Nafiza, just see this, di, how shy she is! Leave it then. We'll go by ourselves.'

'Even if he is looking disorderly, it doesn't matter. After all, we are related; he's like a cousin to me.'

Holding up their silk saris so that they wouldn't trip over, they climbed up the stairs. They were old-fashioned, steep wooden stairs, so they went up carefully, fearful of falling down. Upstairs, the smell of flowers coming out of the very first room indicated that the bridegroom must be there. Nafiza opened the door and thrust her head in, to see. Sikander was lying on the bed, smoking a cigarette. When he saw her, he immediately sat up, saying, 'Come in, Macchi.'

'What are you up to?' Nafiza asked. She entered the room followed by Mumtaz. He invited them both to sit down. Mumtaz sat down on one of the chairs there, while Nafiza went up and sat on the bed next to him as if she had a special right. She gazed at him, and then winked and smiled.

'Why are your eyes all red, have you been awake all night? All by yourselves in this upstairs room, besides! You must have run about and played catch,' she teased.

Sikander was wearing a silk veshti and banyan. A gold chain sparkled around his neck. Nafiza and he were of the same age. She had a teenaged son. He was only just married. She remembered the days when they were in school together. He had lived in this very house at the time.

'Pach!' he said crossly, in answer to her. 'I've married this baby calf of a girl, and am having a hard time. Go on with you!'

'Well, don't carry on about it! You could have married me, couldn't you? At that time you refused, for no good reason,' she challenged him.

He answered playfully, laughing at her, 'What would I have done with you? What was the good of your being pretty? You were too short for my liking.'

'Too short? Me? A fine thing to say!' She touched her chest, looking surprised. 'Short or tall, if everything else is right, it wouldn't have mattered, would it, Macchaan? It wasn't in your destiny; what to do!' She feigned a great sigh, as if pitying him.

Sikander pointed to Mumtaz and asked, 'Why is this lady sitting here silently?'

Mumtaz had been quiet so far, feeling shy for some reason. Nafiza turned to look at her, and then said to Sikander, mockingly, 'Oh, poor thing! She never knows what to say.'

Mumtaz laughed at this. Sikander, appreciating her good looks, said, 'Please wait a moment.' He rose up, put out his cigarette and flung it away through the window. He returned and sat down again on the bed, saying, 'Please accept my apologies for smoking in front of two beautiful ladies.'

'Well, let's get to the point, and say why we came. Now tell us the truth, Macchaan. What happened, exactly?' Nafiza came out with it directly.

He was somewhat taken aback, but answered with equal directness, 'Oh, all that is done.' He shrugged his shoulders in a proud gesture.

'If it's all done, then why do you sound so resentful, calling her a baby calf and a baby lamb?'

'Is it all right just to do it? Come on, mustn't she show even a little enthusiasm,' he complained. 'And she's so very shy. She really gives me a hard time.'

Nafiza said, trying to hearten him, 'I'll make her shyness vanish into thin air. Just wait and see.'

'You have a go. But she won't come round, you know.' He sounded quite certain of it.

'Just you wait. See if I don't sort her out and send her to you. You are going to be surprised. So what will you give me in return?'

He took her up on that. 'I can only give you what I have, surely. You are very welcome to it, if you want it.' Mumtaz joined in their laughter, until the whole room echoed.

'Very well; we'll go now,' Nafiza said getting to her feet. 'Macchaan, eat well while you are in your mother-in-law's house. You need to keep up your strength.' She winked at him again, and came out of the room.

'I'll also say goodbye,' Mumtaz said, following Nafiza.

Sikander called after them, 'Do visit often, Macchi, while I am here.'

They came down the wooden stairs and went out into the street, through the back door. As they were walking home, Nafiza said with an air of concern, 'I need to tell you something. You won't take it amiss, will you? I don't at all like the way your husband is making so much of that Abdulla. Why should he be so close to a man who marries a new wife every year? I'm afraid he's going to say one day that he too is prepared to marry again. It's like the evil spoiling the good by association.'

Mumtaz was infuriated by Nafiza's apparent concern. 'Keep your jokes and mockery to yourself. My husband is not the kind of person who goes sniffing after others.' She spoke quite sharply. Although she did not show any change of expression, Nafiza felt Mumtaz was pointing a finger at herself, and she was distressed. She walked home, hurt that what she had said out of genuine anxiety should have been misunderstood.

❧ 44 ❧

Wahida lay on her bed, utterly limp and burning hot. Kader had just arranged for the doctor to come and see her. The doctor had declared it an ordinary fever, and prescribed a medicine accordingly. When he said that, Wahida had wanted to shout out what it was that had made her ill. But she was helpless; she could only mutter angrily to herself.

None of the things that had happened recently made sense to her. She could not remember ever having seen an unfamiliar male face since the day she first menstruated. She had never been aware of her mother or Chitthi having a bath unexpectedly, at dawn. Her parents, and her Chitthi and Chaccha always behaved with restraint in front of her, as if it were wrong to chat and laugh intimately between themselves in her presence. From the time she was a child, her mother had taught her to cover her body when she had a bath, and never stare at herself even accidentally. But now, everything seemed to be upside down. Her mother was telling her to be on her own with a man, to sleep with him. She sent people to Wahida who blamed her for not behaving properly towards her husband, and advised her on how she should be with him. What had happened that within a week the same people who had frightened her, and kept things covered up, were now showing things to her openly and brazenly? She lifted her right hand which lay limply by her side, and felt into the neck of her blouse. She touched the tali strung with black beads. Did it have such force, she asked herself. When she realized that the very day this was placed around her neck, everything changed for her, an unbearable shock broke through her, making her shudder all over. She had a confused sense of being in a totally unknown world.

Behind her tight shut eyes, the scenes she had seen on TV replayed themselves, as if on a mental screen, shocking her yet again. Desperately she attempted to keep her eyes wide-open.

With a strenuous effort she kept at bay the nausea she had felt on seeing those naked bodies. Yet the features and forms of the man and woman kept filling her mind and memory. However hard she tried, she could not obliterate some scenes which had appeared for a few minutes alone.

What had shocked her most of all was the excitement she had seen on Nafiza's and Mumtaz's faces, as they watched those scenes with her. For some reason, those two had not been very friendly with each other, as if there had been some ill feeling between them. All the same, they had relished those scenes sufficiently to exchange oblique remarks and comments. Some of the things they had said continued to sound in her ear, robbing her of peace of mind.

Wahida's anger was directed most of all against her mother. Why did she allow this obscenity? None of this need have happened, if she had refused to let them show the cassette. Would she go to any length to ensure that Wahida was comfortable with her husband? It had only succeeded in making Wahida ill. Did Rahima understand what she had done? Of course she must understand. How could she not? It was Rahima's consequent guilt and regret that stopped her from talking to her daughter properly, or even coming near her. Wahida knew this. Her head ached.

As soon as she fell ill, Sikander set off home. 'What business have I here, when you are not feeling well? Rather than sitting at home doing nothing, I might as well go home,' he had said, feeling aggrieved. She felt unhappy that he had spoken like that. For no reason at all, she had an instant's vision of the cinema-hero husband who stayed by the side of his sick wife, ministering to her. She wondered repeatedly, whether there was any reason at all for her to like him.

It seemed that he possessed not a single one of the attributes that she had wished for, in a future husband. Her heart and mind refused to accept that Sikander was truly her husband now; it seemed to her that it was a stranger who lay with her. She could not prevent the questions that came to her, 'Who is

this? What business does he have here?' Neither did she know
how to put an end to this chaotic state of mind. She tried to
console herself with the thought that only six days had gone
by; that in the course of time, everything would work out. Yet
it was a cause of grief to her that the experience of sex, which
should have been a matter of joy, would – at best – become
something to which she grew accustomed. We learn to endure
anxiety, grief, hardship and pain only by accepting them
through habituation. Was this relationship too, going to be
like that? In that case, what sort of hell would it be, for her?
Did she possess enough strength for such endurance?
Tormented as she was by a thousand anxieties and questions,
she thought suddenly of her father-in-law. She, who had been
as carefree as a bird, was burdened by all these worries and
problems within the space of a week of marriage. How could
this have happened? Hating to be in such a state of confusion,
she lay prone on the bed, shutting her eyes tightly in an attempt
to sleep.

⌒ 45 ⌒

Sainu was giving the twins their bath. This task was
easier now, since she had cropped off their hair, following
Farida's advice. In earlier times, on days when she was due to
wash their hair, she would start on her complaints from
daybreak. All the time, there would be oblique remarks aimed
at Mumtaz. Nowadays, Mumtaz realised, she wasn't subjected
to quite the same nagging. From where she was standing in the
courtyard, she watched for a while, to see whether the
bathroom door was being opened. It didn't look as if the baths
would be over just yet. Mumtaz thought for a while. She wanted
to take some fish curry to Nafiza, before Sainu was finished.
Nafiza was just next door; she could step across and return in
an instant. But what if Farida was on the lookout? No, Farida
was saying her prayers. It would take her a while. Nafiza loved

a curry made of the ayira fish that Suleiman had bought that morning.

Mumtaz thought of her altercation with Nafiza, a couple of days ago. I must have a cursed tongue, she chided herself; why on earth did I speak to her like that. Her indiscretion gnawed away at her. The gift of the fish curry would be an excuse to put things right between them.

Mumtaz was not without doubts about Suleiman. If she failed to produce a child quickly, it would not surprise her too much if he did, indeed, marry again. The thought terrified her. Even the previous night he had said as if it were a joke, 'Nowadays, I only sleep with you because I want a child. That's all I think of.' The words had bitten into her. After he said that, she could not remain in his arms. She pulled herself away and lay at a distance from him. She wanted to brush away his touch — which had seemed so pleasing just a short while ago — from her body. It distressed her that he was so unaware of her feelings. She wept for a long time, without his knowledge.

It further annoyed her now, that he had determined on marrying Farida to Aziz, without expecting Mumtaz to state her opinion about it. Startled by the creak of the bathroom door as it opened, she came to herself, left the courtyard and went back into her room. Sainu would stand the two girls in the courtyard, rub them dry with towels, and change their clothes. She disliked watching this, and so she entered her own room and lay down. She felt weary. She tried to remember how many days had passed since she had menstruated last, and therefore could not say her prayers. Counting on her fingers, she calculated that it must be twenty-two days. She must be careful now to lie down and rest enough, and not to strain herself. Zohra and Rahima had advised her not to run about too much or work too hard during the last days of her monthly cycle. But in all this time, it was only now that she felt such a desperate need to conceive a child, and such fear. Was she right to be so fearful? She knew that it would not be a big deal for him to find another woman, and this made her very anxious. Yes, she decided, her fear and anxiety were indeed valid. It would be a good thing for her to take it easy from that very day. She knew that Sainu would never stand for it if she lay in bed and ate her meals without doing any house work, and planned that it would be best for her to go to her mother's house for a while.

Once again she thought of Nafiza. Mumtaz didn't know whether Nafiza was aware that Aziz was going to be married, and would leave the country soon after that. She was bound to be shaken by the news. Mumtaz was eager to tell her about it, and watch her expression change. Although she knew it was callous of her, she was impelled by that eagerness to leave her room. Once again she came out into the hall.

Farida had gone up to the terrace, probably, to hang up the clothes. Sainu was sitting on the thinnai in the courtyard, drying her children's hair. She looked up and asked Mumtaz, 'Why has Suleiman not come home for his meal as yet? He usually returns straight after the Luhur prayers.' As far as Sainu was concerned, the family was allowed to eat only after her son had been served.

'I have no idea,' Mumtaz replied. She went into the kitchen, picked up the dish in which she had poured the fish curry, and hurried out by the back door to Nafiza's house.

* * *

Nafiza had not expected to see Mumtaz enter her house all of a sudden, and looked at her enquiringly. 'It's nothing important,' Mumtaz said, placing the dish on the thinnai, and sitting down on the floor.

'Adé, why do you sit on the floor in your prayer sari,' Nafiza scolded, going to fetch a mat which she shook out and laid down.

'It doesn't matter; I've sat down now.' Mumtaz crossed her legs and made herself comfortable.

'What's this? It looks as if you've brought me something?'

Nafiza took the dish and peered into it. 'Is it fish curry?'

'Yes,' Nafiza said proudly, 'I brought it because it's your favourite.'

Nafiza looked at Mumtaz directly. 'Does your mother-in-law know? She wouldn't have the heart to share it, would she?'

'I brought it without her knowledge, of course,' Mumtaz boasted, and then bit her tongue as if she realized she had made a mistake; as if her affection for Nafiza had driven her to tell the truth, even if it were a mistake.

Nafiza's expression changed at once.

By way of making peace, Mumtaz went on, 'What if she knows? The woman won't say anything.'

Nafiza looked as if she were staring at a disgusting object. She was greatly annoyed with Mumtaz for having brought the curry. Was she so poverty stricken and in need of free meals? 'Why do you belittle me like this? Take it away. Do I go about begging for food? What is food anyway, it only turns into shit,' Nafiza spoke with extreme resentment. Again she said, 'Please take this and go away, you'll be doing me a great favour.'

Mumtaz was profoundly embarrassed. Why on earth had she admitted that she had brought the curry without her mother-in-law's knowledge? After a moment's silence, she said, 'This comes out of my husband's earnings. Don't you think I have a right to it, too? No, I won't take it away. Please just keep it, and don't say any more.' She sounded as if she were pleading.

They were both silent for awhile. Nafiza was aware that Mumtaz's conscience was uneasy. She had been unhappy ever since Mumtaz had spoken to her in that way, some days ago. It irritated her that the woman had come over now, voluntarily, in order to prove her affection. All the same, she was reluctant to break off her friendship with Mumtaz. She knew that were she to do that, there would be no one else she could turn to. Both women were friendly with Sherifa, it was true, but they could never share with her the jokes and banter which they exchanged between themselves. Nor would it be wise of them to do so.

Mumtaz was perplexed by Nafiza's silence, and wondered whether she should announce her news. Although she was still eager to watch how Nafiza might react, she was worried that it would only worsen the atmosphere which was already so uncomfortable. Not knowing what to do, she looked up at Nafiza's face, and then downward at the floor. 'Where's Ahmad? He doesn't seem to be about. Hasn't he come home yet?'

Nafiza understood Mumtaz's discomfort. Realizing after all, that it was up to her to speak naturally, and put her at her ease once more, she said, 'Oh, Ahmad? He's gone to stay in town until the end of the school holidays. I feel as if the house isn't pleasant anymore.' She assumed a sad expression.

Mumtaz nodded in agreement. After a while, she asked again, 'And where is Ahmad's father? Isn't he coming home for his meal?'

'Oh, he's gone on business to town; he's had to order stock. That's why I didn't even make a kuzhambu. I've just cooked the rice. Rafiq only likes curd with his rice. Why go to a lot of trouble, just for one woman?'

Mumtaz again agreed vehemently. 'Too true. Why cook anything special when the men are away? Might as well just eat what there is to hand.'

Nafiza asked, 'I hear that Wahida has a fever. Did you go and see her?'

'Not yet. I must go today. Rahimakka said it was watching the cassette that brought it on. It seems Wahida was quite angry with us.' Mumtaz laughed.

'Fine; if it was so disgusting, then why did she agree that we should show it to her daughter? She could have put a stop to it, couldn't she? It really is astonishing. Girls who are much younger than Wahida sleep with their husbands, don't they? Don't they have babies? Why must this one alone be so stubborn?' Nafiza spoke crossly. She was greatly irritated by Wahida's extreme modesty, and the reason for her fever; it also struck her as very odd.

'Too true. Here's my sister-in-law, Farida, who can't wait to get married; she is ready for everything. What is Wahida doing, keeping herself under wraps as if she is so precious!' It struck Mumtaz suddenly that here was an opportunity for her to tell Nafiza about Farida's forthcoming marriage. If she missed this chance, it might be difficult for her to speak about it. So she hurried on. 'We are going to arrange a marriage for Farida. Her brother has decided on the bridegroom.' She stopped short after this preamble.

Just as Nafiza was about to ask who it was, Mumtaz gave out his name. 'He plans to marry her to Aziz, and then take Aziz away with him when he goes back, abroad. Keep this to yourself. We haven't said anything publicly, yet.' She looked closely at Nafiza, eager to note what she might give away.

Her news thundered against Nafiza's heart. Was Mumtaz just being provocative, or was she telling the truth? Greatly bewildered, yet careful not to betray any emotion whatever, Nafiza remained silent.

Mumtaz was disappointed that her news produced no great effect. Was Nafiza really not shaken by it, or was she clever enough to hide her feelings? She looked again at her sharply, then turned her gaze away. Suddenly, she lost interest in the affair. She realized quite clearly that there was nothing more to be said by either of them, and that it was time for her to leave. 'I must go now, Nafiza,' she said, 'Mother-in-law will be looking for me.' She pushed open the back door and went out into the street.

Nafiza sat where she was, watching her. The next instant she rose to her feet, entered the bedroom, fell on her bed and began to weep.

* * *

Nafiza wept, her face buried in Aziz's lap. For a long time he had been trying to console her. He had been very hesitant about telling her his news, but she had found it out by herself, somehow. It wasn't easy for either of them. The plain fact was that they must part now forever: it was this that made her weep. He was well aware of the cause of her grief, yet he could see no other choice for himself. It was a big thing for him to be offered a bride who came from a better placed family than his, and taken into partnership abroad, as well. Let the community gossip as it pleased. He did indeed love Nafiza. But the two of them had always known that their relationship could never be a lasting one. If he were to lose this opportunity, another one might never come his way again. And he was in no position to refuse this chance – surely sent by Allah – to better himself.

He patted her back gently, trying to comfort her. His lungi was wet with her tears. He began to think that she believed that her incessant tears would persuade him to reject the marriage offer. He could not remember there ever having been any promises or demands on either side, in the love between them. On that day, however, her tears seemed to demand something from him.

Although he was aware that her tears rose from a terrible grief and loss, he began to feel mildly annoyed. It was true that she could never assure him of stability or certainty in their relationship; and it was equally true that he had never expected such a certainty. Struggling always at some kind of precipice, they had never known at what instant their relationship might tip over the edge, scatter away and vanish. Allah alone was privy to that. And it was Allah who had shown him the way forward now. The thought gave him hope. He was not prepared to be shattered, as she was. Nor could he give up his entire life for the sake of a relationship which could not go beyond a certain point. Not knowing quite how to make her understand this, he sat there silently, letting her cry her fill.

She mouthed something in between her tears. The words were lost, buried in his clothes, but they rose and fell, as if she were reciting something. It sounded like a prayer. His flesh crept, and he could not bring himself to listen to what she actually said. He tightened his legs, allowing the words to be lost inside his clothes. Suddenly, still weeping, Nafiza scratched him with her finger nails, trying to enforce her protest. Smarting from the pain, at once he grabbed hold of her and flung her off from him. Surprised and frightened by his anger, she sat up and stared at him. His words came out instantly. 'Chi, do you call yourself a woman? Can't you understand my position, in the slightest?'

He must have shocked himself as well as her. When he realized what he had said, he could not believe what he had done. Nafiza said very quietly, 'Get out'. For an instant she wondered whether those words had actually been uttered by a man she had held so dear. Then she repeated, 'Just go.' His eyes pleaded for a last chance to show her all the love he had felt for her through all these years, but she ignored it. Saddened and ashamed that she had allowed herself to be so distressed, she said, 'Please go; don't cause me any more pain.'

After he had left, feeling humiliated, cringing within himself, her tears stopped completely. She had been weeping because of her anguish that her relationship with him was about to break. Now she thought of it with disgust. She breathed hard as a sudden, hot anger streamed through her from the top of her head down to the soles of her feet. Her breasts heaved, and her jacket was wet through with sweat. Her body felt as heavy and still as a corpse. At that one moment, all the loneliness and emptiness which she had sought to avoid throughout her life crowded in on her. The afternoon's heat had lessened along the street; Rafiq peeped in through the open door, then ran in and flung himself on to her lap. She lay down for a long time, holding him to her, breathing in the smell of dust which came off him.

* * *

Much disturbed to find the house in darkness, Bashir felt his way along the walls until he reached the switch in the hall, and turned on the lights. The house which lay coiled up in the darkness now unrolled into the light and Bashir, still anxious, made his way towards the bedroom and pushed open the door which had been left half-closed. The light from the hall fell into the room though the open door, and he stood there for a minute, gazing at Nafiza as she lay across the bed, with Rafiq clinging to her. He closed the door again, leaving it very slightly ajar, and returned to the hall. He stood still, undoing his shirt buttons.

It was just past eight. She did not sleep at such a time, normally, he reflected, as he took the shirt off, placed it on its hanger, and sat down on the sofa. He remembered what Suleiman had just told him. A little while ago when he was walking towards the hauz for his olu ablutions before the Maghrib prayers, Suleiman had come up and embraced him and greeted him. 'Asalaamu alcikum! Anné, we are going to finalise our arrangements for my sister's wedding. It will happen next week. Be sure to join us.'

Delighted to hear the news, Bashir asked eagerly, 'Is that so? When? Who is the bridegroom?'

'The bridegroom is our Aziz. Where else will we go?' Suleiman spoke hastily if a little wearily. 'Everything is to be finalised next week, on Friday. My mother would have told your family as well. You must all come.' He walked off towards the hauz.

Freeing himself from this memory, Bashir plunged into a whirlpool of thoughts. Could there be a connection between Suleiman's news and the fact that Nafiza lay asleep at such an unusual hour? Ché, it couldn't be, he told himself, refusing to allow that thought to surface in his mind. Whatever suspicion lurked somewhere within him, he could not acknowledge it openly.

All the same he was restless and floundering, in a state of confusion and helplessness, unable to understand what had happened. Why was she like this? How had he failed her? How could she not realize that he would intuit the reason why she lay there so broken-hearted, and how profoundly painful that would be, for him? Despair and helplessness made his throat choke. A dog went past the street, its howl loud and clear.

He could not even decide whether he was hungry or not. Not knowing what he should do, he went through the back of the house into the open courtyard, and sat on its paved floor. He stared up into the sky. Clusters of stars, looking as if they heaped up against a dark-blue sky, seemed to laugh down at him, so he lowered his eyes and gazed at his feet. The day's heat, still stored in the paving stones seeped into his feet, and slowly filled his whole body. His mind was still tossing about, tormented, so he rose to his feet and walked up to the well. He squatted down, knees drawn up, on the washing stone laid into the well's parapet wall. He tried to calculate for how long she had lain on that bed. The iron bucket, sitting on the parapet wall was still full of soaking clothes. She must have intended to wash them. He was struck by a sudden anxiety. Had she and Rafiq eaten their mid-day meal? No, they certainly would not have done so, he told himself, and was filled with compassion. How could she ruin her health in this way? Troubled by this, he stood up and began to hurry inside. Then, struck by a sudden thought, he turned and went into the kitchen instead.

At the sound of the door opening, baby mice scampered out of sight; the sudden light alerted the cockroaches, which disappeared into their hideouts. Realizing that the mice and cockroaches would make themselves at home only when they were sure that no one had been about for some time, he went up to the cooking hearth and lifted the lid off the pot to see if there was any rice left. She must have cooked it at mid-day. When he saw that it was full, not a single spoonful had been removed, he felt himself grow a little angry. If she wouldn't eat, should she deprive the child as well? He left the kitchen and returned to the bedroom. But when he saw her lying huddled there, on one side of the bed, even that slight anger vanished like smoke. His heart melted as he woke her up, calling, 'Nafiza, Nafiza.' His voice was very gentle.

ℭ 46 ℌ

Madina had a stack of books in her arms. She came
running into Rabia's house, hiding the books loosely
under her davani. She went to Wahida's room straight away,
and dropped them with a thud into her lap, and gasped out,
'My Anni told me to give them to you.' She ran away again.

Rabia, who had gone on some chore, was just returning to
the house. Madina rushed up to her, caught her hands and
said, 'Come on, let's play.'

Rabia gazed at her friend, her face looking drawn. For the
past few days she had been thinking about Ahmad a great deal.
She was deeply depressed because she didn't know when he was
due to return. She only partly understood why she needed him
so much. That look of distress stayed with her permanently.

Madina caught hold of her and shook her hard. 'Why are
you looking so strange? Come on, let's go and play,' she said
once more. She winked and smiled mischievously. 'Come, I
want to show you something.'

It was nearly the end of the Asar period, almost time for
Maghrib. Rabia tried to smile, in an effort to match Madina's
excitement, but failed. 'Hurry up,' Madina said, dragging
Rabia and racing toward the terrace of Rabia's house. Rabia
followed her and began climbing the stairs. Madina turned
round quickly, and gazed about her, to check whether anyone
had seen them. Clearly it pleased her that no one had noticed
them: as soon as they were upstairs she locked the door to the
terrace. She pulled away her davani and drew out a book which
she had tucked into her jacket. She sat down on the floor, her
back to the wall, and held the book out, inviting Rabia to take
a look. Rabia's unhappy expression changed as she sat down
close to Madina and took the book from her, eagerly. It was
still light enough to see quite clearly.

There was a picture of a half-naked woman on the cover of
the book, displaying her breasts without even a shred of cloth

upon them. Instantly, Rabia looked up at Madina. How on earth had she got hold of it? Madina said, 'Mumtaz Anni gave me a lot of books to take to Wahidakka. I took this from the pile and hid it away.' Madina smiled proudly.

'Without anyone's knowledge?' Rabia was astonished.

'Of course!'

Rabia's fear was greater than her curiosity. 'We're finished if they find out. They'll kill us,' she said.

Madina was nonchalant. 'I'm telling you they don't know.' And so they began to turn the pages. The pictures chased Rabia's fear away. They read the stories in the book, spelling out the words. Gradually they understood the riddle of sex just a little, and found it of absorbing interest. The notion of nakedness, which had frightened her all this while, changed somewhat, and began to excite Rabia.

She came to herself with a start, and tried to understand what was happening. Above her head, flocks of birds were flying home to their nests. A pale moon seemed to be staring down at her, making her feel self-conscious. As if it realized her embarrassment, the moon was trying to hide away among the swiftly moving clouds. The red paving stones which had soaked up the sun all day began to feel hot against her, even through her clothes. She was anxious she might pick up some kind of urinary trouble. Even worse, she was beset by the fear that instead of reading the Koran or the Taghlim, or reciting the Yasin at Maghrib time, here she was committing a grave sin. She reminded herself that if Periattha were to come home suddenly and find she had gone elsewhere instead of saying her prayers, he would call her a saithaan and scold her.

She thought of the Hadith that he had quoted the day before. According to it, it was the Devil who always tempted us; if we manage to escape him, we can be assured of a place in heaven where milk and honey will flow like rivers, and where thousands of houri women would serve the men and make them happy. Immediately, the question had arisen in her mind: Will there be houri men to serve the women? She had been too frightened

to ask Periattha this. She would ask Periamma today, and find
out. Ahmad would surely tell her, if she were to ask him. She
remembered that he wasn't there, and felt sad again.

The darkness filling the terrace didn't frighten her as usual,
she realized; it had changed instead, into a friendly presence.
She remembered what had happened the day before. As they
were on their way to buy badam fruit, Madina asked her, 'Why
are you so quiet? Did your Macchaan bother you again or
what?'

Rabia shook her head violently. 'Ché ché! I never go
anywhere near him, anyway.' She had begun to feel reluctant
to talk to anyone about Sikander. It seemed to be derogatory
towards Wahida. Hereafter she could not think of him as a single
man or a stranger, but someone who was closely associated with
Akka. She had realized that all the respect he was accorded by
her family was because of their love for Wahida, not because of
any quality of his own. She was aware that each member of the
family feared that any criticism or ridicule of him might only
fuel Wahida's antipathy towards him.

'In that case, why won't you talk to me,' Madina repeated.

'Oh, it's nothing.' Rabia was silent for a moment. Then she
said, 'The street isn't much fun without Ahmad, is it?' She had
expected Madina to agree, and was shocked to see her friend
redden with anger. She was frightened by this. Why did she get
so angry at the very mention of his name? She couldn't
understand it. Why was it so difficult for Madina to be friendly
with both Rabia and Ahmad? Rabia, after all, loved both
Madina and Ahmad. Madina was so affectionate towards Rabia,
but she was always furious with Ahmad. What was the problem
between them? Rabia walked on, trying to work it out.

Madina snapped at her, 'You only like that corpse of a fellow.
Go and marry him.' She sounded disappointed and cross. After
that there was no need for words between them, as they walked
on.

Now Madina held her closely in her embrace. Rabia was
small and slim enough to fit easily into Madina's arms. Unable

to move away, she imagined Ahmad's touch along with Madina's, as if to separate and understand the difference. She was certain that there must be a difference, although she could not say exactly what it was. She also knew she needed both of them and their affection.

They were both startled by someone shouting in the street to someone else. It was quite dark now, Rabia realized. 'Come. let's go down. It's very late,' she said, anxiously. Wahida would be leaving for her husband's house, after the mid-day feast the next day. Rabia wanted to go and talk to her for awhile. Heaven knew when she would come back. Zohra had said it would be only after the fortieth day, when her lap would be filled with silk for the last of the wedding rites.

Madina took no notice of her words. Rabia looked up at the sky once more. It looked beautiful with clusters of grey clouds bordered in a pale-yellow light. Akka always loved to look at the skies. Almost everyday Rabia would join her as she lay on the bed in the courtyard, gazing at the sky and listening to the radio. Wahida would point out the shape of the clouds: a hunch-backed old man, a pregnant woman, a baby monkey. Since she got married and went away, she never listened to the radio, and she never even came out to the courtyard. Rabia wondered, did you lose interest in all this once you were married?

Even in the semi-darkness, Madina looked very peaceful, sitting beside her. From a distance, the cinema songs which were broadcast before the evening show, came floating on the air towards them. Madina said, in a voice full of yearning, 'They are showing a very good film today. There's a goat in it, which does a lot of tricks. Uma told me.'

Her disappointment was infectious. 'But they've decided at the mosque that we are not allowed to go, so how can we see it? If you're a man, you may go. Or if you're a Hindu like Uma, you may go. But what can we do,' Rabia complained. If anyone dared to break the rule, no Hazrat nor Nattaamai would ever enter their house to say the Fatiha on any occasion, good or bad. They would not be allowed to join in any community function. Rabia knew that Suleiman was responsible for all this, but she said nothing because she didn't want to hurt Madina. It was her father who always spoke against Suleiman. He even had a nickname for the man: Allah's Guardian.

Zohra had asked, looking wide-eyed and innocent, 'What does that mean, please?'

'You idiot,' he had said, rolling about with laughter, 'Can't you work out that much? You tell me, who is it who cares for and looks after the whole world? Isn't it Allah who does that? Now, do you know who safeguards Allah? Who but our Suleiman! That's what he thinks he is doing, guarding Allah. Hence the name, Allah's Guardian. What do you think of that?'

Now half the townsfolk had forgotten Suleiman's real name and called him only by his nickname. It must have even reached his ears by now, Rabia thought.

'Never mind,' Madina was saying, 'Faridakka is getting married, did you know? Aziz is to be the bridegroom.'

Rabia frowned as if she were wondering which Aziz she meant.

'Ada, it's that man who visits Ahmad's house quite often.'

'Oh, him?'

'He's poor, of course, but Anna says, what does that matter. He's going to take him abroad, soon after the wedding, so that he can earn well.'

It seemed to Rabia that Madina sounded unhappy about this news, rather than joyful, as she should be. 'Poor Farida,' she said. 'She's getting married after all this time, but her husband will go abroad immediately after the wedding. How can she be happy?'

'She too will be like my sister-in-law, reading all these books and writing letters.' Madina put her right hand to her mouth and giggled softly. Rabia didn't know what else to say, and sat there quietly, gazing at the mountain at the edge of their town, now sleeping in the darkness. The darkness seemed to surround it most densely, where its cone-shaped peak almost touched the sky.

* * *

That mountain was just next to their school. You could begin to climb it just past the school's playground. She had always wanted to climb right up to the top of it. She constantly pestered people about what you could find there. Knowing that her wish grew the greater everyday, Ahmad said to her one day, 'Will you go with me? We'll climb it together.'

When she asked him, wide eyed, whether he really could climb such a high mountain, he said, 'Pooh! Call this a mountain? This Ahmad can climb much higher ones!' He tugged at the ends of his collar with both hands, pulling them up stylishly. Eager and frightened at the same time, she nodded her head at once, agreeing to go with him.

'One thing though. That saithaan isn't allowed to come. It's got to be just you.'

She knew at once who he meant, and nodded her head once again. The next day, as she set off to climb the mountain as soon as school was over, she lied to Madina for the first time. She said she was going to borrow some notes from Ahmad, and would come home later on.

Iliaz and Ahmad were waiting for her at the base of the mountain, just past the playground. They had leaned their satchels against the rocks that lay about, piled one on top of the other. The sun was still scorching and the heat struck her face making her grumble at it. Ahmad, meanwhile, plucked her school bag from her, and leaned it beside theirs. She was not frightened at all and was quite prepared to follow him anywhere. It was a courage born out of her belief that he could protect her against any possible harm.

She had only one remaining worry. Would he make sure she reached home before it was dark? When she asked him this, he said carelessly, 'Pooh! Do you consider this a mountain? We can get up there and back in a trice!' The way he said it delighted her, and made her trust him implicitly. Full of that trust, she looked up to the mountain top. True, it was only a small one. There were only a few trees and shrubs; they were scattered about and not densely crowded together. This made her feel much less afraid. They began to climb up.

The lower slope was full of rounded rocks. Ahmad looked about at the large rocks and smaller stones everywhere, and noticed how many of the trees and shrubs were stripped bare. He told her, laughing, 'Goats and cows must have been grazing here. That's why the trees look bald, as if a barber has shaved them.'

The stones hurt her feet, through her sandals. The heat seemed to follow them without any let up; the sweat ran down her face and neck. The two boys, however, went ahead enthusiastically, not aware of any of these hardships. She stood still for a moment to rest her legs, and looked up once more. The mountain seemed to loom above her and she was struck with fear, suddenly. She looked at the cactus plants and the trees whose names she didn't know. The thought struck her suddenly that there might be snakes lurking about, and she was frightened. It surprised her that Ahmad and Iliaz were finding this climb such a pleasure.

After they had gone a bit further, Ahmad turned round and called, 'Ei, why have you stopped? Hurry and catch us up.' She was astonished and delighted that his voice echoed and rang around the mountain. Even though she didn't need to answer, she shouted from where she was, 'I'm coming'. Thrilled at the way the mountain threw their voices back at them, the two boys began to shout, 'Ohoho', as they ran on. Rabia breathed hard as she ran, hoping to catch up with them. She had to stop every now and then to free her long skirt as it caught against the thorny bushes.

She finally caught up with them when they stopped and waited for her. She said, 'This mountain is not at all as I expected.' All the colours she had noticed from a distance had dissolved away, and the light gone. There were no clustering trees and no shade; only the sun's heat, rocks, and thorny bushes. It didn't seem like a mountain at all.

Ahmad said, 'This is what they call a mountain, di. I know, though, it isn't how you imagine mountains to be. Look there, you can see a second mountain behind this one. That's really super, but you can't go there: that's where there are lots of deer, foxes, tigers and even pythons and everything. Here there's nothing like that; but then, you don't have to be frightened.' He tried to make the best of it, as he did not like to see her disappointment. It embarrassed him that she might think he had boasted rather too much about the mysteries hidden in the mountain, and how it was a mere trifle for him to climb it. Once she said that the mountain wasn't such a big deal, he couldn't make any more great claims. He was quiet, thinking of ways in which he could rid her of her disappointment.

Iliaz stood there, unaware of any of this, wondering if there was an adventure they could embark upon. He kicked at the steep path with his sandaled foot once or twice. Then he announced, taking the lead surprisingly, 'Let's go and pluck kalaa fruit.'

Both boys shouted together, 'Let's see whether the kalaa fruit is ripe!'

Again it was Iliaz who ran towards it first, calling out, 'See, on that bush, right next to the cactus!' He sounded as if he had spotted some rare object.

Rabia noticed that Ahmad's face had fallen. She realized that he was envious that Iliaz had found out something Ahmad himself had not, and was showing it to Rabia. Did Iliaz become some kind of hero just because he had discovered the kalaa bush? Her affection for Ahmad would never lessen by a jot, she told herself. She would assure Ahmad of that, after Iliaz went home. She walked up to the bush.

She longed to pick the fruit growing on the dense bushes, but hesitated because there might be snakes lurking there. Ahmad said to her, 'You just stay here. I'll go and pick the fruit.' He and Iliaz pushed aside the bushes and began to fill their pockets.

After a while she too lost her fear and went next to them, tightening her skirt about her, and tucking it between her thighs. As she began to pluck the fruit, Ahmad cautioned her, 'Be careful, there might be thorns.' Then he called out again excitedly, 'Look there at that picchippu shrub, it's covered with flowers.'

Both Iliaz and Rabia turned and looked in the same direction. Ahmad was delighted to see the joy flooding her face. The clumps of plants, just beginning to wither, were covered with buds. Rabia went up to them on her own, and began to gather them into her hands. They would open by the evening, but already covered her fingers with their scent. She gathered them with a great show of excitement, just so that Ahmad should feel pleased with himself.

After this, all three collected plenty of the bright red seeds which had fallen from a gundumani tree. They were very beautiful: black on top and blood red beneath. Rabia realized just then that the heat was no longer direct; a gentle breeze was blowing. Nothing stood in its way, and it circled them again and again. Now it fell against her face with a rustling sound. It pulled at her hair. It lifted her skirt and made it flap about. She gathered the skirt together and held it firmly between her thighs, saying, 'It's getting late; let's go.' She turned round and looked downwards to the base of the mountain.

From the mountain, all the houses in their town looked tiny and beautiful, She stood still, amazed; filled with a strange joy. She tried to work out which of those houses was hers. They all looked the same, all tiny; she was disappointed. There was something else that was puzzling. From the terrace of her house she could see the mountain so clearly, but from the mountain she could not distinguish her house. She thought for a bit, and told herself, 'Of course, the mountain is a thousand times bigger than our house, after all.'

She began to climb down, saying, 'Let's go, I'm thirsty now.'

Ahmad stopped her. 'Wait, let's catch a few scorpions.'

'Scorpions?' she screamed.

'Of course,' Ahmad's voice was casual and haughty.

'Where are they?' she asked, fearfully.

'Oh, somewhere.' He asked her to get off from the large stone on which she was standing. She climbed down and stood a little distance away, watching him, her face dark with fear.

Ahmad began to shift the rock, using all his strength. It gave slightly and then moved. He took one hand away from the rock and drew out a matchbox from his trousers pocket. Holding it half-open with his left hand he rolled the rock with his right hand. The rock rolled over easily, having already moved out of its fixed position. The tiny scorpions stuck to the underside of the rock began to run helter-skelter. Immediately he found a stick with which he held down the tail of one of the scorpions, making it impossible for it to move. All the rest of them scurried away into the bushes. Rabia was frozen with shock, having involuntarily taken a couple of steps backwards.

He gave her a gleeful and victorious look, then winked at Iliaz, as if to say, 'What do you think of that'. He placed the half-open matchbox in front of the scorpion, still trapped by the stick, and struggling. He loosened the stick slightly, and just as soon as the scorpion entered the matchbox, he snapped it shut. Then he leapt up and down, shouting with delight at having caught his scorpion.

Rabia had reached the very pitch of fear. Too terrified to put her feet down on the ground, she asked, 'Ahmad, do scorpions live only underneath stones?' Her mouth was dry and she could hardly speak.

'Where else?' he asked, even more nonchalantly than before, as if he were applauding himself for the feat he had accomplished in front of her.

'Under every stone?'

'Of course. So what?'

So what might have happened if one of the stones on which they had trodden had rolled away? The very thought of it made her quake. She had been told how painful a scorpion's sting could be. Supposing it happened here on this mountain? And she had not told anyone she had come here! Terrified, she said, 'I'm frightened to stand here, but how will I climb down? There are rocks and stones all along the way; how can I put my foot down?' She was almost crying as she said this. She wished, somewhat foolishly, that a plane might appear suddenly and carry her through the air.

'Scaredy cat!' Ahmad said. 'See, this is why I shouldn't bring you up the mountain.' Casually he stowed away the matchbox into his pocket. 'OK, OK, come on. Place your feet on the ground and avoid all the stones. Come on then. I meant to catch another four or five scorpions, but look at the state of you!' He began to hurry down the mountain. Surprised at the ease with which they were climbing down, she followed treading carefully.

That evening when Zohra heard of her adventure, she scolded her soundly, saying, 'Supposing you had gone and got your first period when you were climbing the mountain?' Rabia remembered this along with her mountain climbing adventure, and also how the next day all the school children teased her about the graffiti they found, written with thorns on the fleshy cactus leaves: Ahmad's name and hers, linked together.

❧ 47 ❧

The pain in her lower belly stopped Wahida from getting up from her bed, while the burning sensation in her urinary tract made her suffer the more. She pitied herself more than usual, and the tears streamed from her eyes. She felt as if she had arrived at a huge forest from which there was no escape for her, hereafter. She wished she could fall on her mother's lap and weep loudly, but pushed away that thought immediately, resolved never to do it. What sort of mother is she, she muttered to herself, her disgust even making her forget her pain for a moment. She asked herself whether she could ever look at her mother again. Anyway, why did Rahima consent to her daughter's marriage, when she wasn't entirely satisfied about it? Had Rahima resisted it steadfastly, Wahida would not be in this state today, enduring all the difficulties of this house and family. Wahida's anger turned into accusations against her mother.

She felt another spasm of pain in her lower belly like a bolt of lightning, and she called out softly. Sabia had poured sesame oil over her lower belly, that morning, and told her to massage it in. 'When you first have sex with your husband, it will hurt like that. You'll feel that burning pain in your lower belly, like a painful urinary infection. Rub this in; you'll feel all right soon,' she said.

She couldn't feel the slightest affection towards Sikander. She was also surprised that this did not seem to bother him. It pained her that she could not accept him in her heart, and she knew that it was this that made her body suffer too. But it pained her the more that he seemed indifferent to her suffering, or indeed didn't even think about it.

She had been surprised, the day before, when he took no notice whatever of the dark-blue sari with white flowers which suited her so well. She did not actually want him to compliment her on her looks, but was irritated, all the same, that it never occurred to him to do so.

Whatever sari Sabia wore, Sayyed was sure to express his pleasure in it and compliment her the whole day, making Wahida want to cover her ears. It amused her that at his age, Sayyed took such delight in Sabia's old face. Yesterday Sayyed had summoned Wahida and made her sit by his side, praising and enjoying her pretty sari. It had only repulsed her, making her resolve never to wear anything pretty.

She knew nothing at all about Sikander. Was he given to drink? Might he drink, and then come home and beat her up? Did he smoke? Did he have any other bad habits? It was not because of any serious fault in him that she disliked him, but because of trivial and mundane matters.

It was his behaviour and manners that put her off so much. The husband of her imagination was courteous and gentle. There was no comparison with the real man who did know how to be sensitive towards his new bride. Why did he act in so crude a manner towards her? Did he never learn anything from the cinema, even?

Hunger gnawed at her, on top of her stomach ache. She had felt too shy to eat properly, ever since she came to this house. Rahima could never bear it whenever Nuramma came to them, hungry. She would serve her a meal, at once. If she were only to see Wahida now, lying here, limp with hunger! Grief choked her, when she thought of it. When she was at home, Nuramma would come and ask for food sometimes. She always wanted to eat the moment she was hungry. Rahima would say, 'The menfolk haven't come home yet from their prayers. We'll eat in a little while.'

Nuramma would scold Rahima fondly, 'Why, are men's stomachs special then? Don't we feel hungry, too? Just serve me my share, thayi,'

Rabia and Wahida would watch her eat, from their hiding place. Rabia could never get over it. She'd whisper in Wahida's ears, 'Why, Akka, how big a stomach can this woman have? It must be as big as a cauldron, otherwise how will it hold this much rice?'

Wahida would be quite as surprised and shocked, and she would amuse herself by calculating how many of her own meals would equal that one serving of Nuramma's. Nuramma in turn, would be abashed by their gaze if she saw them, and say, 'Adi, you girls, don't watch me eat and cast an evil eye. It would be a fine thing if I just played with my rice like you people with your tiny stomachs.'

As soon as she finished eating, Nuramma would raise her hands and stay in that position for half an hour muttering her private prayers. Wahida would wonder what it was she was pleading to God for. Even Zohra and Rahima would exchange mischievous glances at the sight of her.

When her father and Chaccha returned from the mosque and saw the spectacle of Nuramma at her prayers, they would be overcome with laughter. His handkerchief pressed against his mouth, Chaccha would ask, 'It's a special alms meal today, is it?'

As soon as she heard them, Nuramma would finish her prayers in haste, and agree, 'Yes, attha.'

Chaccha would summon Zohra and ask her in Nuramma's presence, 'You cooked an extra measure of rice today, for Nuramma's sake, I hope?' He would speak without betraying the slightest trace of mockery.

Nuramma, only partly aware of his mocking, would say, 'They are queens; they appeased my hunger; may they live well.' And with this blessing, she would go home.

Wahida felt repeated stabs of pain in her belly. Ever since she came to this house, on the one hand she felt too shy to eat; on the other, the goings-on in that household stopped her from being able to eat. It was Sabia who cooked every meal. Because her husband had come home from his long stay abroad, she made it her business to show off her culinary skill and cooked all kinds of dishes. There wasn't a single meal at which meat was not served. She knew her daughter-in-law could not cook, so she gave her a number of little jobs to do in the kitchen. Sabia always had a handkerchief tucked in at her waist, while she cooked. When the wood smoke filled the kitchen, her nose often streamed, and she pulled at her handkerchief all the time, and sneezed into it. She would then squeeze the tamarind without washing her hand. She had a habit of tasting the kuzhambu cooking on the stove, and then stirring it with the same spoon which she had put into her mouth.

At such times, Wahida's stomach turned. She imagined the

kuzhambu boiling with Sabia's spittle and phlegm mixed into it. How could she bring herself to eat, after that? Yet it was imperative that she eat. Very often, Sayyed would force her to sit down and eat with him. 'You come and eat with me. Your Kuppi and he can eat later,' he would say. He would invite her to sit next to him on the mat, and help her to the variety of dishes laid out in front of them. He'd fill her plate with mutton and chicken, saying, 'Eat well! How are you going to manage if you are so thin!'

Meanwhile, Sabia would sit opposite them watching Wahida's plate, eagle-eyed, wondering if she was going to eat everything up. Knowing very well that she was under her surveillance, Wahida shrank within herself. Already she was put off eating by Sabia's style of cooking; now when she read the meaning in Sabia's eyes, as she watched her, she wanted to get up at once. Sayyed would pull her down, scolding her lovingly, 'What a woman you are, such a poor eater!'

His so-called 'love' irritated her beyond endurance. Forced to say something because of Sayyed's stubbornness, Sabia would chime in, 'Eat well, our goddess; if you grow thin, I'll have to answer to your mother.'

Wahida made no answer, but simply moved the rice around her plate with her fingers, trying hard to get rid of the notion that she was eating food polluted by Sabia's spittle. Had she ever drunk from a cup or tumbler which someone else had put to their mouths, she asked herself, either in her own home, or at school? She could not remember a single occasion when she had done so. Nor had she ever shared a sweet or snack which anyone else had bitten through, even if they had used a cloth.

The tears flowed from her eyes involuntarily, and she buried her face in her pillow. She knew that the look in Sabia's eyes as she watched her was hostile and rejecting, and she felt humiliated by it. She knew that the respect and dignity accorded her in her own family had vanished here, in this house. She remembered the trouble her mother always took to get her to eat. She had never been moved by any of it. Rahima had taken her rejection as a rejection of her love, too. She would say, 'Your body needs the strength. How will you grow up into a woman, otherwise?' Those sorrowful words echoed to her from a distance.

It was nearly time for the Luhur prayers. If she did her ablutions now, it would be just in time for the call to prayers. She struggled to sit up in her bed. Her hair was tangled. Had her mother been there, she would have oiled it for her and combed it out. Because she wasn't eating properly, she was finding it difficult to go to the toilet properly. Yesterday, she had passed blood, besides, and this frightened her. She had repeated her ablutions again and again before completing her prayer cycle.

She had been afraid that once she was married, her mother-in-law might be cruel to her; she had not known what kind of a man her husband would turn out to be. But she had not known what kind of problems she would actually face, and which of them would prove the most difficult. She was overcome by a terrible weariness. Once again she thought of her mother, and longed to see her and weep; yet she knew perfectly well that it would be of no use. The last time she went home, there was one occasion when she lay on her mother's lap weeping, trying to say a few things about Sikander to her. Rahima had looked at her serenely, gently stroking her back. After a while she took her in her arms and comforted her. She said, 'Look here, from now on Sikander is your husband. Nothing is ever going to change that. Understand this first and foremost. Don't be like a child, complaining that he snores, or talks to women, or smokes cigarettes. You are not a child anymore; you have the status of a man's wife. Let us say he is a man of good character; if you talk about him out of turn, people will not respect him. Do you understand?' She was silent after that, as if there was nothing more to be said. Wahida thought she detected a trace of bitterness in her mother's voice, but did not any more have the courage to seek proof of it by looking at Rahima's face. Wahida felt a surge of pity for her mother. Perhaps it was wrong to distress Rahima by sharing with her, her own sorrows. She ought to not make her anxious about her daughter's unhappiness. She stopped weeping, after that.

She looked at the clock again before getting up, at last. The call to prayer sounded. She ought to stay still while it was being said, so she sat quietly where she was, hands laid together, ready to say her prayers. The fading henna on her hands reminded her once again that she was married; once again she felt that fear within her belly. She counted on her fingers and calculated that fifteen days had passed since her wedding day, and sighed deeply. It felt as if a long, long time had gone by.

She heard the door being opened, and turned round to see Sayyed standing there. She rose to her feet in a hurry, pulling the sari well over her head, and stepped to one side, respectfully. She asked herself why this man had to turn up, when she was in agony already; but her lips murmured politely, 'Welcome, Maamu. Asalaamu aleikum'

'Thank you, let me come in,' he said, entering the room and sitting down on the bed. Immediately he made a show of being upset. 'Adada, I've gone and sat down in my clean praying clothes! Well? Is there any pollution on the bed?' He spoke as if he were making a joke. His teasing tone made her cringe and, not wishing to answer, she lowered her eyes.

Sayyed looked around the room for a moment, as if seeing it for the first time. Satisfied with what he saw, he remarked, 'It's well furnished, isn't it?'

Still not wishing to say anything, she murmured, 'Mm', and nodded her head.

'Why do you keep standing? Come and sit down,' he urged her. He insisted she do so, much against her will. Finally she sat down, cowering away at a corner of the bed. She couldn't see a way out, and had begun to fear he might actually pull her by the hand and force her to sit.

Sayyed gazed at her. She could feel his eyes going all the way through her from her head to her feet, and tried – but failed – to shrink even more into herself. His eyes groping at every part of her body, he said, 'Sabia told me, you have a stomach ache. Did it hurt a lot, then?'

The impotence and salacious eagerness reflected in his voice and expression threw her into complete confusion. She was speechless with shock. There was an open look of voyeuristic pleasure playing on his old face; he seemed totally oblivious to what she might think of him. After a moment's silence, he began again. 'Don't worry! At first it will hurt a lot, definitely. Besides, you are very young. He's not like that, he's a rough fellow, and a big man. So it must have been difficult for you. But say you grit your teeth, it will come out all right soon. What do you say?' He looked at her closely, as if eager to know how she felt; as if he wanted her to believe that he was saying all this out of concern for her. Even though he must have seen she was tense with fear, he ignored it, intent on carrying on with what he was saying.

'Take my case. I'm past it now; I can't do anything. Even if I want to, I can't. But your husband isn't like that. He's in his prime. So it's you who must give in and go along with him. Say you take to bed complaining it hurts. It will be hard on him, won't it, poor fellow! Here he is, just married.' He was struggling to find the words to say what he actually intended.

She was still in shock; unable to escape from the dreadful situation in which she was trapped. Close to tears, she bit her lip and tried to hide her distress. His short form, wrinkled face and narrow eyes gave him the look of some unrecognizable animal. She realized, with a kind of horror, that behind his pointed beard, his fez and his prayers there was an extremely unpleasant man.

'Why won't you say anything? What's the matter?' As if he wished to comfort and reassure her, he leaned over and patted her on her back.

Taken aback by this, she turned around, muttering, 'Nothing, it's nothing.' No other words would come to her.

Pleased to have got her to speak, he started again. 'In those days, when I was a new bridegroom, I was very lively. Now of course, I'm old, and not up to anything. In Ceylon, there are these Sinhala women who hang around; available for a fiver or a tenner. There we were, trying to make some money, all of us young, having left our wives behind. In those days, we didn't have the money to pay these women. We worked all the time, in order to make good. Now there's the money, but the youth has gone. Can't do a thing.' He gave a great sigh, full of frustration. He went on, 'I have a friend there. More or less my age, he is. He goes to those Sinhala women even now. But what can he do? What good is it just to have the urge? Those women will just touch him and stroke him, grab his money and send him home. Poor man,' he said, as if full of sympathy for his friend.

It was immediately apparent to her that this was not a real friend, but an imaginary one who reflected Sayyed's own impotence and frustration. She was astonished at herself, wondering how it was that young as she was, she had understood at once who he was actually talking about. She realized that she had changed utterly, in just fifteen days.

How was she to live out the rest of her life? How had it become necessary to ask herself this, at so early an age? Was it just because she was married? The thoughts whirled round in her mind. Again she felt as if she were caught in a mouse-trap.

Even Sayyed could see by now that Wahida was much disturbed; only he hadn't a clue why that should be. He stared at her with narrowed eyes. It seemed to her that he was struggling with his desires as he watched her, looking like an aged wolf. Taking advantage of her silence, he went on. 'Listen to this. I'm not up to anything now, but do you know how many women I slept with in my youth? You'll think, what, this old fellow?' He smiled and winked. 'Do you know what I was like in those days? I was a lively one! Do you think I was a lazy layabout like your husband? When I was first married, I didn't leave Sabia alone for a month, you know that? Night or day.'

'She was only ten years old at the time, she hadn't even menstruated. But even then, look, she was prepared to please me and I was never disappointed. And then, lots of women in this town were after me. I was quite a playboy; I could handle them all.' He was giving her all these details about his personal life in a confidential voice.

She felt nauseated by all this. If he went on a moment longer, she was afraid she would throw up. Her heart beat fast and her thin frame trembled, as she tried to control herself. 'I have to say my prayers', she murmured. She herself wasn't sure whether the words had passed her lips.

At last he gave up, realizing that she was not paying attention to his frustrations nor enjoying listening to his tales. The expression on his face betrayed his profound pity for himself and repulsion against his own body for no longer being able to function in the way he wanted. Even so, Wahida noted, he was finding it difficult to go away. She was desperate for someone to rescue her from such an ugly situation. Persuaded at last of her state of anxiety and tension, he rose to his feet and walked off wearily, carrying with him all the rest of the fantasies and hopes he had wanted to pour out to her. As she watched him go she thought to herself that he was pitiable, after all.

☞ 48 ☜

At midnight, unable to sleep, Wahida stood in the little terrace adjoining her bedroom, gazing down at the street aimlessly. It was only a narrow street. Very close to Sabia's house, and facing west, stood the magnificent one-storey house Ismail Nanna had built. Even though more than fifty years had passed since then, it still looked new; there was nothing dilapidated about it. Both its entrance and the veranda surrounding the first floor had fine woodwork and murals. The floors of the entire house were of marble. Sabia Kuppi had built her own house, according to Rahima, intending it to be even better than Ismail's. But although it was huge, this house didn't have any beauty or grace. Rahima would say, 'What is a house? It's the people who live in it who make it what it is.' Wahida's glance swept over the street. It was so quiet, it was frightening. Apart from these two one-storey mansions, all the other houses were little ones. As she watched, wide-eyed, for an instant she thought she would die of shock.

Not willing to believe what she saw, she rubbed her eyes hard, and looked down carefully. It was Firdaus; she was absolutely certain. Why on earth was she going into the house opposite theirs? And at midnight, too? And then she understood, beyond any shadow of a doubt. She swallowed hard to ease her dry throat, and as if to aid her understanding. She had been standing there all this while, thinking of her own position and weeping, but now she felt a different emotion taking hold of her. It overtook and brushed aside all considerations about herself, turning into shock and then intense anger at Firdaus.

'Chi, what sort of woman is she,' she muttered to herself. 'How can she bring herself to do this?' At the same time, she wondered why she was so angry. Was her fury more than she ought to feel? She was only a young girl. Had she suddenly become knowledgeable enough to judge Firdaus, and condemn her?

In the silent darkness, she turned her head here and there, still staring into the street. It seemed even more quiet than usual. Or was she imagining it? It was amaavaasai that night, no moon to be seen in the sky. She wondered for a moment whether anyone else had seen Firdaus going into Siva's house. After a moment's consideration, she realized that no one would have had the chance to see her and was relieved, strangely. Sikander was fast asleep, having made his usual demands on her. She had come out into the terrace adjoining their room, unable to sleep because of his loud snoring. She could never sleep if there was the slightest noise in the room. Before she was married, she could sleep in comfort and alone. Was it possible now? There was nothing for it but to get used to the noise, she thought, bitterly.

Once, when she had come home from her Nanni's house, Rahima had begged, 'Come and sleep with your Attha and me tonight.'

She had refused, stubbornly. 'No Amma, my clothes might slip off me at night.'

Her mother often came and stood by her bed at night, and watched her. She always lay in the same position, waking up in the morning exactly as she lay down at night. Her hair was exactly as she had combed and plaited it before she went to bed; the bed clothes as if they had been freshly spread. The skirt pulled down to cover her heels; the davani tucked in tightly and covering her chest. Her mother would scold her lovingly, at times. 'What a girl you are, what does it matter if you move your arms and legs when you sleep? Don't you ever wake up at night to go to the toilet? If you sleep in such a rigid position, how will the blood circulate freely in your body? It must be why you sprain your neck so often.'

So her mother knew perfectly well that Wahida wasn't telling her truly, why she wouldn't sleep in her parents' room. It was because her father snored loudly, right through the night. She had often said, 'How on earth do you manage to sleep in all that noise, Amma? If it were me I wouldn't stay here for even one minute.'

Smiling bitterly, she thought of Firdaus again. How desperate and driven she must be! How daring of her to do this! But whatever it was, it was all wrong, she told herself, frustrated and angry. She was very distressed when she thought of Zohra. What would she do if she were to know of this? Wahida forced herself to imagine it. She was in no doubt Zohra would murder her sister. Suddenly, Wahida was in a frenzy to go down immediately and warn Firdaus of this. Afraid that in her impulsiveness, she might wake Sikander and give the game away, she calmed down a little. She tried to reprove herself for such an extreme reaction on her part, She was afraid that in her agitation she might do something rash and foolish; betray them, and cause them great harm.

Although she was held back by the fear of what might happen if this affair became public, her whole self was seething, unable to endure what was going on. She lifted her right hand and touched her forehead and neck. To her surprise she felt cold and chill. She pushed away her fantasy of confronting them and stared down, once again, at the street, and the steps leading up to Siva's front door.

The street was motionless, dense with darkness, making her fearful. At the corner of the street, a reddish coloured cow stood by the tap, chewing cud. The stench of its urine came past her nostrils. Whose cow might it be? Surely it must belong to Saithoon, who sold paniyaaram. She was the only one who kept a cow; everyone else in the town kept buffalos, and Sabia would only buy milk from her. Every time she came to Sabia's house, she would boast for hours about her cow's intelligence, as if she were showing off her own child. After she had gone, Sabia always complained, 'She keeps one wretched cow, and goes around boasting about the beast!'

Why did Saithoon leave the cow to roam about in the street and not tether it in its shed? What if Saithoon should come looking for it? She was afraid of that, yet hoped for it too.

Firdaus had not come out yet. She wanted to go and confront them in their crime and spit at Firdaus. Even if she didn't actually spit at her, she wanted to make it clear she knew what Firdaus was up to. She could not rest until she did this. Driven by the fear she might change her mind, she stopped thinking any further. Quietly she went down the back stairs, into the garden, opened the outside gate noiselessly, walked silently and swiftly to the street in front of the house. She looked about quickly to see if she had been noticed, then hurried to Siva's front door and pushed at it gently. The door was unlocked; it made no sound as it gave. Without any hesitation or fear she walked into the front room. The yellow light of the bulb that had been left on filled the entire room, enabling her to see quite clearly. Her heart was beating fast with an excitement she could not control as her gaze swept over the main room and came to rest at the room which opened to one side.

She was stunned for a moment at the sight of Siva and Firdaus lying together there. The next minute she came to, and spat involuntarily, saying, 'Thuu! How can you call yourself a woman!'

Startled out of their love-making, Firdaus and Siva sat up, cowering against the wall, and stared uncomprehendingly at the sight of Wahida suddenly standing there. As they cringed, overcome with the shame and humiliation of their situation, Wahida turned on her heel and walked out without looking back. She made straight for Firdaus's house, whose front door had been unlocked, went in and stood in the courtyard, waiting for Firdaus to return.

The darkness which filled the widespread courtyard didn't threaten her even a little. She was shaking, as if in some kind of frenzy. Was what she had just done, right or wrong? She tried to stand still and breathe deeply. Was it right of her to break into the middle of their love-making; to insist on staring at them, against their will? The question kept troubling her, and in order to resist it, she gazed round about, at the courtyard, and at the garden and its trees, at a distance. The trees were still; the darkness seemed to gather beneath them, heavily. She heard the cluck-cluck of a hen cheeping faintly, from a corner of the courtyard, where it lay beneath a basket. She looked up towards the terrace of Sabia's house, afraid someone might be there. Her slim form was still trembling.

She heard Firdaus's footsteps sounding softly, and stood up straight, waiting for her. Firdaus, entering her house, shaken and fearful, had not expected to find Wahida there. For a moment she stood absolutely still, stunned. All the same, Wahida could detect no movement at all in Firdaus's face, in that pale light. The way Firdaus looked directly at her, as if to ask, 'What do you want', made Wahida tremble. How could Firdaus stand in front of her, without any show of fear, or any attempt at appealing to her? Wahida was confused and dumbstruck.

Without hesitation, without seeming to tremble, Firdaus spoke clearly, in an indifferent tone. 'You saw it all, didn't you? So why have you come here now?'

The calmness of her voice crushed to pieces all Wahida's assumptions. She had thought Firdaus would plead with her, weep, beg her not to tell anyone. The way Firdaus stood there and asked her question, left her even more confused. After a while, by way of revealing all her anger, she raised her voice and asked, 'Aren't you ashamed of yourself?'

Firdaus answered quietly, 'Please go away from here; don't make trouble for me.' There was bitterness in her voice. She was actually very afraid her mother would wake up, and desperately needed to get Wahida away from there.

Wahida, however, showed no signs of moving. She asked again, 'How reckless you must be! Are you a woman at all?' She stopped short, unable to say anything further.

Firdaus was quiet, not caring to reply. This only provoked Wahida the more. She thought that Firdaus held her in some sort of contempt, refusing even to reply to her. Suddenly she said, like a child, 'Wait; as soon as it is light, I'll tell about you.'

But Firdaus still did not show any fear or resistance; she murmured once again, 'Get away quickly.' She began to walk past Wahida, across the courtyard.

'I won't go. So what are you going to do about it?' Wahida's voice had hardened. She felt herself grow warm, as if her blood was boiling. She felt her legs and voice tremble.

Her tone of voice made Firdaus stop short. She spoke in a

warning voice, 'If you don't go, there might be a terrible consequence. I'm warning you.'

Wahida said, vengefully, 'I'm not going to move, without telling everyone about your behaviour. Wait till sunrise!' The satisfaction of having struck back at Firdaus for having warned her sent a feeling of relief throughout her body.

The darkness that surrounded them, as well as the wind and its moisture had helped to temper, at least a little, the harshness of their exchange. Perhaps, Wahida thought, it was just as well they could not see each other clearly, nor gage the strength of their feelings. Then she realized that her threat had finally registered with Firdaus, and felt an overpowering sense of victory. Her belief that she had brought Firdaus to book, suddenly calmed her down. Her anger and aversion began to vanish away, like smoke. She couldn't understand how that feeling of repulsion that had so overcome her for all this time could just melt away. What was it, exactly, that gentled her? She looked at Firdaus and was surprised by a well-spring of affection and sympathy for her. Once again she was confused. She thought with shame of the reason for her standing there, and wanted to get away at once. In the darkness she couldn't quite find her direction.

After a moment's silence, Firdaus blocked her way as if she were wanting to say something. Quietly she raised her fair-skinned arm which was bare of bangles. 'What did you say? Did you question my behaviour? Before you go and tell everyone, you'd better check out with your Chaccha how your mother behaved with him.' Having said this, loud and clear, Firdaus walked rapidly across the courtyard, gently pushed open the front door, entered, and locked it from inside.

Loneliness descended upon Wahida, as if she were on her own in a huge forest. The last words that Firdaus had flung at her had put her in a terrible confusion, a state of mind such as she had never experienced before. Dawn was about to break. Full of grief, she began to make her way home slowly, dragging her heavy legs.

⌒ 49 ⌒

Firdaus felt faint. Unable even to stand up, she lay on her bed, shrunk within herself. The pillowcase gave off a faint smell of henna flowers mixed with oil, which seemed to penetrate her nostrils. Her long, pale fingers played with and stroked the tassels edging the pillow case. She was thinking of her childhood days.

In those days, she always sucked the thumb of her right hand as she slept. Amina had tried in all sorts of ways to break this habit. Zohra and Amina had watched over Firdaus, night after night, in turn. They would tie up all her fingers together, after she was asleep. Somehow, by morning, her thumb alone would have freed itself. At other times, they had tried rubbing neem oil all over the thumb. When she wept at its bitter taste, Zohra would say, 'You idiot girl! What's the use of your being so beautiful now? If you keep on sucking your thumb, your teeth and upper lip will start to stick out. After that you'll become ugly; no one will marry you.' That voice, so fond and affectionate, still stayed in her memory. How she wished she could return to those childhood days!

It was her mother, most of all, who kept her daughter's beauty in wraps. How many times a week had she done the ritual to cast away the evil eye! When there were women visitors, she would not easily allow Firdaus to come in front of them. She used to sulk and ask, 'Amma, why do you hide me away, even from women?'

'Yes, di; they'll take a look at you, and shoot their mouths off. Afterwards, it will be up to me to waste my time doing the dhrishti against the evil eye.' Although she sounded as if she were complaining, there was an overwhelming pride in her voice too.

Firdaus's throat choked with grief. Where were all these people now? How could their affection and love vanish away? Does even love come to an end? Never mind her mother's anger against her; how could Zohra turn away from her in repulsion?

How could she bring herself to ignore her sister? What had she done that was so terrible? As always, she could not find an answer.

There was a burning sensation in her stomach and chest. She had drawn Death very close to her. The thought beset her that everyone was eager to see her off this world. For a moment she was filled with a sorrow that made her want to cry out aloud. How much she had loved this life! She had never really wanted to leave it. Why must she die? She yearned to open her wardrobe and take out her saris and jewellery, and admire herself one last time. But her body lay helpless and worn out, on the bed.

She thought of Siva. She would never see him again, hereafter. Realizing this, her fear of death grew the greater, and she trembled. At this moment of death, more that anything else she had lost, the thought of parting from Siva for ever was her greatest grief. It was the knowledge that she would never see him again that provoked her to end her life. It was because of him alone that she was prepared to give up all else that she loved in life. So ardently she loved him.

Tears choked her. More than the fact that she was entirely alone and orphaned, her realization that she was being driven off from this world, helpless as she was, urged her towards death. Why was it that this huge world could hold no place for her? Who was hurt by her love, and in what way? She was weary of asking herself these questions.

She thought of Wahida. She regretted having punished her too hard. But why had she turned up here to make trouble? And in return, Firdaus had ensured that Wahida would carry an ache in her heart, for all time. She felt sorry for this, as she had done ever since. But what was the good of feeling sorry about it now? She had brought great harm upon Rahima who had been as loving as a sister to her. She herself was about to die, but she was leaving behind a piece of information which would hurt two people for the rest of their lives.

'Ya Allah,' she murmured, feeling more and more weak.

How did it happen, why did I let it happen, she lamented softly. She couldn't herself take in what she had said. She could not begin to imagine how aghast and pained Wahida must be feeling.

The burning sensation was gathering force in her stomach. Her thoughts turned again to the events of that morning. Amina had been woken up by the hot exchange of words between Wahida and Firdaus. She sat up on her mat, without moving, tense with fury. In the pale night light, Firdaus saw, in Amina's posture, the intensity of her anger. Firdaus stood stock-still at the door, realizing her own vulnerability. Amina's fierce gaze encircled her, was everywhere about her.

Neither she nor Amina could get past that moment. Firdaus cowered against the wall, wishing she could dissolve away into a spirit. She had a sudden thought that she had never truly held on to anything she loved. Amina still said nothing for a long, long while, and this terrified Firdaus. She wanted to go to her, touch her, be sure she was all right.

Unable to move because she was trembling so much with fear and humiliation, she slid down from the wall and sat down against it. Full of guilt and extreme anxiety, she wondered if her mother would actually die of shock. Gathering up all her strength, forgetting even to wipe away the tears streaming down her pale face, like a child she crawled up to her mother, touched her shoulder, shook her gently from fear of hurting her, and said, 'Amma?' At once she found herself being flung away, as if she had been struck by lightning. She was thrown against the wall, like a ball bouncing. Stunned by the blow, she wondered that Amina's arms could summon up such strength. Her head throbbed fiercely, but she was too bewildered to reveal her pain.

Having pushed Firdaus away with all her strength, Amina stood up like a wild animal and shouted in a voice that came from the depth of her belly. 'Are you that far gone, that you'll sleep with a Kafir? You evil creature, were you really born from my stomach? Oh Allah!' Her voice screeched with pain.

She was shaking all over, like a piece of cloth blown by the wind. After that she set about her business without further thought. She mixed rat poison in a tumbler and placed it next to Firdaus. Her voice was loud and clear.

'Today you must die. Or else, I must die. Before it turns into something like that business in Kallupatti.' She sounded fearless, very certain. Firdaus had no doubt that Amina had absolutely made up her mind. Even in her state of confusion, she remembered an event that lurked somewhere in her mind. People had come to know that a Muslim girl of that town had fallen in love with a Hindu boy. The boy was driven out, and the Jamaat met and made their decision about the girl. Everyone there agreed that the parents must give her poison and kill her. The parents, subsequently, forced the girl to poison herself, and buried her at once. Everyone knew that the grave had been dug beforehand, so that nothing would come to the notice of the police.

Firdaus desperate for her life, shook her head stubbornly and screamed, 'I won't, Amma. Leave me alone, Amma.'

But Amina stood by her decision; steadfast and resolute. She knew how much Firdaus loved life. But as far as Amina was concerned, she had no right whatsoever to live anymore. If she insisted she would live, then there would be no other way for Amina to avoid ignominy but to die herself.

Firdaus came running up to her mother, and fell at her feet, clasping her legs tightly. She was desperate that her mother should show her some pity and allow her to live. But Amina's face was set and expressionless. She made no attempt to touch her daughter or lift her up. Firdaus realized that Amina did not touch her, for fear her resolution was shaken. She was prepared to battle for that very thing the Amina was refusing to yield. If there were the slightest shred of love in her mother's heart, she would hang on to it.

Fearful that if she paid heed to her daughter's anguish she might cave in, Amina became more urgent. She was clear that nothing should now stand in her way. In a firm voice she asked

again, 'Will you drink it, or shall I?' Without waiting for a
reply, in a kind of frenzy, she reached out for the tumbler.

Firdaus hurried to her and seized her hands. She swallowed
the contents of the tumbler without hesitation. At that moment
she could see that there was no other way. She drank down the
poison, went to her room and lay down on her bed.

Her throat and stomach were burning, as if on fire. She
swallowed back the pain, determined to die without making a
noise. Even at that moment she could not believe she was
actually dying, nor understand why she had been driven to
this pass. She asked herself again whether it was such a huge sin
for her to be with someone she loved; she had asked this so
often. She wished she could see Siva one last time, but she had
guessed that there might be trouble after Wahida had seen
them, and had told him to leave the town early in the morning.
He had been in a terrible state of shock; more shaken and unable
to cope than she; even more vulnerable. Grief overcame her.
Must she really die? She had been caught up in so many troubles
but had come through all of them; had hung on to life
steadfastly. Was it her mother's threat alone that pushed her
towards death? Was it not also her terrible betrayal of Rahima,
who had always loved her so much?

What a big folly that was! She regretted it with all her heart.
Her betrayal would have dogged her for the end of her days.
She could never again have faced either Rahima or Wahida. If
this business were to come between Rahima and Wahida, she
could not have borne to witness it.

She thought of Zohra and Rabia. What an innocent her
Akka was; how much to be pitied! Hereafter when Rabia came
to this town, Firdaus would not be there to gather her into her
lap and pet her. She tried to think of all the reasons why she
should still live. But to whom could she tell them? Who was
there who would permit her to live? She stretched her legs out,
knowing that at the moment of life's departure, one must not
curl up one's body. She knew she was very near her last
moments. She stared at the photograph of her father, Ismail,

which hung on the wall opposite her. A small yearning came
over her: could he not have protected her?

She thought of the tumbler in which Amina had brought
the rat poison to her. A wide mouthed tumbler. When she was
a little girl, her mother would give her milk in it, never in a
smaller one. She was prepared to quarrel, if any one teased her
saying, 'So much fuss over a girl child!' There had been words
with Sabia Akka, many times. Today Amina gave her the poison
in the very same tumbler. How could she do that? She wanted
to know the answer to that, however absurd it might be. When
she was a child, Amina had combed her hair, fed her, bathed
her, dried her hair so carefully with frankincense. When did all
that cease? Since her talaq? Could all that love turn to hate for
just that one reason? Her mind was slipping. Still she wanted
to hold on to life. Her mind went totally blank. Quietly she
died.

ᖇ 50 ᖘ

It was a Friday; they had all bathed and washed their
hair early in the morning. Breakfast was over, and
preparations were going on for the midday meal. Zohra was
scraping a coconut, Rabia sitting next to her and watching the
fun. Every now and then she pleaded, 'Amma, let me turn the
handle.'

'You be quiet; you'll scrape your hand. You can do all this
when you are grown up,' Zohra admonished, going on with
her work.

Karim normally left the house soon after breakfast, and did
not turn up again until midday. When he returned that day,
so soon, Zohra was first surprised, then, seeing his stern
expression, extremely anxious. He came up to her, then
noticing Rabia sitting there, took her away into their bedroom.

A minute later, Zohra's screams shook the whole house.

Stunned and terrified, Rabia went running in search of her
mother. It was Rahima who brought Zohra out of her faint,
supported her into the car, and accompanied her and Rabia.
Rabia could not understand what had happened. She was eager
to know, but kept quiet, since no one was in a position to explain
anything to her.

The car arrived at her grandmother's town, and came to a
stop at her house. Rabia feared the worst when she saw the
men seated on the benches outside the house. She began to
understand what had happened to her Nanni. Zohra climbed
down from the car and hurried into the house, weeping loudly,
followed by Rahima and Rabia. Everyone there who had been
expecting their arrival, stood up and began to crowd around,
watching with excitement.

Rabia, pushing her way past the women crowding the hall,
was astonished to see her Nanni sitting by the long bench where
the corpse lay. Then whose body was it that lay beneath the
covers? Could it be Chitthi? She began to shake. She had
thought it was Nanni. But how did Chitthi die? Rabia stood
there in utter shock. Zohra fell on her mother's lap and began
to weep loudly. At once, Amina began to weep too. All the
other women there, who had stopped weeping, began again,
unable to bear the sight of the mother's and daughter's grief.
Nobody paid any attention to Rabia, all alone in the house full
of heavy lamentation. Nobody seemed to need her presence
there. It didn't occur to her to weep; she only wanted to know
at once, why her Chitthi was dead. How could her Chitthi die,
when so many old women were alive? She was wracked by the
thought.

A woman who had just come in went up to the corpse and
uncovered the face in order to say a salawat. In that instant it
hit Rabia forcibly that Firdaus was indeed dead. That fair
complexioned face, smooth and round as if made of dough
made Rabia's eyes dazzle. She shut them tightly, as if she would
not allow herself to see. She was always too scared to see dead

people's faces. She had seen a dead face once, and had nightmares for days afterwards, waking up and screaming. But she knew perfectly well that on that day it wasn't out of her usual fear that she shut her eyes.

It was the sight of the lifeless face of someone she loved, who always laughed with her and petted her, that made her tremble. She could not accept that this body which had carried her about and embraced her, this face that had kissed her, should be lying there so still. Even then, the tears didn't come. The question that was paramount in her mind stopped her from crying. How did Firdaus die? She wanted to get out of the room, but could not make her way through the crowds. She went and stood at the foot of the stairs, half-hidden.

A woman pointed at her and said to her companion, 'Look how that little girl doesn't even weep. And how Firdaus cared for her and looked after her!' Rabia overheard this, and continued to stand where she was, weary at heart. At that moment, Wahida entered the room, wrapped in a dupatta which exposed only her face, followed by Sabia. Rabia wanted to go to her cousin at once, but the crowds would not allow her to move.

Wahida stood by the side of the shrouded body, with eyes full of tears, for a moment only. She hesitated a moment more, but because the crowds there would not allow her to sit, she began to make her way back towards the door. She wanted to go away at once, unable to bear the sight of her mother and Zohra weeping in Amina's arms. Sabia too, anxious to take her away from there, set about firmly asking people to move out of her way. Rabia, not wishing to miss this chance pushed her way in their wake, and tried to join Wahida. Wahida, though, covered entirely by her dupatta except for her eyes, head bent low, did not notice Rabia standing there.

Noticing Wahida's quick exit, and Sabia's anxiety to take her away, one woman commented, 'This is astonishing, di, why is she sticking to her daughter-in-law's side like this?'

'Never mind that,' the woman sitting next to her. 'When a death happens in the early morning, why does a close neighbour come to the house of mourning so late? And when they are related, besides,' she complained.

Rabia heard this too, but did not understand the innuendo. It seemed that Wahida had heard it too. She stopped short for a moment lost in thought. But Sabia insisted that she should move, whether she wanted to or not, saying, 'Come on, hurry up.' Rabia was now jostling her way through the crowd, determined to get out.

She arrived at Wahida's house almost unaware of how she got there. When Wahida came inside, having washed her face and her arms and legs in the backyard, she was shocked to see Rabia standing there. She was also overcome with grief. She ran up to her and held her tightly. The lament which forced its way up from the pit of her stomach stuck in her throat at the sight of Sabia. Sabia's face darkened at the sight of Rabia. She looked at Rabia sharply as if to ask why she had turned up here, when she was actually attending a funeral. Then she herself returned to Amina's house.

After she had gone, Wahida raised her voice and poured out all the grief she had kept buried all this time. Rabia, wrapped in Wahida's warmth, began to weep at last. Wahida's tears brought home to her, her huge loss, and she began to weep with grief and fear. But in Wahida's voice there was the shadow of a sorrow which would last for ever.

◠ 51 ◠

After they had taken the body away, Amina lay in a corner of the house, utterly broken. Zohra huddled at her feet. Amina felt as if a huge drama had finally come to an end. The lie she had put about – that Firdaus had been struck by an electric current – had silenced the town to some extent. The laments of the women who had bathed and laid out Firdaus's body seemed to ring in Amina's ears, even now. 'So young and firm she is! Poor wretch, was she born so beautiful only in order to die before her life was even half over?' they had mourned. They had tried to console her by saying, 'Comfort yourself with the thought that Allah always calls to himself that which is most precious to him.' All the same, the truth was that no one could be comforted. The tears streamed continually from Amina's eyes. She still could not believe that Firdaus was dead. How much she had loved this world. In spite of so many difficulties that beset her, how clearly she had demonstrated that she would never willingly die. Amina felt a deep repulsion towards herself. How could she be a mother? The question repeated itself, tormenting her. She was a murderer, she realized, with profound pain.

She could not believe what she had done in the name of family honour. She felt a fierce pain in her heart as she thought of her dead daughter, whose only sin was that she wanted to live. Amina felt she must extricate herself from this pain, or else the hatred she felt for herself would surely destroy her. She sought to redeem herself with the thought that what Firdaus did was wicked beyond belief. She convinced herself that it was a sin that no one could forgive, at any time, and under any circumstances. In this way she persuaded herself to be rid of guilt and to be at peace.

She could hear Zohra sobbing quietly, at her feet. In the silence of the night, that sound seemed to pierce anyone who heard it, to the very heart. Amina gritted her teeth and swallowed back the tears that threatened to break out of her, burying them deep within. Her hands reached out involuntarily, looking for Firdaus who would normally lie next to her. The emptiness that filled that space shocked her and made her tremble. The smell which usually rose from her and the warmth of her young body were gone forever; only a slight scent of incense was still left even after the house had been washed thoroughly, reminding Amina of her daughter's

corpse. However hard she tried to forget, the smell of the incense
lingered around her.

Amina opened her eyes and looked about her, peering
through the pale night-light. She saw four or five women
sleeping there, other than herself and Zohra. Why were they
there, she wondered. Would her loss be the less for their presence
there? She searched for Rabia. It would have comforted her to
see the little girl. It struck her that she had been treacherous
towards Rabia too. Rabia had doted on her Chitthi.

She had wept until there were no tears left in her eyes. But
however great the sorrow, in the end one got used to it, she
told herself. On the one hand she was struck down by the fact
that she had killed her own daughter; on the other hand she
believed she had done right. It could only end this way; there
could have been no other path, she told herself in justification.
Anything else would have been worse, more shameful.

Zohra was still sobbing quietly. Let her weep, Amina
thought; perhaps if she knew all that had happened, she would
grieve a little less. She wanted to comfort Zohra by telling her
everything, but had to be silent and wait for the right time.
Outside, the hen cheeped, tearing apart the garden's darkness.
She could hear the cow chewing on its straw. Hereafter there
was no one to feed them and care for them. Did they realize
that Firdaus was not in the house any more? Why must she
think of such things in the midst of her sorrow? She was still
unable to accept the extent of the anger that had filled her. She
trembled to think how deeply rooted it must have been to push
her into doing so violent a deed. How did this happen to her,
who was normally so composed both in her form and by
nature?

A great sigh rose up from her and died away. She wished she
could confess everything to Zohra immediately and be
vindicated. She might be at peace after that, at least. Besides,
she wanted to assuage Zohra's grief, a little. She believed that if
she were to tell Zohra the entire truth about Firdaus, Zohra
would accept what had to be. But she saw no hope of an

opportunity to speak to Zohra just yet. Amina thought of her
husband and was glad he died without witnessing all these
terrible things. As she remembered him, her eyes sought his
photograph which hung on the wall opposite her bed.
Although it was a photograph which she glanced at everyday,
it seemed to her just then that there was an intensity
smouldering in the eyes, and in the expression on his face. The
keenness with which those eyes looked at her, while the room
floated in the dimly-lit night-light, plunged her into sadness.
She wanted to shake herself free of the anger in that look and
redeem herself from its accusation. She wanted to brush away
his charge that she killed his daughter. She repeated to herself
what the circumstances were and how she had safeguarded the
honour of the family, insisting on the justice of her action.
And yet, heart-broken, she lay prone on her bed, preventing
the photograph from gazing at her.

One of the women sleeping in the room snored, making it
impossible for Amina to stay there any more. A sound like
that of an animal's. She opened the door and came out into
the threshold, wanting to sit for a while in the courtyard. The
moonlight falling there, brought a measure of peace. She sat
down on the thinnai, drawing her knees up. Above her head
the moon crept past, scattering handfuls of dazzling light. The
light spread everywhere: along the paving stones, by the well,
and upon all the bushes in the garden. Startled by an owl's
hoot in the distance, she gazed about her, her eyes coming to
rest on the parapet of the terrace. She frowned in frustration,
seeing it sitting there. Her frown implied that everything was
over now. In earlier times, she would have been quick to chase
it away. Now she sat watching it, motionless. Idly she wondered
what day it was the previous day and realized, after a moment's
confusion, it had been a Friday. She thought of the Friday
celebrations in the town, and reminded herself that for her
family there would be no more such happiness. There would
be no more festivals, she realized, in utter weariness. Silently
she gazed at the plants in the garden, and it seemed to her that

Firdaus was moving amongst them. She narrowed her eyes and stared hard trying to ascertain whether it was really her daughter. No, it was her imagination, she realized. She shut her eyes tightly trying to call up a picture of Firdaus, and failed. But how would Firdaus ever come in front of her eyes again? She would never do so, not even in Amina's dreams. Overwhelmed by a yearning love and guilt at the same time, she began to weep aloud, just as dawn was breaking.

☙ 52 ❧

Wahida stood leaning against one of the pillars in the hall, her arms around it. Sayyed sat opposite her, lounging in an easy chair; Sabia sitting directly in front of him, her knees drawn up, her chin resting against her right hand. Anxiety filled her face. Sayyed kept on staring at Wahida and dropping sly smiles. He would smile at Wahida and then quickly turn his face away. Wahida found this deeply irritating. She wished she could go away from there; she was so tired she could barely stand. Because Sayyed had expressly told her to stay, she did so. Silently she cursed him, calling him a wretched old man. She remembered her mother telling her that if she scolded old people, her own life-span would lessen. Perhaps by scolding this man constantly, her own life-span would decrease until she died, she thought. It might not be such a bad thing, either. She found herself recoiling at the thought of her mother. However hard she tried to prevent her feelings of displeasure, she found she could not, and this worried her.

Sayyed cleared his throat. 'Come and sit here, child,' he said. ' That pillar is not going to disappear; you don't have to stand there hugging it so tightly.' He laughed loudly at his own wit.

It must have annoyed him that neither Wahida nor Sabia laughed with him. He was already distressed by the news from Sri Lanka about the ethnic riots, and the prisoners who had been killed brutally. It annoyed him the more that Sabia was sunk in her own thoughts. He growled at her, 'What is it, woman, has your ship sunk or what, you are lost in your own tragedy! Here I am, worried about all our property there and what has happened to it, and you don't even seem to understand.' The anger in his tone made Wahida afraid.

'Well, well, the lord and master is getting quite agitated. If you have your own worries, so have I.' Sabia frowned at him in reply.

Sayyed stared at her as if to ask what these worries of hers were. Sabia understood, and asked him, 'Tell me how it strikes you. Do you think Firdaus really died of an electric shock?'

'Why do you think about that now? Is that all you are worrying about? And here I was, under the wrong impression that you were anxious about our shop,' he said resentfully. Then he added, concerned to know Sabia's opinion, 'Well, what's your impression, then?'

Wahida noticed that the sudden flash of eagerness in Sabia's face had infected Sayyed, too. She was even more irritated. Sabia, who had been speaking loudly so far, lowered her voice. 'You know what, that whore must have been having a relationship with the fellow living opposite them. Her mother must have seen them. This is what must have happened. Amina is an honourable woman. She'd have scolded her properly. The girl must have drunk poison and died. Don't you think so?' Sabia stretched her imagination to the full and told her tale with great gusto. She looked her husband eagerly, waiting for his response.

Although Sayyed supposed that Sabia's conjectures might be right, he was loath to admit it in front of Wahida, knowing that she could go and report the conversation to her Chitthi, Zohra. At least for the look of the thing, he felt, he had to rebuke his wife. so he said, 'Sh! Be quiet. You shouldn't make up these tales about a young woman.'

But Sabia pounced on him as soon as he finished speaking.

'Oh yes, as if you are a man who knows everything. You be quiet. Nothing happens here without my knowledge. The cow that strays helps itself to all it gets. That fellow Siva's wife was never here. These women will never give up a chance if they can have a man for free. It's a case of each one having a turn.' She spoke in a mocking tone, as if to shut him up.

Sayyed glanced at Wahida and squirmed with embarrassment. As if to change the subject, he said, 'What was that you said? Did you say that women will never give up a chance if they can get a man for free? So is that what you get up to when I'm not in town?' He winked at Wahida and shook with laughter. Wahida, repulsed by the sight of his paunch bobbing up and down by itself, turned her eyes away.

But Sabia was furious with him for asking her such a question, and laughing in front of Wahida. She frowned at him, round-eyed, and made as if to spit, turning her face towards the courtyard, Turning again to face him, she said, 'Who do you think you are talking to? Keep in mind the pride and honour of my family, and remember whose daughter I am. Do you think it was ever written in our destiny or history that our women would stray? A fine thing you said.' She spoke angrily and heaved a great sigh.

Wahida could make out perfectly well that Sabia intended to humiliate Amina's family by comparing it with her own. Her heart filled with pain. Images of Amina and Zohra appeared to her briefly and disappeared. At that time she did not attempt to think of Firdaus; any thoughts of her made Wahida's entire body tremble, and she forced herself to shut them out.

Sayyed was more and more embarrassed. Why was Sabia speaking like this and so boldly, in front of Wahida? Wishing to send the girl away from there, he turned to her and said, 'Please go and make me some tea.'

Wahida set off towards the kitchen, not caring to say anything. She was seething with anger, and controlled herself with difficulty. Asking herself whether Sabia had any right to boast about her family's honour, she struck a matchstick and lit the stove. She herself had observed, since she entered this house, their carelessness in handling food and the way beggars walked past this house alone while Sabia watched them go by without the least embarrassment. She could hear Sabia's voice as she went on talking. She was complaining about the way Amina had brought up Firdaus. Sayyed must have spoken up in disagreement. Now Sabia's voice came, even more loudly as she scolded him, 'You have been living abroad for some years, what do you know? Just shut up.'

From where she stood in the kitchen, Wahida turned round to look at Sabia, who sat directly within her range of vision. Her face was darkened by her bad thoughts. There was a dense darkness spreading over her forehead and cheeks. Rahima often said that it was not just Sabia's heart that had darkened, her face had, too. The milk hissed as it came to a boil, and Wahida took down the tin of tea leaves and made the tea. She considered whether to that day she had ever served her parents so much as a chombu of water. Today, here she was bound to make tea and serve it whenever she was asked, just like a servant, she thought resentfully. She poured out the tea in two tumblers and put out the stove. A smell of kerosene oil rose from it, making her feel queasy. She covered her head properly before picking up the tumblers. If her sari slipped down from her head, Sabia would howl like an animal, 'Doesn't a woman have to show respect? Don't throw away the family honour to the winds!'

Sayyed took the tea that she offered and insisted that she should sit down by him. 'Come here. There are some matters that we have to speak about. So come and sit here awhile.' He held the tumbler with both hands, sucking at the tea with relish. It was clear that the tea was greatly to his liking. He expected his wife to show an equal satisfaction and was disappointed.

'Why have you shoved in so much sugar?' Sabia frowned.

Wahida had expected it. Surely Sabia's head would split if

she could not find some fault with her daughter-in-law.

Sayyed wanted to speak of something else. He stared at Wahida for an instant. His eyes roved over her thin form, and then lowered, having failed to find whatever it sought. Wahida turned her face away, to avoid that gaze which crawled all over her. Sayyed sat up straight and began. 'So tell me what I should do now,' he said, addressing his wife.

Neither Sabia nor Wahida had the slightest doubt as to what he meant. It was obvious that he wanted to talk about the ethnic riots that were going on in Sri Lanka even on the previous day. Wahida plunged into anxiety. It was not the terrible news that came through newspapers and radio broadcasts that caused her grief. Rather, it was her fear that Sayyed would decide to stay at home, giving the riots as a reason. Her one comfort when he overstepped the mark in his behaviour towards her was that he would not be there for long. It shocked her to think this might not be the case.

Sabia thought for a while and said, 'Why do you have to make a decision immediately? Let's wait for a few days and then decide whether you should go or stay.'

It was at that moment that Sikander entered the house. His face was dark with perspiration. His veshti was covered in dust. Hearing his footsteps, Sabia turned round and asked with concern, 'Where have you been, my boy?'

This annoyed Sayyed, who cut in sarcastically, before Sikander could answer, 'The boy has been hard at work, earning his living!'

Sikander's face tightened. He knew why his father was angry, so he stopped for a moment and addressed him directly. 'If there are riots going on there, what am I supposed to do?'

Sayyed kept quiet. He was upset that his son had shown no concern, nor talked to him about the Sri Lankan situation. At the same time, he was afraid that if he were to say anything, Sikander might answer back disrespectfully.

When Sikander had gone to the courtyard to wash his feet, Sabia started to take Wahida to task. 'Can't you see that your husband has come home? Are you going to make him some coffee, or are you going sit there idly? Do I have to tell you even this? And here, hand him a towel before you go into the kitchen.'

Wahida felt ashamed. She wondered why Sabia always spoke sharply to her these days. She remembered how sweetly and kindly Sabia had spoken to her before she was married. She thought too of her words that morning. Wahida was having a bath early that morning. She usually had a bath immediately after Sikander had sex with her at night. Somehow she had fallen asleep on the previous night, and when she was awake, the first light of dawn was breaking. She got up in haste, her weak body beginning to tremble. Her tongue felt dry, and she moved forward, about to drink a mouthful from the tumbler of water on the table. But she remembered her mother's words, 'After you have been with your husband, you must not drink even a mouthful of water without having had a bath. It's a sin.' Hastily she stripped the bed of its sheets and pillowcases, gathered them up and locked herself in the bathroom. Sikander was not to be seen. Hastily she recited the appropriate prayers three times, had a bath and began to soap and rinse out the bedclothes. She knew she had to clean all the places in her room where she had walked around, and was worried about that as well. Someone banged at the bathroom door. She stood stock-still and called out, 'Who is it?' She was overcome with shame; embarrassed that having a bath at such an early hour made it apparent to everyone what had happened in the night. Besides, Sayyed had a habit of touching her hair and asking, 'So, have you had a bath?' However casually he asked his question, she felt ready to die of shame. She had taken to covering her head entirely, until her hair was dry.

Sabia shouted again, 'What, can't you hear me?'

She answered only, 'What is it, Kuppi?'

'You are having a cleansing bath, is that it?' Sabia sounded furious.

'Yes.' The single word was spoken with shame.

'So you wait until it is day-break do you, woman, before you have a bath? Don't you know it is a sin? It's a disgusting way to behave!' Sabia walked away. Wahida's whole body shrank, and she stayed there weeping for a long time. Her tears joined the water spraying from the shower. She remembered that her mother had spoken to her once, about this matter, when she was at home. Rahima's tone had not been harsh or hurtful, but Wahida had been struck by its sternness. It was after that conversation that she had understood how sinful it was to err in this.

Sabia's scolding broke into her thoughts and brought her back to the present. 'What are you day-dreaming about instead of taking him his towel?' Wahida leapt to her feet, blinking, as if she had just woken up.

Sayyed spoke sharply to his wife and in support of Wahida, 'Here, what is the matter with you? You are always finding fault with the child. Can't you shut up?' Of course he had been afraid to speak up. Sabia would not let him off, he knew. And sure enough, she hissed at him immediately. 'No, you keep quiet. You and your mouth, like an owl, hooting.' Then she turned to Wahida and gave her orders, 'Go now, amma. You go and cook the rice for the evening meal. Be sure to put on enough rice for my sahar meal as well: I shall be keeping the Sayyed Ali fast.'

Sikander, coming into the hall at that moment, after having washed his face and feet, took one look at Wahida's face and knew at once that his mother had been shouting at her. At once he came forward and stood in front of his mother. Gently he wiped off the water still dripping from his face. Knowing it was inauspicious to shake his hands, he dried them by burying them in his veshti. His face was red with anger. He raised his voice, clearly intending to rebuke his mother, and said, 'What are you thinking of, Amma? I've been observing you since morning, you've been getting at her constantly. Keep in mind that she is my wife!'

Sabia was completely taken aback. She stared at her son,

who seemed to have flung her off in one minute. Was it really
he? She was deeply humiliated that he spoke in this way in
front of Wahida. Wahida, in her turn, was nonplussed. It
astonished her that Sikander found it unbearable that his
mother was scolding her. Realizing that he was there to speak
up for her, she felt, for the very first time in that house, the
comfort of being protected. Sabia noticed her look of sudden
serenity, and this made her even more furious.

'Did you say that she is your wife? No, I didn't know. How
would I know? I only know it now that you tell me so. And of
course you'll speak up for her, you've got your new bride,
haven't you?' Her throat choked, and it seemed that the tears
would stream from her eyes. She pulled out the handkerchief
that was tucked into her waist and blew her nose.

Sayyed sat quietly, not knowing what to do. He had not
liked it either, that Sikander had spoken like that in front of
Wahida. Sikander, not wishing to stay there any longer,
hastened up the stairs. As he went, he only spoke briefly to
Wahida, 'Come upstairs.'

Wahida followed after him, shrinking with fear. She didn't
dare stay there in the hall. She was too frightened even to look
at Sabia. As she went up the stairs, she could hear her mother-
in-law wailing, 'Did you see what he did? It's all her work.
She's only a little thing, but she's got him eating out of her
hand, with all the lies she's told.'

When she entered their room, he was already sitting on the
bed. 'Come here,' he said, summoning her to his side. She went
up to him hesitantly. 'Don't stand there blinking; sit here,' he
said again, indicating a space beside him. He scolded her
affectionately, 'If you don't have any work to do, why don't
you just come upstairs and lie down for a bit? Why do you go
to those old folk? They'll wear you out with their chatter.' She
didn't answer, but sat there silently, pulling at a loose thread
in the bed sheet, wondering that he could be so affectionate
towards her.

He was still breathing hard from the encounter with his parents. Seeing from the look on her face that she continued to be upset, he went on, 'Don't worry. I'm here, aren't I?' He hesitated after that, unable to find any more words to express his feelings. It pained him to see her at the brink of tears, her face drawn and taut. He said again, 'Haven't I told you? You mustn't worry now.' His tone was almost pleading. Wahida was suddenly sorry for him. She wished he would take her hand and comfort her by stroking her long fingers, still ornamented with henna. But he just didn't know how to show any affection. He didn't even begin to understand how he could make an effort to console her, and could only say again and again, 'Leave it alone now. Don't worry. Hereafter, I'll see to things.' Wahida smiled at him.

Satisfied when she smiled at last, he lay back on the bed with a sigh of relief. 'Good; go and see to your work if you have any,' he said to her, shutting his eyes and returning to his own thoughts. But for the first time in all her days in this household, Wahida felt she was safeguarded. She felt a tiny spurt of affection for the relationship that afforded her that protection, and realized the importance of sustaining it.

* * *

Having resolved to forego even the early morning sahar meal which is normally allowed during a fast, Sabia woke up rather late the next morning. She went and sat on the sofa and began complaining at once. 'I started on this Sayyed Ali fast only for the sake of my only son, that he should have a good life and marry my brother's daughter. I've kept the one-day-a-month fast for fourteen days out of sixteen. And how can he fling me off now! I've kept this fast with such devotion. He knows it very well. Yet he has the heart to kick his mother aside. Did that Allah bless me with a daughter at least? For whom did I save up all my money? For my son, who else?'

It was not right to break off the sixteen month fast without completing it, so Sabia fasted on that day too. Sayyed sat around, unable to make any reply to her complaints.

∼ 53 ∼

Wahida, coming up to the terrace to collect the clothes which hung there to dry, looked across at Firdaus's house, involuntarily. The courtyard was empty and filled with dust. Amina had been admitted into a hospital in Madurai because of chest pains. Zohra Chitthi had accompanied her there. Everyone said that there was no hope that she would survive. Fear built its nest in Wahida's heart. Whenever the thought struck her that she was the cause of Firdaus's death, the tears poured out of her eyes. Had she not seen Firdaus on that night, none of this would have happened. Had she even left it alone instead of following her there, all this might have been prevented. So many things were the result of that impulsive act. Yet the great repulsion she had felt towards her mother that night had all melted away after Firdaus's death. It was a comfort to her that all the hatred she had felt had vanished, without leaving a mark. It was as if nothing that occurred before Firdaus died was of the least importance. She didn't know whether this feeling would last. She thought that hereafter, whenever she saw her mother, she would remember what Firdaus said. She was aware too that there was still some anger left in her, towards Firdaus. When everything was added up, did her going there and confronting Firdaus equal Firdaus telling her about Rahima?

She stared up at the sky. It had started to darken. Patches of grey clouds were lying still all over it. In the distance, the hills lay, shaped like a tortoise and an elephant. Yet another rose like a cone, right up to the sky. She wondered where Firdaus was, right now. She had read in the Hadiths about the paradise called Jannathul Firdaus. Was it possible she might have entered there? No, she would certainly be in hell, Wahida thought. There was no other possibility, given the sin Firdaus committed. And it was right that it should be so, Wahida considered. She made up her mind never again to think about the whole business.

That morning Mumtaz and Sainu had come to visit them. Farida was going to be married, and Aziz was the chosen bridegroom. After giving them this news, Mumtaz had whispered into Wahida's ear, 'Poor Nafiza.' Wahida had not understood what Mumtaz meant, but had nodded her head anyway. Sainu had accompanied Mumtaz. Meanwhile, Sabia hesitated, not quite able to complain about her daughter-in-law to Sainu openly, but not wishing to keep quiet either. Fortunately for her, Mumtaz took Wahida upstairs, asking to see her room.

It was actually Sikander that she had hoped to see, and Sikander himself was aware of it very quickly. Wahida listened silently to their jokes and teasing. Mumtaz was wearing a very thin sari which revealed most of her body. But she seemed not in the least aware of it, as she sat next to him and chatted away familiarly. Wahida did not at all like the way Mumtaz pretended not to notice the way Sikander was watching her and appreciating her beauty. It struck her that Mumtaz assumed that she was only a little girl who wouldn't understand what was going on. Once again she was annoyed with Sikander because of the way he talked to women. But leaving him aside, she could not understand why this woman was flaunting herself in this way. It was the same with the women of this neighbourhood. Whenever they were free during the day, they would gather together in Sabia's house and pass the time away exchanging pleasantries. And just like Mumtaz, they would banter with him, Sabia joining in. Wahida disliked them all at such times. She would tell herself that Sikander was a flirt. Yet when he stood up to his mother in defence of herself, that disapproval melted away, a little at least.

Wahida was confused by her own attitude. Even if she did

not love him, she wished at least not to dislike him. Otherwise, she knew, she would not be able to live out the rest of her life. With a sense of extreme weariness, she shut her eyes. Although it had started to darken, the paving stones beneath her feet were still warm in the terrace. Troubled by the sight of the emptiness in Amina's house and the unbroken darkness of its courtyard, Wahida turned her eyes away. The only way to avoid looking at it would be to go downstairs. But, fearful of Sayyed's presence, she hesitated still. At last, remembering that Sabia Kuppi was waiting to break her fast, she hurried down. People who undertook the Sayyed Ali fast observed it most stringently, she knew. The entire house had been cleaned that morning. But that evening Sabia had yet again washed and cleaned the place where she would sit to break her fast, rinsed out her mat and spread it out. In every household there would be at least one woman who had vowed to keep this fast on one day for sixteen consecutive months. On the sixteenth day, the needy were summoned and fed, and prayers said to mark the end of the fast. Wahida wondered whether on that day at least Sabia would give food to the beggars. It also came to her with some surprise that in no household had she known of men who kept this particular fast. Whatever difficulty a family faced, it was the women who vowed to fast in order to alleviate it. Once when she herself had fallen ill with malaria, her mother had undertaken a three day fast in the name of the saint Mohiuddin. She had asked her mother at that time, whether men never made special vows to fast. She could not remember her mother giving her a proper reply.

Sabia, sitting up on her mat, all ready for her meal, heard the sound of Wahida's toe-rings as she came down the stairs, and quickly lay down again. Wahida, noticing, smiled to herself, made straight for the kitchen, took down the milk from the stove, and began to prepare a kanji of rava. The incense wafting to her from the hall reminded her of Firdaus.

Since Firdaus died, Sabia had begun to close all the windows as well as the front door of her house, as soon as the Maghrib prayers were said at dusk. Besides this, Sabia had placed an iron knife and a broom at the front door steps, just as they did, customarily, in houses where a woman had just given birth, or a girl had menstruated for the first time. They would do this for forty days, in order to keep ghosts and spirits away. Sayyed had teased her saying, 'Why, Sabia, have you come of age only now?'

'You keep quiet. She was a young woman. Who knows how much she held on to life? Her unfulfilled hopes and wishes will never let her stay quiet in her grave. She'll come back, you'll see.' Sabia would begin to shake as she spoke. 'She loved this world so much,' she would complain.

Sayyed would fall about laughing and tease her, 'Of course, people like you have no worldly desires at all, do you?' Sabia would only grimace, implying that he was beyond the pale, and it was no use bandying words with him. Everyday something like this happened, to Wahida's amusement.

The house, with all its windows shut, felt oppressive. In the hall, smoke spiralled upwards from an incense stick which had been inserted into a banana in the plate full of fruit with which Sabia would break her fast. Rings of smoke began to fill the room, making Wahida gasp for breath. When she began to unhook the window shutter, Sabia called out sharply, 'Why are you opening it?' She sounded terrified, as if a ghost waiting outside would enter the house instantly.

'There is no air at all, I was sweating,' Wahida apologised, quickly adding, 'Besides, we won't hear the nagara sounding from the mosque; don't you have to end your fast?'

'I'll hear it all right. You first shut the window. Such concern you are showing!' She added a muttered, 'Useless clod!' before blowing her nose hard.

Wahida's stomach turned. That was the first day she had eaten properly. Sabia had not come into the kitchen because she was keeping her fast. She lay on her bed the whole time. Perhaps she feared that were she to see all the food that was being prepared her mouth would water; she might not be able to resist the temptation to eat. Whatever the reason, she had come nowhere near the kitchen. For once Wahida had been able to eat without feeling sick. She had to laugh at herself and her situation.

Besides she was amused that Sabia, at her age, was so terrified at the thought of ghosts. Wahida reminded herself that Sabia had just called her a 'useless clod'. She too used to be scared to go outdoors for up to a week after there was a funeral in their town. At night, she would refuse even to go out to relieve herself, but lie in bed, gritting her teeth. Rahima used to scold Wahida, saying she could have slept in her mother's room. But now, there had been such a violent death right next door, yet she was not in the least afraid. She was astonished, and wondered why this was so. Why had not Firdaus's death frightened her? Where had all her fear gone? Even the previous night, when she could not sleep, she had gone out of her room and stood outside in the terrace for a long, long time.

Wahida turned around with a shock when someone touched her bottom lightly. Sayyed stood behind her, grinning and saying softly, 'This sari suits you very well.' He tottered past her and went and sat next to Sabia. Sabia gave no sign of taking in his arrival; she was immersed in reading the Koran. Wahida's entire body shrank with shame and humiliation. She felt a sense of burning where he touched her, as if she were on fire. For an instant she glared at him, her eyes giving out sparks of rage. He lowered his eyes as if afraid to meet her gaze, suggesting that he had convinced himself he had acted involuntarily. Wahida swallowed the anger which she could not reveal. She didn't what else to do, how to protest against his behaviour.

She came to herself when Sayyed's voice shook her out of her reverie at last. 'Why are you standing there still? The call for prayers has been said. Ask your Kuppi what she needs, and serve her, amma.' She recognized the note of conciliation in his voice. Sadly, it proved to her that he had not touched her by mistake.

❧ 54 ❧

Rabia lay on the long chair in the hall. She was utterly dejected and sore at heart. Her mother was away at the hospital in Madurai, with her Amina Nanni. There was no knowing when they would return. Her father went to see them every two days, taking them clothes and food. He said to her every evening before he went to sleep, 'Rabia, you can sleep in my room, if you like.' Stubbornly she refused, in spite of the affectionate tone.

It was her mother's warning that always remained with her, stopping her. 'Don't go if your father invites you to sleep in his room. You won't know if your skirt or davani slip off when you are asleep; you don't want that to happen in front of your father.'

'What Amma said is right,' she told herself. 'As Amma always says, "There's no lack of games during the day." But look at me now, there's none of all that; I stay shut up here all by myself. It might be a little less sad if I were with Attha.' Yet she put aside that thought steadfastly. Although both her father and Periamma were especially affectionate towards her, she thought of her mother with a great yearning. She felt as if she had been totally abandoned.

She remembered her Firdaus Chitthi. She called to mind the last time she saw her face. It was dry and smooth, like a doll's. She could not believe Chitthi had gone to a place from which she would never return. It was strange that however much she wept and yearned to see her, she would never again do so. She had thought that one died only when one grew old, that it was the old who died first. She could not understand why Firdaus died when she could have lived for so many more years.

She remembered that Nuramma was still alive. For some days she had not been able to get up. Iliaz came to their house everyday to eat a meal, and carried away some gruel for his grandmother whom he fed. Rabia had gone with him to their house one day. Even before they entered the house, Nuramma called out, as soon as she heard their footsteps, 'Who is it?' When they drew near her, she opened her eyes a little, looked at them and was silent. The whole house stank of urine! Before feeding Nuramma her kanji, Iliaz lit a chimney-lamp and placed it in its niche on the wall. She put her davani to her nose and held it tight saying, 'I'm going, da.'

He looked at her piteously and pleaded, 'Wait a bit. Let me come back with you.'

She felt sorry for him and said, 'All right then, but hurry.' She stood to one side, avoiding the mat on which Nuramma lay. Iliaz tended to come and sleep in Rabia's house while Nuramma lay there all alone, every night. It was Periamma who insisted that Iliaz should not stay alone with her. If her life left her suddenly, in the middle of the night, it would be too frightening for him, she said. So he spread a mat outside Rahima's room and slept in their house. Sometimes when she saw him there, Rabia wanted to cry. She wondered how it must be for him, when she herself felt so bereft because her mother was away for just ten days.

Nuramma opened her mouth to be fed by Iliaz, but whenever she heard footsteps she stopped eating and called out, 'Who is it?' Iliaz and Rabia exchanged smiles. He told her, 'It's always like this. She can hear at once, if anyone goes along the street at any time. Immediately she'll start asking, "Who is it? Who is it?" It happens a hundred times a day. Why should she be bothered, whoever it is?' They were both astonished that she always said this, for she never spoke or moved otherwise.

Periamma had arranged for Asiamma, the woman who attended at funerals, to bathe and clean Nuramma twice a week, and change her clothes. Periamma often lamented, 'They say that you need a son to care for you in your old age. Here this witless woman abandoned both her mother and her orphaned son!'

Rabia thought of her Chitthi once more. She realized that her thoughts of Firdaus were all about the affection her aunt had showered upon her. She was overcome with sorrow when the truth struck her that she would never experience that again, that Firdaus had died so unfairly. Rabia did not ever want to go to that small town again. The girl who told her stories every day, the girl who had carried her in a palm-leaf basket held on her head, from the palmyra grove right up to the house, was no longer in this world. Hiding the tears which poured from her eyes, she lay prone on the chaise-longue and wept for a long time. When she heard Rahima Periamma's footsteps, she wiped away her tears. She knew that her aunt would worry if she saw her weeping.

Rahima came up to her and touched her very gently, to wake her up. 'You must not sleep at this time, Rabia. A girl should not be lying down at lamp-lighting time. Come, get up. Go and see Madina for awhile.' It was clear she was anxious to know whether Rabia had been weeping.

'Nothing's the matter, Periamma,' Rabia muttered. Rahima hurried away from there as if she did not dare to look at Rabia too closely.

Rabia got up and went outside to sit on the front thinnai. Farida's wedding was over. Just as soon as that was done, Madina menstruated for the first time. It was now the fourth day. There were so many questions Rabia wanted to ask Madina about all that, and many things that Madina wanted to tell Rabia. But it was Rabia who hesitated to visit her friend for any length of time. She had no desire to go anywhere, and stayed shut up at home. Only on the previous day, she had spent a little time with Madina. There were a lot of women sitting around her and gossiping. Madina sat in a chair, wearing a silk sari and a lot of jewellery. The entire house was full of laughter and merry-making. Rabia went and sat close to Madina's feet and looked at her silently. Madina glowed with a shy happiness. Rabia was distressed by the thought that from now on they would not allow Madina to cross the threshold of the house. She would not be allowed to go to school again, this year. Rabia remembered that besides that, Ahmad would not

be returning to their town. Nafiza had told them that his
Maama was planning to enroll him in an excellent school near
his house.

The sound of laughter from the crowd of women broke into
Rabia's thoughts. One of the women there winked at her and
said, 'Whose turn is it next? Yours, isn't it?'

Nafiza laughed and said, 'Of course! It's summer time;
perfect for bursting!' They all laughed together, embarrassing
Rabia.

Sainu gave a sigh of satisfaction. 'My daughter did a good
thing,' she said, 'she got past the month of Chitthirai. It is not
auspicious for the family if a girl comes of age or gives birth in
Chitthirai.'

Madina bent down and whispered in Rabia's ear, 'Why don't
you stay here with me until the seven days are over? After all,
your mother is not at home.' She wanted to keep Rabia by her
side, but she knew that Rabia would not stay. She also knew
that even if Rabia agreed to stay, Sainu would never allow it,
so her invitation was half-hearted. In any case, Rabia shook
her head and refused firmly. Her face was tight with anxiety.
Madina hated to see her like that. She felt sorry that she herself
was all decked up when her best friend was so sad. Rabia did, to
some extent, understand how Madina felt.

The heat had decreased as the day darkened, but it was still
humid. Rabia wondered whether she should go across to
Madina's house. She gave up the idea, however, knowing she
must not go there after dark. The street looked bright in the
lamplight. She could see Iliaz standing in the distance, talking
to someone. She could at least go and talk to him. Quietly she
slid off the thinnai and walked towards him. She could feel a
gentle breeze attempting to lift away the cares in her heart and
to comfort her. All the same, she could not but feel she too had
no one to care for her, and had been orphaned, like Iliaz.
Suddenly fearful, she wondered what would happen if she died
then and there, and was extremely sorry for herself and for
Iliaz.

She had been eating a mango one day, when she was very little. She had not bothered to wash her hands and mouth when she finished eating. Instead, she twisted round and wiped her mouth on the shoulder of her blouse while wiping her hands firmly against her skirt. Her mother, observing this, had given her a good scolding. As for her father, he had wiped his hands on her skirt deliberately, after he finished eating, laughing as he did so. Deeply humiliated, she had wept right through that night. She had wanted to die at once. She had gone to sleep, still wondering if it would be best to jump into the well. She felt today the same pity and sorrow for herself.

A beggar woman walked along the street in front of her, begging for food. She wore a sari that was ragged and patched together. She had covered her unkempt hair with the end of it. The breeze blowing past her carried her stench. Rabia wrinkled up her nose and held her breath. What if she too were to be a beggar woman, just like that? The stench that came off her was unbearable, and made her stomach turn. Why was it that there was always this bad smell from muzafirs alone? Why could they not go and bathe in any one of the ponds in the town? Rabia's mother would never let her bathe in a pond; she always said, 'Disgusting; that's where the beggars bathe, di.' Rabia began to walk a little faster, wishing to walk past the beggar woman, and beyond the reach of her smell.

As she passed Iliaz's house, she could hear Nuramma's voice asking, 'Who is it?' She hesitated a moment, but walked on. The question came again, a couple of times, as the beggar woman's footsteps followed hers. The woman, realizing that there was someone in the house, stopped short and began to call out, 'Amma, thaaye, give me some food, amma.'

Iliaz stood further on, talking to Rafiq. She hurried up to them and gestured towards Nuramma's house, saying, 'Ei Iliaz, just look at that.' He turned round quickly, and saw the woman begging. 'Pach! Oh, that? That old lady calls out to whoever passes by. The beggar woman hopes there is someone there who will feed her. OK, let her be.'

Rabia was surprised. Didn't he have a care in the world? How was it that even his mother's departure had not upset him? He was completely absorbed in his conversation. Rafiq said, 'My brother is not going to return to this town. It seems he is going to study in town, hereafter.'

Iliaz's disappointment was apparent. 'Ahmad won't be coming back here,' he repeated to Rabia.

In her turn, she said, 'And Madina won't be going out of her house, after this. Did you know that?'

They looked at each other for awhile, and then turned and began to walk together towards his house. She wanted to hold on to him and weep. She couldn't understand how, suddenly, she felt such affection and sympathy towards him. She wanted to do something specially for him.

In earlier times, during the cold weather months, all the children would gather together in the common ground beside the roadside, in the early morning. Each child would bring some dry leaves or twigs which they would heap together to make a little bonfire. In those days, if Rabia found Iliaz next to her, she always drove him away, saying, 'Get up and go and sit somewhere else.' That was a time when Madina, Ahmad, Razak and all of them were a united group. Madina always scolded Rabia at such times, saying, 'Why do you drive him off like that?' But Rabia held her ground. 'Chi,' she would say, ' he and his ragged trousers!' She wouldn't allow him to join them when they played with spinning tops, either.

The main reason for her annoyance was the kindness that her mother and aunt showed towards Iliaz. It made her jealous that they were equally generous towards him as they were to her; equally affectionate. Periamma was particularly loving towards him, calling him 'Orphan child.' Now, Rabia thought, how could it be that she herself felt such affection for him?

She stopped short, hearing Sherifa's voice ask her, 'Rabia, how is your Nanni? Has your mother not come home as yet?'

'No, Akka, Amma hasn't come home as yet. It seems Nanni isn't quite well as yet. I'll go now, Akka,' she answered, moving

on. She noted the sympathy in Sherifa's voice. The great
kindness with which everyone looked at her and spoke to her
affected Rabia oddly. It annoyed her. Even if she felt sorry for
herself, she did not like it that others should feel sorry for her.

Iliaz, who was walking along with her, stopped for a moment
and took something out of his trousers pocket. He handed it
to her, saying, 'Just look at this.' It was a lottery prize card. He
spread it out to show her. All along the bottom of it were a
series of number in dark blue. At the top were pictures of coins,
interspersed with photographs of MGR and Sivaji.

She looked at him enquiringly. His eyes looked out of his
dark face eagerly. 'Will you choose a number? If I make five
rupees, I can keep it for my expenses.'

It made her pleased and happy that he should ask her, just
when she was anxious to do something for him. 'Of course I
will. Come home with me,' she told him.

They went on. Just as they passed his house, he said, 'Wait a
moment, I'll just light the lamps and come back.'

Rapidly he went in, by himself. Hearing his footsteps, the
inevitable question came from within, Who is it? Rabia stood
waiting for him, full of fear, panic stricken yet again by the
tremor in that voice.

∽ 55 ∼

Wahida was so happy, she could scarcely move. Her
mother was going to arrive that evening and take her
home. She should have come for her on the fortieth day after
the wedding. But Amina was ill at the time, and Zohra was
looking after her in the hospital. So Sabia had arranged to do
the ceremony here, filling Wahida's lap with silk saris. Now,
Amina had been brought home, worn down, looking half her
original size. She absolutely refused to go to Zohra's house.
'Let my life end in the house my husband built for me,' she
declared. Wahida could not bear to look at Amina. She had

heard the expression, 'walking corpse'. It certainly applied to Amina, she thought.

All through the town, people gossiped about Firdaus's death, each offering their own version. Five or six women foregathered at Sabia's house every day, at about eleven in the morning, having finished all their chores. It seemed they had to tell tales about someone or the other, or else they could not live. Sikander always joined them, bantering with them and calling them cousin, or sister-in-law or aunt. For some days they had been talking about Firdaus constantly, imagining in detail what might have happened. Wahida found it unendurable. She murmured to Sikander, 'A well-placed family such as ours ought not to be gossiping about all that goes on in the town; it can only lead to our own ruin.' But he shut her up with a couple of words, 'Don't talk like an old woman.'

She had made it obvious several times that she did not like the way he flirted with these women, but he never gave any signs of taking notice of her disapproval. She felt a great relief that for a few days at least, in her mother's house, she would not have to see or hear these things which so distressed her. Above all, she would not be pestered by the old man. Even the thought of him made her whole self shrink and cringe.

During the past week, one day when Sabia was not at home, he came and sat by her and began to speak casually. He had rolled up his veshti and tucked it up between his thighs, and sat with his knees drawn up. 'The situation there hasn't stabilized, it seems. They are saying so on Radio Ceylon.' He sounded anxious and regretful. 'Heaven knows what has happened to my shop. And look at me, stuck here, not able to find out.'

For a moment, he was sunk in his thoughts, and she quickly took the opportunity to rise to her feet. But he took notice of it immediately and spoke authoritatively, 'Where are you off to? Sit down.'

She was frightened; her tongue was dry. She sat down again immediately. 'You only have to find a moment, you'll lock yourself in with your husband. A fine one you are!' He gave a salacious smile. She was fiercely embarrassed. Sikander was asleep upstairs, in their room. She understood what Sayyed was insinuating. He went on, 'No need to feel shy. I too was like that when I was young. Day and night, we used to stay together behind locked doors.' For an instant he revelled in his memories. He looked ecstatic. 'And was that all? Do you know how many women wanted to sleep with me because I was so handsome when I was young? You think your husband is handsome, don't you? You should ask Sabia what I used to be like. There were so many women who were after me. She knows very well. I used to come and tell her all about them. They were all my own relations.'

Suddenly he lowered his voice into a whisper. He brought his face close to Wahida's and said, 'Don't tell anyone, but I've even had it off with Amina.' As the spittle scattered from his mouth and an evil smell came out of it, Wahida knew for certain that he was lying. She hated him for it. He went on, taking no notice of the expression on her face. 'She used to be very attractive when she was little, and her husband was often away. I was lying on the thinnai one night, because it was so humid inside. Someone woke me up when I was half asleep. I looked up and saw Amina. And don't ask what went on in the store-room she took me to, among all the bundles and what-not. In the middle of it all, she said, Wait a bit, let me make myself more comfortable.' He struck his bare thigh with his right hand and began to cackle.

Suddenly she felt desperately sorry for him because all he could do was to comfort himself by telling her these imagined events. He looked at her as if it did not even occur to him that she might hate him or ridicule him. She thought she would have to use all her reserves of patience to deal with him. She did indeed feel sorry for him, for his impotence and his old age. At the same time, she wanted to be extremely careful not to give him the slightest encouragement, by any expression on her face.

'And then, listen to this.' Sayyed clicked his tongue as if in relish. He was glowing with pleasure. It seemed as if he was taking this opportunity to boast to her of all his sexual feats. 'Just think of it, I never hid even this from Sabia. She knows about every woman I have slept with, to this day. I would never keep anything from her. And she never scolded me, but only listened with interest. What do you think of that?'

Wahida put these thoughts behind her and began to pack her clothes in her suitcase. It was a long time since she had seen her parents. When they came for Firdaus's funeral, they had nodded to her from a distance, and left; it would not have been proper for them to come to Sabia's house. After that, since Amina went to hospital, and Zohra with her, it had been impossible for them to visit her. Wahida remembered how furious Sabia had been because Rabia had come to their house that day, when Firdaus was laid out.

Wahida longed for her mother. She wanted to tell her mother all the difficulties she was experiencing, and weep into her lap. But at the same time the question whether it would be possible to look at Rahima without embarrassment made her panic, bringing her mind to a standstill. She had been floating in a kind of joy because she would see her mother soon. Now the question burst through her, 'Why did she do it?' She tried to control her terror that something might happen to her mother, as it did to Firdaus.

She got up from the bed, stood in front of the full-length mirror and stared at her own reflection. The image she saw there seemed to bear no resemblance to herself. It indicated quite clearly how much thinner she had grown, and this made her anxious. She wondered why she should not stay away from this house; never return to it again. How could she manage that? She had a sudden illusion that many years had passed by since she entered this house, and that many events had come to a conclusion. She was aware that she had come to understand much more about the world since her arrival here. She imagined herself as a knowledgeable middle aged woman. Yet the face she saw in the mirror still had a childish quality about it. There were a couple of pimples which showed up against the light complexion of her cheeks and forehead. It could be because it would soon be that time of the month for her when she was not allowed to pray. She was greatly relieved. Thank Heavens, she muttered to herself. She could not have conceived. She returned to the bed and sat down again, and realized that her fear had ebbed away to a great extent. Even when she menstruated the first time, Sabia had shown her displeasure clearly. Even Sayyed had made his complaints. She had felt deeply ashamed. All the women who lived along their street had come and comisserated. A few had comforted Sabia, saying, 'Don't worry; it will stop next month.' Wahida had been shocked by all this. Something that was her own private affair, which had always been kept hidden, was now the talk of everyone in the town.

This month she would menstruate in her mother's house. There too, she had noticed how the womenfolk would probe and pry into other people's lives. Mumtaz Anni had been pestered to death by them. She knew that they would question her too, continuously. The very thought of it dulled her enthusiasm to go home; yet the relief that she could not have conceived was too great. Nothing in this house was to her liking. She could only resolve that she must go away now, and never come back. Every time she thought of this house, images of Sabia blowing her nose into her handkerchief as she cooked and Sayyed stroking his thighs as he talked salaciously rose in her mind, driving her away.

She opened her wardrobe and began to pack all her jewellery into her case. She was never going to return, so why leave them here? Sabia had given her orders to Sikander that he was to bring back the fortieth day wedding gifts in abundance. 'Your father-in-law has not given all the wedding gifts in the proper way. They didn't even send us a full vessel of athirsam on the wedding day itself. There weren't enough coconuts and fruit either. And what about the seventh day celebration? Your mother-in-law just threw down a hundred athirsam and went her way. How was I to distribute the wedding sweets to all our relations here? They were all asking, why Sabia, aren't there any wedding sweets for us? They are perfectly capable of decking out their daughter in jewellery from head to toe, after all! They claim they are spending lakhs on this wedding; they can't even send their new in-laws the proper sweets. Wretched fellows! Wretched whore of a woman! You just tell that wife of yours that they should do it all decently this time at least.' Sabia poured all this out in one breath.

Sikander gave it back to her sharply. 'What is the matter with you? It's not as if you don't have anything of your own! Anyway, they are not a family of beggars, they are your own brothers, aren't they? They will give you whatever you ask for, won't they?

Sabia blew her nose for a long time after that, lamenting, 'She's got you under her spell, hasn't she? Otherwise you wouldn't talk like this, would you?'

He took no notice at all of what she said. He just walked away, silently. Wahida, standing there and weeping, was very pleased that he had stood up for her family and its honour. But although she was aware of that spurt of affection for him, she knew that there was every possibility it would melt away.

Wahida found it humiliating that Sabia always accused her of having cast a spell on Sikander. She had no idea what Sabia meant by it. Whenever Sabia spoke those words, Wahida could only bring to mind a cinema actress wearing indecent and flimsy clothes, trying to seduce the hero of a film. Sometimes she even wanted to laugh. But usually she just gritted her teeth and counted the days that were left for her here, forced to listen to such nonsense. She thought to herself that her father – who had been so happy in the thought that he had given his daughter into the safe-keeping of his own sister, so certain of his daughter's future happiness that he had not found a reason to come and visit her after she left her parents' home – would surely be shocked at the sight of her, on her return. But he was going to be even more shocked at what she proposed to tell him. She dug out of her memory every instance of Sabia's complaints against her and her family, made a list of them like a child, and tucked them away in her mind. This was a great consolation to her.

☙ 56 ❧

Wahida was surprised to find that her home had changed entirely and was strangely quiet. Zohra's face looked wilted and without animation. Even her mother looked as if she had suffered a loss of some kind. The instant Rahima saw her daughter, half her life seemed to ebb away. Clearly she was half dead with worry about how to restore Wahida's health; but even so, seemed curiously withdrawn and at a distance. Sabia had insisted that Sikander should return home the very next day after bringing Wahida. According to her, if a woman had sex at the end of her monthly cycle, any embryo in the making would dissolve. So she had warned Sikander not to touch his wife during her last week. He was due to go abroad very soon, besides. If a child were conceived by then, he could go away without any worries, Sabia thought.

Wahida was much relieved when Sikander left. If it became certain that she had conceived, Sabia would buy him his plane ticket the very next day and send him off. That would be fine too. He would not come back for two or three years. But the thought that she must bear a child to achieve that was painful to her. When she disliked the man himself, why did she need his child?

Rabia lay on Wahida's lap all the time. She never ventured outside any more. It was she who told Wahida, 'Akka, it seems that Amma and Periamma are going their separate ways. They want to build a wall through the house.' From this one piece of news, Wahida could infer several things. She realized that when Zohra was with Amina at the hospital, she would have been told the whole truth. However she was still not sure whether Rahima's withdrawal from her was because of that, or whether she, Wahida, were imagining all of it. She tried to convince herself that it was indeed her imagination, for surely Rahima continued to be loving and affectionate even when she need not be.

However, she had hoped for some peace and quiet when she came home and Rabia's news was a bitter disappointment. The unnatural silence in the house, and the way everyone went about their business wordlessly troubled and pained her. She had hoped to share her experiences at Sabia's house with her own family and seek some comfort, but was confused now, not knowing to whom she could speak. There were some things that she could not tell her mother. Specifically, she had thought to tell Zohra alone about Sayyed's behaviour and speech. But Zohra went about with such a grim face that Wahida began to wonder whether she was angry with her. It seemed that no one was talking to anyone else properly. True, her mother made her different kinds of soup each day and made her eat. She oiled and combed Wahida's hair; rubbed it with oil and washed it for her. Yet all the time something kept her from drawing close to Wahida. Realizing this, Wahida was gnawed with anxiety. Had Rahima realized that Wahida knew her secret?

By eleven in the morning, all the women who lived along their street finished their chores and began to arrive to meet Wahida: Sherifa, Nafiza. Mumtaz, Sainu and Saura were all there. Nafiza looked care-worn, not as sprightly as before. Wahida remembered what Mumtaz had told her, when she came to announce Farida's wedding.

Each one of the women repeatedly remarked on how thin Wahida had become. Mumtaz asked, laughing, 'Why, di, don't they feed you at all in that house?'

'What a question,' Saura scoffed. 'As if that wretched woman is likely to look after the child properly. Heaven knows how she lashed at her with her tongue.' She stopped short, as if full of concern, expecting that Wahida would agree.

But Rahima had warned Wahida, as soon as she arrived. 'The women who come to visit will ask you about your husband and your in-laws, and pester the life out of you, all ready to carry the ember of one hearth to nine different households. So, whatever they ask, you please just smile and be quiet. If anything you say gets back to your in-laws, there will be trouble.' So Wahida stayed silent, neither agreeing with Saura nor disagreeing.

Sherifa cut in and scolded her mother. 'Unless you hear all the town's gossip, you won't sleep, will you?' It distressed Sherifa greatly, to see Wahida. Her eyes no longer appeared bright. Leave the in-laws aside, had Wahida liked her husband even a little bit, she would not look quite so unhappy, Sherifa thought.

Saura was annoyed with her daughter and complained, 'Look at this one, she can never be happy without blaming me for something or the other.' Then she asked Wahida again, 'Well, amma, have you had your period yet, or have some days gone by since you were due?'

Wahida knew that she was forced into giving an answer and had just opened her mouth when her mother interrupted and said briefly, as if to put an end to the conversation, 'She still has some days to go.'

Although Sherifa and the rest understood why Rahima had spoken up, Saura was not prepared to let go. 'How can that be? She had her period just after she got married. So she should be due just about now.' She tried to count the days on her fingers, bending and straightening them. Struck by another doubt, she turned to Wahida and asked, 'By the way, he has slept with you, hasn't he?'

At this, Rahima's features hardened with annoyance. Sainu, for her turn, laughed and said, 'As if these girls nowadays need to be told how to sleep with their husbands!' Everyone joined in the laughter. Zohra, not wishing to stay there any longer, rose to her feet and disappeared into the kitchen. Wahida reflected remorsefully that nobody took any notice of the sadness in her aunt's face, but continued to laugh and joke as they wished.

The moment Zohra left, Sainu came and whispered in her ear, as if she had been waiting for just that opportunity, 'Do you know anything about her sister's death? They say she took poison and died.'

Wahida began to shake with fear. She shook her head violently as if to say, 'I don't know anything about it.'

Saura put in casually, 'That's what happens if you are impudent enough to go grazing round the town.'

'Come on, just tell us what they are saying over there. It seems your Chitthi has quarrelled with your mother, besides, and is planning on setting up her own kitchen,' Mumtaz persisted.

Wahida knew what she was insinuating. But Rahima answered in her place, once again. 'There is no quarrel at all, as you seem to think. It's just that our men consider it best to separate.' She was horrified that these women should know so much about their affairs, and was anxious to conclude this conversation before Zohra returned.

Sherifa was desperate to change the topic of conversation, but didn't know how. As for Nafiza, she listened to what was being said, but never opened her mouth. Saura began to speak of Firdaus yet again. 'By the way, did that girl come back to haunt anyone? I meant to ask this earlier, but forgot.' Eager as she was, she had lowered her voice, anxious that Zohra should not overhear.

Wahida opened her mouth for the first time, to say, 'Ché ché, there's been nothing like that.' She was reminded of her mother-in-law, who always spoke of this.

Saura began to get bored and irritated. This girl was not going to give anything away. Thinking that she should get away, she asked, 'So what have you cooked in your house today? It must be something special; your daughter has come home.'

Rahima understood from the way Saura asked her question, that she hoped to take something home for her meal. 'It's meat and mocchai beans in a tamarind based sauce. Would you like to take some with you?' She went off towards the kitchen, anxious to send Saura away, by whatever means. Sherifa was deeply embarrassed by her mother, and looked at Wahida as if to say, 'However much I tell her, she never takes it in. What can I do?'

The mid-day call for prayers sounded from the mosque. At once, all the woman fell silent. Saura, who had risen to her feet, sat down again, waiting for the initial call to end.

Saura's request for the curry reminded Wahida of her mother-in-law. Sabia was the same; she always brought home a little of whatever was cooked in the houses she visited. When Wahida and she were working in the kitchen, she had many stories to tell as she chopped the vegetables. Wahida, trying to make out the point of these stories, found that most of them were to do with food. Whenever she recalled an event, she remembered a dish that she had eaten at the time. If the talk turned to the summer heat of Chittirai, she would remark, her mouth watering at her own words, 'You should eat a curry of dal during that month. The new crop of tamarind is just ripe then; and it is during that month that mangos and murungai are all in season. A dal curry comes out at its tastiest then. It's also the season when the ponds dry out, and you get plenty of fish. You get good sized viral fish, too.' In the same way, she would expound on harvest time, and all the sweetmeats made out of the new rice.

When she wanted to describe her father's tenderness towards her, she would say, 'Why, Wahida, do you know how much my father – your grandfather, that is – doted on me? When I returned home to my parents' house, your grandfather would come rushing from his work to see me, in the height of the noon-day heat. And he would never, not for once, come back empty handed. There were always his farm-labourers following him, their arms full of duck and chicken and fish. Just think that all this would have been taken to the mosque and slaughtered all ready. Then he'd make a fuss and drive everyone about their business saying "My daughter will be hungry, hurry up and get it ready." And he'd watch over me while I sat down and ate. He doted on me that much.' She would melt at her own words.

It was the same when she spoke of Sayyed's love for her. 'This father-in-law of yours, do you know how much he loves me? You've seen yourself that he never likes to eat without me. That man will not allow me to eat by myself.' She spoke with pride.

Wahida remarked, 'Of course, when Maamu goes abroad again, he'll have to eat on his own, won't he?'

Unaware of the teasing tone, Sabia answered, 'Of course he must eat on his own when he goes abroad. What can he do about it? Does all life come to a stop because the monkey died?'

It was astonishing to Wahida that nothing seemed to impress Sabia apart from things to do with food and eating. How was it that she could only remember all past events through their association with food?

Wahida wrenched her thoughts away and turned to Sainu, 'Well, Kuppi, it seems that Madina has come of age?'

'Yes, amma. It's as if the over-eager calf has had its leg broken. Come and see the child, one of these days.'

Rahima, coming with a dish of the tamarind curry for Sabia, said, 'Sainu Akka has just pushed one daughter out of the house, and now another one is ready.'

'Yes; what else? Now we have to look for a bridegroom for the next one. We have to collect everything that is needed. We must get started on all that, otherwise it will never get done in time.' Sainu sounded anxious.

'Don't let it get you down. If your other two had been normal, there would have been four daughters to see to. Now it's only two,' Nafiza put in, having been quiet all this time.

'Yes, that is true enough. But better they should leave this world rather than remain in this pitiful state.' Sainu's face tightened with sorrow.

Zohra emerged from the kitchen, wiping her hands with the

end of her sari, as if she had been busy. She came into the hall and sat with the other women. Wahida knew, from her expression, that she did not want the rest to assume she had been hiding.

As soon as Zohra arrived, Saura went up to her, still carrying her dish, and assuming an expression of great concern. 'Well, Zohra,' she said, 'you could bring your mother here and look after her, couldn't you? How is her health these days?'

Wahida found it surprising that this woman who had been pestering and probing her a little while ago should suddenly put on this look of sympathy and concern. At the same time, all the other women assumed appropriate expressions and prepared to listen to Zohra. Clearly, Zohra's grief was renewed by Saura's question and her apparent pity, however doubtful her real feelings. Involuntarily, Zohra's eyes filled and her throat choked. Unable to say anything, she dropped her head in confusion. Everyone there was distressed by the state of her, and sat quietly, exchanging glances.

Wahida was furious with Saura, wondering why the woman was showing so much concern. Rahima watched with anguish as Zohra's wounds seemed to reopen.

Saura went on, with a great sigh, 'What can we say. That was all that young girl had in her destiny. That was all the food and water that was meant for her in this world. There is nothing at all that anyone could have done. How she was, firm as a banana plant. How her hair tumbled down, right to the ground. The sight of it, as they bathed her, tore at the guts of everyone there.' Saura's face was sunk in extreme sorrow. Her voice truly had a timbre of sadness. Wahida observed that all the other faces too reflected that sorrow, as if in agreement. None of them seemed to be pretending, either.

Sainu assumed the right to advise Zohra. She said, 'What has happened, has happened; a life has gone forever. But you have to look after the life that is left behind, don't you? You are your mother's only support now. Will you bring her here and keep her with you, or will you leave her there, all by herself?'

Wahida noticed how strangely Sainu's long face and the long knot at the back of her head wagged up and down as she spoke. She was so absorbed in what she was saying that she had not noticed that her feet were pointing towards the west. Wahida wished she could point this out.

Zohra spoke with despair. 'She refuses to come away, Akka. I've tried my best to persuade her. She insists stubbornly that she will live out her life in the house her husband built for her.' Zohra blew her nose. Her eyes and the tip of her nose were red. Wahida could hardly bear to look at her. She thought to herself that her aunt had surely gauged whether the love and concern the women there were displaying, was real or not.

Saura spoke up in support of Amina. 'What she says is true enough. Whatever the reason, how can she leave the house her husband built for her?' She had stood up ready to leave sometime ago and remained as she was, reluctant to sit down again because of the difficulty in heaving herself up. The room filled with the aroma of the curry she held in her hand. Nobody said anything more for awhile.

'How many more days will you stay here, Wahida? Until Bakr Id, will it be?' Sherifa asked, hoping to change the topic of conversation.

'I don't know,' Wahida shook her head in reply.

'We don't have to keep count of the days when our child comes home to us. Let her stay as long as she likes,' Rahima said.

'Of course you'll say that. But her husband and mother-in-law have to agree, don't they? Hereafter they'll have the last word,' Sherifa pointed out.

'Don't mention that woman. She's not going to make haste to take her daughter-in-law home. She'll save herself the expense, won't she? Miserly wretch,' Nafiza said, ridiculing Sabia. Everyone there had to agree.

At last Saura moved towards the door, saying, 'Well, I must go; it is time for prayers.' One by one, all the women rose to their feet, preparing to leave.

Just at that time, Suleiman, returning from the mosque, heard the noise of the women conversing, and stepped inside the house. As soon as they saw him, Zohra and Rahima stood up in consternation, pulling their saris well over their heads, and welcomed him. Meanwhile, Wahida and Sherifa fled inside, also covering their heads.

'Thank you, I'll come in,' Suleiman said. 'But I noticed two people running and hiding as soon as they saw me. Who were they?' He gave a flick at the sofa with his handkerchief and sat down.

'Who do you think it was? Just your Maamu's daughters, Sherifa and Wahida, that's all,' Sainu assured him.

'Oh, so our girls know how to be modest, do they?' Suleiman widened his eyes, pretending to be surprised. He asked Rahima, 'Has Maamu not returned yet? It seems I'm the first one to come home after the prayers.' He stopped Saura who was trying to leave. 'Wait a moment Mammani, and listen to this news.'

'Well, hurry up and tell us, then,' Mumtaz scolded him affectionately. 'Don't I have to go home and serve your meal?'

Rahima had fetched a glass of buttermilk. Suleiman demurred. 'What is this? Buttermilk? No, thanks, I'm just about to go home.' She insisted, however, and he accepted the glass from her. 'It's very hot isn't it? It's really killing me. You'll never get a climate as pleasant as Singapore's, though.'

'Tell us your news. I must go soon,' Mumtaz scolded him again.

Suleiman took his time. 'Do you people know what's happened? You remember that Fatima who eloped a little while ago?' He paused for a moment and gazed at all the faces around him. Then he announced with a flourish, 'The whore is dead. We have just got the information.'

Everyone there looked both surprised and scared. Clearly, no one could believe their ears. Sherifa and Wahida, listening inside, were shocked by the way he could announce the news of a death with such glee. They looked at each other, trying to take in both the news and the manner in which it was told.

Saura, coming to herself after an instant, asked, 'What are you saying? How can you tell us such an important thing so casually?'

Sainu rushed in with her questions, one after another, 'What happened? How? Who told you?'

Suleiman was even more buoyed up by the effect of his news upon them. He fully intended to use this opportunity to tell them all he knew, and to make the most of it. 'Do you see how Allah has punished her? What did that runaway whore do? What were her thoughts, do you suppose? And look what happened to her. Would He let her get away with it? He knows everything. Is there a secret that is hidden from Him? How mighty is He?' Suleiman said all this with great satisfaction. 'The two of them set up a household in Madurai. Yesterday, she set off for the market. She was run over – we don't know whether it was a bus or a lorry.'

Sherifa was disgusted by the way he told his story with such relish. It was a good thing they did not marry her to him, her Kuppi's son. She felt sorry for Mumtaz, and a great sorrow for Fatima.

'Oh what a terrible thing,' Saura remarked. 'And how did you get to know this?'

'The information was sent to us from the police station there. That fellow asked if her body should be brought here. The Jamaat has sent word that it would be impossible; they could bury or burn it wherever they chose, but they must not bring it here. We have just discussed the affair and sent word. Who knows what they will do to an unclaimed body, bury it or burn it! See what came to her, and how quickly, the whore. I never thought He would give her what she deserved so soon. The Lord is great, isn't He?' He spoke with pride.

Nafiza gave a great sigh. 'Her fate took her to that place. It was destined that Israel should pluck away her life there and then.' She realized that although so much time had passed since Fatima's death was announced, it had not occurred to her or anyone else there to say the prayer for the dead. Raising her voice, as if to remind the others, she spoke it aloud: *Inna illahi va inna illaihi raji han* , From God do we come and to God do we return. Immediately all the other women chanted it together. More than the shock of the news, their faces registered their shock for forgetting to say the prayer. Rahima and Zohra were the most distressed. Nafiza felt she had accomplished something important.

Suleiman, proud that his mission was accomplished satisfactorily, went away, saying 'Asalaamu aleikum'. Rahima and Zohra stood stock still, unable even to reply to his salaam. Mumtaz followed him out. Nafiza said her goodbyes and left. Sherifa and Wahida came out of their hiding, still shocked and silent. Sainu stumbled over her words, 'Well, we can't change her fate, can we? She got the punishment she deserved. He knows all secrets.' She too went on her way, saying, 'Ele, Rahima, bring your daughter over to our house this evening. Let it be her formal visit for Madina's coming of age. Besides, Farida is at her mother-in-law's place now. Tell Wahida to call on her as well.'

When they had all left, Wahida, Zohra and Rahima stood there for awhile, quietly. Then the two older women busied themselves with their work while Wahida's mind filled with pain.

๑ 57 ๑

When she heard from Rabia that the family was splitting up, Wahida went to her mother and asked, 'Is it true, Amma, what she says?' Rahima's heart missed a beat. 'Yes,' she said briefly, slipping away from there like smoke blown away by the wind.

When Zohra made that request, the very day after she brought Amina home, Rahima had no idea what her reason was; she only understood that her sister-in-law spoke out of some anger. Later, when she went to fetch Wahida home, she

visited Amina. Amina clutched hold of Rahima with her thin
hands and wept for a long time. More certain of herself in
Zohra's absence, Amina poured out the truth about Firdaus's
death in complete detail. When she finished speaking, Rahima
shrank within herself, in horror. She left for home without a
word.

How could something done unthinkingly, a long time ago,
turn up in the present, assuming such monstrous proportions?
She could not remind herself of what had happened in the past.
She did not have the strength of mind to do so; she knew that
well enough. She had decided to forget the incident totally,
had refused to allow any confusion in her mind or thought;
yet now she shrank with the shame of it. She struggled hard,
and indeed tortured herself, to ensure that her daughter was
not aware of her continuous sense of guilt. She could not
understand how an error committed a long time ago, for which
she had suffered, repented, and at last forgiven herself, should
become known, so cruelly, at just this time. She felt as if her
heart were like a piece of old cloth, wrung out and limp. She
had no means of knowing what was in Wahida's mind, yet did
not have the courage even to stand in front of her. The fear
that her daughter might hate her haunted her all the time and
kept her awake. During the day she went about without
animation. It seemed to her that she kept her distance from
Wahida, and at the same time, heaped her with love and
affection.

Besides this, she was racked by the anxiety that Wahida was
perhaps not happy in her husband's house. It seemed to her
that Sikander and Wahida did not even talk to each other with
any degree of closeness. Yet she hoped that this was her
imagination, and resolved upon a three month fast for the
sake of her daughter's happiness. She forced herself away from
her thoughts, fearing that her reddened eyes and swollen face
would distress and confuse Wahida. She remembered it was a
Friday, that it reflected badly on the family for her to weep on
an auspicious day and busied herself with her chores. Yet all

the time, she trembled inwardly, imagining that Wahida was watching her closely.

Wahida had washed her hair, and was combing it out. The water dripped off it. Rahima, standing by the hearth, cooking, saw her at a distance and hurried up to her saying, 'Why have you left your hair so wet; won't you catch a cold?' She picked up a towel which was hanging on the line outside, and began to dry Wahida's hair. As Wahida sat in front of her, leaning back conveniently, Rahima hesitated, thought for awhile and finally asked her question. 'Well, amma, how many days is it if you add today? Tell me properly.' Although it was embarrassing to ask this, Rahima thought it was her duty to do so.

Wahida felt shy. Her face reddened; she shrank away. Rahima spoke anxiously, 'Just tell me, amma. It's only I, your mother, who asks. I had been planning to go to the dargah today. I've made a vow to light the lamps there for seven Fridays. I thought I would take you with me this Friday. It might be good to finish it today.'

Since she was a child, Wahida never gave away her feelings quickly, either by expression or gesture. Zohra would say, 'Your daughter is a close one. Has she ever been one to dance or sing spontaneously? Look at mine – she's always prancing about, always singing away. Is she like a girl?' It was not clear whether she was praising Wahida or scolding Rabia. Her face showed pride and annoyance equally. It struck Rahima, suddenly, that Zohra was absolutely right. In the old days, her daughter's silence needed no interpretation; today it could mean a thousand things, she thought, with pain. 'She's an enigma,' Rahima muttered to herself, troubled that Wahida gave no answer. If she could be sure that Wahida was just shy, she would be at peace. But was she silent because she disliked that very idea of bearing a child? Or did she indeed dislike the idea of discussing it with her mother? Rahima just could not make it out. Her hands fell away as if she didn't have the strength to dry her daughter's hair any more. She got up and went into her room, took out some clothes and jewellery for Wahida to wear, and spread them all out on the bed. She hoped Wahida would not refuse her this time.

Wahida, following her, looked about her as if to ask, 'What is all this for?'

Rahima, certain that she must reply to the unspoken question, said, 'It is Friday today. We must visit Farida in her husband's house. We have to look in on Madina. She was so much part of our family, and she's been asking for you.'

Wahida thought of her Chitthi. She could not feel happy about dressing herself up. She put aside everything that was spread out on the bed, saying softly, 'No, Amma. Chitthi is still mourning. I can't feel happy about dressing up in all this. Let it be another day.'

Rahima understood her daughter's hesitation, yet could not agree with her. Wahida too was a new bride. If she could not dress up now, when would she do so? She thought for awhile and then said, 'What can we do about it? Of course I feel badly about it too. But she cannot observe any celebration for a whole year. What will you do all that time?' Rahima was anxious to come to an understanding with her daughter before Zohra could emerge from her bath.

Wahida was firm in her refusal, however. 'No, Amma. How can we get along as a family, then? Can I say one thing to her face, and then do something else behind her back?' Rahima was pleased that Wahida was at least breaking her silence and speaking to her. Perhaps she had been imagining all sorts of things and worrying unnecessarily. She had been wrong, she told herself; Wahida held nothing against her mother. Feeling much happier, she returned to her work in the kitchen without wishing to say anything more. After a while, she noticed that Zohra had come out of her bath, and was helping Wahida to dress and putting her at her ease. The household had not lost its harmony entirely.

* * *

The late afternoon sun fell directly on their faces, burning them. As she walked along, Rahima wiped her face with the dupatta covering her. In a little wire basket she carried the oil for the lamps, wicks, the money offering and her book of prayers. She had vowed to light the lamps at the dargah for seven consecutive Fridays. Saura and Sainu followed her, swaying from side to side. They did not have the ability to keep up with her pace.

Saura struggled to walk, dragging her heavy body. It irritated Rahima to have to walk so slowly along with them. She felt sorry that she had been forced to go with them, for lack of any other company. Zohra had refused to come, following Firdaus's death. 'What's the use? I'm not going to do it anymore,' she declared. Saura and Sainu had pleaded with her, saying it was not good to stop the series mid-way. But Zohra refused to listen. 'There is nothing more that can happen to me,' she insisted.

Sainu had placed her hand over Zohra's mouth and scolded, 'What is this, di, it's a big thing you are saying. You have a young daughter, whose whole life is ahead of her. Don't blurt out all this in your distress. If you stop lighting the lamps now, won't the saints be angry with you?'

Rahima turned round and hurried the two older women. 'Come on, hurry up. The heat is unbearable. Let's get inside the dargah quickly.' She wiped her face again. It was quite inflamed.

'Ss! Just wait a bit, we're coming,' Sainu said. 'It's because you vowed you'd walk all the way there and light the lamps that we have to make this trip in the burning heat. Otherwise we could have come by car, at least.' She made a great effort and walked a little faster. Saura, unable to do even that, trailed behind.

Along with the heat, a hot wind blew, making Sainu feel even worse. 'This is not like the usual heat of Chittirai. It takes it out of you.' She began to complain about Zohra. 'Why is that woman being so high and mighty? Which of us doesn't have her own troubles? Heaven knows what sin her younger sister committed; anyway she's dead and gone now. So what can any of us do about it? Look at this Fatima who went and eloped. Did Allah let her off? Instead of letting it all go, she has to plead her sister's case saying she was such a virtuous woman. And all the time she has this little daughter, bright as a banana shoot.' Sainu gazed at Rahima as she walked on, expecting an answer.

Rahima turned her face away, wondering what possible pleasure there could be in getting her to tell tales. She tried to put a stop to the conversation. 'Akka, I've done my ritual ablutions, so let's not speak now. What do we gain by talking about it, anyhow? And if I break the rules, where will I do the olu ablutions again?'

Her sharp response and her faint indication of displeasure irritated Sainu. 'Oh yes, just remember that we have done our ablutions too, you are not the only one. I know very well that you are not one to give anything away about your sister-in-law.'

Saura intervened at this point, scolding Sainu fondly, saying, 'Listen, Sainu, don't you know this one will never open her mouth? She has such a firm affection for her sister-in-law. Did you imagine it was anything less than that?' She smiled at Rahima, hoping that her flattery might get something out of her. But Rahima merely returned a quiet smile, repeating her daspih prayers under her breath as she walked on.

Because it was the road that led into town, lines of buses, lorries and cars went past them constantly. The heat crossed the town slowly, hesitantly, as if it were unsure of what it was doing. Before them and behind them, there were five or six women, also on their way to the dargah. Rahima was surprised at herself. In earlier times, she never went to the dargah. These were shrines where male saints were buried. She had listened to the Hadiths that Kader cited in regard to them: Women were forbidden go there; and to offer prayers there was to compare the saints who were buried there to Allah himself;

Allah would never forgive that. Rahima asked herself why she had begun to come to the dargah now, without her husband's knowledge. With what belief? Or rather in what state of anxiety and disbelief did she come here?

She was aware that in her anxiety for her daughter's happiness she was prepared to do anything. This was why she had changed. All the vows and fasts she had undertaken – the Sayyed Ali fast, three month fast, the lamps at the dargah, the vow to visit the dargah at Nagore and Yerwadi – all these were only for Wahida's happiness. When she thought of this, she even feared for her own sanity. She longed for the clarity of a single belief that was beyond all this. Sainu too had made a vow in the hope of securing Farida's marriage – that was why she came to the dargah, without Suleiman's knowledge. It was doubtful that she would have survived, without this last hope.

☙ 58 ☙

It was a week since school reopened. Zohra had declared that Rabia need not study anymore. Rabia had pleaded and begged as much as she dared. But Zohra had made her decision the day after Madina menstruated. She said, 'It's enough for you to stay at home, and be a well-behaved girl. Madina is not going to school any more; I don't want you to go alone.'

Rabia said she would go with Uma. Zohra scolded, 'Uma belongs to a Hindu labouring family. You cannot go unless there is someone from our street with you.' Rabia was extremely disappointed by this.

Rahima said, 'She's only in the seventh; don't stop her just yet.'

Zohra was sharp. 'It's impossible,' she said firmly. She wasn't prepared to listen to anyone after that.

Both Rahima and Wahida noticed that Zohra was even more intent than before on disciplining and controlling Rabia. Wahida had even said to her mother, 'That poor child! She's being caged inside the house even before she's come of age.'

Rahima replied, 'You don't know what they are saying in this town about Zohra's family. Even Saura has whispered to me, "Amina's daughter was the same as Amina's sister. It's happening generation after generation, you see. It's not for nothing they say you have to look to the lineage of a family." Zohra is scared to death by all this. She's killing the little girl with her over-protection.'

Wahida was troubled by all this. She remembered that when she went to visit Madina the other day, she had asked eagerly whether Rabia would be going to school anymore. She would be delighted by the news. She had said, childishly, 'If Rabia is here, then we could chat together all the time; I won't be bored at all.'

That year, on the last day of the month of Safar, Rabia had gone to the Hazrat's house after her bath early in the morning and had brought home six or seven mango leaves on which he had written appropriate texts in ink. She had given them to Wahida, saying, 'Akka, wash these off in water, and then drink some of the water and give me the rest.' Rabia had looked eager and anxious at the same time. Just as soon as they had drunk the water, Rabia ran to her mother and asked, 'Amma, may I go with up the mountain this afternoon to walk on the grass, along with all the other women?'

'None of that for you. Suppose you get your period suddenly, when you are up there?' Zohra spoke casually, and busied herself with the special lunch which would be blessed.

Wahida pressed her aunt. 'Why, Chitthi? Why can't you let her go? The whole town is going.'

'You don't understand, Wahida. If she gets her period suddenly and becomes a prey for ghosts and spirits, we can't do anything about it. Let her get married, she can go after that. Last year and the year before that, she was still a little girl, and went as she pleased; no one stopped her. So why complain now?' Zohra spoke with determination.

Wahida could say nothing more. As for Rabia, she dressed

up in her new clothes and put flowers in her hair, but could do nothing other than weep the whole day.

Just before the yearly examination, too, Zohra gave her daughter a difficult time. Wahida remembered with much sadness, how Zohra would nag at Rabia, even if she picked up a book. 'How is it going to help you, to be studying all the time? It's not as if you are going to become a Collector or something, is it? You are going to menstruate this year or the next, and that will be it. Isn't it enough that you just pass? You've got your head in your books night and day. What use is it to a girl? Doesn't your head ache?'

Whenever Wahida advised Rabia to work hard for her examinations, the little girl would answer, 'But Akka, what will I gain by studying so hard? Anyway they will take me out of school very soon.' The regret in the girl's voice pained Wahida.

Zohra had changed; she wasn't as before. The strained expression with which her aunt went about all the time took all the joy out of Wahida's return home. Arrangements had been made already, for a wall to be raised right through the house. Even that morning, various people had come to measure the house. Neither Kader nor Karim said a word openly about the division of the property. They acted as if there was some quarrel which affected only the women.

Apparently, Zohra had said just one thing to Karim, 'I want to bring my mother to live with me. That's why I want us to separate.' Karim reported this to Kader, who agreed that it was reasonable enough. After that, nobody dared to argue against it. Only Zohra, Rahima and Wahida knew the real reason why Zohra was determined to separate the joint family.

Wahida began to feel as if she were in a hellish place. She had hoped to escape from her mother-in-law's house forever and never again leave her parents' house. But she found it unbearable to watch Zohra's aloofness, Rahima's strange reticence and Rabia, brought low at so young an age and lying huddled up next to her cousin, caged within the room. Her mind was in a turmoil, not knowing who to blame. She even thought of returning to Sabia's house, but instantly called to mind Sayyed's features, followed by Sabia's words and her handkerchief, and felt herself tremble.

Rousing herself from her thoughts, she asked herself how many days had passed since she last menstruated. Thirty one or thirty two? Normally she had a regular cycle of thirty days. Why was she late, she wondered, with sudden fear. Involuntarily her hand went up to her forehead and cheeks, touched her pimples, and was satisfied. She went up to the mirror and stared at herself. She stroked the pimple which stood on her cheek, swollen and red. The sight pleased her greatly, and she give a little pinch. It hurt, but was comforting at the same time, though the spot reddened a little more against her light skin. The sari she wore, with its black background, stood out strikingly. She looked much healthier since her return. She tried to remember whether Sikander had mentioned her good looks even once. He fell on her like an animal, at night. That was all. She asked herself whether she wanted him to appreciate her beauty or praise it. She knew the answer to that. No, she did not. She was pleased that this was so. Immediately she thought of how Sayyed pestered her with his supposedly appreciative remarks all the time, and brushed away the memory. She was afraid she would drive herself mad by thinking of this and that. She wished she could talk to someone, and looked across at Rabia, asleep on her bed. It was nearly time for the Asar prayers; she should wake her and talk to her a little. She went and sat on the bed and began to scratch her feet in an attempt to wake her. How could this girl who always asked a thousand questions, and never stood still a moment, lie there, looking so broken and oppressed?

Rahima came in, a plate in her hand. She put it down on the bed, and made to leave, saying, 'Here's some puffed rice for the two of you. After you've eaten it, you can have some tea.'

Wahida stopped her, saying, 'I haven't said my prayers yet,

Amma. Keep it by, outside. It's going to be messy here.'

'As if it's likely the two of you will finish it off,' Rahima complained, leaving the room with her plate. Rabia got up and went to wash her face. Wahida heard her mother's footsteps again. It was a sound she had always loved, since she was a child. She walked as quietly as a cat. Only the gentle tinkle of her toe-rings announced her arrival. She looked up enquiringly. Rahima stood there, hesitantly.

After a moment, Rahima said, 'It's nothing, but you are late now by a couple of days, aren't you? So just stay in bed quietly for a bit. There's no rush to even to say your prayers. You can see to all that later.'

Wahida could see clearly that her mother's face had grown pale before she finished speaking. Why was Rahima so afraid to speak up? She must indeed feel at a great distance from Wahida, in that case. If Wahida were to make no reply, Rahima would sure feel deeply hurt. She said, 'No, Amma; just look at the pimples all over my face.' She was sure her meaning was plain.

Rahima understood what her daughter was saying. All the same, she said, 'Never mind. You take some rest; nothing wrong in that.' She left the room, satisfied that Wahida had at least answered her.

Rabia returned to the room, having washed her face. She lay down once more, her head on Wahida's lap. 'Still sleepy?' Wahida asked, patting her face. 'Get up now; I'll comb your hair for you.'

Rabia sat up without a word, undid her plait and turned around, allowing Wahida to comb out her hair. Wahida took up Rabia's hair with both hands and began combing it very gently so that she would feel no pain. Struck by a thought, Rabia turned round suddenly and looked Wahida in the eye. 'Why didn't you go on a journey anywhere after you were married?'

Wahida remembered that she had promised Rabia to take

her on a train journey somewhere, after her wedding. It distressed her now that Rabia should have kept it in mind, and wondered what to say. But Rabia went on, 'I asked Periamma about it. She told me that if you went anywhere before forty days were over, the ghosts and spirits would smell the scent of flowers on you and grab hold of you.'

It was a relief for Wahida that Rabia had given her own answer. She said nothing, but continued to comb the girl's hair. She saw the lice running here and there, and scolded, 'Look at this, di, you have all this hair, don't you ever comb out the lice?' She went up to her almirah, brought out a fine-toothed comb, and began to comb out the lice.

'Akka, when you comb my hair, it feels just as if Firdaus Chitthi were combing it. It doesn't hurt in the least,' Rabia remarked. 'When I remember Chitthi, I want to weep.' Wahida felt a sharp pain. Rabia went on, 'My Chitthi was so good. She really doted on me, didn't she, Akka?'

Wahida's throat felt choked at the sadness in Rabia's voice; she could not answer. She could only murmured in agreement. The tears rose up to screen her eyes. Quickly she said, 'Just a minute; I'll be back.' She left the room hastily, went into a corner of the hall and wiped her eyes, looking about her all the time. Through the window she could see her mother cooking in the kitchen. Zohra was nowhere to be seen. She was afraid to return to Rabia's side, worried that she might ask her more questions. She decided she must bring up some other matter immediately, but could think of nothing else. It was as if her mind was anchored on Firdaus's memory.

'Akka, please do my hair quickly,' Rabia called loudly. 'Amma will scold me if my hair is loose at Maghrib time; she says that is when the angels are on the look out.'

Wahida, determined to take control of the conversation as she returned to the room, asked, 'Rabia, where's Ahmad these days, anyway? He doesn't seem to be anywhere about.' As she plaited Rabia's hair, Wahida could see her face fall at the very mention of Ahmad. The girl used to play with her friends outside everyday until it was dark. Now, it was all over.

'Ahmad isn't here now, Akka. He's joined a school at his Maama's place.'

Rabia could scarcely say this in a low voice.

Wahida then remembered something else. Mutthu, the driver, was no longer working for them. She had heard he had been dismissed, but didn't know why. She had meant to ask her mother, but had not remembered. She asked Rabia, 'Why did they tell Mutthu to stop working for us, Rabia? Do you know anything about it?'

Rabia was thrilled that Wahida respected her sufficiently to seek information from her. She turned round and asked eagerly, 'Don't you know? Suleiman Anna complained about him to Attha. He didn't like Mutthu, it seems. Attha at once told Mutthu Annan to leave. It seems he is driving a lorry somewhere else. Uma told me.' She sounded truly sorry at this turn of events.

Wahida didn't know what to say. Quietly she finished plaiting Rabia's hair, finishing it off with a ribbon and tassels, thinking to herself that Rabia was only a little girl who would not know anything more. But Rabia turned round sharply, saying, 'Mutthu Annan was very bad, Akka. Farida Akka too. Everyday they used to stand by the window, giggling together.'

A sudden realization flashed through Wahida's brain. She reminded herself of Sainu's complaints the day before. 'We didn't have sufficient time to find a good husband for Farida. We decided to get her married quickly, even if the bridegroom wasn't well placed. It will be a consolation if we can get a good match for the little one, at least.'

Sainu had taken advantage of Rahima's absence to ask, 'Well, Wahida, how many days is it now, that you have missed your period? Come on, you can tell me. Am I an outsider, after all? Who am I going to tell?' Sainu had gone on, 'Listen to this. My daughter-in-law apparently has a womb that hasn't developed properly. It seems the doctor-amma has told her it is doubtful whether she'll be able to conceive. I only have the one son. What will happen to us if he doesn't have an heir? I'm shattered by the thought. Since he heard the news, my boy has dwindled to half his size.' Her voice was steeped in disappointment. She spoke quite loudly, taking courage by the fact that Mumtaz was not there. It seemed to Wahida that Sainu was actually pleased rather than otherwise. She didn't appear to want to hide her news or make a secret of it.

Wahida thought of Suleiman. He might marry again, quite possibly. Like his friend, Abdulla Bhai. Poor Mumtaz, she thought.

As Wahida was leaving, Sainu said, 'Let me know when your husband is coming back. I must give a feast for you both'.

Rabikka and Siddikka had pestered her all through her visit to their house. They had fingered her sari, each piece of jewellery on her and the flowers in her hair, asking all the time, 'What's this? Where did you get it?' They repeated the same two questions a hundred times until at last Sainu chased them away, aiming a blow at each with a cane that she kept for the purpose. At once, Wahida rose to her feet, wanting to escape. She couldn't bear the stench of them, besides. She determined right then that she would never accept an invitation to dinner at that house.

Darkness began to pervade the room, reminding her that she had missed saying the Asar prayers. Full of remorse, she decided that she would say the Asar prayers along with the Maghrib ones. She rose to her feet and went to make her olu ablutions.

◆ 59 ◆

Nafiza climbed up to the terrace of her house in order to turn over the chillies and coriander seeds laid out there, to dry. It was very hot; it would all dry out in a single day. As she bent down to turn everything over, spreading it all out with her hands, she thought she could send it to be ground that very evening. The heat struck like a blow at the back of her neck. She hurried to finish her work, stood up and gazed about her at the town and its streets. There was not much going on in the streets; it was too hot for people to be out. At a distance she could see the tiled roof of Aziz's house. It was only a little house. She thought of him now. She had not met him at all, after his marriage. There had been no opportunity for that. Had he forgotten her entirely? She was filled with sadness at the thought. She could not tell whether too much had been done or said, or too little. In her mind it was just right, and as it should be. Of course, he and she had loved each other very dearly. But they had both always asked themselves how it could last forever. Of course it was true that that their relationship could not be a long-lasting one. It was equally true that it was not possible for him to give up his whole life for its sake.

She did not any longer resent his marriage. She had come to terms with it well enough. Nor was it such a sadness that she did not even see him any more. The most important thing now was for her to be free of other peoples' surveillance. The heat brought her to herself and she climbed down again, wiping the sweat off her face with the end of her sari. She longed to see Ahmad. Why should she not make a visit to see him, tomorrow? The whole town had gossiped to its heart's content over the fact that he had been sent away to study. Saura had hinted very deliberately, in her hearing, 'It's all because he would have got in the way of their business'. It was as if she had been struck across the ear. She raged within herself, 'It's because of her evil tongue that her daughter has turned widow at a time when she should be enjoying her life.' True, Sherifa was a sad, innocent wretch. She never made trouble or quarrelled with anyone. But all the same, a mother's sins came to rest on her children. It was just the same with Mumtaz. After all her jokes and banter, here she was, unable to bear any children. It served her right, she thought, enjoying a moment's pleasure before her conscience started prick her. How could she be so evil, she upbraided herself.

She came downstairs and sat down on the sofa, turning on

her transistor radio. An urgent news report was being read, speaking of the number of people who had died in the ethnic riots in Sri Lanka that day, and how many towns were under curfew. She felt a mixture of pity and annoyance. What a nuisance; they had stopped relaying their usual songs in order to give the news. Once again she thought of Aziz. Since she heard that he would leave for Singapore within a week, she could not help thinking of him. The thought that he might not return for two or three years did indeed provoke in her a desire to see him.

She wondered whether he too thought of her. She told herself that he had a new bride now; why would he harbour thoughts of Nafiza. She was aware of a slight feeling of jealousy within her, towards Farida. All these days she had managed to stop herself from being jealous, but it appeared to have grown within her, in spite of her efforts. Suddenly she felt the need to weep her heart out. It was not the right moment, though. It was very nearly time for Bashir to come home for his meal, after the noon prayers. She wanted to have his food all ready by the time he arrived. She rose to her feet, and pulled out just three of the strands of meat which had been salted and strung out to dry. The meat had dried well and was as hard as stone. She took the strands to the grindstone that was set into the courtyard and struck them hard and repeatedly, with a hammer.

Bashir came home promptly after the prayers were over. Seeing her in the courtyard, he handed her a parcel, saying, 'Here, take this'. Then he hurried inside the house, peeling off his shirt as he went.

'What on earth is this?,' she asked, following him.

'There was a Hazrat at the mosque selling Korans and holy books, so I bought one,' he told her, sinking into the sofa.

She was shocked and distressed by his words and hurriedly put away the book on the sofa. 'You carried it all this distance, should you have handed it to me as soon as you got here? I've gone and touched it when I'm in the wrong time of the month.'

She shouted at him and rushed away into the kitchen.

Bashir picked up the book and touched it to his eyes, then opened the almirah and put it away. He realized that Rafiq was not about and called out, 'Nafiza, where's he? I don't see him anywhere.'

She called back from the kitchen, 'Who, Rafiq? I have no idea. He must be playing in the street, with his friends. He'll turn up right enough, when he is hungry.'

As she spread out a mat and laid out the food, he said, helping himself to rice, 'I came past Nuramma's house, on my way home. She never fails to ask, "Who is it?" It gives me a strange feeling, to hear her. It's a terrible tragedy, isn't it?'

'Yes, of course it's a terrible tragedy,' Nafiza agreed, sadly. 'The girl ran away, only to die. When you think of the fate of that little boy... It's only Rahimakka who looks after them, otherwise it would be difficult for them to manage.'

He mixed his rice with the curry, saying, 'You too are women, but did any of you do as Rahima does? Did you ever send the lad some food?' He began to eat.

Nafiza felt a sharp twinge. She was aware that she had never given anything either to Iliaz or to Nuramma, but she didn't want to admit her failure. 'Yes, but it was in their house that both mother and daughter wore themselves out in service. It is their responsibility to look after them. They've done it so far, but who knows what is going to happen in the future. The family is going to break up, after all.' She added angrily, 'But what are we to say about that woman who abandoned her own child!'

Bashir, too, felt angry towards Fatima, but did not feel able to speak about her openly. He went on eating, while considering whether anything he said about Fatima might be taken as an oblique hit at Nafiza, and serve only to hurt her. He said at last, 'Let's leave it. Allah pays each of us back for the sins we commit. Look how He punished her immediately. Did He allow her to live with that man for even one year?' He was quiet after that.

She was pierced to the heart by the way Bashir overlooked
her own hot words against Fatima, and refused to utter a single
word against her, for his part. She was filled with sadness and
shame. Had he spoken even one word in anger, it would have
been better. It was his generosity in choosing to be ignorant
that she found so unbearable. She wanted to take herself away
from there, immediately. She left the kitchen, on the excuse of
looking for Rafiq. She came outside and flicked away the tears
which had welled up in her eyes, on to the blazing courtyard.
In an instant they had disappeared amongst the hot stones.

๛ 60 ๛

'Allah, your boundless grace,' Sikander said, sitting down
on the bed wearily and stretching out his legs
in relief. Wahida stood next to him, holding a chombu of water.
He was not too dark-skinned, but dark, all the same. A robust
body. His mature face looked smooth. It was obvious that he
had shaved just before his visit to his in-laws. She knew that,
when she stood next to him, her own light skin looked several
shades lighter. Besides, she had a slight frame, as if she could be
broken easily. Unaware that she was observing him, he had
stretched himself out, and was staring at the cross-beam. He
had informed his in-laws that his parents had asked him to go
and visit his wife. She wanted to laugh at that. No sooner than
he arrived, he planned to set off to Chénnai for his visa. It was
Rahima who insisted that he stay for a day at least. Wahida
was ashamed and annoyed, remembering how her mother had
hastened to dress and adorn her the minute he arrived.

Just as her mother finished placing the flowers in her hair,
and made ready to leave, she asked very casually and gently,
'Well, how many days since you were due?' Wahida knew
exactly what she meant, though she spoke obliquely, and felt
ashamed. She put down the water pot on a stool nearby, and
sat down at the edge of the bed. Startled out of his thoughts, he

looked at her in surprise, and asked, 'When did you come up? Is it very late?' He went on, quite kindly, 'Go to sleep, if you are sleepy.' She continued to sit there, without making a reply.

'Attha is complaining all the time because you aren't there. He says there's no one there even to make tea for him. He wants to know when you'll be back.' He believed he had conveyed to her, at least partially, his father's affection for his daughter-in-law. He looked at her with pride, smiling to himself. She, on the other hand, simmered with fury, grumbling to herself, 'As if that man needs me just to make his tea! He drinks tea all the time only to get hold of me.'

Sikander asked outright, 'Is all the news I hear really true?' She stared at him, not knowing what he meant.

'Are you pretending, or what? It seems your family is breaking up? I heard all about it. Did you think you could hide it from me? I know all the news about this town even before you come to know of it. Shall I tell you some more?' he teased her. 'I know it all: how Mumtaz has been possessed by Firdaus's ghost, how that Fatima who ran off got killed, how Farida and Mutthu were caught showing their teeth at each other, and how her brother threatened to take poison and die if she didn't agree to be married immediately. Yes, I know everything. But you won't tell me anything, will you?' He sounded resentful.

Still she wouldn't open her mouth. He was repeating all the gossip about this town; he even knew about this matter of Mumtaz. She was astonished at how all this had travelled to him, as if by bus.

'Look at me, asking you about it all. Are you deaf or what? Go on. Go to sleep if you want.' He was annoyed now. 'My mother has given me strict instructions not to touch you during these days. So you needn't worry. I'm not going to eat you up.' He muttered sharply, 'As if you would be welcoming at the best of times, anyway.' He put a pillow beneath his legs, and stretched himself out.

She lay down next to him without a word. She was distressed that since the moment of his arrival, he had not spoken one word of affection to her. He had asked her all these unnecessary things. What kind of creature was he, she wondered. How could there be a person such as this, without any knowledge of how to speak or act affectionately? She had shut eyes and was thinking that he didn't even know how to behave to his wife, when he shook her by the arm, gently. She opened her eyes, surprised, and asked what was the matter.

'You aren't asleep yet are you? Your husband comes to you after a whole week's absence, couldn't you have spoken a couple of words in affection? You could have asked how I am. Stupid thing! It's just my fate.' He struck his forehead lightly with the palm of his hand. His voice was full of disappointment.

She was shocked. It had never ever struck her that his feelings were the same as hers; that he too resented the way she behaved towards him and thought it not right. Surprised by this, she felt a stirring of sympathy for him.

He continued to grumble at her. 'Even on a good day you don't show any interest in anything. As if I can expect any conversation out of you just for today. In Singapore, I can just trip over Malaysian women, ready for it, for just five and ten Singapore rupees. There was a woman who worked in my shop; she was desperate to be with me. And here you are, calling yourself a woman.'

She saw from his expression that he really did speak out of considerable experience, and the little sympathy she had felt for him vanished. 'Chi, what sort of man is this,' shrinking within herself in disgust. She battled to suppress the tears which threatened to pour out in spite of her efforts. She rolled over in the bed and turned her face sideways, to avoid his eyes. His complete disregard of her cut her to the heart.

He got up from the bed, switched off the light, and came and lay down again. He lay very close to her, and the smell of perspiration coming off him made her feel sick. She turned over and buried her face in her pillow, trying to avoid it.

He began again. 'Well, tell me, is it true that Mumtaz was possessed by a ghost?'

Would his head burst if he didn't find out the truth about that business, she wondered. Her stomach churned, preventing her from replying to him.

'Does it hurt even to say a word in reply?' he asked, muttering something else to himself.

She rose up silently, drank a mouthful of water, and then chose one of the bedcovers which were stacked on a stool by the wall. She was aware that he was watching her closely now, in the pale light, but taking no notice, she shook out the cover with all her strength, and spread it out. Then she returned to the bed and lay down again. She wished she could take herself away to another room, but silently covered herself right up to her face. She tried to go to sleep, but could not. She consoled herself that at least the sheet would stop her from hearing his words.

She was aware of his sudden anger at her withdrawal. She could feel him moving away. It must have upset him to see her covering up her face, but he accepted it quietly. That was a great relief to her. She realized that she felt less sick. Under the sheet it was entirely dark. She imagined herself floating in that protecting darkness.

At last he turned to one side and was deeply asleep. She began to feel choked from staying under the cover for so long, so she put her head out gently and took a deep breath. The jasmine in her hair had flowered, and its scent was filling the room now. A breeze blew in from the open window. Because the window was right by the bed, she could see into the street. From her upstairs room, the cemetery could be seen clearly, the graves lit up by the light shining there. The more recent graves were still raised mounds, while the older graves had sunk into holes. From the time she was a child, she would never open this window when she came upstairs. Now she gazed at the cemetery without fear. She thought bitterly that the stories she had heard and the fears that had etched themselves into her mind were as nothing to her now. Did anxiety drive away even fear?

She turned her gaze away to the rest of the street. The street light glowed, off and on; the entire street was quiet. All the people living there belonged to trading families. Everyone was asleep by ten, and awake for the early morning Bajar prayers. In the old days, even after everyone had gone to bed, Nuramma went about until it was late, even at midnight. Because she kept a cow whose milk she sold, she kept awake at night, giving it food and water, and talking to it. Wahida's uncle, Karim, always made fun of Nuramma, saying she went about all night like the ghost of Mohini. All the street dogs were terrified of her. She never left a single one alone, throwing stones at them and even breaking their legs. There were many dogs who prowled about the town that had been maimed by her. Rahima and Zohra often wondered how she could do this so pitilessly. When she walked about at night, not a single dog would come near the street, having worked out from a distance that she was there. She, for her part, would grin victoriously when she saw this, and call them obscene names. Everyone was astonished that she never seemed to need to sleep, but walked around the streets as if in search of something secret. Now, she was bed-ridden, making them all wonder if this is where unfulfilled desires take you. And now there were four dogs running together along the street. It seemed to Wahida that they were intent on some purpose, wandering about so very freely.

Her gaze returned to the cemetery. A high wall had been raised around it, and its wide gates were locked. The walls were built to protect the graves, after the bodies of children had been dug up by dogs sometime ago. Inside the walls, lines of coconut palms swayed in unison as the breeze blew, as if possessed by ghosts. It felt as if it was just yesterday that the saplings were planted. They had grown so tall in just a few years. Her aunt Zohra always said, 'They are a strong variety; they'll grow very quickly.'

She thought of Mumtaz. She had visited them just once at Sabia's house, to invite them to Farida's wedding. She could not understand how or why Firdaus's ghost should possess her. Wahida too had been there. Why did it not possess her rather than Mumtaz who had come there just that one day? Sainu said, sarcastically, 'She must have really taken to this girl.' According to Sainu, the ghost had thrown Mumtaz into a terrible frenzy the other day. Wahida could not believe it; at the same time she could not disbelieve it either.

Zohra had been furious when she heard about it. She raged, 'Just let me hear anyone saying that Firdaus's ghost is wandering about; I'll finish them off once and for all.'

Wahida could not understand why she was so angry until Rahima explained. 'It's only people who have an excessive love and desire for this world who return as ghosts.'

Greatly troubled by these thoughts, she shut her eyes tightly and tried to free herself of them.

～ 61 ～

Madina and Rabia were sitting together in a corner of the terrace. A strong wind blew on their faces, tossing their hair about. They were both silent, not sure what to say to each other. The decision to build a wall through their house had filled Rabia with a sadness equal to what she felt when Firdaus died. Besides, she who was used to running about as she pleased had now been stopped from going to school; her mother would not even allow her to go into the street all that much. It upset her greatly. In earlier times, they would all go to the cinema together – she, Uma, Ahmad, Iliaz, everyone. Nowadays, Madina would not be allowed to go. Nor, for that matter, could any of the women of their community go to the cinema. She could not understand how everything had become so unbearably sad. Had Ahmad been there, it might have been different. But she had no idea when he was likely to come back. She wondered whether he missed her too.

Madina pinched her thigh lightly, bringing her to herself. Rabia stared at her in bewilderment, then recovered herself, laughing. 'You seem to be deep in thought,' Madina remarked.

There were lots of things she had wanted to say to Rabia. But they had not been able to talk to each other properly since Firdaus died. Then Madina had menstruated, and there had been no time at all to see each other or talk at any length. It was only that day that Rabia had sought out her friend. Madina was distressed by Rabia's anxious and distraught look. She wondered what the matter was with Rabia. How she could share her experiences with her unless she showed some interest. 'What is the matter with you?' Madina asked again.

'Nothing,' said Rabia. 'Where's your sister-in-law? I don't see her about.'

Her question embarrassed Madina. She stalled for a moment, wondering whether she should come out with it or not. Then she said, 'That is… a ghost is haunting her, so we've sent her to her parents' house.'

How did a ghost haunt you? The gossip that she heard about Firdaus having become a ghost filled Rabia with pain, and a desperate desire to understand what that meant. She was not prepared to believe it. Yet she was absolutely certain that Madina would not lie to her.

Madina, for her part, did not quite understand it either. Yet, the sight of Mumtaz Anni on that night, in a frenzy, her hair streaming about her had made her own hair stand on end. The very memory of it made Madina grow tense with shock now, and Rabia, sitting next to her observed it clearly. After that, Suleiman started to sleep in a separate room, every night. Nobody would speak to Mumtaz anymore. At last, Sainu said to her, 'You had best go to your mother's house until you have recovered completely.'

Mumtaz did not wish to go away. Yet it must have upset her that every evening the ghost possessed her, that Suleiman and the rest were terrified at the sight of her at such times, and although she was herself during the day, nobody would speak to her. She had gone, voluntarily. After that Suleiman refused even to visit her. And Sainu did not ask him to do so, either. All this seemed very odd to Madina. At lunchtime, the day before, her mother had raised her usual lament. 'I have only one son and heir. Your wife wasn't capable of producing a single child so that this family may survive. Her mother tied this barren girl to us and went about saying, "I didn't realize what I did marrying her into that family. Now she'll have idiot children, poor thing." And here she is, incapable of bearing a single child, idiot or not.'

'Leave all that,' Madina said, brushing off these thoughts. She didn't wish to tell Rabia any of this. To change the topic she said, 'Rabia, shall I tell you how it was when I menstruated?' She was desperate to share it all with Rabia, and surprised that so many days had gone by without her doing so.

'Mm. Tell me.'

Rabia's lack of interest held Madina back a little, but she pretended not to notice it, and pressed on. 'When I went to the toilet that day, I noticed quite a dark blood stain. Do you know, when I saw it, the life seemed to go out of me. I began to tremble, not knowing who to tell, who to ask. I thought something terrible had happened to me. In the end I washed myself thoroughly, and decided to keep quiet.' She stopped, disappointed that Rabia had not interrupted with her questions. She was also irritated that Rabia continued to be so withdrawn and glum-looking. But she also felt sorry for her friend, and so she put her arm around her shoulder, and asked affectionately, 'What's got into you, di?'

Rabia pulled herself together at once, and said sadly, 'Nothing, really. You know they've stopped me from school, don't you? It's just that. And then, they're going to build a wall through our house, tomorrow.'

Madina understood how she felt. She was silent for awhile. She had heard her mother and Nafiza saying to each other that Rabia's mother and aunt had quarrelled. So she put on a knowing look and asked, 'It seems there is a quarrel in your family? I heard about that.'

'No, it's not that, Madina. It doesn't at all seem as if there's been a quarrel. It's only Akka and I who seem upset about it.'

Rabia sat there with her chin against her right hand, in a very grown-up way. Then she spoke hesitantly, 'Madina, I'm going to ask you something. Will you answer me truly? It is my mother I feel so sorry for. She gets so upset and furious if anyone asks her about Firdaus, and whether it is her ghost that is haunting Mumtaz.' She stopped and then asked, anxious for some kind of confirmation, 'How can they be sure that the ghost is my Chitthi?'

Madina did not like to look at Rabia's anxious face, so she bent down and drew lines on the terrace floor with her fingers silently. Then she nodded as if it was only right for her to confirm what she knew. 'But I am sure. That evening, when Annan entered their room, Anni shouted loudly at him, "Get out, you dog; don't touch me." At once, my mother and I ran and stood outside their door. Annan opened the door and came out, saying, "Amma, just look at this." Amma went inside, terrified. Mumtaz Anni was in a corner, sitting with her face buried in her knees. Amma asked her, "Amma, good lady, who are you? Where do you come from?" I could see that Amma was trembling all over with fear. Then Mumtaz Anni lifted her head, looked straight at Amma and shouted out in a frenzy, "I am Firdaus, di." All of us fled from the room, then.'

A look of guilt flashed across Madina's face, as if she had just done a great wrong. Added to that was her anxiety that she had caused Rabia much grief by answering her question and confirming her doubt.

They were both quiet, after that. Dusk was falling, spreading an extraordinary yellow light across the skies, beautiful to see. Everything, everywhere looked yellow. Even their faces reflected the yellow light. Since Madina came of age, she had stayed indoors; she had gained a little weight and her skin had lightened, making her look very pretty, Rabia noticed. She felt a sudden happiness at the thought that she too might grow prettier and lighter-skinned when she came of age. Once again she thought of Ahmad, and how pleasant it would be if he were

there. She laid her head on Madina's lap and gazed up at the
sky, as if trying to learn something.

⌒ 62 ⌒

Zohra's throat ached from swallowing back her tears.
She went into the kitchen, dipped a chombu into the
earthenware water pot and drank. The cold water slid down
her throat, soothing it. Her gaze fell directly on the bricks
heaped up at the front entrance of the house. The wall had
been raised halfway across the courtyard. It would be finished
in a couple of days. Because it was a large enough house they
had measured up all its rooms and its courtyard and divided it
into two equal halves. It was decided, after proper
consultations, that the houses of the elder and younger brother
should face in particular directions. Because of this, that part
of the courtyard which contained the well came to Rahima.
Zohra asked for a well to be dug at once on their side, too. But
Karim was adamant. 'It appears that Wahida might conceive,
any time now. If that is certain, then we mustn't dig a well
right now. Wait for a while, let's see.'

Zohra was annoyed and angry, but could say nothing. The
two brothers had been very stern with the women. Kader
summoned them and said, 'Misunderstandings happen
between women; it's not unusual. It's a big thing that we have
been united as a family for so long. Heaven knows who cast an
evil eye on us; may Allah protect us! But let me say one thing.
The house is divided, but the family always works as one. Let it
be so until Rabia is married, when I intend to spend exactly the
same amount as I have done for my own daughter's wedding.'
That was his last word. After that, no one said anything.

Before the wall was begun, Kader said to Zohra, 'Look,
amma, take whatever you need to set up house on your side.
None of us will object. And for Allah's sake forgive us if during

all these years there has been any inequality in our dealings.'

Rahima was silent throughout. Zohra could not believe she was truly forbearing and muttered to herself, 'Deceitful woman! She's venom, through and through.'

The kitchen, bathroom and toilet were all three on Zohra's side of the house, and only the well on Rahima's side. It was decided that a new kitchen and bathroom would be built and a new well dug out of their joint finances. Except for the well, the other work had all begun. Kader told his brother, 'Please switch on the pump and help yourselves to water at any time, every day.'

Zohra alone could not agree. She had tried to insist stubbornly that the well should be dug immediately, afraid that it could be postponed for up to a year. But he had stopped her as if with one blow across her mouth. Zohra hand stroked her right cheek involuntarily. She lamented to herself that it was his wrongdoing that caused all this trouble in the first place, and turned her anger towards Rabia. 'Why is this wretched child so fond of that slut? She sticks to the woman like a leech! How on earth am I to pluck her away?' she muttered to herself.

Karim made it worse by provoking her every now and then. 'What's the good of your being so hostile towards her? Your daughter dotes on her, don't you know that?' He knew perfectly well that it wasn't just to bring her mother home that Zohra was bent on dividing the family. In earlier times, Zohra had often felt totally dependent and helpless. She had begun to think that if she were not able to have her way in this one thing at least, life would be meaningless. Now she felt a spurt of harsh satisfaction that she had achieved her wish.

She thought of Firdaus, suddenly. It was as if her eyes had forgotten her face. Her throat choked, when she remembered that Firdaus did not even appear in her dreams anymore. Firdaus was angry with her sister, that is why she kept away, Zohra thought. When Firdaus was alive, it was Zohra who had been angry and kept away. Why, she had even, in her obstinacy, refused to allow Rabia to visit Firdaus. Zohra wept, blaming herself for being so stubborn towards that innocent child. She thought how Firdaus, in her last hour, had no one to come to her aid, and could not control her tears. Sitting in a corner of her room, she buried her face in her lap and tried to swallow her sobs. She was not prepared to allow Rahima to hear her weep; not for an instant.

She heard someone calling out to her outside her door, and came out, wiping her face firmly with the end of her sari. She saw Mariyayi there, with a container of milk. she took the milk from her and went into the kitchen. Mariyayi gazed at her and then at the growing wall and was silent, her eyes sad. Thinking her own thoughts, she sank down on the washing stone set into the courtyard. She came to herself only when Rabia ran in from the street, flopped into her lap and gave her a hug.

⌒ **63** ⌒

Rahima stirred the rice with a spoon, and picked up one grain to test whether it was cooked. It felt as if it wasn't quite done. She poured in a little more water into the pot and blew on the fire until it blazed up. The tears poured from her eyes, both because the smoke irritated them and because her heart was heavy. Ever since the wall started coming up, Wahida seemed to be heart-broken. Rahima had no idea what was in Wahida's mind, since her daughter would not confide in her anymore. She wept at the thought that Wahida had distanced herself in disgust.

It distressed her that Sainu or Saura or Nafiza would come to her in turn, and then go to Zohra, asking questions, probing, trying to make them talk. They always made a pretence of concern. They would say to her, 'Why, Rahima, you have a heart of pure gold. Look at the way she has flung you aside, what a business it is!' To Zohra it was a different tune, 'It's the quiet ones who ruin the whole town, they say. It's a good thing you realized that in time.'

Kader summoned Rahima and Zohra and said very sharply, 'Look here, both of you. There will be people who will go any length to find out what is going on amongst us. The truth is that we are separating amicably. But don't either of you blurt out anything and disgrace us all. If that happens, I will stop at nothing.' Karim knew his words were directed at Zohra in particular, and she understood that, too.

Rahima was frustrated by her realization that one could never judge others properly. How close Zohra had been to her at one time. And now, how hostile!

The rice boiled over with a hissing noise. The fire underneath was extinguished; smoke rose from it. Rahima broke pieces of firewood, stacked them into the hearth and blew steadily to start the fire again. She tried the rice again, saying to herself, 'I must get myself a gas stove now at least, instead of being frightened to death at the thought.' Once again she rubbed her eyes, sore with the smoke, with the end of her sari.

She could hear Sainu's voice in the street, calling out to someone. The fear that she might come into their house surrounded Rahima, like the smoke. The minute she entered she would begin her questions. 'How many days since Wahida was due?' 'Is it true she is vomiting?' 'Have you tried a hot bath?' And not just Sainu. Saura, Nafiza and all the rest, they all asked the same question. Sometimes she even told them to mind their own business, speaking sharply. But the very next day they were back, asking the same thing again. She, at least, felt embarrassed by her rudeness, but they didn't seem to mind in the least.

She remembered she must strain the rice. She held the rice-pot with a piece of cloth and strained away the water by setting it aslant, balancing the lid against the blow-pipe to steady it. She went into Wahida's room to see what she was doing. Wahida had darkened the room by shutting all the windows.

Rahima saw her daughter lying curled up, at the edge of her bed, and felt fear clutching at her lower belly. Why was Wahida so unhappy, she thought, with anguish. How could a newly married girl be so utterly listless? Was this all her life was going to be? The questions pierced her heart and her head began to throb with a splitting headache. The tears spurted from her eyes again. At once she wiped them and went about her chores.

꩜ **64** ꩜

For two days, Sherifa had not left her bed. She lay on it, her face swollen with tears, her body weakened from lack of food. Her sister, Raihana looked after the baby. Saura was in the same state, weeping in her room. For Sherifa, it was no great hardship to fast, but she wondered how her mother could refrain from eating. Food was her whole world, her life, her everything.

Sainu had visited them two days ago, asking that Sherifa should agree to a nikah with Suleiman. She had complained to her sister-in-law, Saura, that Mumtaz was haunted, and she would never bear children. What was more, she would not allow Suleiman anywhere near her at night, but drove him away. From the moment she left, Saura began her incessant plea. She wept, and did everything in her power to force Sherifa to agree to the nikah. At last, both women had taken to their beds.

'Your Attha is old now; once he is gone who will be there to look after this family? How will you live out your days without a man's support? Your sister stands here with her bald head; who will care for her? Your brother is only a helpless child, who will teach him what is right and what is wrong? If your life is sorted out, if you are happy, the very thought of it will add at least a few more years to your Attha's life. Suleiman is from our family, and he will surely take us under his wing. And who would have thought we would ever have the chance to marry

you to my own brother's son. It's as if Allah himself sought
you out. Don't refuse this, amma,' Saura had pleaded, sitting
by the bed head.

The very sound of Suleiman's name infuriated Sherifa. That
look of malice on his face as he told them about Fatima's death
in Rahima's house that day had made her dislike him greatly.
Now he had decided to marry again, as soon as his wife showed
signs of illness. Disgusting man, she thought to herself, proud
that she herself was still loyal to her husband's memory.

She considered all that Saura said, to try and persuade her.
Her concerns were valid enough. But whatever reason she had,
how could her mother bring herself to harm Mumtaz, the
neighbour they had known for so long? It didn't seem to cause
her the least embarrassment. As far as her mother was
concerned, Sherifa must be married, one way or another. She
was prepared to do anything to that end. She thought about
the fact that a family would indeed suffer all sorts of difficulties
without a man's support. Four days ago, they had received a
telephone call from her father. He had a slight pain in his chest
and had seen a doctor. They had asked him to come home
immediately, but he had refused saying he could not leave his
work. It had been the same with Sainu Mammaani's husband.
But he had died abroad, and they did not even bring his body
home. Saura had recalled that as well, as she wept earlier. When
her father left this time, Sherifa had said to him, 'Why do you
have to go again? What you have earned so far is enough for
us. You are getting old now. Who do you need to earn for,
now?'

But he wouldn't listen. 'No, I can't stay even a minute
longer. Nothing is going to happen to me. Allah will look after
me.'

Saura had said then, 'Leave it; he can't let go of his worldly
desires.' She knew him well enough. It was Sherifa who prayed
to Allah for her father everyday, as if she were holding his life
in her hands. Today, she was in anguish, having heard he was

ill. But for Saura, the news brought other worries, and reminded her of her responsibilities.

Sherifa tossed in her bed and gave a deep sigh. She remembered how her status as a widow caused them so much trouble last year. Every year, during the month of Rabi'ul Avval, the month of the Prophet's birth, directly after the Maulud – the series of hourly recitations held for a period of ten days – was over, all the families in the community were asked to make a contribution to a feast. A husband and wife together made a unit, and were asked to donate a hundred rupees to the mosque. Those who had the means had to give a sum of money as a gift, separately. The Nattaanmai used the money collected in this way to buy several sheep which were slaughtered in the mosque, and then cooked in a number of big cooking pots. They calculated that one cooking pot would serve ten units. Each pot was then carried to one of the ten families, and one person from that particular family shared it out appropriately. On that day last year, they shared out the lamb curry in the courtyard of Sherifa's house, and it was Sainu who presided over this rite. She sat by the cooking pot, stirred the curry, collected the meat pieces in a dish, and began to portion it into the vessels that were laid out in front of her. The aroma of the curry stopped them all from noticing the late morning heat in the courtyard. Each one stood by the side of the vessel she had brought and watched Sainu, without once blinking. Nafiza, Zohra, Fatima, Saura and all the rest of them seemed to think that even if they moved slightly, Sainu might make a mistake. Sainu read out from the note sent by the mosque, listing the portions allocated to each one. In due time, she called out, 'This portion is the widow's portion: half for Sherifa and half for me,' and placed the portions in the appropriate dishes.

Immediately Saura's face darkened as if in shock. It was as if she had been reminded brutally of something that had lain hidden for a while. She raised a great wail, lamenting 'Lord, how could you do this to me! Here I am, a vavarasi with my husband alive, having to see with my own eyes my daughter receiving a widow's share.' She had flung away her own portion, without caring that it had been blessed at the mosque. Everyone present felt her grief and shared it, but they were all embarrassed at the spectacle she made of herself. At that time too, Saura had wept for a whole week following the incident, pleading with Sherifa to marry again.

Remembering all that, Sherifa told herself that on this occasion too, Saura would continue to weep for a week. After that, things would be as usual. All the same, the question rose urgently in Sherifa's mind, whether it was going to be possible for her to live alone all her life, controlling her desires and feelings. She thought again how painful every night proved to be, how hard she had to try, to overcome her frustration. Would the memory of her husband and her love for her child be sufficient support for her, for the rest of her days? She lay still on her bed, overcome with confusion, not knowing what she should do.

Although she said all the prescribed prayers everyday, followed the Koran and the Hadiths, and never failed to keep a weekly fast, somewhere in her heart and mind those feelings and desires lurked still, never giving up their hold. Everyday, when she lifted up her hands in prayer, she asked for the same thing. Always she pleaded to be set free of worldly desires and attachments. Why did Allah not show her any pity? When she thought about it, she could not but be angry with him. Full of frustration, she sat up and gently leaned her feet on the ground. Her legs shook and she could barely stand; she clung to the side of the bed. Her head was spinning, and she thought she would faint. She felt a great fatigue, as if everything in her body had been squeezed out. She thought she might as well brush her teeth and drink some water. She looked out of the window and saw a boy running past Nuramma's house. Immediately Nuramma called out from within, in a weak voice, 'Who is it?'

Sherifa went into the bathroom and began to brush her

teeth. She began to gargle and spit out the water, watching her face reflected in the bathroom, and observing that it was scarcely recognizable. She filled her mouth with water until her cheeks were puffed out. The muscles of her face ached because she had not eaten for two days nor talked to anyone; she tried to relax them by holding the water in her mouth and spitting it out. She watched her reflection as her cheeks expanded and contracted again and again, and her eardrops set with stones swung backward and forward.

When she was first married, she had seen a picture of an actress, on the cover of a weekly magazine, wearing a pair of eardrops exactly like this. Immediately she had craved for a similar pair and shown Salaam the picture. 'Of course, little sister, I'll have it made for you at once,' he said. He had summoned the goldsmith, shown him the picture and asked him to copy the design exactly. When he called her 'little sister', teasing her fondly, she always felt shy. Always, when they were happy, he would tease her by calling her that. 'Aren't you ashamed of yourself, di,' he would say, 'would anyone marry their brother? If you think about it, doesn't it make you want to die of shame?' He loved to provoke her playfully. Sherifa washed her face, her head filled with various thoughts and anxieties.

65

Wahida, opening her eyes just a little to see who had come in, met her mother's eyes and was greatly moved. She noticed how her mother's beautiful and serene face had changed; how these days it was always drawn with anxiety, and found it unbearable. Realizing that she herself was the cause of all her mother's troubles, she shut her eyes again, tightly. If only she had never gone out to the terrace that night, or at least had not seen Firdaus…? Even though her eyes were closed, she could picture those scenes clearly. Not wishing to see them again, nor be reminded of them, she snapped open her eyes again. How good it would be if only one could fling away unwanted memories like goods that were no longer needed! It was astonishing that even though she tried to pluck them out by their roots, they still put out shoots and grew large enough to torment her. If only there were some way to forget it all and find happiness elsewhere! But that seemed impossible. Thoughts of her husband just added to her anxieties; she felt no other emotion towards him.

The thought that her life had turned into a disaster brought her to the brink of tears yet again. However much she tried to reconcile herself to her situation, she could not avoid the questions that echoed in her mind: Is this all? Has everything come to an end? Is there no alternative to this? She was resolved on one thing alone: she would not return to her husband's house. However much they tried to persuade her, she would refuse that life. Since she did not experience the least happiness there, why should she go and live in that house, as if she were deliberately opting for a home in hell? She had been loved and cherished in this household; so now what compulsion was there for her to go and be a servant in another?

She remembered Sayyed's gaze roving all over her body with relish and Sabia's eyes keeping watch over her as she ate, and buried her face deep in her mother's lap. She imagined how her mother's face would plunge into even more sorrow when she heard Wahida say it was not possible for her to live in her husband's house. She began to tremble.

Rahima was aware of her daughter shuddering momentarily, and then growing still, and was frightened. She shook her slightly, asking, 'What is it, amma, what has happened?'

Wahida opened her eyes slowly and looked up into her mother's face. She spoke a single word, 'Nothing', shut her eyes again, and was silent for a while. Again she murmured, 'Amma'.

Rahima realized that Wahida was trying desperately to find the words to speak to her. In her turn, she was terrified of hearing what she might say. Her throat felt dry, her tongue seemed to twist about. She stammered out again, very tenderly, 'What is the matter, amma?'

'That is, Amma...' Wahida began again, 'I don't want to return there. Let me stay here hereafter.'

Rahima half understood what Wahida was saying, and asked again, 'What are you saying, amma?' She sounded as distressed as Wahida had expected she would be.

'It's true. I will never go back there again, never. I don't like anyone there. Please don't send me back there, Amma.' She buried her face in her mother's lap and began to weep.

Rahima put her hand against her daughter's back and hugged her close, not knowing what to do. Did the girl not know what she was saying, or did she know only too well? Whatever it was, she wanted to comfort her, and so she said, 'Very well, amma. You don't have to go there again. You just stay here.' But Rahima's heart was greatly troubled.

Wahida lifted her head and looked up at the mother's face. She saw there a terrible and uncomprehending anxiety. For a moment she was filled with pity for her. All the same, even if she caused her mother pain in the process, she was determined to speak out and not suffer in secret. She would not hide things any longer. Gaining courage with this thought, she said, speaking of Sikander in the singular, not in the respectful plural, 'I don't like him, Amma. And Sayyed Maama is a lecher. I don't want any of them.'

To Rahima, it seemed as if Wahida were talking like a child. What use was it to speak like this, now that she was married? On one hand, she worried about how to make Wahida understand this; on the other, she was full of guilt at having pushed her daughter, knowingly, into such a hell-hole. She was deeply saddened by it all. Now what alternative could there be for Wahida? The only honourable course for her was to spend the rest of her days with her husband. Otherwise she would end up ruined, like Firdaus. All these thoughts went through her head and made her speechless.

Wahida was disappointed that her mother had not yet spoken a single word of comfort to her. She buried her head more deeply into her mother's lap as if she understood the absolute necessity of getting an appropriate answer from her. She felt as if she would only escape from her situation if she had at least one person who could speak up for her.

Rahima stroked her daughter's head, gently. She spoke at last, trying to make her understand the reality. 'Very well, amma. You need not go there. You can stay on here, if that is what you want. Let us agree that your husband can visit you here as he pleases. But you must not address him disrespectfully. That would be wrong-doing on your part. Is it so wrong of him to talk to other women? Doesn't your Attha speak to his kinswomen? But you must speak to him openly, tell him what is in your mind; it is up to you to reform him. These days, men listen to their wives, don't they? You mustn't come and complain about him. If he knew this, how distressed he would be!' Her voice was full of sympathy for Sikander.

Wahida had guessed that her mother would speak like this and attempt to make her come to terms with her situation. Would any mother wish to see her child cut herself off from the possibility of a respectable life? Of course Rahima would do all that was in her power to make Wahida accept her marriage. But Wahida too became more obstinate in her determination not to discuss it any further.

She jerked her head away and sat up. She knotted up her hair, which had fallen loose. She found herself growing intensely angry with Rahima for taking Sikander's part unconditionally. She was aware that the pity she felt for her mother a little while ago was draining away, leaving her empty and hard-hearted. It came to her quite clearly that there was no use in pleading her case any more. She thought of Mumtaz, suddenly. Sherifa and Suleiman were to be married the following week. Yesterday, Sherifa had told her about it, weeping: Saura had threatened to kill herself unless Sherifa agreed to the marriage. Wahida wished that she had been haunted, instead of Mumtaz; it might have been the means of her redemption.

She got up from the bed, hoping she would feel better if she washed her face. She left the room without looking at Rahima. The bright daylight dazzled her eyes. Her eyes had become used to the darkness of her room, and she rubbed at them, preparing them for the light. Just as she realized that it was nearly time for the Luhur prayers, she heard the radio blaring from Sainu's house. The twelve-forty news from Delhi was being read by a woman with a deep voice. Just as she entered the bathroom and began washing her face, the woman announced that there was severe rioting in Sri Lanka; that hundreds of innocent Tamil people had been killed and several towns were under curfew order. She listened carefully, remembering Sayyed. Definitely, he would not be going back there. However, it was not of the least concern to her, she thought; after all, she was never going back to her in-laws. The thought gave her courage as she began her olu ablutions.

As she began to rinse out her mouth, she felt slightly dizzy. She stopped and steadied herself against the wall, wondering what was the matter. Her stomach churned, and the saliva poured into her mouth. When she bent down to spit it out, the vomit rose from the pit of her stomach, and her breakfast of iddlis poured out of her, undigested, scattering everywhere. She began to vomit again and again, it seemed, unstoppably. Involuntarily she wetted herself, the urine soaking her petticoat and sari, through and through. She could hear her mother running up to the bathroom and knocking on the door. Then the sound of it dimmed, as if it came from a great distance. She slid down against the wall and sat down on the floor, clasping her legs tightly. It came to her that a life had taken form inside her. She placed her hand against her lower belly. She could feel nothing. Her mother was still knocking on the door, but she was unwilling to open the door, and did not move. She began to understand one thing. What she had hoped for so desperately was not going to happen. Realizing the necessity of accepting that truth, she raised her voice and began to weep loudly.

ℂ 66 ℂ

From the moment she heard that Ahmad had come home, Rabia's feet would scarcely touch the ground. It was Iliaz who had brought the news. When he came to fetch some iddlis from Rahima Periamma, he had called her aside, quietly, and told her about it. 'You go and visit him at his house. Tell him I'll go there this evening, when I've finished at the shop.' he said. She finished her breakfast in a great hurry, went into her room and opened her wardrobe door, wondering which of her skirts and davanis she should wear. When she pulled out her best clothes, the wooden doll fell out from among them. She stared at it for a moment, then picked it up and held it tightly against her. She pressed its face against her chest, petting it. She felt a thrill of joy all through her, as if Ahmad himself had embraced her. Quickly she hid it away among her clothes.

She shook out the skirt and tied its strings around her waist. She had had a bath on the previous day, and did not have to do so again that morning. She slipped on her blouse hurriedly, doing up the buttons as far as she could reach and tucked the davani about her and into her waist. Grabbing her comb in her hand, she ran through the gap in the still incomplete wall calling out to Wahida, 'Akka, please do my plaits.' Wahida sat up in bed, ran her fingers through her hair and knotted it. Rabia noticed the tiredness in her face, but was in no state to take any account of it.

'What's the hurry, di?' Wahida asked, taking the comb from Rabia, and doing up the buttons which were left undone, without waiting to be asked. Wondering why Rabia was suddenly so happy after so many days of listlessness she asked,

'You seem to be in a hurry to set off somewhere?'

'No, nothing like that, 'Rabia said, adding, 'Amma keeps telling me I mustn't come here anymore.'

Wahida was quiet as she attended to Rabia's hair. Rabia was disappointed that her cousin made no reply, but didn't say anything further. Silently she leaned back, allowing Wahida to continue combing her hair. She was angry with herself for having told Wahida what her mother had said. 'Saniyan,' she scolded herself. She thought of how Wahida didn't even smile so much, nowadays. In the old days she used to keep Zohra's transistor radio at her bedside, and listen to songs all the time. That too, had stopped entirely. Rabia was perfectly aware that all this had happened since Wahida got married. She waited quietly.

When Rabia rose to her feet, her hair combed and plaited, Wahida said, 'Your face looks as if a whole tin of oil has been spilt over it; go and wash it.'

'Very well, Akka,' Rabia said, going into the newly built bathroom, instead of returning home. In the soap-dish there was Lux soap, from abroad. She reached for it eagerly, thinking of Sikander. He must have brought it, she thought, squeezing it between her hands and rubbing her face. After she had gone over her face at least ten times, the soap suds between her fingers assured her that she looked bright enough, and she came outside and wiped her face on the handloom towel hanging on the line outside. She breathed in the sharp smell of whitewash. It reminded her of fast days and the month of Ramzan. She went back into the room and began to powder her face. Not satisfied that she looked pretty enough, she smoothed the powder puff over her face again and again.

She heard someone say, 'Yes, of course you look pretty,' and turned round quickly. Seeing her Periamma standing there, she dropped her head shyly and ran outside.

She went past Madina's house quickly, treading softly in case she was seen on her way to Ahmad's. She breathed a sigh of relief when she was safely past. The door to Ahmad's house was closed. Even as she climbed the front steps, the blood rushed to her head and her heart beat fast. She thought her breath would stop for sheer joy. She pushed the door open gently and went inside. Ahmad sat on his bed, swinging his legs. As soon as she entered, he stopped, looked up and stared at her. She imagined that she had changed utterly, and that he was shocked to find he could not even recognize her. She looked closely at him, and saw that he had grown quite a bit taller. He wore long trousers and a shirt; there was a watch around his wrist. His face had the sophisticated look of well-read town boys. She felt a sudden hesitation to go near him, or even to say his name, and stood still.

He took the initiative, and called out to her, 'Come here, di, why do you stand there?' He went on, with surprise, 'How did you manage to grow so much in such a short time? And what is this I hear about you not going to school anymore?'

Pleased that he spoke to her in his usual way, she ran up to him eagerly and stood by his side. At that moment, Nafiza came into the room and teased, 'Welcome, my daughter-in-law, what's the news? Have you come to see your bridegroom?'

Rabia grew red and dropped her head. Aware that Ahmad was looking at her, she bowed her head a little lower.

'Why aren't you going to school?' he asked again. 'Actually, I'm off there myself, right now, to get my Transfer Certificate. My Attha will join me there later. Come on, let's both go together, now.'

'Me?' Rabia hesitated. For a moment, her fear of a scolding from her mother flickered across her face. But she realized that he would soon go back to his uncle's place, and wanted to stay with him so long as he was here. She didn't allow herself to think any further. 'Yes, I'll come,' she said. 'Wait just a moment, I'll tell them at home.' She didn't wait for a reply, but ran home. Even then, she kept a wary glance on Madina's house.

Zohra was in the kitchen, frying something. Rabia ran to

her room, took out the wooden doll from her wardrobe and tucked it into her davani, against her stomach. Then she went to her mother, walking casually and unhurriedly. Through the clouds of smoke she said, 'Amma, I'm going to Madina's; don't go looking for me.' She left the house without any show of haste.

Once outside, she began running again towards Ahmad's house. She was greatly relieved that her mother had not said anything to prevent her, but knew that the chief reason that Zohra had let her go was because she preferred Rabia to go to Madina rather than stay in the house with Wahida. In the old days she would have scolded her for going to Madina all the time; now she said nothing.

Ahmad had come out into the street, waiting for her. She ran up to him, and they began walking together. 'Where's Iliaz?' he asked.

'He's working in our shop these days, parcelling up the groceries. He's at home only on Sundays. Sad, isn't it?'

'I don't see that girl about. Where's she gone?' His voice sounded sharp.

She understood who he meant, but felt too shy to explain.

'Are you deaf?' he scolded, looking at her as if he expected an answer.

Not able to get out of it now, she stammered, 'That is … she.. has come of age now.'

'Is that so,' was all he said, walking along as usual. By that time they had gone past the library, and reached the back of the school. Her face filled with delight at the sight of the school.

Ahmad glanced at his watch in a grown up way. 'Attha said he would come only after eleven. Come, let's go and sit under the trees by the side of the mountain, until then. It's only a quarter past ten, now.' He walked on, ahead.

The school playground had no surrounding compound wall, and they could see that it was completely empty; there were no children about. She told herself it was because the first lesson must only just have started, and went with him to the tamarind tree that stood at some distance. A cluster of four trees stood there, casting a cool shade.

They sat down together under the trees. The thought of her mother made her tremble. Ahmad, sitting next to her, said, 'There isn't another school like this one, is there?'

She was quite speechless; in a daze of joy and shyness. She only wanted to enjoy to the full the experience of being alone with him.

'Why won't you answer me? Why have they stopped you from going to school? Don't you mind?'

'There's no reason. Except that there's no one of my age to walk to school with me. Yes, of course I mind,' she said, looking down. She felt shy to meet his eyes. Happiness flowed through her from head to foot, and she could scarcely contain herself. Secretly, without his being aware, she felt for the wooden doll. She wanted to show it to him and remind him of many things, but her shyness left her tongue-tied. She couldn't talk to him as easily as he could, with her. She turned her gaze toward the mountain side. Cactus plants clustered in lines, a little distance away. One of the plants was full of bright red flowers. She remembered suddenly that the roses were in flower in their garden, and she had not plucked them for her hair. She had been so anxious her mother would scold her that she had quite forgotten about the flowers. Uma always said that she looked pretty with roses on either side of her plaits. It might have pleased Ahmad too. What a pity she had forgotten!

Realizing that her gaze had not left the cactus plant, Ahmad asked, 'What are you thinking about?'

'Nothing,' she said, startled.

Her expression must have communicated something to him. He stopped whatever he was about to say, and hurried up to the cacti. 'Come here,' he gestured to her. She went up to him, trembling with excitement, and looking about her. He smiled at her and bent among the cactus plants, as if searching for something. His hand brushed against hers lightly, sending a thrill through her. She realized at once what he was looking for and was filled with an unnameable joy.

She was much more familiar with that place than he was, so she walked up at a particular plant, bent down and looked carefully. 'Look, here...,' she called out excitedly, but swallowing her words halfway through, overcome yet again.

'Where?' he asked eagerly. He came next to her, saw on the cactus leaf at which she pointed, her name and his together, and laughed. That laugh made her feel very proud. In some way it had been established that he still thought of her. She was comforted by that and very content. She wanted to enjoy that sense of relief by herself, and returned to the shade of the tree.

After a while he came and sat by her again. He took out his handkerchief and wiped the sweat off his forehead and neck. It seemed to her that all his actions were done deliberately, for her sake; this too pleased her. He folded his handkerchief once more, put it away, and drew out something else. He spread open a small paper packet and held it out to her in the palm of his hand. The packet was full of small coffee coloured sweets, each individually wrapped. 'Help yourself,' he said. She demurred, feeling shy to eat in front of him. He scolded her fondly, 'Go on, I told you to, didn't I?' She reached out and helped herself to a single piece. 'Go on, eat it,' he ordered her. 'These sweets are from abroad. My Nanna sent them. Try it and see.' He unwrapped a piece and popped it into his mouth. She began to eat hers very neatly and soundlessly.

He looked at his wristwatch again. 'It's very nearly eleven. You wait here. I'll go to the Headmaster's office and see whether my Attha has come.' He got up, dusted off the seat of his trousers and set off towards the school.

Rabia watched him go, then stood up and went to the cactus plants again. She was surprised that she did not feel in the least afraid, although there was no one to be seen for some distance. She squatted down to examine the names joined together and realized that it was Ahmad who had written them there. Her heart filled with joy.

When he returned, she was waiting for him under the tree, gazing at a couple of boys who were climbing up the mountain to graze their cattle. As they started back towards their homes, Ahmad asked, 'What are you hiding underneath your davani?'

She looked down at herself and realized he had noticed the bump sticking out at her waist. She squirmed and said 'Nothing.'

'You are hiding something, aren't you?' he asked again.

She thought then that if she missed this chance there would not be another and so she slipped her hand inside her davani and brought out the wooden doll she had kept hidden. 'Look, it's this. It's yours, isn't it? I brought it to return it,' she told him. She blushed and was half dead with shame by the time she said all this.

For a minute he looked at her and the doll, in turn. All sorts of memories were flickering in his mind, it was apparent. 'You are returning this? To me? Oh no. Keep it for yourself. I won't need all this there,' he told her, smiling very affectionately.

They walked on silently, after that. when they reached his house, Ahmad said, 'I have to leave this very evening. I'll return only after the exams, for the holidays. So I'll say goodbye now, all right?'

She stood there for a while after he went inside, choking with grief. She felt as if something had been ripped away from her body. When she went home, she saw with shock and incomprehension that the wall was complete. With weary steps she went to her room and lay down, curled up on her bed. Her fingers were entwined tightly about the wooden doll.